PENGUIN BOOKS
Christmas with the Engine Girls

Daisy Styles grew up in Lancashire surrounded by a family and community of strong women. She loved to listen to their stories of life in the cotton mill, in the home, at the pub, on the dancefloor, in the local church, or just what happened to them on the bus going into town. It was from these women, particularly her vibrant mother and Irish grandmother, that Daisy learnt the art of storytelling.

By the same author

The Bomb Girls

The Code Girls

The Bomb Girls' Secrets

Christmas with the Bomb Girls

The Bomb Girl Brides

The Wartime Midwives

Home Fires and Spitfires

Keep Smiling Through

A Mother's Love

Christmas with the Wartime Midwives

Christmas with the Engine Girls

DAISY STYLES

PENGUIN BOOKS

PENGUIN BOOKS

UK | USA | Canada | Ireland | Australia
India | New Zealand | South Africa

Penguin Books is part of the Penguin Random House group of companies
whose addresses can be found at global.penguinrandomhouse.com

First published 2023
001

Set in 12.5/14.75pt Garamond MT
Typeset by Falcon Oast Graphic Art Ltd
Printed in Great Britain by Clays Ltd, Elcograf S.p.A.

The authorized representative in the EEA is Penguin Random House Ireland,
Morrison Chambers, 32 Nassau Street, Dublin D02 YH68

A CIP catalogue record for this book is available from the British Library

ISBN: 978–0–241–99871–7

www.greenpenguin.co.uk

MIX
Paper | Supporting
responsible forestry
FSC® C018179

Penguin Random House is committed to a
sustainable future for our business, our readers
and our planet. This book is made from Forest
Stewardship Council® certified paper.

For my wonderful mother,
Emily Redmond, a Bolton Bomb Girl!
Always remembered, always an inspiration. Miss you . . .

1. Ruby

Late summer 1941

'Sh-shhh, lovie, shhh,' Ruby whispered as she laid her three-month-old son down in his cot, gently tucking him up and resting her head against the wooden bars. She smiled adoringly as she tenderly stroked wisps of dark hair from Archie's warm pink cheeks. 'Just like your dad,' she sighed. 'He would be so proud of you, sweetheart,' she added as she reluctantly rose to get ready for her early morning shift at the Bell Works factory in Hucknall, across town from the red-brick terraced house she shared with her mother and sister in Nottingham.

So far, her husband George hadn't even seen his son. Stationed with his infantry unit somewhere in England, he had not been given compassionate leave when Archie was born. After the retreat from Dunkirk the previous year, troops were being trained in preparation for posting overseas. On the home front, following the RAF's victory in the Battle of Britain the previous summer, the nation, battered as it was, would never accept defeat. The same firm resolve sounded from one end of Britain to the other – there was absolutely no thought of ever giving up. Every man and woman openly declared that they would rather die than accept a tyrant as their leader. It was a conviction that had grown even greater after the Blitz on London and other major cities.

Sitting at her little vanity dressing table, with a picture of George in pride of place beside the fluted mirror, Ruby's thoughts flew back to the reports of the awful night – nearly a year ago now, she reflected – when Hitler's plan to turn Coventry into a fireball had swung into action. On a moonlit night, when it was bright enough for the Luftwaffe to see the traffic moving around, the city was subjected to an eleven-hour continuous bombing campaign, the aim being to knock out Coventry as a major centre for wartime production. It was rumoured that the attack was Hitler's revenge for the RAF air raid on Munich, a city he dearly loved. Five hundred tons of explosives and thirty thousand incendiaries were unleashed, pounding ancient Coventry, over and over again, until the glow from the burning ruins could be seen as far away as Birmingham. And as if that wasn't bad enough, over five hundred innocent civilians were killed in the constant, brutal bombardment. Children and babies, God help them, just like my baby sleeping peacefully, Ruby thought as she threw her son a last loving look, before hurrying downstairs to find her mother making tea and toast in their small back kitchen.

'I 'eard the little lad in the middle of the night,' Ruby's mum said anxiously.

Feeling guilty that her ailing mother was losing her much-needed sleep, Ruby quickly apologized. 'Sorry, Mam, did he wake you?'

Looking pale and drawn, Ruby's mum quickly shook her head. 'Don't fret, mi duck, I was already awake, worrying about one thing and another,' she confessed.

The sight of her mother's worn expression and her

formerly dark hair, now heavily streaked with bands of grey, made Ruby's heart contract with pity. A strong woman with indefatigable energy, her health had radically declined after the death of her youngest child, her only son, Derek, who had been killed at Dunkirk. As if the poor woman hasn't got enough to bear without the burden of helping me to raise my son, Ruby thought miserably.

'Mam, I could go in late if you need to catch up with your sleep?' she anxiously suggested.

Her mother flapped a dismissive hand in the air. 'You'll do no such thing, young lady,' she quickly told her daughter. 'Now drink your tea and get along with you,' she urged. 'If we all took time off for no good reason, we'd never get anywhere, would we?'

Obediently swallowing her hot tea and nibbling toast smeared with white margarine, Ruby did as she was told. In between eating and drinking she went through Archie's day.

'I changed Archie before I gave him his bottle, so he'll probably sleep for a good hour, then wake for another feed. I've left it all ready,' she added, nodding towards the draining board where bottles of freshly made National Dried Baby Milk were arranged.

'Sweetheart, I've reared three children, I know how to look after a baby,' her mother reassured her.

Ruby pushed back her flimsy wooden kitchen chair and rose to go. 'I know,' she blushed. 'I just hate leaving him.'

Seeing her eldest daughter so dejected, her mother slipped an arm around Ruby's slender waist. 'Course you do, lovie. He's a lovely little lad, good-natured and content, he's a credit to you.'

Ruby's shoulders drooped. 'I wish I could look after him

myself, I wish George was here to get to know his son – I wish this damn war had never started,' she blurted out, before she could stop herself. Seeing the look of anguish that flashed across her mother's face, Ruby could have bitten her tongue off. At least she had a son to hold, while her mother had lost her only boy in the fight for peace.

'Don't we all, love.' Her mother sighed as she refilled her cup with strong tea. 'Don't we all.'

Catching sight of the clock on the kitchen wall, Ruby hurriedly grabbed her coat, gas mask and snap bag.

'I'd better get a move on,' she said, visibly flustered, as she gave her mother a quick hug before dashing for the door. She passed her younger sister in the hallway, on her way into the kitchen.

'Oh, Rita,' Ruby reminded her sister. 'Don't forget to take Archie out in his pram when you get home from school. Mam will need a break by then, even if it's only for half an hour.'

Ruby shrugged on her coat and half ran, half walked through Hucknall's winding terraced streets as the sun slowly rose in the soft, early September morning sky, throwing a rosy light on the countless red-brick houses that backed on to cobbled lanes where rag and bone men on carts pulled by stocky ponies regularly plied their trade. Ringing a brass hand bell and calling out 'rag 'n' bone!' or 'any old iron!' their raucous calls brought people rushing to their doors with their unwanted items. Ruby had been born and grew up in this tight-knit community. She knew everybody in their street and beyond; she had attended the local Protestant school, leaving at fourteen to work at the Bell Works engineering factory, building posh Humber cars and the popular Hillman Minx. Even in those pre-Spitfire assembling days it had been a dirty, grubby job, but Ruby had always been a regular little grease monkey – as a kid she'd loved fixing broken bikes, enjoyed the challenge – and the pay was good, far better than a shop job.

It was at one of the Bell Works' dances, when she was only sixteen, that Ruby had first met George Fields. Tall, dark and handsome, with twinkling blue eyes, he had a warm, wide smile that melted Ruby's heart the moment she laid eyes on him. Young and awkward, she was hovering shyly at the back of the canteen, which for the evening had been transformed into a dance hall illuminated by slowly turning silver-glitter globes with a stage for the band, bright with twinkling lights. Nervously sipping lemonade, Ruby was watching the bolder girls flirt and chat with young local lads, never for a minute imagining that anybody would be attracted to her. She was innocently unaware of how good-looking she actually was, with long curly brunette hair that framed her pretty face, dominated by large thoughtful deep-blue eyes fringed with dark lashes. Her youthful body was tall and muscular; she had always loved playing rounders and walking for miles in the Peak District, which had kept her fit and athletic. Long-legged and slim, Ruby perfectly suited the duck-egg blue crêpe dress that was fashionably short with a nipped-in waist, emphasizing her small pert breasts and slim hips.

When George, who was even taller than her, tapped her on the shoulder, Ruby jumped in surprise. Nodding towards the dance band, who were blasting out 'Begin The Beguine', the well-built young man with broad shoulders and a warm smile politely asked, 'May I have this dance?'

Blushing furiously, Ruby followed him on to the dance floor. When George touched her fingers, she felt an electric shock sensation run through her entire body. Intoxicated by the band, and the boy whose arms were encircling her body, Ruby moved and swayed among the throng of other dancers, all caught up in the music and abandoning themselves to a feeling of complete happiness. Giving no thought to rationing, long shifts, food shortages or the ever-present threat of enemy action, the dancers circled around each other, hugging, kissing, laughing, simply living in the moment. When the dance number came to an end there was a loud groan of disappointment, nobody in the crowd wanted the magic to stop, least of all Ruby, whose hand was being held by George. When the band played the opening chords for 'Jumpin' Jive' the place exploded. Laughing, George swept Ruby off her feet and spun her around before putting her back down again.

And so the night went on, with one popular song following another, until as the enchanted evening came to an end the waltzes started up. With her head resting against George's shoulder and her arms around his neck, Ruby lost herself in the slow rhythm of the music. In a romantic daze, the final dance, simply titled 'Yours', made her tremble with the overwhelming emotions that were coursing through her body. When the lights flashed up and the music faded, the dancers blinked as if awoken from a spell. Turning to George, expecting him to say a simple goodnight, Ruby's happiness was complete when he asked, 'Can I see you again soon?'

'Yes, please,' Ruby eagerly replied.

And until the war started, they were barely apart for

more than a day at a time, getting engaged at eighteen and married at twenty-one. They were best friends as well as devoted lovers. Saying goodbye to her handsome young husband, proud in his soldier's khaki battledress, queueing on Nottingham railway station to board a packed train with hundreds of other new recruits, Ruby felt her heart breaking. But like millions of other women saying farewell to their boyfriends, fiancés and husbands, she kept her feelings to herself – sending her beloved off with a brave smile on her face and a prayer on her lips.

But now, two years into the war, she was bringing up a child on her own, and depended on her ailing mother for childcare. Clocking on at the Bell Works with a stream of other women starting the morning shift, Ruby was glad she was employed as an engine girl. Building Spitfires could only help hasten the end of the war – and bring George home to her and the little son he had not yet even seen.

2. The Bell Works

After clocking on in the large tiled factory entrance hall, Ruby joined the queue of women heading towards the female cloakroom where, amid the usual companionable banter, Ruby changed into her work clothes.

'Bloody 'ell!' one girl exclaimed. 'Did you hear there's another load of young pilots arriving at the Polish airbase in Hucknall?'

Audrey, Ruby's closest friend, unmarried and desperate for a boyfriend, grinned.

'The more the merrier, I say.'

'Shameless hussy!' Annie, the female overseer, rebuked her from across the changing area.

Audrey threw Ruby a cheeky wink, lowering her voice.

'If we were all like her, we'd never even have a blasted boyfriend – and we certainly wouldn't have any fun.'

Glancing nervously towards Annie – to whom she was loyal, despite the woman's sharp tongue – Ruby pressed a finger to her lips. 'Shhh!'

Having worked with Annie for years, Ruby knew better than most how dedicated to her work – and, more recently, the war effort – she was. A middle-aged spinster who lived with her ailing ninety-year-old mother, Annie gave unsparingly to the Bell Works and the factory's output of aircraft that she firmly believed would win the war.

Her zeal often irritated the workers, especially the

younger girls who dismissed her as cranky or bad-tempered, but Ruby – in her typically warm and generous way – respected Annie's steadfast dedication. Wriggling her shapely bottom into her heavy work overalls, Ruby reflected that life had to be more than just a route march, Audrey was right, people needed fun to take their minds off the constant fear the nation lived with. It seemed like the younger you were, the more fun you needed, she thought as she adjusted her green polka-dot turban that contrasted prettily with her rich brunette curls.

Her days of fun had been curtailed when she waved her young soldier husband off to fight on Europe's battlefields. Becoming a mother and taking on the responsibility of rearing a young child had sobered Ruby up, but that didn't mean she had forgotten the giddy days of falling in love, of walking out hand in hand with her boyfriend, kissing in the moonlight and dancing to the strains of the romantic ballad 'I'll Never Smile Again'. She was glad she had so many wonderful memories – which she was quite sure Annie didn't have. There was no space in Annie's strict routine for frivolity or romance, which was why the overseer came across as cranky and judgemental when, in fact, she was simply doing her best for her country.

'Righty-ho, ladies,' Annie called over her shoulder as she left the changing room. 'Let's get down to business.'

With Annie's rallying call ringing in her ears, Ruby hurriedly checked her reflection in the only mirror available. No longer dressed in a pleated skirt and cardigan with her long hair swinging around her shoulders, Ruby marvelled at the difference a change of clothes made. Now wearing masculine work clothes, she cut a completely different figure to the girl who had walked through the streets of Hucknall half an hour ago. But the tough hard-wearing dungarees suited her strong lean body – and more importantly, they gave her the freedom of movement to clamber into the metal fuselages that she generally worked inside, fitting engines into aircrafts straight off the assembly line.

After double-checking to make sure that Annie had left the room, Ruby reached for the lipstick she kept in her pocket. Audrey caught sight of her friend applying her favourite Victory Red lipstick, and grinned. Like many of the other young female workers, war or no war, the girls never failed to gloss their lips before starting work, often swapping different fashionable brands with friends so that they could experiment with various popular colours. Audrey, who was a bit of a make-up specialist, insisted that as a sentimental act of loyalty a girl's make-up had to complement her boyfriend's uniform – not that any of them could afford the time or money for such subtleties, but it was always a bit of fun to share their make-up with each other, especially if Audrey was overseeing the process.

'If your boyfriend is an RAF man, your make-up colours should be softer to match his blue uniform – natural rose lipstick and cream rouge, with a soft English peach foundation. If your man is a soldier boy in khaki battledress, you should be using vibrant colours to reflect his kit – vivid rouge, flaming reds for your lipsticks, and a deep-peach face powder,' she explained now to Ruby, with great confidence.

Mary, one of the youngest girls on the shop floor and

very much an innocent mummy's girl, gave a dismissive snort.

'Who the heck's got that kind of money to go along with all that drivel?'

Audrey, well used to Mary's judgements, rolled her eyes. 'Depends what your priorities are,' she muttered.

Losing track of time as the conversation about rouge and foundation rolled on, Ruby realized with a start that if she didn't get a move on she would miss the precious mug of tea that she looked forward to before her shift started. Ruby hurried out of the ladies' changing room and joined her fellow workers sitting around canteen tables hurriedly drinking tea, in between taking drags from their cigarettes, as they waited for the factory hooter to announce a change of shifts.

When the hooter sounded, the exhausted night team – who had started work at 8 p.m. the previous night – appeared, bleary-eyed and yawning, as they nodded wearily at their replacements. Watching them go on their way, Ruby marvelled at the sheer tenacity of the women she worked alongside. Assembling Spitfires to keep up with the Luftwaffe's Messerschmitts required ever-improving engineering techniques that designers and pilots were constantly finessing. Women who had formerly stayed at home or worked in shops and offices were now employed on large-scale wartime production lines, doing work that was both gruelling and relentless. The noise on the workshop floor alone – the din of heavy machinery, a cacophony of drilling and bolting that never ever stopped – was enough to strain anybody's nerves. With the nation on a wartime footing, the Bell Works operated three hundred and sixty-five days a year to meet the demand for Spitfires; mercifully, there was the incentive of a good bonus for overtime, but the pace was unquestionably blistering.

Occasionally when Ruby watched a pilot test one of the aircraft that she and her team had sweated and slaved to create, her skin prickled with pride. To see something made of metal, beaten and drilled into shape, riveted and hammered by engine girls just like herself, take to the air and soar like a bird was a deeply thrilling moment. Ruby marvelled at the makeover she had been a part of – taking a metal skeleton clamped to a jig, a cramped carcass that she and her colleagues had crawled around inside, securing sheet-metal panels with hundreds of screws, and transforming it into an airborne Supermarine Spitfire. The transformation brought about by a team of skilled engineers – who were constantly advancing aerodynamic technology – and the dedicated workforce, always took Ruby's breath away. Sadly, the grim reality was that however many planes the Bell Works pushed out, just as many were brought down by the enemy, landing in balls of fire in watery graveyards deep in the North Sea and the Channel. The constant need for more and more war planes had to be met. For every one that got shot down, another two were needed to replace it. The task was simply endless – sometimes it even seemed impossible – but it had to be done, Ruby told herself every single day of her working life.

As the day-shift crew walked on to the factory floor, they passed the weary night shift they were replacing. Nods and smiles were exchanged as girls who had grown up together in Hucknall and gone to school with each other in happier pre-war days crossed paths. In teams around the clock this small army of engine girls worked on assembly lines; bolting, drilling and riveting sheet metal on to Spitfire aluminium frames from the nose to the tail. Taking up their allotted posts on the numerous assembly lines that ran in close ranks, the morning shift swung into action. The weekly roster pinned up in the canteen dictated which crews were working together and which assembly lines – wings, nose, tail, cockpit, fuselage – they were assigned to. Apart from the wings, which had their own separate shed out in the yard, large enough to accommodate the span of several Spitfire wings, the assembly lines were concentrated on the Bell Works' vast echoing factory floor.

This week, Ruby was on fuselage duty with Audrey, next week she might be riveting in the wings shed with young Mary, or on the cockpit assembly line, possibly training up a new girl. Ruby's steadiness and patience, combined with her speed and accuracy with a pneumatic drill and riveting gun, made her an excellent teacher; as an older experienced hand she was often called upon to help new engine girls learn the ropes. As things stood right now, there just weren't enough women to keep up with the growing demand for more fighter planes. Female volunteers were slowly joining the workforce in Hucknall but there never seemed enough women to meet the demand.

The sooner female conscription is legalized the better, Ruby thought as she slid her long slender body into the narrow metal fuselage that would soon house the cockpit and engine. Winking at Audrey, who was already hard at work bolting sheet-metal panels into place, Ruby called out over the hammering din of heavy machinery, 'Shove over, duck, make way for me.'

Though Audrey couldn't hear a word, she perfectly understood, shifting her hips sideways to make room for Ruby to wriggle into the cramped space, where she hunched over and hunkered down. Gripping the heavy pneumatic riveting gun, Audrey gave her friend the thumbs up sign.

The two women crouched close together, working in concentrated silence, until the siren shrilled out three hours later for their morning tea break.

3. Whitby

Starting the day, getting ready for work, was one of Lillian Palmer's small pleasures. Not that she liked early morning shifts at the Dolphin Hotel where she worked in Whitby. Lily loved her sleep and had to have two alarm clocks to wake her – as well as her dad shaking her before he took his fishing trawler out to sea almost as soon as the sun rose every morning. But once she was awake, and after she had downed her first strong cup of tea of the day, Lily paid meticulous attention to her presentation. Always wearing a uniform – a smart, black and white waitress's dress modelled on the same design as the Lyons Café famous 'nippy' outfit – relieved her of the problem of worrying about what to wear for work, but that didn't stop Lily from paying particular attention to her make-up and hair. Twisting her long, naturally blonde hair into a fashionable victory roll, much sported by popular film stars, Lily applied mascara to the long lashes fringing her stunning, large silver-grey eyes. After applying her favourite Revlon pink lipstick to her pouting Cupid's bow lips, Lily rubbed rouge along the line of her high cheekbones to emphasize the daintiness of her sweet heart-shaped face. Standing before her small dressing-table mirror in her neat little bedroom overlooking Whitby harbour – presently loud with the shrill call of seagulls wheeling in the bright blue winter sky – Lily smiled at the finished effect.

'You'll do, Miss Palmer,' she announced.

Slipping into her uniform, which she ironed every night before she went to bed, Lily smiled as she admired the completed look. Small and trim, she had shapely hips, fine legs and small high breasts. Lily was confident that she was pleasing to the eye, a fact she enjoyed but never overplayed. It had been drilled into her by her mother that 'pride went before a fall', so Lily had never let her looks go to her head. And really, how could she? Coming from a working-class fishing background, with a father who worked long hours to keep his family housed and fed and a mother from a stern Methodist background, she had been strictly brought up to respect herself, and others too. Her older brother, Hugh, a new recruit in the RAF, had inherited their mother's religious fervour, while Lily had inherited her father's mischievous sense of humour and curiosity about the world around her. Useful characteristics in the hotel business, where Lily thrived. In the years since leaving school, Lily had worked her way up from chamber maid to head waitress at the Dolphin, where she was popular with everyone, customers and staff alike.

Hurrying through the narrow cobbled streets of the little fishing port perched on a north-westerly promontory overlooking the North Sea, Lily inhaled the morning air, rich with the salty tang of the sea and freshly landed fish in laden vessels bobbing on the water. She loved this time of the year, when the seasons changed and summer gave way to autumn. The sea air, still warm with the last kiss of summer, was fresh and pleasant, though the golden leaves on the trees lining the esplanade hinted at a change in seasons. Squally weather would soon blast the little harbour and autumn tides would lash the rocks on the sandy beach. As usual, seagulls wheeled overhead, diving down and squabbling over pickings from gutted fish thrown over the sides of fishing boats. The fishermen (these days reduced to a few men deemed as 'essential workers') had seen Lily grow up. They called out greetings as they waved and winked at the bonny lass who always smiled and waved back.

'Morning. Good catch?'

'Fair to middling. Mind how you go on yonder cobbles, lass, high tide's left 'em right slippy and wet.'

'I'll watch my step,' Lily called back as she confidently threaded her way around the fishing nets laid out to dry. 'Have a good day.'

Breezing into the Dolphin, Lily brought the same cheery spirit into the quiet hotel where the cleaners were busy vacuuming carpets and emptying the fire grates. Her wide smile, the swing of her hips, the busy *tip-tap* of her well-polished, black-heeled shoes and the sheer joie de vivre that she emanated always lifted everybody's spirits, from the hotel manager to the lift boy. Hurrying into the staff cloakroom, Lily hung up her coat, quickly checked her hair and make-up and made for the kitchen where breakfast was in full swing.

'Get yourself a cup of tea before you start serving up,' Chef instructed. 'You young 'uns are all the same these days, thin as pins with no flesh on your bones.'

Lily giggled as she poured herself a cuppa from the big black teapot, always on the go, on the vast industrial stove where Chef was frying sausages that looked more like cardboard than meat.

'Slap a couple of these on a butty,' Chef urged. 'They're not as bad as they look – mostly breadcrumbs mixed with sage and onion, and somewhere in there is a bit of ground pork mince.'

Squashing a sausage between two slices of bread, Lily added a scraping of HP Sauce before sinking her small white teeth into the sandwich.

'Mmm, they're hot and peppery,' she said as she wiped her hands. 'Now to work,' she announced as she headed for the swing doors that led into the elegant dining room with tall bay windows giving magnificent views of the North Sea and Whitby's sweeping promenade.

A fellow waitress on her way into the kitchen gave Lily a meaningful wink.

'Watch out for that grey-haired travelling salesman at table sixteen, he's after anybody in a skirt,' she warned.

Lily circulated breakfast menus to tables already filling up, at the same time deftly avoiding the salesman in the fear that he might indeed have every intention of stroking her shapely bottom.

After breakfast had been served, Lily and her best friend, Vera, cleared away, wiping down the tables, and resetting the cutlery for the lunchtime session.

Seeing Vera's glum expression, Lily edged closer to enquire, 'What's up, lovie?'

Her friend's tender expression caused a tear to roll down Vera's face; grabbing a handkerchief from her uniform pocket, she quickly wiped it away.

'It's Wilfred.'

Lily's heart lurched; Wilfred was Vera's fiancé, only nine-teen, the complete love of the young girl's life. He was currently away training with his regiment.

Lily chose her words carefully. 'Have you had bad news?'

Dabbing her blotchy red cheeks, Vera exclaimed, 'NO! That's just it, I've heard nothing from him since his last leave.'

Lily stared at her incredulously. As far as she recalled, Wilfred had been gone for some time now, possibly as long as six weeks.

'Maybe it's the forces' mail,' she suggested. 'You can wait months for a letter from abroad these days, especially if the censors get their hands on it.'

'I know that,' Vera answered wearily as she flopped into the nearest vacant chair. 'To be honest, I'm worried about a lot more than that,' she blurted out. 'Wilfred's changed . . .' she dropped her voice to a whisper. 'He's sex mad since he joined up.'

Recalling the shy but polite young man with mousey-coloured hair who looked like he wouldn't say boo to a goose, Lily couldn't imagine how he could possibly have put a foot wrong.

'He never stopped pestering me all the time he was home. Said it was my duty as his fiancée, Catholic or not, to . . . you know,' she blushed. 'Do it.'

Again, Lily had trouble imagining gawky Wilfred pres-sing his young fiancée to go against her moral principles.

'And did you do it?' she asked cautiously.

Vera cupped her face in her hands and cried some more.

'On his last night home on leave, I did,' she confessed.

Lily smothered a gasp, not because she was shocked

by the idea of sex outside of marriage, quite a few of her friends had sex with their boyfriends whenever it was possible, but they were all a lot more worldly-wise than Vera – who was, to put it mildly, a bit slow on the uptake.

'I hated it,' Vera blurted out. 'It felt wrong . . . and it bloody hurt too.'

Putting an arm around her friend's shuddering shoulders, Lily comforted her.

Vera stumbled on. 'We didn't, you know, use anything,' she said, at which point Lily's heart sank. Surrendering her virginity without taking precautions seemed a sure-fire recipe for disaster.

'Have you had your monthly since?' Lily gently enquired.

Vera shook her head.

'No,' she answered, almost inaudibly. 'Do you think I might be expecting?'

Put on the spot, Lily answered carefully, 'You'll know better if you miss another one. I've heard other women saying there are signs you should watch out for, like feeling sick.'

'I have felt a bit sick in the morning,' Vera told her miserably.

'Maybe you should try and see a doctor.'

Vera responded in alarm.

'I can't do that, Lil, I haven't got the money to pay a doctor. And anyway, what if mi family were to find out that I've been seeing a doctor behind their backs? Wouldn't they immediately be suspicious?'

The tense conversation came to an abrupt end when the head porter bustled in, waving the lunchtime menus.

'Chef's compliments,' he ostentatiously announced.

'Soup of the day, pea and mint, game pie – probably rabbit – served with roast spuds and sprouts, followed by jam roly-poly and custard. A bargain for one shilling and sixpence!'

Throughout the busy day Lily's thoughts constantly drifted to Vera. Hers was no uncommon story, she knew of two other girls who'd got themselves in the family way. One had married her sweetheart and kept her baby, while the other had been sent away to a mother and baby home in the Lake District. Worried about Vera, Lily wondered what her friend would do if she was in fact pregnant; she didn't imagine the poor girl would get much support from her family.

Serving teas took Lily's mind off Vera's problems. With a winning smile, she mollified fractious children with promises of an ice cream and endeared herself to older couples by topping up their teapots with hot water so they could spin their afternoon tea out a bit longer. As she monitored all the various goings-on in the popular Dolphin restaurant, Lily thanked her lucky stars that she had so far not given her heart away. Of course, she'd had plenty of boyfriends; the most significant (before he was conscripted) was a good-looking engineer who regularly came to fix the hotel's dodgy heating system. They had enjoyed long walks on the beach and a few meals out in Robin Hood's Bay, just a few miles down the coast, all of which Lily had enjoyed until, sitting on a bench just below the memorial that marked Captain Cook's departure for the South Seas in 1768, the young engineer had proposed to her. Flabbergasted, Lily had spluttered her apologies, she wasn't ready for marriage, she told him, but managed not to add least of all to a man she had met barely six times. Indignant and offended, the engineer had left her on the bench. When she returned to the Dolphin, she was told he had packed his toolkit and left in a hurry.

Even now, Lily shuddered at the thought of getting married – maybe one day, in the dim and distant future, but not now while she was young, with the world (albeit a war-torn world) at her feet. She wanted to live, embrace life, and maybe travel, possibly move on to a posher hotel down south, with better money and more responsibility, which would further her career. Though there was a war raging, that didn't stop lovely Lily from dreaming.

'You only get one life,' she often told herself. 'Better make the most of it.'

4. Domestic Quarters

Standing in the cold wind, Ruby shivered as she buttoned her winter coat right up to her chin. She, Audrey and Mary had joined a small crowd of Bell workers on a bleak building site to the rear of the vast factory yard, part of which gave on to the runway where newly built Spitfires were tested before they were dispatched to airfields around the country.

'Bloody 'ell!' Audrey murmured. 'I'd rather them than me.'

Ruby couldn't have agreed more. The rows of prefabricated buildings presently being assembled looked bleak and unwelcoming in the driving grey rain. Though clearly needed, these newly erected domestic quarters for incoming female workers from other parts of the country didn't exactly look homely and welcoming.

'They'll soon be needed, when outsiders arrive to swell the ranks of our Hucknall workforce,' Audrey pointed out.

'Conscription's not compulsory yet, but I bet it won't be long coming. With our men fighting at the front, women will have to jump into their shoes and help run the country.'

'Especially here in Hucknall, building war planes around the clock, we can't knock 'em out quick enough. Mind you,' Audrey grimaced, 'I'm not keen on having strangers cluttering up the place.'

'Don't be daft,' Ruby chided. 'It'll ease our workload and

help the war effort – anyway, like I said, conscription's still not compulsory.'

'Not *yet*,' Audrey retorted. 'I've been reading about women who are keen to get stuck in and do their patriotic bit, they're not hanging about waiting to be told what to do, they're jumping before they're pushed.'

Mary looked puzzled. 'What're you talking about, Audrey?'

'Quite a lot of women aren't waiting until female conscription becomes law. They want to make their own minds up about where they're going to work for the war effort.'

'You see, lovie,' Ruby patiently explained, 'women will inevitably be called up, whether they like it or not.'

Causing nervous Mary even greater alarm, Audrey elaborated.

'They might be sent to join the Land Army, or they could become munitions workers, shipbuilders, mechanics, engineers, air-raid wardens, fire-engine drivers. With our men away fighting, us women will be needed to run the country.'

Mary's face blanched in horror.

'I don't want to get called up,' she gulped.

'Don't worry about it, lovie,' Ruby soothed. 'You're already doing essential war work here at the Bell Works – building fighter planes is an essential job.'

Looking visibly relieved, Mary gazed at the rows of half-built prefabs.

'I wouldn't like to live there myself, there's not enough room to swing a cat.'

'They say they're building different sizes,' Audrey told her friends. 'Two, and even three bedrooms – and they will all have an indoor privy, which might be a luxury for some.'

'Depends where you're coming from,' Ruby said. 'If you're a toff from a comfortable big house with all mod cons then you might see a tin prefab – indoor privy or not – as a bit of a comedown in the world.'

'On the other hand, if you're used to a water pump in the backyard, where you have to break the ice every morning just to have a wash, you might see it as going up in the world,' Audrey pointed out.

Sighing wistfully, Mary murmured, 'I'd love an indoor lavvie. We've got three privies down our back alleyway, lined up, side by side. I've always been terrified of falling down one of them big black holes and landing in God knows what.'

Waving a hand in all directions, Audrey continued, 'They say they'll be extending the site. There'll be Nissen huts all over the place, housing a medical block, communal bathrooms, even a laundry and a little chapel.'

'I'd much rather be at home with mi mam,' Mary muttered anxiously.

Audrey gave her a playful dig in the ribs. 'Don't worry, mi duck, you'll be all right to stay with your mam.'

Gazing at the grim sprawling site, Ruby wondered when conscription would become law. It was only a question of time before the Prime Minister harnessed the female workforce, many of whom would be forced to leave their homes, families and domestic jobs in shops and offices. Ruby was glad that the Bell Works was near to home and her baby, and that she was working alongside so many women she had grown up with. She was happy to be an engine girl, a woman who worked on the assembly line building fighter planes to defeat the enemy. There was no doubt that the

Bell Works was the right place for her. How women leave their kiddies behind and move to another place to do their bit for the war effort beats me, she thought. Thank God I'm right here at home in Hucknall.

Chilled by the easterly wind that was whipping around the yard, the little crowd of women returned to the canteen, eager to grab a cup of tea before the siren called them back to their benches.

'All I can say is, I'm glad I'll be going home to my own bed tonight,' Mary said with obvious relief.

'Don't speak too soon,' Audrey joked. 'If we're pushed to do extra hours, we could finish up in one of them prefabs.'

Panicking, Mary exclaimed, 'I'm not leaving mi mam. I'd hate to live with strangers.'

Seeing the girl looking panic-stricken, Ruby flashed a 'shut up!' look at Audrey.

'Just ignore Audrey,' she smiled. 'You should know by now how much she likes to tease people.'

Looking grumpy, Mary muttered, 'Humph! I don't think it's that blinking funny.'

Deep in thought, Ruby returned to work on the shop floor. Deafened by the combined sounds of bolting and hammering, she concentrated hard on drilling metal plates on to the sides of the aircraft's fuselage, which was secured to a jig. With the ceaseless din of the assembly line pounding in her ears, Ruby joined Audrey in the body of the plane. She was almost on autopilot as she considered her future options. If Audrey was proved right, and production were to increase – and realistically, how could it not in the circumstances? – would she too inevitably be working even longer hours? Strong and fit, she could physically do more hours if necessary – and as Audrey had pointed out, the bonus for overtime was very attractive – but she wasn't the only person in the equation. There were Archie and her mother to consider. Her mother couldn't possibly do any more than she was already doing, and anyway, Ruby told herself, she wouldn't push her. But if she and her other colleagues were forced to work round-the-clock shifts, she would have no choice but to book Archie into a local day nursery. One thing was clear, Ruby could *definitely* not stop work. It was her moral obligation, her bit towards beating the tyrant Hitler. God, she thought to herself, how much harder was it going to get? Already they were struggling with household bills – especially fuel, which right now was a vital commodity needed for industry and warships. Domestic distribution would be a low priority, but how would they get by if they were both cold and hungry?

The long gruelling day was broken by welcome tea breaks, when the girls could at least hear themselves speak. Gazing glumly at her grey-coloured sandwich, Mary groaned.

'Mi mam's only gone and packed me jam butties!'

Knowing how dirt-poor Mary's family were and how her mother struggled to bring up six children, the youngest under a year old, Ruby immediately offered Mary a round of her own corned-beef-and-piccalilli sandwiches.

'Here, help yourself.'

'Ta very much,' Mary said gratefully, as she eagerly accepted the offered food. 'I know we're poor,' she muttered, 'but I can't get through a day's work in this place on jam butties.'

Seeing Mary's eyes resting longingly on her remaining sandwiches, Ruby said tactfully, 'Swap yours for mine – jam will make a nice change.'

Leaving Mary to get on with her dinner, Ruby slumped back in her metal chair and closed her eyes. She was grateful for the comparative peace of the canteen; Joe Loss's orchestra playing out on the overhead radio was soothing compared with the racket of the shop floor.

'Bad night with the baby?' Audrey enquired as she lit up a Woodbine.

Ruby shook her head.

'It's not Archie, it's mi mother that's troubling me these days. I think I'm wearing her out with all this babysitting,' she confessed. 'The thought of our hours increasing is worrying me sick, I really can't ask Mam to do more.'

'Aye, it's tough all round,' Audrey sympathized. 'Not even mothers and babies get off light when there's a war on.'

5. Jump Before You're Pushed

After a long and busy shift at Whitby's Dolphin Hotel, Lily walked home deep in thought. Earlier she had served afternoon tea to a smart young woman and her middle-aged parents in the hotel's elegant dining room overlooking Whitby's quaint old promenade. Placing a plate of neatly cut cucumber sandwiches and a pot of tea on the table where they were sitting, Lily had not been able to help but overhear some of their conversation.

'Really, darling,' the grey-haired, softly spoken mother had fretted. 'It seems precipitous to make the move now.'

Responding to his wife, the older man had said in a much louder voice, 'I agree with your mother, dear, as far as I'm concerned, you'd be wise to wait until you get your call-up papers.'

The attractive young woman, smartly attired in a military-style tweed coat and matching tweed hat, had looked distinctly uncomfortable and wriggled awkwardly in her seat.

'I thought we'd agreed to have tea together in order to take our minds off me joining the Auxiliary Territorial Service,' she'd said impatiently. 'I'm twenty-one, surely I should be allowed to make my own decisions.'

When she returned to the table later, with rounds of toasted tea cakes and coconut macaroons, Lily had sensed that the mother, though tearful, seemed nevertheless resigned, while the father huffed and puffed into his large bushy grey moustache, muttering all the while, 'I still don't believe there's any reason to rush into things – female conscription will come soon enough.'

For the rest of her shift the family's earnest conversation had spooled through Lily's head and now, heading home, it was still running through her mind.

Walking along the harbour wall with Captain Cook's imposing statue standing high above her, the fine figure confidently looking towards the southern horizon where his destiny lay, Lily wondered about her own destiny and where it would take her. North, east, south, west? Once conscripted, she could be sent anywhere to do her bit for the war effort; some jobsworth in a municipal office would decide her future, without consulting her or her wishes. Did she want to build ships, or harness carthorses to a plough and work the land? Or would she join the canary girls in munitions factories, building bombs and ammunition? Hearing the low drone of an aeroplane overhead, Lily stopped to gaze up at its progress out over the North Sea. With houses blacked out and street lights turned off, Lily watched as the faint outline of the aeroplane disappeared behind a bank of dark cloud. Always interested in aircraft, Lily wondered what the plane might be – a Bristol Beaufighter perhaps? Where was it heading? she wondered. What was its load? Who was the pilot? And what airfield had it flown out of? Aware of a tingling sense of excitement running through her veins, Lily had a sudden realization. She knew what she wanted to do for her country.

'I want to build aircraft,' she thought. 'I want to be an engine girl!'

*

Ironically, a few days later, Lily had a very similar conversation with her parents to the one she had overheard while serving tea to the family in the Dolphin. After Mrs Palmer had remonstrated at the idea of Lily volunteering for war work, Mr Palmer said, 'I can see that the lass has a point.'

Clearly annoyed that her husband wasn't backing her up, Mrs Palmer cried, 'Don't be ridiculous! Why does she have to rush things?'

Lighting up his old pipe, Mr Palmer took a few lugubrious puffs before he responded calmly, 'So she gets to pick what she wants to do.'

Smiling, Lily quickly nodded her head. 'Dad's right, female conscription is inevitable, we're hearing about it all the time these days,' she pointed out. 'It's sensible to choose the kind of war work I want to do while I've got the chance.'

Now tearful, Mrs Palmer exclaimed, 'But building planes, that's no job for a lass!'

'Women are already building aircraft, Mother,' Lily reminded her.

'She's right, you know,' Mr Palmer agreed. 'With the majority of our male workforce away fighting, who else could be building them? Ships, tanks, cars – and trains too, for that matter.'

Highly agitated, Mrs Palmer continued, 'There's no planes being built here in Whitby – she'll have to go away. Leave home,' she added on a sob.

'If she's called up, she might well have to go away anyway,' her husband reasoned.

Keen to avoid conflict between her parents, Lily stepped

in. 'There's a war on – there's no dodging the bullet when it comes to female conscription. I'm making a decision while I'm free to do so. I really don't want to find myself doing a job I hate, possibly in a place I hate too. You must see the reasoning in that, surely?'

Nodding, her mother stuffed the handkerchief she had been using to dry her eyes back into her pinafore pocket.

'Aye, I do,' she said resignedly.

Mr Palmer rose to stroke his beloved daughter's long silver-blonde hair.

'I'm proud of you, Lily, just make sure you choose wisely.'

Even though Lily believed she had chosen wisely, she was nevertheless taken aback when just a week later she returned home from the Dolphin Hotel to find a buff envelope addressed to her propped up on the hall table. Hurrying into the hallway to greet her daughter, Mrs Palmer nodded in the direction of the envelope.

'It arrived this morning, just after you left for work. You'd best open it,' she urged.

Sitting at the kitchen table, Lily read the letter. It was short and to the point.

'I've been sent to a factory in Nottingham, a place called Hucknall.'

'Doing what?' her mother enquired.

Lily shook her head in confusion. 'It's not very clear; just assembling machinery, hopefully for aircraft, that's what I specifically asked to do when I applied. Though I didn't specify any town or city – that seemed less important.'

Later, when her father read the letter, she asked, 'Do you

think I will be working with planes, Dad? You know how mad I am about them. After volunteering to do something I've got my heart set on, I'd be really disappointed if I was put to work doing something else.'

Her dad gave a knowing grunt. 'If whoever sent that letter were specific, and the letter fell into the wrong hands – just remember, there are spies everywhere these days – Jerry would have a field day.' Seeing Lily's anxious expression, he added, 'Try not to panic, lass, it's all about dispersal these days.'

'What's that got to do with anything?' his wife asked impatiently.

'It's an important policy,' Mr Palmer explained. 'Don't you remember what happened only a year ago, when the Luftwaffe bombed the Spitfire factory in Southampton?'

'I remember,' Lily recalled. 'The factory was destroyed and over a hundred workers were killed.'

'Aye, that's what comes of having all your eggs in one basket,' Mr Palmer said darkly. 'Since then, the government have spread the workload here, there and everywhere in order to keep the location of aircraft plant a secret. I reckon there are quite a few workers on assembly lines up and down the land who don't even know what they're actually assembling.' Seeing his daughter's crestfallen expression, he quickly added, 'Stop your fretting, lass, if you've specifically stated your preferred line of work, I'm sure that will be taken into consideration.'

Sucking in her lips, Mrs Palmer sighed, 'Eeh, our lass, I'll miss you, and so will your dad. We were both hoping that when you did get called up, it would be somewhere local so you wouldn't have to leave home. Still,' she said, as she took a deep shuddering breath, 'we won't be the first family saying goodbye to their daughter. Everybody is making sacrifices these days.'

Giving her anxious mother a big hug, Lily smiled. 'Cheer up, Mum, with a bit of luck I might be home for Christmas!'

6. Prefab No. 8

By the end of September, with only a week to go before she left for Nottingham, Lily had a lot of goodbyes to say in the hectic days that followed. On hearing of Lily's imminent departure, nearly every customer gave her a hug or a squeeze; a few old ladies particularly devoted to the pretty little waitress they had grown fond of actually wept when they kissed her goodbye.

'They'll never get another lass like you. You always know where we like to sit, and you never stint on topping up the teapot with extra hot water,' they said. 'Aye, the Dolphin will be a poorer place without you, young Lily.'

The staff were even sadder than the customers.

'Best waitress we've ever had,' the manager announced at Lily's farewell drinks party, where all invited were served sweet sherry in tiny little glasses. 'Nothing's ever been too much for Lily, always keen and willing to help, with a bright smile and never a word of complaint.'

Overcome by all the compliments and high emotion, Lily was almost glad when the week came to an end and she walked out of the Dolphin for the last time; all she had to deal with now was actually leaving home and her parents. Standing with their daughter at Whitby station, Mr and Mrs Palmer tried their hardest to be sensible. But when the thundering steam train roared into sight, Mrs Palmer wept openly on her husband's shoulder.

'Now, now, lass, pull yourself together, or else you'll have our Lily bawling too.'

'I'll miss you so much, sweetheart,' Mrs Palmer cried as Lily climbed on to the train. 'Write as soon as you get there.'

Waving from the open window, Lily called back, 'I will, Mum. As soon as I get an address you can reach me at, I'll let you know right away – I promise.'

'Do that, lovie, I'll be worried sick until I know you're in your own digs,' her mother fussed.

As black smoke gushed from the steam engine's funnel and the train started to slowly rumble forwards, Mr Palmer called out, 'Take care of yourself, lass.'

Waving until they were out of sight, Lily watched her parents disappear in a blast of black engine smoke. She finally slumped back into her seat and sighed. What had she let herself in for? Despite all her brave words – joining up earlier than was actually required of her – sitting in a dark and smoggy train that continually pulled over into sidings in order to let more important trains pass by, Lily wondered what on earth waited for her down south in Hucknall, at the end of the line.

After connecting with a troop train in Leeds, followed by a long journey to Nottingham, Lily caught a bus to the Bell Works. She stood in the marbled Edwardian entrance hall, watching the many workers continuously coming and going across the vaulted, echoing space. It was clearly the clocking on and off area at the beginning and end of their shifts. Wondering where she should go, and who she should report to, the pretty and obviously confused newcomer immediately caught the foreman's roving eye.

'Hello, mi duck,' Sid Sharp said, in a thick Midlands accent, as he approached the hesitant young woman. 'You look like you've lost a fiver and found tuppence,' he chuckled.

Fumbling for a letter in her coat pocket, Lily explained, 'I've come here to work.'

'Oh, aye,' Sid nodded. 'Let's tek you to't manager's office and he can decide what to do wi' you. I'm Sid Sharp, work's foreman, by the way,' he added jovially.

After being welcomed by the manager, Mr Lovelace, Lily was allocated her accommodation.

'Prefab Number Eight,' the manager told her. 'I'll walk you over there,' he volunteered.

Following the manager across the sweeping factory yard, Lily stumbled in the darkness. She was grateful for a guide to show her the way.

'We daren't light up the place, too dangerous – the Luftwaffe got wind of Southampton's aircraft industry only last year, blew the place sky high, that's why we try to keep our location off the radar. We don't want that happening here in Hucknall to our aircraft industry, do we?'

Mr Lovelace led her into a small prefab that was freezing cold and echoed with the sound of their voices. He switched on a dim light before elaborating on the work she would be doing.

'You'll be building Spitfires, Miss Palmer, you've been sent to the Bell Works to assemble fighter aircraft.'

Lily's relief and happiness were palpable. She knew exactly what a Spitfire was, and though she had applied to work on aircraft she hadn't quite let herself believe it would actually happen. This was exactly what she had hoped for, and the reason she had made the sacrifice of leaving home, but Lily was nevertheless suddenly overcome. 'I only hope I'll be good enough,' she dithered.

Laying a key on the table in the bare kitchen, Mr Lovelace smiled. 'You'll soon pick it up, though I have to warn you it's hard, repetitive work with little variation, there's not much chopping and changing attached to the job – or, for that matter, to the daily routine. What we do expect from our engine girls is skill and accuracy. Never forget, pilots will be flying the planes you're assembling, so you are very much needed on the factory floor,' Lovelace assured a somewhat overawed Lily. 'Now then, this here's the key to the front door. You'll be on your own for the time being, but it's a two-bed, so somebody will probably join you soon; workers are slowly arriving. You can get yourself breakfast in the factory canteen before you start work tomorrow morning. If you're hungry now after your long journey, you could pop over there for supper,' he suggested.

Lily quickly shook her head. 'No, thank you, Mr Lovelace, my mother packed me enough sandwiches for a week, and I had a flask of tea too, so I'm fine,' she assured him.

'Welcome to the Bell Works, I hope you'll be happy in your war work here, Miss Palmer,' Mr Lovelace said before he left Lily to explore her new accommodation.

Looking around the tiny prefab, Lily's heart sank. It was depressingly sparsely furnished: two narrow single beds, with bedding folded neatly on top, in the front and back bedrooms, each with a rickety old wardrobe and a pine chest of drawers. Blackout curtains covered the windows, making the rooms – lit by dangling bare bulbs – dark and gloomy.

'At least there's a decent bathroom,' Lily thought as she inspected the newly installed bath, sink and lavatory, in a small room just off the main hallway.

The freezing-cold front room, furnished with only a utility mock-leatherette sofa and an armchair, had a small metal fireplace and in the fully equipped kitchen stood a metal table and four metal chairs.

After a quick wash in cold water, Lily boiled up a pan of water and filled the hot-water bottle her mother had given her before leaving. Taking off her warm winter clothes, she slipped into her winceyette nightie and then dived into bed.

Lying on a mattress as hard as a plank, Lily said through her chattering teeth, 'My new home, *brrrrrr*, Prefab Number Eight.'

After a grim night in her icy bedroom, Lily reported in for work at seven o'clock the next morning. Using the card she had been issued with, she clocked on alongside several other women, most of whom nudged each other as they threw sly sidelong looks in her direction. Yet again mystified as to where she should go next, Lily was grateful when a lively red-headed woman with violet blue eyes and a wide gap-toothed smile steered her by the elbow out of the entrance hall.

'I can see you're a new girl,' she said cheerfully as she led Lily into the canteen.

A large Bakelite radio, positioned on a high shelf, was blaring out Glenn Miller's 'Little Brown Jug'.

'Sit yourself down, mind you sit this side of the serving hatch,' Lily's companion advised. Dropping her voice, she whispered, 'Over here is where the likes of us, the *newcomers*, sit.' She said the word with scorn. 'That's what the Hucknall lasses call us behind our backs – they're not that welcoming, if the truth be told. I do believe they think we arrived with the plague or summat,' she giggled. 'Give me two ticks and I'll get you a brew and summat to eat before the hooter goes. I'm Jeannie Bradshaw, by the way.'

Waiting for her new friend to return, Lily surreptitiously took in her surroundings. The vast canteen was cluttered with numerous metal tables and chairs where the workers, mostly women, sat; some were smoking as they chatted over plates of toast and mugs of tea. Before Jeannie re-appeared with their breakfast Lily was aware of eyes staring at her across the space and heads being nodded in her direction. Relieved to see Jeannie (who was at least smiling and welcoming), Lily realized she was famished when she saw the plate of toast that Jeannie set down before her.

'I haven't eaten since I was on the train travelling down here yesterday,' she admitted as she polished off her round of toast before willingly accepting some of Jeannie's.

'You've got to keep up your strength in this place,' Jeannie confided. 'It has to be said, there's enough grub, plain and simple but plenty of it, day and night. How far have you travelled?' she asked.

'Whitby. Where do you come from?'

'Bolton,' Jeannie answered as she leant in closer to whisper. 'I've not been here long, arrived only last week. Like you, I decided to offer my services to King and coun-try,' she grinned. 'It seemed like a good idea at the time, not waiting to be given my marching orders, but now I'm wondering why I rushed it,' she concluded grimly.

'Why?' Lily asked nervously.

Nodding towards the other side of the canteen, Jeannie muttered darkly, 'Like I just said, the locals aren't exactly welcoming.'

Lily's lovely silver-grey eyes opened wide in amazement. 'But we're all in this together.'

'Try telling that to that miserable lot over yonder,' Jeannie grimaced.

'That's ridiculous!' Lily exclaimed.

Jeannie nodded as she lit up a Woodbine. 'More and more volunteers are arriving by the day, so they're going to have to lump it,' she said harshly.

Lily's heart sank; feeling homesick was bad enough, but living in a hostile environment where you blatantly weren't wanted would be just awful. Determined to get some sort of explanation, she asked, 'Do you know why they might resent us?'

Jeannie shrugged. 'I've no idea. Believe me, I've tried to get to the bottom of it, but nobody is forthcoming with the truth. I've smiled and nodded, tried chatting, even asked if I could join them as I was on my own when I first arrived. They let me, but they all clammed up, so I didn't do that again.' Visibly brightening, she added, 'I've not been here long but assembling an aircraft is quite a thrill. So far, I've enjoyed the cockpit assembly line the best. I mean,' Jeannie added with a shy smile, 'it's the place where the pilot sits! Just thinking about him flying a plane I've helped to assemble sends a shiver up and down my spine; it makes me feel proper proud and patriotic,' she confessed.

Lily, with her passion for aircraft, beamed back. 'Oh, I can imagine,' she exclaimed. 'The cockpit is the centre of aircraft operations; I'd love to work on that section.'

'I've overheard some girls talking about how proud they are to be assembling Spitfire wings, they obviously get a kick out of that. It's not something I've experienced myself, but I'm looking forward to working in the wings shed.'

Again, knowledgeable Lily responded enthusiastically.

'It's the wings that give the Spitfire its unique silhouette, and the aerodynamics that make it the best aircraft in the air. I hope I get a chance to work in the wings shed too.'

Laughing, Jeannie responded, 'Don't worry, lovie, we're regularly moved around the factory. It all depends on the weekly roster and which assembly line you're assigned to. Over time you'll cover all the divisions – cockpit, fuselage, nose, tail and wings. You'll get your chance to experience all the different processes that go into building a Spit.' Seeing Lily's wonderful silver-grey eyes blaze with excitement, Jeannie grinned. 'There's nothing quite like seeing a Hucknall Spit fly out of here and take to the skies.'

'Heavens!' Lily exclaimed. 'With all the patriotic pride and commitment here, I'm amazed there's so much animosity in the workplace.'

Jeannie nodded in agreement. 'I totally agree – but sadly, the bottom line is the local lasses just don't like us, simple as that.'

Speculating, Lily said, 'Do you think they resent us taking their jobs?'

Jeannie shook her head. 'No, there aren't enough women working here in the first place; there's plenty of jobs to go around.'

Looking thoughtful, Lily came up with another suggestion.

'I wonder if the Hucknall lasses think that us newcomers get given the best jobs?'

'That doesn't make sense; we're all basically doing the same thing – assembling different parts of a Spitfire. All the jobs are rotated on a weekly basis. Every engine girl gets a stab at working on all the different assembly lines, nobody can cherry-pick, you go where you're sent.' Sighing, Jeannie shook her head again. 'Though we're physically thrown together building Spits, there's no way that we socialize outside of the job – not even in the canteen. The locals sit on one side, and us new girls sit on the other.'

Looking disappointed, Lily said, 'What a shame. We could learn so much from the girls who've been assembling planes longer than we have. I never imagined I'd be walking into a working environment where I wasn't welcome.'

Suddenly scraping back her chair, Jeannie muttered, 'Aye, aye, brace yourself, here comes Annie Barnes, our overseer. Be on your guard, she can be a right cow.' Swiftly moving away, she left Lily alone with Annie.

The overseer didn't even trouble herself with any polite introductions.

'Are you the new girl, Lily Palmer?'

'Yes, pleased to meet you,' Lily answered, with her sweetest smile, which had no effect on the grim-faced woman.

Responding with a curt nod, she barked, 'Follow me, I'll show you to your workstation.'

Hurrying after Annie, Lily was shown into the ladies' changing room where she was issued with work clothes.

Annie pointed to the rows of shelves. 'Dungarees, woollen shirt, boots – pick your size and get changed.'

Petite Lily rummaged around before selecting the

43

smallest pair of dungarees she could find. Holding them up to her slender frame, she couldn't stop herself from bursting out laughing when she saw that the crotch of the garment actually came down to her knees.

'These are men's clothes!' she exclaimed.

'They're all men's clothes,' Annie answered sharply.

Gazing down in dismay at the dungarees she was still holding up to herself, Lily said, 'But they don't actually fit.'

Annie shrugged. 'Find something that fits as much as possible and get a move on, I haven't got all day.' Leaving Lily fumbling about with the clothes on the shelves, Annie exited the room, calling over her shoulder, 'See you on the factory floor in five minutes.'

To Lily's relief, Jeannie appeared in the changing room just after Annie had left.

'I can't find anything that fits me,' Lily wailed.

Jeannie grimaced. 'We all have the same problem. Even though they're dressing women for the job, the powers that be insist on buying men's clothing.' Bursting out laughing at the sight of diminutive Lily drowning in her dungarees, she cried, 'Heck! They're a terrible fit.' Jeannie, stouter and taller than Lily, slipped into her own work clothes and fastened the clips on her dungarees. 'I'm twice the size of you and these things drown me. They're heavy too, trailing around your ankles. You'll have to make some alterations when you've got time.'

Realizing there was little choice, Lily settled for an enormous pair of dungarees that she had to roll up three times so she didn't trip as she walked. Seeing her reflection in the small mirror over the communal sinks, Lily couldn't believe she was the same girl who only the previous week had worked at the Dolphin Hotel wearing a dainty black and white waitress's uniform with a crisply ironed apron and a lace-frilled cap. Groaning inwardly, Lillian fastened the laces on her big heavy work boots. Before they left the changing room, Jeannie thrust a red cotton polka-dot scarf into her hands.

'We might look rubbish, but we have to keep standards up somehow – put this on, like this,' Jeannie explained as she tied her green polka-dot scarf into a knotted turban on top of her head. 'And finish it off with a dash of lipstick – Victory Red is my favourite,' she giggled as she passed her cherry red Maybelline lipstick to Lily. 'Brightens up our day if nobody else's,' she laughed.

7. Spanner and Hammer

When Jeannie led Lily on to the factory floor, the bewildered newcomer gazed up at the aircraft, all in different stages of assembly, and caught her breath in astonishment. To one side of the vast echoing space, technicians and draughtsmen, mostly older men past conscription age and some young female technicians, were labouring over plans and designs, while at the other end of the factory Spitfires secured to jigs were being constructed. Seeing the gleaming metal fuselages taking shape – the nose, the cockpit and tail – made Lily shiver with sheer excitement. She presumed that once the wings had been fitted and the Rolls-Royce 'Merlin' engine put through its final tests, the finished aircraft would be wheeled out on to the runway to await collection. Imagining a completed Spitfire – one that she had helped to build – roaring down the runway and taking to the skies raised goosebumps on Lily's slender arms.

The noise level all around her was completely deafening. The combined sounds of metallic banging, clanging, battering, drilling and bolting literally made her ears ring. She turned to Jeannie, trying to make herself heard over the din.

'Where do I go?'

Waving a hand in the air, Jeannie mouthed, 'Can't hear you.'

When Lily felt a hand grip her arm, she jumped in surprise.

'This way,' Annie said as she indicated that Lily should follow her.

In a daze, and feeling like her ears would explode, Lily made her way around the vast factory floor. The space was divided into areas in which aircraft kits in various stages of assembly were ranged in rows as far as the eye could see. Lily knew from the cinema newsreels that thousands of planes were needed to wage a war that was predicted to be fought predominantly in the air. Slowing her step to gaze around, she gasped at the enormity of the task created by such a massive operation. Realizing she needed to quicken her pace in order to catch up with the overseer, Lily filed past assembly lines where crews of engine girls wearing the same ghastly over-sized dungarees were straddled across aircraft tails and noses, crouched inside cramped cockpits, or working at a higher level on fuselages supported on precarious metal jigs.

Seeing Annie beckoning to her from an open doorway, Lily followed her out into a draughty concreted yard where the supervisor rattled through procedure with the bewildered newcomer.

'Crews work in pairs. You might not always be paired with the same engine girl but you will get to know your crew, as teamwork is essential here. You'll do the same thing, day in and day out, albeit on different sections of the aircraft – your work will include riveting, drilling and bolting cockpits, fuselages, tails, and working on Spitfire wings and noses, which come in pre-made kits. Your task is to excel at your work until it becomes second nature to you; something you could do in your sleep. Always keep your mind on your task, sloppiness could cost a pilot his life,' she said grimly. 'Teamwork, speed, accuracy and efficiency are what we expect of our engine girls here in Hucknall.'

Though she had longed for this task, Lily suddenly felt overwhelmed and panicked. 'I've always loved aircraft,' she blurted out. 'I'm interested in the engineering side of things too. I'm keen to learn more,' she added, with her most charming smile. 'It would be really useful to talk to the engineers and learn more about the workings of a Spitfire.' Seeing Annie's disapproving expression, she added rather self-consciously, 'If that could be arranged, of course – it's important to me that I do my best for my country.'

'That's as may be, but this isn't a college of learning, young lady, we're here to assemble aircraft parts and build war planes at speed, we can't have workers thinking they can study while they're on the job. The best workers here are the fastest, the most skilful and the most experienced. They learn from hard graft and experience – we don't tolerate hangers-on.'

Stung by Annie's harsh words, Lily remonstrated with her. 'I'm only saying I'd like to learn more about the whole process – greater knowledge and understanding must help new engine girls in the long term?'

Annie rolled her eyes impatiently. 'For the time being you'll work with Jeannie on the fuselage assembly line.'

Lily nodded. 'We've already met. She's kindly been explaining how things work here.'

'She's taken to the work and got the hang of things without mithering for preferential treatment,' Annie grumbled.

Then she said, rather begrudgingly, 'I'll see if one of the engineers can spare you a few minutes later on.'

'That would be very kind of you,' Lily answered civilly.

Obviously annoyed, Annie added, 'Though it has to be said, we Hucknall workers learnt the job on the spot. Nobody taught us,' she explained, with a disapproving sniff. Abruptly turning away, she said, 'Let's get back inside.'

Lily followed the overseer back indoors. She was beginning to realize that Jeannie's advice on the 'them' and 'us' situation was spot on.

How on earth did things get so bad? Lily worried.

Once more on the factory floor, all thoughts other than concentrating hard on the task at hand simply fled. Yet again, Lily reacted to the clamouring noise that made speech impossible. How would she ever learn anything if she couldn't even hear what she was being told to do? After directing her to Jeannie, who was crouched low in the narrow confines of an aircraft's fuselage, Annie walked away, leaving Lily clambering up a ladder that gave on to a scaffolded jig to support the aircraft's carcass.

Dropping nervously into the metal shell, Lily crept on her hands and knees towards Jeannie, who was holding a large pneumatic drill in her right hand. Realizing that words were wasted in a situation like this, Lily closely watched her friend drilling holes into a long slim sheet of shaped alloy that formed one of the many sections making up the undercarriage of the fuselage. Lily was thrilled to be at last inside the heart of a Spit; she felt privileged to be working on these beautiful planes, she was proud of their name and prowess and what they were already achieving in the skies over Europe. As she crawled after Jeannie and watched her drill a series of neat holes in a metal seam, Lily realized she was already looking forward to working on all the different assembly lines, which would give her greater knowledge and insight into the aircraft she loved most.

Breaking through Lily's thoughts, Jeannie indicated that they should retrace their steps to the spot where they had started from, at which point Jeannie replaced the pneumatic drill with a riveting gun which she used to secure the metal section she had just drilled into place. At the end of this procedure Jeannie indicated that they should work in tandem – Jeannie would do the drilling, leaving Lily to do the riveting. Feeling extremely tense, Lily reached out for the riveting gun dangling from a line suspended from the ceiling, momentarily staggering under the weight of the hefty tool. Previously, the heaviest thing she had ever lifted in the workplace was a hotel lunch tray loaded with plates of meat and two veg; this cumbersome device was altogether another challenge. Gingerly balancing the riveting gun in both hands, Lily used it to rivet the sections she'd watched her friend so expertly drill. Pressing down hard on the gun, she felt her whole body resonate under its power; terrified of making a mistake, Lily concentrated hard on keeping the gun steady. Seeing Jeannie observing her at work, Lily turned to her friend with a questioning look.

'Is this okay?' she mouthed.

Grinning, Jeannie gave the thumbs up. Relieved that she was doing the right thing, Lily threw her a grateful smile before returning to her riveting. Working diligently alongside her new friend, Lily's back and knees began to ache from bending and crouching for such a long period of time. Briefly glancing up from her task, Lily was struck to see so many women, engine girls just like herself, working on Spitfires, all with the same fixed, concentrated expression on their faces, all focused on the same backbreaking job that they believed might help bring about what they most hoped for – the end of the war.

After what seemed like hours, the hooter shrilled out for a break. Indicating that Lily should follow her, Jeannie crept out of the fuselage and descended the ladder propped up against the jig. They threaded their way across the factory floor to enter the canteen area, where the noise level dramatically returned to normal.

With a heartfelt smile, Lily exclaimed, 'Thank God for that!' Realizing that she had spoken in the overloud voice used on the factory floor, embarrassed Lily dropped her tone to a more normal level. 'I don't know what I would have done without you, Jeannie. To guide me,' she added, as they joined the queue at the canteen hatch where strong tea and bread with a thin scraping of margarine were being doled out. Cheerful Jeannie shrugged as she loaded their tray.

'That's all right, lovie, we all get dropped in the deep end to start with. Granite-faced Annie dumps us on the job, then leaves somebody else to show us the ropes.'

Though a little embarrassed, Lily couldn't help but respond excitedly, 'I'm really fascinated by how an aircraft gets assembled. I was hoping once I got settled in that I could find out more – learn about the process of building aircraft. I even mentioned it to Annie,' she admitted.

Jeannie threw her a knowing grin. 'Humph! I bet that went down like a lead balloon?'

Lily grinned back. 'She wasn't impressed.'

'Realistically, I can't see anybody sparing the time to do that – everybody is so crazy busy here. Maybe that's the nature of the job,' Jeannie considered. 'We're just cogs in a wheel – we all do our different bits as best we can, as quickly and skilfully as we can, with no questions asked.'

'That's more or less what Annie said when I asked her about some kind of training. She looked like I'd just landed from Mars!' Lily laughed. 'She said Hucknall girls don't make a fuss, they just get on with it. Heck, I hope Annie doesn't think I'm too big for my boots, asking questions, wasting her time.'

'Stop mithering yourself, lass,' sweet Jeannie smiled. 'It's normal when you start a new job to get some sort of basic training. The technical department at the far end of the factory is crawling with engineers. Why shouldn't they spare us a bit of time, if it helps make for a better and safer end product? I bet they'd queue up to spend the time of day talking to a bonny girl like you,' she teased. Plonking their tray down on an empty table, Jeannie groaned as she gazed miserably at the grey-coloured bread and the pale margarine on their plates. 'God, what wouldn't I give for a chip butty or a meat and potato pie.'

'Rationing or not, we used to serve lovely food at the hotel where I worked,' Lily sighed wistfully. 'Fresh fish, scallops, crab, sometimes lobster, and always homegrown veg, pies and desserts too, all created by Chef in the kitchen. He could work miracles with very little.'

'STOP! STOP!' Jeannie cried. 'It's torture to hear you describe all that lovely grub.'

After quickly downing her strong black tea, Jeannie

lit up a Woodbine. She thoughtfully blew out the smoke before returning to the original subject they had been talking about.

'To be honest, there have been times when I've thought of going to Mr Lovelace to complain about how casually we newcomers are treated. From my experience, and from what I've seen of him, I think the works manager is a fair man, but I don't think he's fully aware of what's going on in his factory. How we're just dropped in at the deep end.'

Reflecting on her recent experience, Lily said thoughtfully, 'We're constantly being told we're not producing enough aircraft to beat the Luftwaffe. The government will need more workers to meet their targets, which means drafting in more workers. As the numbers build up, there's got to be a better training policy in place.'

Jeannie gave a cheeky giggle. 'Annie Barnes won't be best pleased.'

Lily shrugged. 'Tough luck, is all I can say.'

8. Hot Cocoa and a Warm Fire

In the days that followed, Lily, exhausted beyond words, barely noticed the bleakness of her new home, Prefab No. 8, nor how lonely she was. Though she wondered what it would be like to have a person to share her digs with, she also worried about it. Lonely as she was, at least at the end of a long and gruelling twelve-hour shift she could go home and go to bed, instead of chatting politely to someone she had been delegated to live with – someone who she might not even like very much. On her own she could rest her aching body and the throbbing muscles she never even knew she had.

'Probably better this way,' she said to herself as she made her way home. Clutching her gas mask, she hunched her shoulders against the bitterly cold winter wind sweeping across the dark yard that led to the domestic quarters. 'At least I've got time to adjust to the job. Of course it would be nice to have a housemate who I got on with, but that's the luck of the draw.'

Chilled to the bone as she was, Lily would always wash off the grease and the grime of the working day before she went to bed. In her happy and carefree former life in Whitby she would have looked forward to a bath at least once a week, tepid maybe, but still a bath, with bath bubbles and soft towels, and her silky Lauren Bacall dressing gown to slip into once she had towelled herself down.

These days it was a strip wash in a freezing-cold bath-room where the very last thing she wanted to do was take her clothes off. Nevertheless, Lily forced herself to have a proper wash every night before she tumbled into bed in her long, warm winceyette nightie, buttoned up to the neck to keep out the draughts that seemed to blow through the prefab rather than around it.

First, she would scrub away the metallic grit and dirt lodged in her fingernails. Then, using a cold flannel, she would wipe down her dusty and grimy body. It wasn't a pleasurable experience, but the feeling of being clean at the end of her ablutions was so satisfying it was worth the effort of stripping off and all the discomfort that went with it.

Bone weary and tired at the end of her long shift, Lily was waiting for the kettle to boil so that she could fill up her hot-water bottle. She laid her overlong dungarees on the kitchen table and carefully snipped a good six inches off each leg. After putting her hot-water bottle into her single bed, she settled down with her needle and thread in front of the fire that she had lit in the grate as soon as she arrived home. Luckily, kindling was freely available – which was a blessing for the prefab inhabitants, as a fire in the sitting-room hearth was the only source of heat. The rest of the rooms might be chilly, but the sitting room warmed up nicely over a few hours. Wishing she had a wireless set to keep her company, Lily recalled evenings at home when she had listened to the news on the family's Bakelite radio. Sitting in comfy old armchairs before a crackling fire, the family always gathered to drink cocoa as they listened to the news. Though the news had been on at work, it was drowned out by the clatter of scraping chairs and tables and the combined babble of voices in the canteen. With the promise of earning good money, Lily was determined to save up for a wireless, not just for the pleasure of hearing popular music – which she loved to dance to, even if it was on her own – but she also liked to keep up with the war news, particularly when it came to the success of aircraft battles in the skies over Europe.

Glad that she had brought her sewing kit with her, Lily popped a thimble on to her finger in order to push a needle through the thick fabric of the dungarees. She had hastily taken them up and tacked them on her first night home from work, but the rough stitching had worn loose, and they were now in need of more serious alterations. Absorbed in her work, she made a mental note to herself: she would make more effort to turn the prefab into a home rather than just a bolt-hole. A lampshade over the dangling bare bulb would make a difference, and maybe she could brighten up the grim, bog-standard utility sofa with pretty cushions and a bright cover. Glancing around the bleak room, Lily considered how a few little ornaments on the mantel shelf would liven the place up, and a bright rag rug would go well in front of the fire. She was sure she could pick bits and bobs like that up at a local jumble sale, but when would she have the time to queue? When she wasn't working, she was likely to be too exhausted to go shopping. Anyway, living alone she would be the only one to appreciate any interior design changes. Was it really worth the effort just for her own personal satisfaction? The arrival of a housemate might inspire me, Lily considered, as she finished hemming one leg of her dungarees before chewing off the thread and starting work on the second. What's happened to me? she chastised herself. Once so neat, so proud of my looks, my clothes, my hair and my surroundings. After just a few days' work there was simply no time to fuss over minor details like her appearance. Anyway, it didn't matter what she wore because as soon as she got to the Bell Works she would change into the standard (male) uniform and inevitably look like the back end of a bus! Well, at least I won't be tripping up now that these trousers are shorter, she thought gratefully, and I won't be as hampered by them inside a cramped cockpit where space and ease of movement are always at a premium.

Yawning, Lily laid aside her sewing and went into the kitchen to pour milk into a saucepan to heat. Mixing cocoa powder in a cup, she recalled the conversation she had had with Jeannie on her first day. She caught the milk before it boiled over, poured it on to the cocoa powder, then made her way back into the sitting room. She wondered about the divide between the local workers and newly arrived workers like herself. Surely, they must realize that extra hands would significantly lighten the workload? In fairness, Lily thought, she had seen some Hucknall women throughout the day who seemed less hostile. One tall, striking woman with lovely thick brunette hair and sparkling blue eyes had smiled at her in the changing room, and the shy young girl with her had thrown Lily a furtive half-smile. She could only hope that things would improve as more women arrived and the workforce bonded – after all, they had one common cause that united them, which was to build Spitfires to beat the enemy. There could be no better motivation than that. Thinking of the tiffs she had regularly witnessed at the Dolphin Hotel in Whitby, when staff had clashed or a new employee annoyed an established member of staff, she knew from experience that time was a great healer. Hopefully, it will be the same here in Hucknall, Lily thought as she finished her hot drink.

Standing up, stretching her slender young body, she guiltily realized that she hadn't penned the letter she had promised to write to her parents. Lily looked around for a notepad and pencil to take to bed with her.

Once snuggled under the blankets and eiderdown, with the bedside light switched on, Lily started to write her letter home.

Dear Mum and Dad,

Just to let you know I arrived safely in Nottingham and I've been allocated prefab accommodation. You'll never believe it, Mum, we wear men's dungarees for work, two or three times too big for us! I had to take up my pair six inches, they were dragging on the floor and tripping me up. I'm so grateful that you taught me how to sew when I was little, I didn't appreciate it then but I do now. You wouldn't begin to recognize me, your smart fashionable daughter in dungarees and a spotty headscarf, though I did notice today that the engine girls here make a point of wearing lipstick, usually bright red, it seems to be part of the uniform. I'll have to get a new lipstick when I have some time off, as the ones I brought from home are mostly pink.

You'll be relieved to hear that I got the work I requested – I'm assembling aircraft! You'd take to it quicker than me, Dad, at least you can fix your fishing boat's engine when it conks out. I haven't a clue! I work alongside hundreds of other women; newcomers like me, and local lasses from Hucknall. We work in crews assembling different aircraft parts — nose, cockpit, tail, wings — then the finished fuselage is fitted out with controls, and of course the beautiful engine from Rolls-Royce. I can't wait to see one of those famous Merlin engines! Once the aircraft leave the factory, they are then sent where they are most needed. That's top-secret information we workers aren't privy to, but being nosy I'd love to know the destination of the aircraft we build.

The factory where I work is one huge assembly plant — the noise level is indescribable. The constant din of riveting and drilling echoing around the factory floor stopped me dead in my tracks on my first day at work. You literally can't hear yourself speak. We communicate by mouthing and miming; believe me, it's hard work starting a job when you can't even speak! I was paired up with a nice girl called Jeannie, from Bolton in Lancashire. She's a new volunteer, like me, and we're on the same production line for the time being, which is good, as you need somebody you trust to show you the ropes when you start. It was Jeannie who taught me how to rivet and drill long lengths of metal alloy on to a fuselage. It sounds proper grand, building aircraft, but really, it's hard work, repeat, repeat, repeat, in cramped conditions, holding heavy pneumatic tools that, at first, I thought I would drop. If I carry on like this, soon I'll have muscles as big as Robert Mitchum! It's tough but necessary work, though I think we would benefit from a bit of training, which I rashly mentioned to my crabby supervisor who was not impressed. Her attitude seems to be 'like it or lump it' — sink or swim — which, to be blunt, isn't very helpful.

On a lighter note, my new friend Jeannie mentioned they have dance nights here in the factory canteen. You both know better than anybody how much I love dancing, but to be honest I can't imagine where I'll ever get the energy to dance after a twelve-hour shift. And anyway, where would the fellas come from? There's hardly any here on-site, and those that are here look even older than you, Dad. Anyway, with that cheeky remark I'll say goodnight.

Your loving and devoted daughter,
Lily xxx

PS: I've noticed that workers are already applying for leave over the Christmas period. I have too, nothing ventured, nothing gained! But as you can imagine, everybody will be wanting time off then, especially the locals with families, they're sure to get first dibs.

9. Edna Yates

After spending a long day crouched underneath a fuselage, riveting sheet metal on to an undercarriage, Lily arrived home to find a stranger sitting on the utility sofa in her prefab's bleak sitting room.

'Hello,' said the stranger as she sprang to her feet when Lily walked into the room. 'I hope you don't mind,' the newcomer spluttered. 'They gave me a key and told me to let myself in. Oh, I'm Edna, by the way, Edna Yates from Wigan.'

Genuinely delighted to have a housemate, Lily smiled warmly as she returned Edna's handshake.

'Lily Palmer,' she said as she dropped her gas mask on to the sofa and went to hang up her coat. 'Can I get you a cup of tea?'

'Oh aye, I'd love a cuppa,' Edna answered eagerly. 'I feel like I've been on that blasted train for a week, it stopped everywhere down the line – places I never even knew existed. Not to mention the times we were shunted into sidings to let the priority trains pass. I've only come from Wigan, but I feel like I've crossed the bloody Equator,' she chuckled.

While they waited for the little kettle to boil on the small electric stove in the kitchen, Lily showed Edna to her new bedroom.

'The beds are as hard as rock,' she said apologetically. 'And these prefabs are freezing cold.'

Edna surveyed the room.

'I've known worse,' she said. 'At least I have my own room, and an indoor lav and running water, better than a two-up two-down with an outdoor privy and a hand pump in the backyard, which is what I've been used to. The kitchen's all right,' Edna continued when they returned there to brew the tea and make beans on toast.

'Sorry, that's all I've got in,' Lily confessed. 'I eat most of my meals in the canteen. Anyway, there's never a minute to shop, as you'll soon find out for yourself.'

'I'm grateful for small mercies,' Edna said as she hungrily polished off two rounds of beans on toast and several mugs of strong tea.

Surprisingly relaxed in the newcomer's company, Lily took to Edna right away. A plump, cheerful, no-nonsense northerner, with humorous brown eyes, dimples in her pink cheeks and a ready smile, she promised to be easy company. After they had finished their supper, Lily helped Edna unpack her few belongings into a rickety chest of drawers.

'I hope you've enough room for your things?'

Edna burst out laughing. 'To be honest, I've not brought much,' she smiled. 'Just some tops and skirts, and a dress or two.'

'Believe me, you won't be needing them,' Lily informed her. 'We're supplied with work clothes.'

'That's handy like,' Edna responded.

'I wouldn't go that far,' Lily laughed. 'Completely unsuitable – terrible men's dungarees, and big woollen shirts. I've had to alter all of mine.'

Back in the cosy sitting room, with a pot of tea brewing by the fireplace, Edna lit up a Woodbine.

'So, why did you choose to leave home and come here?' she enquired.

After explaining her motives, Lily asked the same question.

Edna gave a heavy sigh. 'Well now, thereby hangs a tale. I've got a two-year-old daughter, Kathleen.' Leaning over, she drew a small picture frame from her capacious battered black handbag.

Wondering where this story was going, Lily gazed at the black and white image of a little girl, with exactly the same dimpled cheeks and dark eyes as her mother.

'She's the spit of you,' she murmured.

'Not so chubby as her mam, thankfully – and I hope not so daft,' Edna said, with a grin. Sighing, she continued, 'Poor little sod – she had to be evacuated to the Lake District for her own safety, with us living so near to Liverpool as we do.'

Lily gave a sympathetic nod. 'Liverpool's been really badly hit.' Feeling genuinely sorry for her new housemate, Lily said, 'I'm so sorry, you must miss her dreadfully.'

'I do, but Liverpool's not safe for a kid.'

'It must have been awful saying goodbye to her,' Lily commiserated.

Edna blinked back tears.

'I can tell you it were no fun seeing her off on't train, just two years old and screaming the place down. Some bossy cow with a posh voice scooped her up and carried her off. It's not like you can explain much when they're that little,' Edna continued. 'How can you begin to tell a little 'un why you're sending her away to live with a complete stranger? I know us women have to give up our kids so we can do our bit for the war effort, but it's not fair – and that's a fact.' Taking a deep breath, she moved on. 'Any road up, once I knew our Kathleen was safe and sound I opted for war work here. I've not had much of a life,' she admitted. 'After leaving school at fourteen I started working in a clothes factory, where I met my husband Jack. We were courting by sixteen, married at eighteen, by the time I was nineteen I was expecting and living with my mother-in-law in Wigan. Moving south and working in an engineering works seemed like a big adventure,' she concluded, with a shy smile.

Edna paused to accept a top-up of tea from Lily before continuing. 'Like you, I jumped before I was pushed, plus I knew that when conscription comes in, I definitely didn't want to do farming or nursing. I don't know much but I am curious about engineering. Though in truth you never know where you'll be sent, do you?'

Lily nodded. 'Dad told me that for safety's sake the armaments industry is scattered far and wide – parts are assembled in warehouses and factories all over the country. Some people working in the industry don't even know what they're assembling,' she added incredulously.

'It's a clever wheeze to keep Jerry guessing.' Edna grinned, before she got down to brass tacks. 'Anyway, I'm looking forward to this new experience, I'm excited, in fact. Tell me straight, what's it like working here?'

Lily raised her pretty arched eyebrows.

'I have to warn you,' she started, 'so far, the natives haven't been that friendly.'

'Why's that, then?' Edna enquired.

Lily gave a resigned shrug. 'I've not been here long enough to get to the bottom of it, but there's definitely an atmosphere.' Seeing Edna's baffled expression, she added, 'You'll see for yourself tomorrow.'

The following morning, Lily led Edna across the dark chilly yard to the Bell Works, where they both clocked on alongside many other women. Lily, who had already changed into her own work shirt and dungarees, suggested they find work clothes for Edna. Like Lily, her new friend was astounded when she saw them.

'They're *enormous*!'

'You don't have to tell me,' Lily laughed. 'Just find something that fits as well as you can, and I'll help you alter them later when we get home.'

Coming out of the changing room, walking stiffly in an outfit that was miles too big for her, Edna joked, 'I never thought I'd complain about summat being too big, normally it's t'other way round, but you could fit a bus in here alongside me.'

Hurrying into the canteen, Lily urged, 'Come on, or we'll miss our breakfast.'

Over mugs of tea and the usual hot toast spread with unappetizing margarine, Lily introduced Edna to Jeannie. She was delighted to see that they immediately bonded. The three of them, all straight-talking northerners, looked likely to form an easy friendship, which was a blessed relief for Jeannie. Living alone in a prefab on the site, and the first of the three to arrive, it was a real pleasure for her to finally meet some women she could see becoming friends. Their jolly breakfast was interrupted by Annie Barnes who, leaving a group of women she had been chatting and laughing with, approached Edna's table.

'Are you the new girl?' she asked.

'Aye, that'd be me, fresh from Wigan and happy to serve,' Edna said, with a bright enthusiastic smile.

Her warmth and bonhomie were totally lost on the overseer.

'Humph!' she grunted as she turned her back on the newcomer. 'Come this way.'

Jeannie, who had already been at the whip end of Annie Barnes' curt manner, nodded in the direction of Lily, sitting next to her at the canteen table.

'I hope you'll treat Edna nicer than you did my friend here when she arrived.'

Looking indignant, Annie glared at Jeannie who unflinchingly held her gaze.

'I don't know what you're referring to,' she declared.

'I've seen you acting nice as pie to your pals over yonder.' Jeannie nodded in the direction of the local girls on the other side of the canteen. 'You spend time with them on the factory floor, helping and advising. You *definitely* don't do that with us newcomers. You seem to begrudge us your time, like you can't even be bothered.'

'This is an essential aircraft-producing factory, not a social committee! I haven't got time for fine talk and long explanations.'

'I'm not looking for anything other than a welcome to strangers who have travelled a distance to work here alongside your local workforce,' Jeannie said sharply. 'We might not be from around here, but we are patriotic.'

Looking directly at Lily, Annie snapped impatiently, 'Us Hucknall workers, unlike you newcomers, don't ask to be trained up by our overworked engineers.'

Stunned and embarrassed, Lily gaped at Annie. So there it was: offence had been taken because of her polite request to have the simplest, most basic training for the work she was expected to do. Red-faced, she immediately apologized.

'I didn't mean to upset anybody. Really, I just want to do the best I can,' she said earnestly.

Annie gave a dismissive shrug. 'Here, we just do as we're told and get on with the job,' she bluntly concluded, before walking away.

On the factory floor, watching from the confines of a cockpit they were fitting out, Jeannie and Lily saw Annie Barnes lead Edna towards a fuselage supported on a jig. She would be working with the tall good-looking brunette Lily recognized as the woman who had previously smiled at her in the ladies' changing room.

Hours later, when the hooter sounded announcing the morning tea break, Jeannie and Lily were able to hear first-hand how things had progressed with the new recruit.

'We saw Annie teamed you up with that nice Hucknall woman, the one with the lovely brunette hair,' Lily observed. 'She's the only one that manages to throw a smile our way,' she added, with a resigned smile.

'Ruby, she's called, she's really nice, well, as much as I could tell in there.' Rolling her brown eyes, Edna cried, 'Hell fire! The noise. I thought I'd burst my ear drums. At first I didn't know what to do, I had no idea what was going on, but Ruby was patient and explained things to me – not that you can hear yourself speak in there. I had to lip-read what she said, of course, which was really tricky

67

to start with, but I eventually got the drift. Mind you, when I picked up that riveting gun, I got the shock of my life, what a weight! Ruby took me through the drilling and riveting, stage by stage, she was an excellent teacher.'

Relieved, Lily said, 'I'm glad it went well for you. I don't know Ruby personally, but she seems a lot friendlier than most of the Hucknall girls. I was lucky enough to have Jeannie to show me the ropes.'

Looking suddenly excited, Edna continued, 'I'll tell you summat, though – I loved being inside that aircraft, half-finished as it was. I felt a thrill run through me like I was doing something really special and important.'

'I know just what you mean,' Lily said, with a shy smile. 'Even before I came here, I've always loved the look of Spitfires, much more than any other fighter planes. They look so light and graceful.'

Jeannie gave a little snort of laughter. 'Ours are only half-built, ladies,' she reminded her enthusiastic pals.

Lily was undeterred. 'But when you're working in that cockpit, you can't help but wonder who'll be flying the aircraft, and hoping they'll survive. It gives me goosebumps, just talking about it,' she admitted.

'I think you've been watching too many scary war films,' Jeannie scoffed.

Ignoring her scepticism, Lily continued, 'Really, don't you think it's amazing that something built of metal, riveted and bolted, fitted with wings, a propeller –'

'Oy! Don't forget about the engine,' Edna interrupted. 'A Spitfire would be going nowhere without a Merlin engine.'

Undeterred, Lily rolled on. 'A machine, completely earthbound, that takes to the air and flies like a bird because of what we have done, what we engine girls have had a hand in creating!' she concluded.

Seemingly unimpressed, Jeannie stubbed out her Woodbine.

'Well, I suppose that's one way of looking at it,' she said as they headed back on to the factory floor.

10. The Factory Floor

The next morning, Ruby had a cuppa with her close friends, Audrey and Mary, in the canteen.

Settling down opposite each other at one of the many metal tables, Audrey asked, 'How was it, working alongside the new girl yesterday?'

Ruby grinned. 'I don't need to tell you that we didn't do much talking.'

Fully aware of the deafening noise level on the factory floor, Audrey gave a knowing nod.

'She – her name is Edna, by the way,' Ruby explained, 'worked really hard, once she'd picked up what was expected of her. She got on with it, without any complaints.'

Audrey exchanged a knowing look with Mary, who had remained silent, before she grunted, 'Humph! I can't believe the cheek of them new girls. Annie told me that one of them blinking newcomers, the bonny little blonde lass, expected some sort of training – I call that preferential treatment myself.'

'REALLY?' Mary gasped.

'Annie said the new girl had asked for a word with the technicians, said she was interested in aircraft and would like to learn more on the technical side, honest to God!' she cried as she dramatically threw up her hands. 'Talk about wasting time, chatting to bloody engineers before getting down to a bit of hard grafting.'

'We didn't get that kind of molly-coddling,' Mary retorted.

'That's right – it was in at the deep end. And no complaining,' Audrey added.

Interrupting them, Ruby tried to be reasonable. 'If I'd had the chance, I'd have asked for advice from the engineers – there's enough of them around,' she reminded her friends. 'When I started, I was too young and nervous to even think of asking questions. But to be honest, it would have been reassuring to have had some professional guidance. I was terrified. I didn't know how hard to press on the riveting gun, or how deep the bolt holes should go. It was Annie that taught me everything I know, bless her.'

'Exactly!' Audrey exclaimed. 'You learnt on the job, and there's no better skilled riveter than Annie Barnes. She taught you, Ruby, and then you taught someone else, and so on it goes.'

'That's right – it was *you* that schooled me,' Mary reminded her friend. 'That's the way we do things here at the Bell Works.'

Rolling her eyes, Audrey scoffed, 'Before we know it, the new girls will be asking to fly the blinking aircraft!'

Being of a more philosophical nature, and having already worked alongside two of the new girls, Ruby tried to de-escalate the mounting prejudice.

'I agree we all help each other; as you say, that's always been the Hucknall tradition – and actually it's not uncommon in other factories. But there is a significant difference,' she pointed out.

'And what might that be?' Audrey asked.

'They're not like us, who started working here straight after leaving school.'

'More's the pity,' Audrey muttered unkindly, under her breath.

Ignoring her nasty comment, Ruby pressed on. 'I'd say the majority of the newcomers are in their twenties or older, and I'd guess they've all worked in other areas of business. Maybe retail or tailoring, in cotton or woollen mills, and I bet they all had a rudimentary training wherever they worked. So why wouldn't they naturally make enquiries about training when they arrive in a new place? They probably think it's the right way to go about things. Just cos we operate in the same way that our mothers did, dun't mean to say it's the right way. The world doesn't revolve around Hucknall, you know.' She smiled as her words sank in.

'I suppose not,' Mary said meekly.

Feeling a bit sorry for her sweet friend, who always avoided trouble and confrontation at all costs, Ruby added with a smile, 'Listen, mi duck, I don't care two hoots who builds the aircraft the nation urgently needs – they could come from Mars, for all that it matters to me. Just so long as we improve our aircraft output to beat the Germans and win the war, that's all that *really* matters in the end, isn't it?'

Mary nodded slowly. 'Point taken,' she conceded. Then, casting around, she nervously whispered, 'You'd better not let Annie hear you talking like that. You know how much she likes things done the Hucknall way.'

Draining her mug of tea, Ruby replied, 'Annie's a patriotic woman. She'll come around in her own time.'

*

A few hours later, side by side within the tight confines of a cockpit, Ruby paused briefly in her task of drilling a series of neat holes along the long metal section they were working on. Wiping grime from her face, Ruby suddenly spotted Annie Barnes bearing down on Jeannie and Lily, who were working on a fuselage cradled on a wooden jig. From what she could make out at a distance, Annie's body language indicated that the overseer was furious. Gesticulating, she ordered the two women out of the aircraft and then frog-marched them off the factory floor. Heavens, Ruby thought. What on earth has put Annie in such a filthy temper?

It didn't take long to find out. When the hooter blasted out for break time, the row going on in the canteen was fast gathering momentum. Annie was in full throttle, relating her complaint to Sid Sharp. The foreman, dressed in his long brown canvas coat, was rising nervously up and down on the balls of his booted feet.

'Now, now,' he said in his low growly voice. 'What's all this about?'

Glaring at him, Annie snapped back, 'These two have all but ruined a fuselage.'

'That's a bit of an exaggeration, Annie,' Lily politely pointed out. Blushing to the roots of her silver-blonde hair, she added, 'We were riveting a long metal sheet section when I lost control of the riveting gun. I think it may have overheated, perhaps I should have stopped to let it cool down, but I was concentrating so hard on getting the job done I just pushed on, until suddenly it was red hot. I couldn't hold it a minute longer, and lost control.'

'Their work was shoddy, a downright disgrace. You

should see the state of the metal section they were working on,' Annie sneered. 'It'll need completely replacing.'

Galvanized by Annie's attack on her ineptitude, Lily immediately went on the defensive. Though she was angry and humiliated by Annie's accusation, she kept her voice firm and steady.

'Could I just point out that we have had no training or preparation for this work. I'm sorry for losing control – a simple word of warning on the dangers of a riveting gun overheating might have helped me avoid the incident. As it was, I made a mistake for which I apologize. I didn't come here to make mistakes,' she passionately declared. 'I want to do my best and work for my country!' Gazing directly at her supervisor, Lily added, 'I actually mentioned to Annie when I first arrived here that I would appreciate a bit of training, it would certainly have benefitted me on this occasion. I know from experience that ignorance often leads to accidents.'

Sitting at a table not far away, but still within listening distance, Ruby gave Audrey a nudge.

'Oh, heck, trouble at mill,' Audrey tittered.

'Shhh,' Ruby hissed. 'I want to hear what Sid's saying.'

Still stinging from being so publicly humiliated, Lily boldly pushed her point home. 'When I started work as a waitress in a hotel I was trained up for the job.'

Sid's bushy eyebrows shot up. 'Hang on a minute, lady – we're making war planes not bloody cream cakes,' he retorted. 'We haven't got time for life's little niceties here at the Bell Works.'

Looking smugger than ever, Annie vigorously nodded her head.

'Are you aware that workers can be fined for wasting time and not keeping up a steady pace of work?' she snapped.

'I appreciate we have to keep up with our vital output,' Lily agreed. 'But if we do a job badly, simply because we don't have the know-how or the basic training, isn't that a waste of time too?'

'What the hell?' Sid exclaimed, now thoroughly frustrated, as he turned red-faced to Annie. 'Has nobody given the lass any training?'

Looking distinctly cross, Annie muttered, 'I put her alongside one of the riveting lasses.'

Quick off the mark, Lily added, 'I was partnered with my friend Jeannie Bradshaw. She's not been here that much longer than me. She did her best to teach me the ropes, but I could barely hear her speak.'

Now thoroughly incensed, Annie cried, 'We can't stop production every time somebody needs an explanation.'

Seeing her friend struggling, Jeannie jumped in.

'Lily's not the only newcomer who's asked for training before we get chucked in at the deep end. We'd all really appreciate a bit of guidance, but so far our requests –' she rolled her eyes in the direction of Annie – 'have fallen on deaf ears. I was lucky, I was allocated to an experienced engine girl, Ruby Fields, who kindly guided me through my first day.' Jeannie now had the bit firmly between her teeth. 'You could talk us through the procedure in the canteen, or out in the yard, rather than on the factory floor,' she protested. 'At least here, we wouldn't have to lip-read or bellow at the top of our voices to communicate.'

Sid threw Annie a suspicious look. 'Don't you go through the drill with them?' he barked.

75

Seeing Annie shift uneasily, Lily pressed on. 'Believe me – we *really* do want to get things right.'

Sid gave a decisive swagger before thrusting his hands into the pockets of his brown coat.

'We'll sort out a bit more training for you new lasses,' he announced. 'But right now, if you don't mind, I'll have a word with Annie *in private*.'

With all eyes levelled on them, Lily and Edna queued up at the canteen counter for their tea while Sid took Annie into his office just off the shop floor. Five minutes later, she came out with a face like thunder.

Smothering a smile, Jeannie said with undisguised glee, 'Looks like she got a right ticking-off.'

Looking grim, Lily muttered under her breath, 'Let's hope she doesn't take it out on us and make life even more difficult than it already is.'

11. Archie

Later that week, when Ruby arrived home exhausted after an all-day shift, the house was ringing with the sound of Archie sobbing his heart out. Seeing her younger sister, Rita, frantically marching up and down the hall, bouncing Archie in her arms as if he were a football, Ruby snatched up her wailing son and held him close, throwing her sister a grateful look. Soothing him with kisses, she shrugged off her coat and then sat down on a kitchen chair where she accepted the bottle of baby milk that Rita waved in front of her.

'It's still warm,' her sister said.

When Archie's frantic sobs subsided, Ruby popped the rubber teat between his lips. 'Shhh, darling,' she murmured as her son latched on and hungrily sucked the milk. Turning to Rita, who was hovering nervously, Ruby whispered, 'What on earth's going on? Where's Mam?'

'In bed,' Rita explained. 'She's had a funny turn. When I got home from school, she looked like she was going to faint. I managed to get her upstairs, then Archie started bawling his head off. I didn't know what to do for the best,' Rita admitted, with tears in her eyes. 'Look after Mam or sort out Archie.'

'You did so well, lovie,' Ruby assured her. 'Pop up and see how Mam is now, while I finish feeding Archie, will you? If she's asleep, don't wake her up,' she quickly added.

Sitting by the kitchen grate, Ruby smoothed down her son's damp curls, smiling tenderly at his long dark lashes fanning out over his warm pink cheeks as he finally fell into a deep peaceful sleep. Gently carrying him upstairs, she laid Archie in his cot, then crept across the landing into her mother's darkened room where Rita was anxiously hovering.

'She's awake,' Rita told her big sister as she crept out of the room.

'Is that you, Ruby?' her mother called out.

Sitting on the edge of the bed, Ruby said softly, 'How are you, Mam?'

'Better,' her mother answered feebly as she struggled to sit up. 'I've no idea what came over me, I hadn't even got the strength to get up out of the chair and see to Archie when he woke up. Is the little lad all right?' she asked anxiously.

'He's fast asleep, went out like a light after his feed.'

Putting on a brave smile, the older woman said, 'I'll be right as rain tomorrow.'

Hearing the feeble tremor in her mother's normally strong voice, Ruby knew for sure this was not going to be the case. Knowing her mother would resist any suggestion of going to see a doctor, Ruby took the decision to make a medical appointment for her mother the next day.

'I've got the day off tomorrow,' she lied. 'You needn't worry about Archie, just get some rest.'

When her mother, usually so stubborn about her commitment to minding her grandson, didn't argue, Ruby knew for sure that she must be feeling very poorly indeed.

'Can I get you anything, dear?' she asked.

'A cup of tea would be nice.'

'Stay right where you are – I'll bring one up for you.'

Early the following morning, Ruby gave a note saying she was sick to a neighbour who also worked at the Bell Works. She made sure her sister got off to school, then left her mum sleeping peacefully in bed as she tucked Archie up in his big old Silver Cross pram to set off for town, warm in her winter coat and hat. Her first stop was the local doctor's surgery, where she managed to make an appointment for her mother later that day. Her mother (who hated any fuss) would put up a fight, so Ruby knew she would have to force her to the surgery – but if necessary, she was prepared to do that, in order to get proper professional advice.

Unused to being out and about during the day, she enjoyed the brisk walk through the park, which was virtually empty on a lovely golden autumn morning. Nevertheless, Ruby enjoyed watching the ducks' antics on the pond, nipping and chasing each other before indignantly flapping their wings and flying away. She imagined longingly what it would be like to walk Archie to the pond every morning; she would bring bread to feed the ducks, and Ruby would teach her son to say, 'Quack! Quack!' She was missing out on so much, she thought sadly. These baby months would fly by, and before she knew where she was Archie would be a toddler. The war took away so much: quality of life, peace of mind, and time to watch children grow up. Life was so harsh these days. The constant reminders of death, loss, hunger and the daily grind of food rationing had rapidly reduced human expectations to their lowest level. They were all fighting for one sole aim – victory over Fascism – and though the nation was galvanized, it was hard not to look back on those golden pre-war days that now seemed like a rosy dream of dim and distant times.

Realizing she was dawdling, Ruby quickened her pace. When she arrived at the local Hucknall day nursery, she asked a young nurse in a starched blue uniform if she might have a word with Matron. Soon she was being directed to her office for a chat, leaving Archie in the care of the nursery nurse. Though Matron was polite and welcoming, Ruby got the distinct impression that she ran a tight ship, expecting mothers to drop off and pick up on the dot, something which immediately troubled Ruby. She knew only too well how unpredictably long the shifts could be at the Bell Works.

'I'm afraid we're strict about timekeeping,' Matron said.

'I'm sure I could manage,' Ruby quickly assured her. 'If you have a place.'

'We'll take Archie just as soon as there's a place for him,' Matron said firmly.

Trying to hide her disappointment that there wasn't an immediate place, Ruby added, 'Archie getting a nursery place would take a lot of pressure off my mother who's been looking after him. Do you have any idea how long it might take for a place to come up?'

Matron gave an understanding nod.

'I'm afraid it's impossible to tell at the moment; but we will be in touch as soon as we can help you. Now, have you checked the cost of keeping Archie here?' she asked bluntly.

Ruby gave a quick nod. 'Yes I have,' she answered, with

a confidence she didn't feel. 'I'm sure I can manage the fees.'

'Well then, we look forward to seeing you, hopefully very soon, Mrs Fields,' Matron concluded.

Walking back home with Archie, who was now restless and eager for his next feed, Ruby felt pleased that she had visited the nursery and met Matron. Nevertheless, she was worried about what she would do before a place came up. The nursery wasn't subsidized, there were no special dispensations for working mothers, even ones building vital aircraft, and managing the fees, despite what she had said to Matron, would be a problem. Right now, her earnings kept the entire family going. We'll have to make things stretch, she thought, it will be worth the sacrifice if only to give Mam a break – and after all, that's the whole point of the exercise, taking some of the strain off Mother's shoulders.

Making the most of her day off, Ruby insisted that her mother stay in bed until the afternoon, then she suggested they could go for a nice stroll with Archie in his pram. Spreading a little rug in front of the fire, Ruby played with her son. Delighting in his growing strength, she smiled as he reached out for his little toys, kicking his chubby legs and gurgling with excitement. It was such a joy spending precious time with Archie. Her days, so taken up with her work, allowed no time for long leisurely playtimes with her little boy. Catching an expression on her baby's face that poignantly reminded Ruby of her husband, she reached into the top drawer of the sideboard where she always kept a pen and notepad. With one eye on Archie, presently chewing his teddy bear's ear, she wrote . . .

My darling love,

Oh, how I miss you. I do hope and pray that you are well and safe. Archie's growing so strong, thank God, you would be thrilled to see him, he's the spitting image of his gorgeous dad.

I know you have enough on your plate, sweetheart, but it would help me to see straight if I could tell you how things are going at this end. In a word, tricky. Mother's not been herself recently and yesterday had a more serious turn. The grief she suffered after the death of our Derek at Dunkirk weakened her normally robust constitution, and the subsequent child-minding she took on when we had Archie has just become too much for her. I'm worried there might be something else wrong too, and am hoping to get her to see a doctor. Of course, she argues she's fine, but when I got home yesterday, Mother was in bed and our Rita was quite literally left holding the baby. I've been looking at a local nursery but there's a waiting list and I've got to think of a way to give Mother a break. She'll insist she's fine, you know what she's like, she'll work till she drops, so I'll have to handle the situation delicately so as not to offend her, but I've made my mind up, things simply can't go on as they are.

War news is deeply troubling, it's bad enough that the Nazis took Kiev but to murder so many innocent Jews in the process, nearly thirty-four thousand dead, it's incomprehensible madness to me; that a race can be despised so much you want them annihilated. And now reports are coming in of the Nazis taking Odessa as they make their advance on Moscow. God help any innocent Jews they find along the way. I wonder how you are, my darling, and where you are? I understand that these are sensitive times, and you have to be sparse with information, otherwise the censors would seize your letters, but every time I hear news about troops being posted overseas my heart skips a beat. I think, is my George there, or has he been moved on?

Wherever you are, I pray God keeps you safe and you'll come home to us soon, I count the days to our reunion.

It's been lovely having a day at home with our son, but it's back to work tomorrow. I wish I could steal a few more days off, but I'm already feeling guilty about not going in, though in fact we have a bigger workforce these days. New conscripts are arriving from all over the country, living in prefabs on the factory site, often far away from home. I feel sorry for them actually. Separated from family and living in a new town while learning how to build aeroplanes is a lot to have asked of you, but realistically it's going on all over the country, women learning a new trade in a strange town where they know nobody at all. I'm ashamed to say the arrival of new girls at the Bell Works has gone down like a lead balloon. The local girls, my friends included, aren't so keen on the incomers – and they, as a result, aren't so keen on us. Can't say that I blame them; we've not exactly rolled out the red carpet.

I won't burden you further with my tales of woe. When I think what you and your mates must be going through, I feel ashamed of my own petty problems. I just miss having you here to talk to, that bright reassuring smile of yours always chases all my cares away. I can't wait for your next leave, sweetheart. Do you think you might get some leave at Christmas? Just think of the joy we'd have together on Christmas morning, waking up to open presents (tiny ones, of course!) with our little boy and then going to church in the snow, singing carols to Archie on the way. I know it might be impossible, but there's nothing wrong with hoping!

All my love,
Your devoted adoring wife,
Ruby xxxxx

*

As Ruby had predicted, her mother was annoyed with her daughter when, during their short afternoon stroll, they stopped in front of the Hucknall surgery and Ruby announced that she had made an appointment for her mother to see the doctor.

'I've never heard such fuss and nonsense,' her mother remonstrated as Ruby scooped Archie out of his pram and carried him into the waiting room along with her protesting mother.

Luckily, cheerful Archie was a great diversion. By the time everybody in the waiting room had commented on what a bonny strong lad he was, it was Ruby's mother's turn to see the doctor. After listening to her chest, pulse rate, heartbeat, and thoroughly examining the older woman, the doctor sat back in his chair.

'Life's taking its toll on you, my dear,' he said, with a kindly smile.

'On us all,' she replied. 'We've all got our burdens.'

Used to old ladies who would rather die than admit defeat, the doctor spoke gently. 'You need to start taking things easy, your breathing's laboured, and your pulse is weak.' Turning to Ruby, who was trying to get a hank of her long hair out of Archie's iron grip, he added, 'I can prescribe a tonic that might help, but more than anything your mother needs to rest.'

Guiltily nodding her head, Ruby said, 'Yes, I know, but try telling Mother that.'

Writing out a prescription, the doctor continued, 'Try this and come back and see me before Christmas, let's see how you're coping then.'

Once outside, Ruby's mother again expressed her displeasure, but Ruby held her ground.

'I'm following the doctor's advice, Mother, even if you're not,' she said as she settled Archie back in his pram, and they began their walk home. 'I won't allow you to run yourself into the ground on our behalf.'

'Then tell me who else is going to look after the little lad, if not me?' her mother remonstrated.

'I've put Archie's name down for a place at Hucknall day nursery, in town,' Ruby informed her. 'As soon as a place comes up, he'll go there,' she said, in a voice that brooked no argument. Stopping briefly to give her mother a kiss, Ruby said with tears in her eyes, 'I love you too much to want to lose you, Mam.'

Up bright and early the next morning, back in charge of her kitchen, Ruby's mother waved her off, all the time insisting she was feeling much better after her rest. For all her mother's determination to carry on as normal, Ruby was even more determined to initiate change after the doctor's appointment. Recalling seeing architect's plans pinned up on the canteen's notice board, detailing the new domestic site that was under construction at the back of the Bell Works, Ruby spent time examining the new development. Her keen eyes soon picked out the large site for the proposed residential block where she saw there was a building block labelled 'NURSERY'.

Dear God, how come this has skipped my attention, she thought, as she peered even more closely at the plan. This could be the answer to all my problems. A nursery for Bell Works babies, right next to the factory.

Determined not to waste a minute, Ruby hurried over to the domestic building site during her dinner break, still in her heavy work clothes. Finding the foreman of the works in a shed, boiling a kettle of water over a gas ring, Ruby immediately said, 'I've been looking at the plans for the new domestic block and I see there are outlines for a nursery.'

'Aye, you're reet, it's over there, yonder, not finished yet, as you can see,' the man said as he jabbed a finger over his shoulder.

Ruby gazed in surprise at a single-storey red-brick building that was presently being fitted with a slate roof.

'Oh, it's half-built already,' she exclaimed.

'Stone floors were laid this week, we'll have the doors and windows in soon, then the decorators. After a lick of paint, the place will be open for business in about a month, I'd hazard a guess – unless Hitler decides to bomb it on his way to London,' he said, with a grim chuckle.

Impressed, Ruby murmured, 'Goodness me, a nursery on the works site will be a godsend.'

'Orders from the top.' The foreman rolled his eyes as if he were referring to the Almighty. 'If we're to get women to come and work at the Bell, they'll need their kiddies looking after, so it makes sense, dun't it?'

Keen to get an exact date out of him, Ruby pressed on. 'So, the nursery could be open for business in a month's time?'

'Mebbe,' the foreman answered.

Thanking him for his help, Ruby wondered who she should see about putting Archie's name on the list. Admittedly, he was already on the town nursery's waiting list, but she'd much prefer him to come to the nursery attached to the factory, though her mother's deteriorating health might force her to take the first place that came up. Hopefully, her mother would soon be relieved of all her gruelling responsibilities, and Archie, if he did get a place at the Bell nursery, would be in a building just across the site from where she was working. Hungry as she was for her mincemeat and onion pasty that she had asked Audrey to keep for her, Ruby nevertheless headed to the admin block where she asked the secretary in charge about the new Bell nursery.

'We've opened a register if you want to put your son's name down,' she was told. 'You'll be pleased to know that the Bell company will subsidize places for their workers' children. Building planes is high-priority work, and we need women to build them – it makes sense that babies are taken care of properly while their mothers get on with their jobs.'

'Indeed it does,' Ruby instantly agreed.

12. Ferry Girls

As the completed Spitfires grew in numbers in the factory's vast stack yard that gave on to the runway used for take-offs and test flights, Sid went around with a face like thunder.

'We can't have 'em piled up there waiting for the bloody Luftwaffe to take a pop at them,' Lily overheard him say to Mr Lovelace, the works manager, who was ultimately in charge of dispatching the aircraft to airbases with the highest priority.

'You don't have to tell me that, Sid,' Mr Lovelace muttered tensely to the foreman. 'I've been on to the ministry every day. If Gerry gets an aerial shot of that yard, they'll bomb the lot to buggery! They should've been shifted long since.' Gazing at the rows of Spitfires with the autumn sunlight bouncing off their shiny wings, he added, 'If some of them don't get collected soon, we'll have no space for the new Spits coming off the factory floor. The very last thing we need is a slowing-up in our output. We'll be in big trouble with the powers that be, if that happens.'

Curious about the planes she had helped build, Lily made a point of questioning Sid a few hours later. Knowing that it was impossible to talk clearly on the factory floor, Lily tracked Sid down during a tea break in the works canteen.

'Where do our planes go when they leave here?' she asked eagerly.

Sid rolled his eyes. 'Well, I'd say that were top-secret information, but let's put it this way, they go where they're most needed.' Inhaling deeply on his Capstan cigarette, he continued, 'Lincoln, Norfolk, Suffolk. The problem is getting somebody to fly 'em out of here. We can't rely on RAF pilots to do the job, well, not unless they're grounded from official duty. We have to rely on ferry girls these days.'

'Ferry girls?' Lily queried.

Sid nodded. 'Aye, lasses who fly planes.'

Lily's lovely silver-grey eyes flew wide open. 'GIRLS! Women fly planes out of the Bell Works?'

'Aye, they don't take off and fly on their own, you know,' Sid joked. 'We've even had lasses turn up here who've never flown a plane before. But needs must, when the devil drives,' he winked. 'Though they might only have driven a truck or a lorry, after a few goes up and down the runway and a quick spin with an instructor, they'd be dispatched and off they'd go. Brave, if you ask me,' he concluded as he stubbed out his cigarette, then rose to leave. 'We're hoping a few might show up soon and help us offload some of our supplies. They're usually on the snooty side, often posh girls who have good connections with the bigwigs.'

'Really, Sid,' Lily scoffed. 'That can't be true.'

'See for yourself,' he shrugged. 'They're often here, having a drink of tea in the canteen before they take off. Generally keep themselves to themselves.'

Determined not to miss any ferry girls who might put in an appearance, Lily kept her eyes open for any new visitors. She was thrilled when, just a few days later, she walked into the canteen and saw two women she had never seen before sitting at one of the many metal tables, at a marked distance from the rest of the workers. Wearing tweed trousers, dark polo-neck sweaters and oversized leather bomber jackets thrown casually over their shoulders, they lounged in their chairs, oozing style and a kind of glamour that Lily had never seen before. When she had imagined what it would be like coming face to face with a ferry girl, she had thought that she would ask lots of questions about what it felt like to be flying a brand-new Spitfire, but looking at these stylish girls in the cold light of day, Lily realized they were way out of her league. For the first time in her life, Lily felt distinctly inferior. What would she, a hotel waitress, have in common with women of their calibre?

Jeannie, under- rather than over-impressed, rolled her eyes in the direction of the visitors.

'Who are them two snobs?' she muttered.

'Ferry girls,' Lily answered knowingly.

'What're they when they're at home?' Jeannie asked.

'They fly planes out of here, take them to RAF airfields,' Lily explained.

Jeannie gave a dismissive grunt. 'They needn't look so snooty. It's us that build the planes in the first place.'

'I think they're brave,' Lily sighed. 'Imagine flying one of our aircraft out of here, how thrilling would that be?'

'Hell fire!' Jeannie laughed. 'Building them is hard enough – I certainly don't want to fly one. Not that I doubt the quality of my work,' she quickly added. 'But I'll leave the flying to the specialists.'

Catching sight of Sid approaching the ferry girls, Edna gave a low chuckle, 'Aye, aye, Sid's moving in on the ladies – he never could resist a pretty face.'

Sitting at a distance, Lily and her friends were unable to hear any words of the exchange between Sid and the visitors, but it was obvious that the foreman's usual flirtatious routine was not going down well.

'It looks like Sid's been given short shrift by the toffee-nosed lasses,' Edna remarked.

'Oooh, Don Juan won't like that,' Jeannie laughed.

With his face flaming in indignation, the foreman, unused to being so brusquely fobbed off, indicated that the ferry girls should follow him out of the canteen.

Agog to see what would happen next, Lily excused herself by saying she needed to pop into the ladies' toilets. 'Won't be a minute,' she told her pals.

When the coast was clear, Lily slipped out after Sid. He was now leading the ferry girls across the yard. Stopping in front of a row of Spitfires, he produced two sets of keys. When he handed them over, the women dismissed him with a businesslike nod. Lily ducked into a dark corner as Sid, still flushed with indignation, stomped back into the building.

As soon as he was out of sight, Lily slipped out of her hiding place just in time to see the ferry girls hoist themselves into the cockpits of their assigned planes. Pulling on goggles, they seemed relaxed and confident as they familiarized themselves with the controls. Turning towards each other, they gave the thumbs up sign, then one of the girls rolled her plane out of its parked position and headed for the runway. At this point, Lily forgot all about keeping out of sight. Mesmerized, she stood on the side of the runway, watching in wonder as the Spitfire lifted and took to the skies like a graceful silver bird. Before Lily had time to get her breath back, the second ferry girl pulled out on to the runway and, after gathering speed, she too lifted her plane, soaring high into the arching blue sky where the two planes, going in opposite directions, peeled off to the left and right. With the sun glinting on the wings, they blazed bright in the clear autumn blue sky before disappearing behind a bank of fluffy white clouds.

Standing on the runway, listening to the sound of the Spitfire engines fading away, Lily was transfixed. In a moment of complete clarity, she knew that one day she *had to* fly a Spitfire for herself; building them was no longer good enough, she needed to sit in the cockpit and operate the controls, she needed to roll her own Spitfire down a runway and take to the skies. She needed to learn how to fly.

13. Kind Thoughts

In a daze Lily returned to work. All through the afternoon she worked long and hard beside Jeannie, bolting and riveting sheet-metal strips on to the carcass of the Spitfire they'd been appointed to that morning. Though the work was seemingly monotonous, working in sync to bolt and rivet sheet metal on to the fuselage that would soon be a fighter plane was, in fact, deeply satisfying. The more Lily did the task, the quicker she was; and the longer she spent doing it, the more confident, experienced and accurate she became. In her pre-Bell Works days she had imagined that she would be working on different tasks throughout the day, but now she realized that the process of repeating the same task, over and over again, led to an excellent eye for detail and a greater speed of production. With her growing knowledge, Lily thrilled to the idea that this was no longer a metal carcass, soon it would be fitted out with a brand-new Rolls-Royce engine, wings would be added and a propeller. It would take to the air like a bird, just as she had seen the ferry girls' planes soar high beyond the clouds.

Later in the shift, during their last tea break of the day, gulping down tea and a plateful of spam butties, Lily finally came out of her Spitfire daydream to realize that her friend Edna was upset. Guilty that she had been preoccupied with her own fantasies, Lily immediately reached out to Edna.

'Lovie, what is it?'

Unable to speak, Edna shoved a grubby letter across the table. 'Read that, I've been keeping it to myself,' she choked. 'It arrived this morning.'

Dear Mrs Yates,

We're afraid to say that we have had to move your daughter to another home. The household in Kendal where she was initially housed has become overcrowded with evacuee children who all became infected with chicken pox. Your daughter Kathleen, being the youngest, was most vulnerable, so we have immediately removed her to a local cottage hospital where she will be cared for until we can find more suitable accommodation for her. We will keep you duly informed . . .

Folding Edna's letter, Lily murmured, 'Poor little thing, I hope she's okay.'

Checking the date at the top of the letter, Jeannie remarked, 'It's taken long enough to get here.'

'They sent it to my Wigan address, it's been posted on,' Edna explained. 'But you're right, Jeannie, it's nearly a month since it was posted, so God knows where our Kathleen is now.'

Seeing Edna's devasted expression, Lily blurted out, 'I think you should get on a train to Kendal and try to find out who is looking after your daughter, and how well she's recovering from chicken pox.'

Jeannie nodded. 'Lily's right, surely you can get a few days off on compassionate leave?' she urged.

Wiping tears from her eyes, Edna gave a bleak smile. 'Well, I've not been here long,' she said hopelessly. 'But I'll talk to Mr Lovelace about it. He is the work's manager, so it's really down to him.'

'How much time off do you need?' Jeannie asked.

'If I can get good connecting trains, I could do it in a day, though it would be a long day.'

'No time like the present,' Lily urged. 'Go and see if you can have a word with Mr Lovelace right now – tell his secretary it's urgent.'

Straightening her turban and wiping her hands down on her dungarees, Edna rose to her feet. 'Wish me luck,' she said as she walked away.

When she had gone, her friends exchanged an anxious glance.

'You hear some terrible stories about little kiddies who've been evacuated,' Jeannie murmured.

'I know, I was thinking just the same thing,' Lily confessed. 'Not that they're all treated badly or neglected,' she added guardedly. 'There are some very good carers out there. It's just the overcrowded conditions that you read about, and the lack of communication between separated families. Little Kathleen is so young, she needs her mother.'

'Pity she can't be taken care of down here, closer to Edna,' Jeannie mused.

Lily looked thoughtful. 'Do you remember seeing details of a nursery building on the Bell Works domestic site plan?'

Jeannie shrugged. 'To be honest, a nursery wasn't at the forefront of my mind when I looked at the plans,' she smiled. 'I didn't fail to notice a laundry and a picture house – and communal bathrooms, which I am very excited about.'

Still focused on her train of thought, Lily continued.

'Just imagine, if Edna could bring her daughter down here, she could be looked after in the works nursery – when it's completed, of course. I'm sure local women will be using it too, even though they all live hereabouts, it'll be handy for so many to have a nursery right here on the site.'

'That's all well and good, lovie, but where would the little lass live?' Jeannie enquired.

'Here in the prefab,' Lily immediately responded. 'It's Edna's home, after all.'

'I'm not sure I'd want to be sharing a prefab with somebody else's baby,' Jeannie said honestly. 'Would you be happy with that, Lil?'

'I don't think I'd mind, but first things first,' pragmatic Lily responded. 'Fingers crossed that Edna gets time off and is allowed to see her daughter.'

'You could suggest it later, when Edna's clearer about the way forward, get the ball rolling,' Jeannie urged.

Half an hour later, Edna rejoined her friends.

Looking at her expectantly, Jeannie asked, 'How did it go?'

In answer Edna gave the thumbs up sign. 'I can't believe it. They've got some new volunteers due to arrive, so they're letting me leave for Kendal tomorrow.'

'That's marvellous,' Lily exclaimed happily. 'I'll help you pack when we get back to the prefab.'

Edna couldn't help but smile. 'I'm only going for the day,' she pointed out. 'Oh, I can't wait to see her, I've been worrying myself sick thinking who's looking after Kathleen and how she's feeling.' Turning to her friends, she added with tears in her eyes, 'It's horrible when you can't take care of your own poorly child.'

Giving Edna a gentle pat on the arm, Lily said, 'I'm sure she'll cheer up at the sight of you, sweetheart.'

Edna gave a miserable shrug. 'That's if she even recognizes me.'

Trying to stay upbeat, Jeannie added, 'The most important thing is you're there with her,' she insisted. 'You'll be able to see for yourself just how she is and exactly who she's with.'

'Yes,' Edna agreed. 'Even if it's a bit of a rush, hopefully I'll be with Kathleen all day, and maybe I can find something out about where she'll be going next.'

Keeping her thoughts to herself, Lily didn't mention the possibility of Kathleen coming to Hucknall. She imagined a lot of plans would need to be put into place before that could happen, but the more she thought about it the more she liked the idea of Kathleen living in Prefab No. 8 with her mummy.

14. Comings and Goings

While Edna was away in Kendal, Lily kept her eye on activities in the yard, where even more completed planes were accumulating, in the hope of seeing more take-offs from the Bell Works runway. That morning, Lily and several other women, Audrey included, noticed three RAF pilots walking across the yard with Mr Lovelace.

'Oooh,' Jeannie teased when she saw Lily's eager expression. 'Who have you got your eye on?'

'I was looking at the planes, not the fellas,' Lily bridled.

'That's what they all say,' Jeannie scoffed. 'Mind you, nobody can deny they're easy on the eye,' she conceded as she admired the three young men in smart RAF blue uniforms.

Seeing a flutter of excitement among the females in the canteen, Sid barked, 'Come along now, ladies, have none of you seen a man before?'

Casting a disparaging glance at the overweight, middle-aged foreman, cheeky Audrey retorted, 'Not one as young as them in months.'

'Forget the view,' Sid retorted. 'If you waste all your time staring at fellas, your tea will go cold.'

Later in the day, the three pilots lounged comfortably in the canteen, drinking tea and smoking roll-ups, basking in the attention of a number of female workers who flirted with them and badgered them for cigarettes.

'Just look at them,' Jeannie sniffed. 'They really do think they're God's gift.'

'Not as far as I'm concerned,' Lily replied. 'Big-heads have never been my sort.'

Throwing her a curious look, Jeannie asked, 'Who *are* your sort?'

'I like clever, sincere men, with an opinion and a mind of their own.'

'Brainboxes?' Jeannie chuckled.

'They would have to be fun too,' Lily quickly added. 'I couldn't bear a man who takes himself too seriously.'

'Hmm,' Jeannie mused as her eyes raked over the visitors, watching them soak up the flirtatious smiles and playful banter. 'Them three over there are taking themselves very seriously.'

When the pilots finally rose and sauntered off into the yard, Lily didn't follow them as she had the ferry girls; the last thing she wanted was to have them think they had a fan trailing them. Instead, she observed their movements through the factory window, watching closely as they boarded their aircraft. One by one, the pilots rolled them out down the runway, gathering speed until they took to the air, then banking high before disappearing behind rolling grey clouds. Though it was nothing like as thrilling as watching the ferry girls take off from the side of the runway – where she had been only yards away from the aircraft, with the wind in her face – it was nevertheless breathtaking to see, even on a cold, misty autumn day.

Returning to work, Lily felt an unexpected thrill as she worked diligently inside the hollow fuselage. Scrunched over double, as she was for most of the working day, she focused hard on her task. Accustomed now to the level of noise, which initially she had thought intolerable, she handled the weighty pneumatic drill and riveting gun with confidence. Having built up muscles she never even thought she had, Lily was acquiring the strength and skills to work for long, concentrated periods of time. In truth, she actually enjoyed the rigour of her exacting work. Badly riveted metal plates could lead to a pilot's death – something they were repeatedly told, over and over again.

'Concentrate on doing the one job effectively,' Sid told his workforce. 'Don't over-complicate the task, repeat and repeat and repeat, until your timing and accuracy are perfect. You're a small cog in a big wheel, make sure you do your job well.'

The more knowledgeable Lily became about her assignment the more she realized she wanted to learn about the mechanics of assembling a Spitfire. When she did finally have a brief training session with one of the engineers – thanks to Sid, who kept his promise – she was desperate to ask more general questions about how an aircraft took off, how it stayed airborne, how far it could fly on its fuel tank. Having already got stick from Annie about wasting the professionals' time, she didn't in fact dare to ask further questions, worried that Annie and Sid would accuse her of overstepping the mark. So she limited her questions to what went on on the factory floor and how she could best increase production. To appease her growing curiosity, she bought aircraft magazines from the newsagent's shop in town and read them avidly in bed every night; memorizing details of Spitfires, Mosquitos and Hurricanes, she would fall asleep often with the aircraft magazine still clutched in her hands.

Excited by the prospect of understanding aircraft better, Lily decided it might be wise to avoid pestering an engineer, which might get her into trouble. Instead, she would visit the local library on her day off. She did consider picking the brains of one of the technicians who drew up complicated plans and diagrams, though she knew that information and manuals would not be bandied around during wartime, for fear of them falling into the wrong hands. Consumed with a growing curiosity, Lily wisely cautioned herself. Her friends already knew she was keen on aircraft in general, but if they discovered she actually wanted to learn how to fly a Spitfire they would certainly think that she had lost her marbles!

Edna joined Lily and Jeannie in the canteen on her return from Kendal.

'Hell fire,' she wearily yawned, 'I spent more time in draughty corridors on packed trains than I actually spent with mi daughter.'

'How was Kathleen?' Lily asked as they set down their tea and toast on a canteen table.

Drinking deeply from the mug of piping-hot tea, Edna answered miserably, 'She didn't even recognize me. She just clung to the old granny lady she's now billeted with. No matter how hard I tried, she refused to make eye contact, avoided looking at me. It was so upsetting, much worse than I ever imagined.'

Looking puzzled, Jeannie enquired, 'I thought she was being taken care of in hospital?'

'I thought so too, but now she appears to be living with an old couple. They were nice enough, but the house was small and cold. I wasn't there for long, I had to see the welfare lady who organizes housing for the evacuees before I got the train back. It was all so rushed and miserable.'

'The poor little thing is probably in shock,' Lily murmured. 'Trailing around from one family to another – what can you expect?'

'But it's awful when your own daughter doesn't even know you,' Edna cried, tears gushing from her dark-brown eyes. 'God . . .' She groaned as she dropped her head into her hands and sobbed. 'What is this bloody war doing to families up and down the land?'

Jeannie and Lily exchanged a desperate look. What could they say or do that might cheer up their heartbroken friend?

Recalling their previous conversation, Lily spoke rather hesitantly. 'We were talking yesterday about the nursery that's being built here on the works domestic site,' she volunteered.

Staring out of the grimy canteen window at the bleak building site that was expanding by the day, Edna asked gloomily, 'What, out there?'

'I don't know where exactly,' Lily admitted. 'I just remember seeing some plans pinned up in the canteen.'

Catching Lily's drift, Jeannie quickly chipped in. 'Stands to reason, when you think about it. There are bound to be loads of women working here in urgent need of childcare.'

Lily nodded. 'I'm sure clever Mr Churchill has worked out a strategy to support working mothers, he must appreciate how much he needs women in the workforce these days.'

Not at all cheered by her friends' words, Edna grumbled,

'That's as may be, but when will it happen? And even if it did, and I could get a place, would I be able to bring my daughter here to Nottingham, to live with me here rather than with a stranger in Kendal?'

Knowing that she had no immediate answer to Edna's troubled question, Lily said firmly, 'There's only one way of finding out, so go and make some enquiries at the general office. And while you're there, ask Mr Lovelace about accommodation for Kathleen. You can't be the only worker on-site who needs advice on family housing. Seriously, Edna, that's got to be your next move.'

Though bone weary after her long and depressing journey, Edna nodded in agreement with her friends.

'Thanks for your advice, you're both right. I'll definitely make enquiries but . . .' Her voice broke as emotion overcame her. 'Right now,' she sobbed, 'my biggest problem is who's looking after my little girl.'

Seeing Edna visibly drooping after her long journey, Jeannie and Lily hurried to hug and console their weary friend, desperate to cheer her up. After offering hankies and more tea, Lily said with a bright smile, 'Here's some more news – the Bell Works are organizing a dance night for this coming Saturday. That should take your mind off your miseries.'

Picking up on the thread, Jeannie added, 'One of the girls told me they're going to smarten the place up with balloons and decorations. Create an atmosphere that doesn't have even a hint of meat pie and chips,' she joked.

Not quite in the party mood, Edna scoffed, 'And who will we dance with? Local lads that dislike us as much as local lasses?'

'Hopefully not,' Jeannie responded. 'There's a Canadian airbase nearby, so maybe they'll ship in some handsome Canadian airmen who'll dance us off our feet all night.'

Wondering if Jeannie hadn't been indiscreet, Lily cautiously asked, 'That's if you're in the mood for dancing, lovie?'

Edna shrugged. 'Like Jeannie just said, it might take mi mind off all mi cares and woes.'

As the conversation continued between Jeannie and Edna, Lily fell silent. If she had just travelled up and down to Kendal on packed and grimy trains and been met by a daughter who didn't even acknowledge her, a dance night would be the last thing on her agenda.

15. A New Lease of Life

Though Jeannie lived on her own in a nearby prefab, she regularly visited her closest friends in Prefab No. 8 after work hours.

'I prefer being here than living on my own,' she admitted as all three friends sat around the crackling fire drinking strong tea.

'I wish there was room for you to move in here with us,' Lily said wistfully.

'Don't be too hasty,' Jeannie grinned. 'If Edna gets permission to move young Kathleen to Hucknall, she might end up living here too. Any luck with your enquiries at the general office?' she asked as she turned to Edna.

'I did speak to Mr Lovelace about accommodation,' Edna told her. 'The poor fella's a bit addled, juggling building Spitfires and constructing a new domestic site, he's got a lot on his plate. He's made an appointment for me to see the domestic accommodation, and he also pointed out that I'll need official permission from the welfare officer in Kendal to remove Kathleen and bring her here.'

'That's all sound advice,' Jeannie replied.

'Absolutely,' Edna agreed. 'I don't want to drag my daughter away from Kendal without being absolutely sure that she has a loving and secure home here with me in Hucknall.' Glancing fondly around the room, she said curiously, 'I wonder what our Kathleen will make of this prefab if she ever comes down here to live with me?'

'I'm sure the little lass will love it,' Jeannie enthused. 'Lily's made it really nice and homely. If Kathleen arrives for Christmas, we could make it even nicer with decorations and a little Christmas tree.'

A radiant smile lit up Edna's tired face. 'What a lovely thought, Jeannie! You're right, Lil's done a lovely job, the way you've got the place arranged, with all your little homely knick-knacks. And you've always got a fire going – there's nothing like a fire to make a place feel welcoming.'

The prefab's warm, welcoming atmosphere was all down to Lily. During her rare periods of time off, she had popped into local second-hand shops to buy little ornaments, or queued in jumble sales on wet Saturday mornings to purchase rugs, sofa throws, some pretty old-fashioned crockery, even a mirror and a few pictures to hang on the wall.

Usually, if they weren't too tired after work, the three friends would sit drinking tea by the fire while listening to the radio. Sometimes, when their favourite band came on – particularly if it was the Andrews Sisters singing their favourites, 'Pennsylvania 6-5000' or 'Beat Me Daddy, Eight To The Bar' – they would spring to their feet and dance around the sitting room until, out of breath, they collapsed back into their chairs. On the Friday evening before the dance, they had music blaring out of the wireless as all three women were planning their hair and make-up. After discussing the advantages of a victory roll hairdo, as opposed to long swinging locks, they tried out each other's lipstick – Lily preferred Max Factor's Cardinal to Edna's first choice, Maybelline's Cherry Lips – plus mascara and panstick make-up, before turning their attention to the clothes they would wear. Jeannie was the first to show off her dance dress, a rather faded plum-coloured taffeta dress with a black lace trim around the scoop neckline.

'It's the only dance dress I've got, a bit dull, I know. And it definitely doesn't do ow't for my red hair either,' she grimaced. 'But it will have to do.'

Looking at the rather old-fashioned full-skirted frock, Lily said with a positive smile, 'Maybe not, but that rich plum shade brings out your big blue eyes, and it goes well with your clear pale complexion. You could always liven it up with a sparkly necklace or a nice brooch,' she tentatively suggested.

Jeannie gave a self-deprecating smile. 'I don't fancy myself as a beauty,' she said humbly. 'I don't think for a minute that a nice frock is going to bring fellas buzzing around me. Folks will just have to take me as they find me,' she said realistically.

Lily, who valued Jeannie as a good friend and trusted her for her straight talking and loyalty, quickly responded, 'You underestimate yourself; any man would be lucky to have you.'

Embarrassed by her friend's complimentary words, Jeannie blushed. 'Nice of you to say so, Lil.'

Wide-eyed Edna exclaimed, 'Don't you want to find a man?'

Jeannie gave a shrug. 'That'd be nice, but I don't have high expectations.'

Looking at her friend's genuinely kind face, Lily thought Jeannie really did underestimate herself; she had lovely shoulder-length golden-red curly hair, laughing pale-blue eyes, freckles dotted her little pert nose, and her wide mouth always had a ready smile. And with her fuller figure and shapely legs, Lily was sure that a lot of men would find Jeannie extremely attractive.

When it came to Edna's turn to show off her dress, she left the room. To her friends' complete astonishment, she re-appeared minutes later bearing a large cardboard box.

'I sent off for this before I came here,' she admitted as she lifted the box lid and revealed a stunning red satin dress.

Lily and Jeannie, momentarily speechless, could only gaze in awe at the dress Edna held up against her body.

'Oh my goodness!' Lily managed to splutter. 'It's *gorgeous*!'

'I've never seen anything like it,' Jeannie gasped. 'Try it on.'

Dashing into the little bathroom, Edna re-emerged a few minutes later looking more like a model than an engine girl. The low square-necked bodice settled flatteringly on her wide shoulder blades, showing off her large breasts, while the fitted top plunged into a tight waistband from which the full skirt, with big side pockets, ballooned out.

'I just love it!' Edna declared as she twirled around in front of her friends.

'It's beautiful,' Jeannie exclaimed. 'You look like a film star.'

Overcome with curiosity, Lily asked, 'Where did it come from?'

Looking embarrassed, Edna said, 'From a catalogue.' Distinctly self-conscious now, she blurted out, 'You're probably wondering what a married woman like me is up to, buying posh frocks and getting all excited about going dancing.'

'We're not here to judge you, Edna,' Jeannie murmured.

Edna threw her friends a guilty look. 'It's just that me

being married, and a mother at that, I thought you might be thinking that I'm not conducting myself as I should. I feel guilty for saying it, but leaving home and that old dragon of a mother-in-law I lived with has given me a new lease of life.'

Lily looked puzzled. 'To be honest, I don't feel like that – in fact, I still miss home comforts and my old job.'

'That's just it, Lil, I've never had home comforts, as you call them,' Edna explained. 'Living with my mother-in-law in Wigan was hell. When Jack was around, the old bat just about managed to behave herself, but once he was called up, my God, she turned into a tyrant!' Reaching out for her packet of Woodbines, Edna lit up a cigarette and inhaled deeply. 'She watched my every move, even read the love letters Jack wrote to me.'

'That's a bit much,' Jeannie sympathized.

'It really was,' Edna quickly agreed. 'He's such a shy lad, always dominated by his mother, but with a tender heart and a sweet smile. Even though we were officially courting, he hardly dared kiss me, took about a month before he held my hand.' She smiled tenderly as she recalled her innocent young boyfriend. 'His mother always resented him walking out with me, thought I wasn't good enough for her son, but Jack was loyal; he said he loved me, and I was the only girl for him. The old bugger criticized everything I did, I couldn't do anything right. Jack defended me, but she always shouted him down. When he was called up, things went seriously wrong. She repeatedly told me I was a bad mother – not fit to take care of a child – even though I was trying my best. I loved my little girl so much, but I really began to doubt myself. Not that the old bat ever lifted a finger to help,' Edna declared.

'Where was your own mother while all of this was going on?' Jeannie asked.

'She died of TB when I was in my teens. The irony is that I was left to bring up three kiddies younger than me. I managed to rear my brothers and sister, but according to my mother-in-law I couldn't rear my own child.'

'Did she ever volunteer to look after Kathleen?' Jeannie enquired.

Edna let out a hoot of laughter. 'You've got to be joking! That would have meant getting off her backside and actually doing something rather than sitting around all day grumbling and complaining. Anyway, even if she had offered, I would never have left my little girl alone with her.'

Gazing at the red satin dress, which Edna had taken off and laid carefully across the arm of the sofa, Lily cautiously ventured, 'It's hard to imagine that you ever thought of buying a glamorous dress like that, with your nasty mother-in-law around.'

'It was a mad impulse, an act of defiance,' Edna declared. 'When I saw it in the catalogue, I just had to have it. Even if I hid it away from snooping eyes, I could peep at it and dream of wearing it one day.'

Still astonished, Jeannie murmured, 'How on earth could you afford such a thing?'

'I saved what was left out of my wages after I'd sent money to Kathleen's carers in Kendal and paid my mother-in-law what she grabbed from my pay packet every week. I saved and saved, then I secretly treated myself for the very first time in my life.'

'Sounds like you deserved a treat,' Jeannie quipped.

'Well, now you've got the dress of your dreams you might as well make the most of it.'

'Don't you worry, I intend to,' Edna shot back. 'I'm looking forward to wearing it tomorrow night.'

Wondering if Edna's husband fighting for his country would be pleased to hear that his wife was going out in a gorgeous dance frock, Lily wisely kept her mouth shut.

Breaking into her friend's thoughts, Edna asked, 'Come on, Lil, what are you going to be wearing?'

'Something Mam made for me last year,' Lily replied. 'It's in the wardrobe, I'll fetch it.'

When Lily returned carrying a pale-blue velvet dress, her friends exclaimed in delight.

'Oh, Lil, it's the perfect colour for you,' Jeannie cried.

The fitted dress, with covered velvet buttons running all the way down the back, had a nipped-in waist, a deep sweetheart neckline, long tight sleeves, and a swishy flared skirt.

'I can't believe your mother made it,' Edna declared. 'It looks like a proper professional job.'

Lily gave a proud smile. 'She's clever with a needle is my mum,' she said. 'She used to make all my clothes. Heaven only knows what she would say if she saw me in my oversized work dungarees.'

Jeannie smiled in admiration. 'That shade of light blue goes beautifully with your eyes and hair.'

'Mum's got a really good eye for fashion; she chose the fabric, and the design too. It fits like a glove, though to be honest I've barely worn it,' Lily said.

'Well, now's your chance,' Edna responded with a gleeful smile. 'We'll all be able to dance in our best frocks tomorrow night till we drop.'

16. Dance Night

On Saturday night as Lily, Edna and Jeannie prepared for the dance, they were as giddy as children getting ready for a party. With Joe Loss & His Orchestra's music blaring out from the radio, they took it in turns to bathe in tepid water, after which they dried themselves in front of the fire in the prefab's cosy sitting room, this time with Frank Sinatra crooning on the radio. After slipping into their dance dresses, the girls combined all their make-up – lip liner, lipstick, mascara, eye liner, face powder in little silver compacts, panstick and rouge. Lily and Jeannie were astonished to discover that Edna – who, as far as they understood, had only been to about three dances in her entire life – was a dab hand when it came to applying make-up.

'How did you learn to do it so well?' Jeannie asked, as Edna smoothed a dot of rouge on to her cheekbones, then deftly blended the cream in with her fingertips so that it merged perfectly with the light tan-coloured Max Factor foundation cream she had already applied.

'I love fashion and beauty, they're my secret vice,' Edna admitted with a girlish giggle. 'I used to read the fashion magazines my workmates in the clothing factory left lying around. We were always messing about with make-up in our dinner breaks.'

Lily giggled too. 'We were the same at the Dolphin Hotel

where I worked in Whitby. Whenever any of us got some new make-up, the rest of us would buzz around like bees. We were always borrowing and experimenting. I especially like Maybelline and Elizabeth Arden products. Ah, those were the days,' she sighed wistfully. 'I used to feel so feminine, made-up with my hair in a victory roll, tripping around in my pretty uniform and my black round-toed heels with a little leather T strap across the top.'

'We have to keep reminding ourselves that we're still young women,' Edna said staunchly. 'Even if we do look a bloody mess in men's dungarees, we never fail to wear bright red lipstick, and we make a point of wearing colourful turbans to perk ourselves up. Engine girls have their pride too,' she said with a swagger.

Lily threw her a fond smile. 'Honestly, Edna, you should go on a propaganda poster promoting female conscription.'

Edna struck a bold heroic pose, flexing her right arm as if she were gripping a riveting gun, and declared, '*DO IT FOR KING AND COUNTRY, LADIES!*'

Lily and Jeannie couldn't help but burst out laughing.

'I wish I'd got a camera!' Jeannie spluttered.

Returning to the important job in hand, Lily squinted as she peered into the mirror over the fireplace.

'The light's so bad in here,' she grumbled. 'I can't see well enough to do my eye liner.'

'Give it here,' Edna said, as she took control and with a confident flourish applied the dark liner. 'There, you look stunning, you'll snap up a fella the minute you walk into the room.'

Noticing that Jeannie had suddenly gone quiet, Edna asked, 'What's up, lovie?'

Blushing, Jeannie answered, 'To be honest, dancing and all the palaver of dressing up is really not my thing.'

'Did you never go dancing when you lived in Bolton?' Edna cried.

Jeannie gave a shrug. 'Maybe twice, at the Palais in the town centre, but really, I preferred just being with my girlfriends from school; we used to go for long walks on the moors, or we'd meet up after work to watch a film at the local picture house. It was a quiet life, but I liked it that way.'

Thinking that Jeannie might suddenly lose her nerve and bolt, Lily quickly reminded her friends, 'We can't go anywhere without our nylons.'

Flourishing a black pencil, Edna grinned. 'Backs to me, please, ladies.'

Turning around, Lily and Jeannie obediently raised their skirts so that Edna could trace a black crayon line down their bare legs.

'Don't fidget,' she warned, 'or the line will go wobbly.' Stepping back to admire the finished result, Edna gave a satisfied smile. 'All done. Hopefully, from a distance nobody will ever know you're not wearing the finest nylons.'

When Lily had traced a black line down Edna's shapely legs, the three friends linked arms, Edna in the middle with Lily and Jeannie either side of her. Taking a minute to admire themselves, they smiled at their reflected image in the mirror over the fireplace; three young girls in their best dresses, hair curled and waved, faces bright with hope, eyes shining and happy.

Delighted by the transformation, Lily declared, 'Engine girls no more.'

'For one night only,' Jeannie joked. 'We're just like Cinderella.'

'Until the clock strikes midnight,' Edna cried as she headed for the door. 'Let's dance until we drop!'

As she held the door open wide for her friends to pass through, Lily noticed that Edna wasn't wearing her wedding ring.

When Lily, Edna and Jeannie swung into the canteen decorated with balloons, coloured bunting and twinkling fairy lights, they hardly recognized the place. The party of workers, some technicians and engine girls who had volunteered for the job of transforming the canteen into a ballroom, had gone to a great deal of trouble to create a romantic atmosphere. The warmth inside and the soft lighting contrasted with the cold autumn night outside, and the mirrored balls hanging from the ceiling shed beams of silvery light on to the dance floor. Combined with the strains of the dance band warming up, it all sent shivers of excitement running through the girls' veins.

Once they had hung up their coats in the ladies' changing room (and reapplied their lipstick), the three women stopped dead in their tracks when they saw how many men were in the room. Young men from the local RAF station mingled with recently arrived Canadian airmen dressed in smart grey and navy-blue uniforms – and a few local Hucknall lads in their de-mob suits or khaki uniforms, who looked a lot less impressive than the overseas visitors. As the band struck up 'Deep Purple', a wave of men moved across the room, eager to find a partner.

Seeing Edna eagerly moving forward, Lily felt suddenly anxious. 'Be careful, lovie, don't go doing anything silly.'

Throwing back her head and tossing her newly waved long dark hair, Edna grinned, 'I'll be careful, Lil, but that won't stop me from having fun!'

Not wanting to join the surging horde on the dance floor just yet, Lily took a few steps back and noticed Jeannie was also nervously backing away. Drawing her friend into a corner, Lily said, 'We don't need to dance right away. We can take a minute to get acclimatized,' she joked.

Jeannie threw her a sweet gap-toothed smile. 'I told you I wasn't keen on this kind of malarkey. I like a laugh, as you well know, but dancing and flirting leave me stone cold, added to which I've got two left feet. If anybody asks me for a dance, they'll regret it in five minutes flat.'

'The Hucknall girls are out in full force,' Lily observed as she recognized some local women.

'Funny,' Jeannie mused. 'They keep their distance from us even on a dance floor.'

Scanning the room, Lily observed, 'I don't see that nice Ruby woman – she's the only one so far who's managed to raise a smile for us newcomers.'

'Mebbe she has a family,' Jeannie suggested. 'You wouldn't go dancing on a Saturday night if you had a family at home, would you?'

Catching sight of Edna twirling around on the dance floor, Lily raised her eyebrows.

Reading her thoughts, Jeannie whispered, 'I know what you're thinking.'

Whispering back, Lily said, 'I only hope Edna knows what she's doing.'

Sneaking a glimpse at Edna, now in a dreamy waltz embrace, Jeannie generously added, 'At least she's having a happy time, dancing in her best red dress, the belle of the ball. Really, Lil, she can't be the only married woman dancing here tonight.'

Lily gave a shrug. 'I suppose you're right,' she agreed. 'Stay where you are, and I'll go and get us both a shandy.'

While she waited for her drinks to be served, Lily noticed two RAF pilots, with their flying jackets thrown carelessly over their uniformed shoulders, propping up the bar.

'God Almighty,' one of them scoffed. 'This is a bit of a homespun affair.'

'Makes me long for the lights of Soho and Mayfair,' his fellow drinker boomed. 'Hell, those were the days. Women all over a chap, I'm not even sure these lasses would understand a word we're talking about. Nice enough, but rather rough around the edges, don't you think?'

Bristling at their unkind comments, Lily threw a dirty look in their direction.

'Come along now, old fella,' his companion reprimanded him. 'If you can't beat 'em, join 'em, I say. There are quite a few impressive fillies here tonight. You never know, your luck might be in,' he added as he gave his friend a meaningful dig in the ribs.

Suddenly catching sight of Lily, with her long silver hair swinging over her lovely heart-shaped face, the airmen immediately came to attention.

'Hello there,' one of them called out. 'Can I buy you a drink?'

Reaching for the shandies that had finally arrived, Lily ignored his offer.

Taking in Lily's slender body and arresting blue velvet dress, the airman added with a persuasive smile, 'What will it be now?'

Giving him an icy stare, Lily answered, 'I don't think from what I've just overheard that I'm quite up to scratch for the likes of you two gentlemen!' Then turning on her heel, she walked away with her head held high.

When Lily returned to the table where she'd left Jeannie sitting forlorn and uncomfortable, she was astonished to find her now happily engaged in conversation with a tall lanky young man with a shock of auburn hair. Smiling at her blushing friend, Lily set Jeannie's drink down on the table.

'Thanks,' Jeannie said, clearly flustered. 'Er, this is Frank.'

Frank stood up to politely shake Lily's hand. 'Very pleased to meet you.'

Taking in his honest blue eyes, wide grin and a hand grip that was so firm it made Lily wince in pain, she said, 'You too, Frank.'

'I came over to ask your friend to dance, but she wasn't so keen, so we're having a little chat instead,' he babbled on. 'To be honest, I'm a bloody awful dancer miself, so I'm not complaining.'

'I'll leave you to it,' Lily said diplomatically as, glass in hand, she slipped away from them – thinking to herself, well, Jeannie seems to be getting on just fine considering she was a nervous wreck less than half an hour ago.

Unfortunately, the sandy-haired RAF officer she had just turned her back on was in keen pursuit of her. Seeing him making a beeline for her, she ducked behind a crowd of dancers. Hoping to skirt along the back of them and hide in the ladies' toilets, in her haste Lily bumped into another uniformed man and felt warm beer splash on to her best dance dress.

'Hah!' Lily exclaimed as cold beer trickled down her chest.

'*Przekięty!* Damn, so sorry, please. What can I do?' the flustered man exclaimed as he took out a clean white hand-kerchief to dab off the beer. 'So stupid,' he said, in an accent she didn't quite recognize.

Worried about where the handkerchief might next land on her body, Lily quickly stepped away from him.

'Really, stop,' she cried. 'It's entirely my fault.'

'No, but you have lovely dress, now ruined,' he fretted, as he continued to try to wipe away the beer stains around her neck and shoulders.

Relieving him of the handkerchief, Lily said, 'Please, let me do it! There,' she announced, 'that'll do.'

'But, but . . .' he continued to fluster.

Looking at him for the first time, Lily was suddenly struck by his height. At least six foot tall, he had beautiful golden-blond hair, cut short, but which still fell beguilingly over green eyes fringed with long lashes. Hoping to bring the accidental mishap to a conclusion, she insisted, 'Look, it was only a lemonade shandy, it'll wash off I'm sure. Just forget it.'

Smiling down at Lily's delicate upturned heart-shaped face, the young man – clearly impressed by her looks – murmured incredulously, 'You have eyes the colour of argent, silver.'

Lost for words, Lily gave an embarrassed shrug.

Collecting his thoughts, the young man clipped his heels together and gave her a smart salute.

'I am Oro Chenko, Lieutenant in Polish RAF.'

Lily gave an intrigued nod. 'Ah, yes, I thought I detected a slight accent. And there's something about your uniform – it's a different shade of blue,' she added as she squinted to get a closer look. 'And you have eagles on your silver buttons.' Looking up, she politely added, 'I'm Lily Palmer, by the way. So, where are you based?' she asked.

'My Polish squadron is in the RAF base in Hucknall.'

'Goodness,' she murmured, 'I never even knew there was a Polish RAF base here.'

'We fly together with your airmen, although,' he added, with a flash of pride in his eyes, 'we Poles fly best.' Extending his hand, he gave another bow. 'Please, will you dance with me now?'

Charmed now by his dazzling smile and gentle modesty, despite their bad start, Lily smiled and took his hand.

'Perfect timing,' she said. 'My favourite waltz song.'

His arm circled her tiny waist and he led her on to the heaving dance floor to the strains of 'Yours'.

Pressed against Oro, Lily abandoned herself to the romantic music and the mood of heightened excitement in the air. Forgetting about how homesick she had felt on her arrival in Hucknall, how bewildered she had been when first faced with the gaping skeleton of the Spitfire fuselage she was expected to work on, how intimidated she had been by Annie's obvious dislike of outsiders . . . it all faded away as she waltzed in a dream world. For a sweet brief time, Lily escaped grim reality as she spun across the floor with her head pressed against Oro's broad shoulder. As the conductor waved his baton, Lily smiled shyly up at

Oro whose handsome face was caught in the soft light of the turning silver orbs.

Smiling down at her, Oro murmured, 'Beautiful Lillee, you dance like film star.'

As the dreamy waltz ended, Glenn Miller's 'In The Mood' blared out.

Throwing Lily a mischievous grin, Oro said, 'Can you jive like a film star too?'

'Try me,' she teased.

Before Lily could catch her breath, Oro, holding her firmly by the hand, twirled her around the dance floor, with Lily responding instinctively to his expert dance moves. The ever popular 'In The Mood' gave way to 'Pennsylvania 6-5000' and 'Boogie Woogie Bugle Boy'. Lily and Oro continued to whirl around the dance floor, which was filling up fast with even more couples. Eventually, desperate to quench her thirst, Lily suggested they got a drink from the bar.

When Oro handed her a brimming glass he joked, 'Beer, this time I'll be careful not to throw it on you!'

After gratefully taking a few mouthfuls of shandy, Lily took the opportunity to ask Oro a few questions about his life as a pilot. 'I envy you,' she confessed.

'Why?'

Smiling shyly, she admitted, 'I build planes, but I have a secret ambition to fly an aircraft.'

'You want to fly?' he exclaimed.

Blushing, Lily blurted out, 'Actually, I would *love* to fly – if I ever got the chance.'

'Women can fly planes like any man, there's not so much difference,' Oro said, without any hint of condescension.

'Maybe,' she chuckled. 'Except I really haven't a clue.'

Oro grinned. 'I'll teach you.'

Taken aback, and frightened that she might drop the glass she was holding, or this time spill the contents over him, Lily carefully set it on the bar.

'How on earth could you teach me?' she gasped.

'Simple, I take you up in my plane and we fly.'

'B . . . b . . . but what about official permission?' she spluttered.

Again, Oro gave a shrug. 'I teach you in a practice run, it's not unusual, people are always training.'

'Really?'

'Really,' he agreed. Then, grabbing her by the hand, he exclaimed, 'Come, dance again.'

Her head spinning with excitement, Lily once more took to the floor – this time to the Andrews Sisters and their ever popular 'Beat Me Daddy, Eight To The Bar'. Losing all her inhibitions, feeling totally carefree, Lily threw back her head and laughed with pleasure. She might be building Spitfires to fight the enemy tomorrow, but right now she was going to dance until she dropped.

17. The Morning After

The following morning, bleary-eyed Edna kept herself very much to herself. Though she could hear Lily pottering around in the prefab, she avoided getting up and greeting her. Realistically, the way she was feeling – dizzy and nauseous after one too many port and lemons – she was glad it was Sunday and she could lie in bed longer than usual. With her head throbbing, Edna's eyes drifted around her bedroom to alight on her stunning red satin dress, which she'd flung carelessly on to a rickety wooden chair.

'God!' she groaned as she recalled swirling around the dance floor in the dress, then pressing her body against Ken's and feeling the sweep of his hands on her. He really was a very persuasive man, Edna thought ruefully. In the dark yard during dance breaks, where they'd headed to cool down, the pair of them had ended up embracing. Ken had even suggested they slip into an empty shed to enjoy 'a bit of privacy', as he put it. Though Edna was weak at the knees with desire, she had staunchly resisted.

'I'm not that kind of girl,' she had protested.

Sliding his hands through her long dark hair, then kissing her bare shoulders, Ken had whispered, 'Oh, I think you are, baby.'

Though Edna was pleased that she hadn't given in

to Ken's persuasive charms, he had left her aching with desire. Married though she was, Edna had never experienced powerful, passionate love-making, the kind she was certain strong, forceful, confident Ken would offer. Jack, though tender and gentle, had always been hesitant, and who could blame him? In their bedroom right next to her mother-in-law's room, with the old woman snoring or noisily using the commode, they had been furtive and shy. Between the two of them, Jack's inexperienced fumblings and her awkwardness, they hadn't exactly been left gasping for breath. It was almost a case of 'the sooner this is over the better'. But it was different with Ken, she sighed, even his kisses could last for minutes. Shivering with guilty delight, Edna imagined what it would be like to lie naked in Ken's arms, allowing him to stroke her body and kiss her where she had never been kissed before. Blushing at her racing thoughts, Edna forced herself to leave her warm bed and go into the freezing bathroom. Briskly washing herself in cold water, she vividly recalled arranging a date with Ken before they went their separate ways after the dance.

'Let's get together for a drink in town this week,' he had suggested as he kissed her goodbye.

Keen to see him again, an excited Edna had immediately agreed – a date, she thought guiltily to herself, she wouldn't be sharing with her friends in a hurry.

In the prefab's cosy sitting room Jeannie and Lily sat chatting companionably by the crackling fire. After gratefully taking a mug of steaming-hot strong tea from Lily, Edna devoured some bread and marge before facing the questions she knew would come from her friends.

Jeannie, who had just popped in for a chat and a catch-up gossip, asked with a teasing smile, 'So, where did you get to, you dirty stop-out?'

'I got detained,' Edna said as she lit up her first cigarette of the day.

'By that Canadian fella you were with all night?' Jeannie asked.

'We did have a bit of a chat after the dance finished,' Edna admitted.

'Edna!' Jeannie cried. 'You're a married woman.'

Looking awkward, Edna prevaricated. 'I said a chat, Jeannie. Anyway,' she shrugged, 'what the eye doesn't see the heart doesn't grieve over.'

Lily wriggled uncomfortably in the battered old leatherette armchair close to the fire. Having remained non-judgemental during their previous conversation on the subject of Edna's marriage, she felt she could no longer keep her thoughts to herself.

'How do you think your husband would feel if he found out what you were up to?' she bluntly asked.

Edna slowly exhaled, before answering. 'He wouldn't be happy, to put it mildly. But,' she added sharply, 'he's not going to find out – is he?'

'I'm not going to tell him, if that's what you mean,' Lily replied.

'Me neither,' Jeannie quickly added.

'But that's not really the point,' Lily continued.

Stubbing out her Woodbine, Edna snapped, 'So, what *is* your point, Lily?'

Now thoroughly uncomfortable, but determined to finish what she had started, Lily pressed on.

'Your husband is fighting for his country, Edna . . .' she stumbled. 'It just doesn't seem, well, right.'

A heavy silence descended, broken by an indignant Edna jumping to her feet, her cheeks blazing and flushed.

'I talked to you about being given a new lease of life, only a few days ago,' she recalled. 'You said then you weren't judging me, but now, after you've seen me having a bit of fun at the dance, it sounds like that's exactly what you're doing.'

Resisting the urge to say, you've gone a lot, lot further than just letting your hair down, Lily protested, 'It's not *judging*, Edna.'

'Then what is it, Lil? You tell me.'

Lily's head drooped in embarrassment. 'Concern,' she murmured.

'Thanks, but you can keep that to yourself,' Edna declared, before she stormed off back to her bedroom.

Glancing at Jeannie, Lily groaned softly. 'Heck! I've gone and put my foot right in it.'

'If you hadn't, I probably would have,' Jeannie replied honestly. 'It really is a bit much.'

'But saying something makes me sound like a right little prig.'

'An honest prig,' Jeannie smiled.

Finally allowing her feelings to show, Lily burst out, 'It's not right, playing around while a man's life might be on the line.'

'It's absolutely not right,' Jeannie agreed. 'But Edna's made no secret of the fact she's making up for lost time.'

'Marriage is for life,' Lily retorted staunchly. 'It doesn't matter whether you're sixteen, twenty-six or fifty-six.'

'Don't go telling that to Edna,' Jeannie winked. 'The mood she's in, she might throw something at you!'

Purposely changing the subject, Lily remarked, 'That young man you were with last night seemed nice enough.'

'Frank,' Jeannie beamed. 'He was very nice.'

'And he didn't mind not dancing all night?'

'No!' Jeannie exclaimed. 'He was as happy as I was to sit and chat over a few glasses of shandy. We did dance the last waltz, though,' she added shyly. 'When it was dark, and nobody could see us. We trod on each other's toes so much we both got a fit of the giggles . . .' She grinned, before blushing crimson and blurting out, 'Frank kissed me just before the lights came up.'

'Oooh, you little tinker!' Lily teased.

'Oh, Lily, it was lovely,' Jeannie confessed. 'I'm not used to fellas – generally speaking, they get on my nerves – but Frank's so modest and understated. He immediately put me at my ease; before I knew it, I was telling him all about my life in Bolton, talking nineteen to the dozen about working in the mill and walking on the moors. I must have bored the poor lad sideways.'

'He looked far from bored to me,' Lily assured her starry-eyed friend. 'Did you make arrangements to meet again?'

Jeannie beamed. 'We did, we're going to the local picture house in Hucknall next weekend, just before his leave ends.' Giving a little sigh, she added, 'He's just the right kind of lad for me, straightforward, lively and fun, pity he's going away so soon. I really enjoy his company.'

'At least you're going to the pictures, that's something to look forward to,' Lily smiled.

Smiling back, Jeannie teased, 'And what about you, with that gorgeous Polish pilot?'

Now it was Lily's turn to blush. Saying his name with obvious pleasure, she smiled. 'Oro, he's very nice.'

Jeannie gave a loud hoot of laughter. 'Nice! Only the best-looking man in the room. You two made a lovely couple on the dance floor.'

Lily's smile widened as she recalled the pleasure she had felt, pressed close in Oro's arms, with the smell of his aftershave in her nostrils and the feel of his firm hand on her back as he guided her skilfully across the dance floor.

'So, did you two kiss before the lights came up?' inquisitive Jeannie enquired.

'No! Not like you and your new friend, Frank,' Lily cried. 'I was hoping we would, but Oro was very formal. He bowed at the end of the dance and shook my hand.'

'Oooh, very princely and romantic,' Jeannie chuckled.

'We arranged to meet up, though, just as soon as we both have a day off. We swapped addresses. He's in walking distance, just up the road in the Polish camp, so we can easily drop each other a line.'

There was a frosty atmosphere in the prefab for the rest of the day, with Lily and Edna giving each other a wide berth, but the following day, once they were back at work on Monday morning, it was impossible to remain huffy and offended. As they worked along the length of a jig fitted with pre-drilled holes indicating precisely where their line of rivets should go, they inevitably bumped and nudged into each other. Their close proximity eventually broke the ice.

When the hooter blasted out, Lily gratefully descended

the steps from the jig, then headed to the canteen with Edna. It was here that Lily turned to her friend and said, 'Edna, I'd like to apologize.'

Visibly relieved, Edna gave an embarrassed nod.

'Me too, Lil, sorry for being such a madam. And . . .' she added self-consciously, 'I do get what you're saying, it's what anybody would say if they caught me, a married woman, flirting with another man. But at the risk of repeating myself – this is a new lease of life for me. Of course, I love my husband, but we're more like pals than lovers. We were hardly out of school before we got wed.'

Pausing to pick up their mugs of tea and much-needed chip butties at the canteen counter, the girls hurried to the nearest vacant table.

Edna continued the delicate conversation. 'Let's be honest, Lily, we're never going to agree on this, so let's just say, it is what it is, and stop the argy-bargy.'

'But before we move on, and before you think I'm always on the moral high ground, I just have to say something,' Lily announced. 'Of course I worry about Jack finding out, or the possibility of your actions somehow having an impact on your daughter, but I'm not judging *you*. I can see why you want to have a new lease of life, as you put it, but it's . . .' Feeling nervous and not wanting to reignite the row, now embarrassed, Lily's voice trailed away.

'I know I *am* being selfish, I can't defend myself!' Edna declared, before blurting out, 'I just want to dance and get dressed up and *live* a little! For God's sake, this blasted war does funny things to all of us,' she said as she swiped telltale tears from her eyes. 'Sometimes, I hardly recognize the woman I used to be.'

Lily gave a heavy sigh. Edna was right: the pitiful, tragic waste of war had changed them all.

When Jeannie joined them a few minutes later, also clutching a mug of tea, she quickly picked up on the mood.

'Have you two made friends?' she asked sweetly.

'Aye, there's not enough time to argue in this place,' Edna chuckled. 'When you're working literally hip to hip, bum to bum,' she grinned, 'you just can't bear a grudge for long, can you?'

18. Audrey

Ruby hadn't attended the Bell Works dance. First of all (unlike Edna), she had no interest in dancing with any-body but her beloved husband, and second (as Lily had suggested), whatever free moments she had she wanted to spend with her baby – who, as far as Ruby was con-cerned, was a lot more fun than any jitterbug or foxtrot. Nevertheless, she was very keen to hear from Audrey (who was full of it) how the evening had progressed.

'Oh, it were smashing,' she grinned, eager to tell her young friend all about it. 'With neither of you two there, I was lucky enough to pal up with some other local lasses.' Turning to Mary, she added, 'You would have liked it, Mary. Why didn't you turn up?'

The shy girl gave a dismissive shrug.

'I like spending my spare time with Mam,' she confessed.

Audrey rolled her heavily made-up eyes.

'What a set of mates,' she chuckled. 'You prefer your mother's company, and Ruby prefers her son's – I don't stand a chance with you two.'

'Well then, it's lucky you have other friends,' Ruby said sharply.

Catching her reproving look, Audrey said to Mary, 'So, lovie, how did you spend your Saturday?'

'We did a bit of shopping down the market, then after our tea – spam fritters and chips – we listened to the radio.

Mother really likes Tommy Handley and *ITMA*. I like the news best,' Mary added. 'After that, we finished our Ovaltine and had an early night.'

Looking distinctly unimpressed, Audrey said, 'Rather you than me, lovie.'

Wishing that Audrey would stop teasing poor Mary, Ruby asked, 'Was the dance band good?'

'Smashing! They played all the favourites tunes – Glenn Miller, Joe Loss, The Andrews Sisters, Frank Sinatra – the floor was packed all night.' Pulling down the corners of her mouth in a disapproving grimace, she added, 'Them new lasses were straight on the dance floor, the minute the band struck up.'

'I suppose they've as much right as us to have fun,' Ruby said fairly.

Audrey raised her eyebrows. 'If you say so.'

Curious, Mary asked, 'Were they wearing nicer frocks than our lasses?'

Audrey's eyes flew wide open. 'Oh, aye. They've got much nicer clothes than us Hucknall girls.'

Ruby burst out laughing. 'That can't be true, Audrey. There's a war on, same rules apply to all – clothes are rationed.'

Audrey gave an indignant shrug. 'I can only tell you what I saw, which is that quite a number of them outsider women were dancing in posher frocks than us on Saturday night.'

'I bet that girl Lily – you know, she's pals with the one I worked with when she started here, the girl with the long silver-blonde hair – I'm sure she looked pretty,' Ruby remarked.

'I know who you mean,' Mary recalled. 'She looks gorgeous enough in her work clothes – she must have looked stunning all dressed up.'

Lowering her voice, Audrey said, 'She did, but it wasn't her that stole the show. It was that tall friend of hers – the one with the long dark hair,' she explained. 'She looked like a blinking film star.'

Knowing that anybody who loved dancing longed to look like one of the famous starlets of the day – Audrey Hepburn, Sophia Loren, Lauren Bacall – Ruby asked, 'What was she wearing?'

Audrey had no problem recounting the details of Edna's show-stopping dress. 'A beautiful red dress with a square-necked bodice that fitted like a glove; it had a tight waistband, big side pockets, and a full skirt that ended mid-calf. Seriously, I don't know anybody here in Hucknall who could afford a dress like that,' she said, with an envious sigh. 'It looked like something that royalty would wear. It's not like she's even good-looking, but that dress made up for everything. She was with a handsome Canadian all night.'

Seeing her friend's wistful expression, Ruby said with a generous smile, 'I'm sure you looked lovely too, duck.'

Audrey gave a resigned shrug. 'Oh, aye, in an old black crêpe frock handed down from my eldest sister.'

Knowing what a great dancer vivacious Audrey was, Ruby said kindly, 'I bet you danced your socks off.'

'I did, for sure, and there were enough fellas to go around too.'

'Did anyone take your fancy?' Lily asked.

Audrey gave a chuckle. 'Yeah, a posh pilot with wandering palms,' she replied. Seeing young Mary's baffled expression, she explained, 'His hands were everywhere, lovie.'

Blushing to the roots of her mousey-brown hair, Mary gulped, 'I hope you didn't let him take advantage of you, Audrey?'

'I wouldn't have minded so much if he hadn't let slip, mid-grope, that he was engaged. Honestly – fellas – out for all they can get!'

'Not all of them,' Ruby corrected her friend. 'My George is always a gent.'

'Lucky you,' Audrey scoffed. 'They're few and far between these days. Anyway,' she continued as she lit up a Woodbine, 'how did you spend your Saturday night?'

'Babysitting Archie, he's teething,' Ruby replied. 'I was determined to give Mam a break, so I made sure I minded him all weekend.'

Ever thoughtful, Mary gently asked, 'How is your mother now?'

Ruby shook her head. 'Not great, not that she would ever let on how she's feeling, she keeps soldiering on.'

Mary gave a fond smile. 'My mother's the same, there's something about that World War One generation. Tough old birds.'

'I'm desperate to lighten her load,' Ruby admitted. 'But that can only happen once I get our Archie into the new Bell Works nursery. Honestly, the sooner that nursery opens the better.'

'It's certainly taking shape,' Audrey remarked. 'I had a look the other day on my way home. From what I could see, it looks just about finished to me.'

'I regularly speak to the site manager,' Ruby informed her

friends. 'He said they've already appointed a matron, and he's personally shown her around the building.' Crossing her fingers, she said fervently, 'Please God, let it be up and running soon.'

'So, your little Archie might be one of the nursery's first customers?' Mary smiled sweetly.

Ruby gave a hopeful nod. 'I keep imagining what it would be like, pushing Archie here in his pram and dropping him off just across the way from where I'm working.' She sighed wistfully.

'It would be very convenient,' Mary agreed. 'You could even pop over and see him during your breaks. Let's hope Archie is one of the first to get a place.'

Ruby shook her head. 'No, I wouldn't pop over,' she said firmly. 'It would only upset the little lad, seeing me coming and going. He'll need to get used to the nursery staff, and the other babies too.'

'He'll probably have plenty of company,' Mary said fondly.

'And Mother will finally get the rest she needs,' Ruby said, with a heartfelt sigh. 'It'll be a huge relief not to have to trouble her any more.'

'There are lots of mothers and grannies, not to mention aunties and neighbours, minding other women's kiddies these days,' Audrey chipped in. 'The government will be needing a lot more nurseries if they want more women of child-bearing age to do men's work.'

'Mother says the Women's Land Army are providing the country with a lot of the food we eat,' Mary piped up.

Audrey grimaced. 'Hell fire, I don't envy them!' she exclaimed. 'I'd rather be here in Hucknall, working with a pneumatic drill and covered in engine grease, than milking cows or ploughing muddy fields.'

'I agree, I'd rather be an engine girl than a land girl. At least I get to stay with Mother,' Mary said, with an emotional catch in her throat.

'You and your mam, you're joined at the hip,' Audrey smiled.

Tears sprang into Mary's big blue eyes. 'The bond's got stronger since Dad died,' she murmured. 'She relies on me a lot more these days.'

Audrey gave her friend's hand a squeeze. 'You're a good lass,' she said warmly.

Looking thoughtful, Ruby added, 'Us women will be running this country very soon, even the young Princess Elizabeth is doing her bit to keep up morale. Remember her on *Children's Hour*, urging us all to have courage? I bet she'll join up just as soon as she's old enough.'

A patriotic girl to the core, Mary said, 'Their parents have set them the best example. The King has said he won't leave London, and we know that Queen Elizabeth won't leave the King – and the Princesses won't leave her. It's reassuring to think we're all in this together.'

'It's impressive the way the King and Queen go up and down the country supporting their subjects,' Audrey agreed. 'They're suffering, just like us – not like Edward VIII, who took himself off rather than toe the party line.'

'He was honest enough to admit that he couldn't do the job without the woman he loved,' Mary reminded her friend.

'Tch!' Audrey scoffed. 'He just thought he could pull a fast one and boss the nation into thinking it was the best thing for their future King, but he reckoned without public reaction – not to mention his own family's disapproval. We're a lot better off with King George VI and Queen Elizabeth; they might live in a palace but they're hard-working, down-to-earth people who have their subjects close to their hearts.'

Putting the royal family to one side, Mary thoughtfully returned to the original subject.

'When will you tell your mother about the nursery?'

'There's no point in talking about it until the place is up and running, and Archie's been offered a place,' Ruby replied. 'Even though it'd be the best thing for her, I know she'll seriously take it to heart. I'm really worried about offending her,' she added anxiously.

Mary gave a sympathetic smile. 'From what you've said, it's the best all round.'

Ruby nodded. 'It's the *only* way, Mary,' she agreed. 'But will Mother see it like that?'

19. Good Riddance to Bad Rubbish

Corresponding by letter, Edna and Ken fixed a day for their first date. Edna was filled with secret delight, counting down the hours to their meeting and fretting about how she could actually get out of the prefab without Lily guessing what she was up to. Later in the week, desperate to see Ken, she lied to her friend about where she was going.

'I'm just popping over to one of the new girl's prefabs,' she told Lily, who was sitting knitting by the fire. 'She's got a little boy who's been evacuated to Wales, so we thought we'd swap notes.'

Though this wasn't a blatant lie – the woman did exist, and she did have a little boy who had been evacuated to Wales – it was still only a half-truth; in reality, she was heading out to meet Ken in The Nag's Head, in Hucknall. Feeling dreadful about lying to her sweetest friend, but driven by an urge that completely overwhelmed her, she applied her make-up after leaving the house, so as to avoid awkward questions.

Edna spent a couple of hours with Ken in the smoky pub before he walked her home. Anxious that she might be spotted by one of her workmates, she insisted that they go their separate ways before they even got as far as the factory gates.

Stopping in one of the cobbled side streets, she said, 'This is fine. I can make my own way home from here.'

'This is even better,' he murmured as he drew her into a dark backstreet where he pressed her up against a wall.

They kissed and clung on to each other, until a couple passing by startled them and they sprang apart. Breathless, Edna agreed to another date before they parted.

'Come on, honey, make the most of it,' Ken whispered in her ear. 'Life's too short, let's have some fun while we can.'

After their first date, several more followed, each one more heated and passionate than the one before. Telling no one of her secret affair, Edna was fully aware that she was spinning two sets of lies: one to her friends, and one to Ken (who had no idea that his girlfriend was married). She continued to use her new friend with the evacuee child in Wales as her excuse to slip out and meet up with Ken. As their dates became more frequent, and the time spent with him ran into hours, it became harder to explain her late return home; sometimes it was so late that Lily was tucked up fast asleep in bed, which was a huge relief for guilty Edna.

Though it was increasingly clear to Edna that her boyfriend was only after one thing, she knew that she was just as guilty as him – except he wasn't married (as far as she knew), and she was. The night Ken asked her out to the local picture house, to see Charlie Chaplin's gripping film *The Great Dictator*, Edna told her friends that she was in fact going to watch the film with her new-found friend. On her way to meet Ken, thoroughly ashamed of herself for lying to Lily and Jeannie and deceiving them, Edna decided it was time to come clean and tell her friends the sordid truth – even though she knew they would both strongly disapprove and, for sure, they would be offended by the string of lies she had told them.

'I can't live with myself doing this any longer,' she realized as she hurried through the streets of Hucknall.

Sitting in the picture house, in the back row in the pitch dark, kissing and cuddling along with other amorous young couples, Edna was barely aware of the film, gripping as it supposedly was. As the evening progressed, Ken's advances had steadily become more demanding, more exciting, to such an extent that Edna was finding it hard to resist. After the film concluded and the courting couples emerged blinking into the bright light that suddenly illuminated the picture house, Ken led Edna into a nearby park. They fell on to a bench where Edna, used only to her husband's clumsy fumblings in the dark, was swept away by her lover's passionate kisses.

'I love you, sweetheart,' Ken murmured as he traced kisses down the line of Edna's neck. 'Be mine forever,' he urged as he expertly undid her bra and felt her breasts.

Though Edna resisted, her struggle was brief, and in the end, she gave in.

'I'll always take care of you, honey,' Ken promised as they made love on a damp bench in the dark.

But Ken never did keep his promise.

After that fateful night in the park, all communication between them ceased. Knowing Ken's address, Edna considered writing to him, but after some thought decided against it. She had behaved badly – like a tramp, her mother-in-law would have said – but she wasn't going to crawl to Ken.

'I've had my bit of fun, and it's clear that Ken got what

he wanted too. Do I really want to rekindle the flame, when I know what a swine he is?'

The more she questioned and chastised herself, the more Edna realized what a fool she had been. As shame set in, she felt lonely and isolated; nevertheless, she couldn't bring herself to confide in her friends. In the end, desperate to offload her misery, she told them late one night. Opening a bottle of brandy (Ken's final gift to her, courtesy of the local black market), Edna poured them each a stiff drink and then poured out her story.

'I know I've been played for a fool,' she cried. 'And I lied to you both, repeatedly, I'm so ashamed,' she sobbed. 'I can never apologize enough for deceiving you both.'

The silence that followed her confession spoke volumes.

'He obviously moved on to pastures new, once he got what he wanted,' Edna blurted out.

'You could regard that as a good thing, that you've seen him for what he really is,' Jeannie reasoned. 'Unless he's broken your heart in the process?' she asked cautiously.

'It's not my heart that's broken – if anything, it's my pride,' Edna explained. 'We were both as bad as each other. You can't have forgotten what I said to you both on the dance night, when I first met him?'

'That you were looking forward to a new lease of life,' Lily vividly recalled.

Edna nodded. 'I felt justified at the time. I seriously thought that I had been short-changed while I was young, and I was due one last fling.'

'Yes, you did say something along those lines,' Jeannie replied.

'I remember neither of you were impressed, but that didn't stop me.'

Taking a deep breath, Lily said bravely, 'I think the best thing you can do, Edna, is to see this as a chapter in your life that's closed – and for the good too.'

Picking up on Lily's line of thought, Jeannie asked, 'And you're quite certain it's over?'

'It's over all right,' Edna acknowledged bitterly.

'Then, if you don't mind me saying, good riddance to bad rubbish,' Jeannie declared.

Nodding solemnly, Lily added, 'I agree, so long as there are no repercussions.'

Draining the last drop of brandy in her glass, Edna prayed there would be no 'repercussions', as Lily tactfully phrased it. This was a chapter of her life she had no intention of reopening.

20. Oro Chenko

Lily didn't have to wait long before she received a letter in the post from Oro. There was one for Edna too. While her friend dashed into the kitchen to make a pot of tea, Lily gazed dreamily at the firm elegant handwriting on the white envelope she was clutching.

'You look like the cat that's got the cream,' Edna teased as she reappeared with a loaded tray. 'Who's it from?'

'The Polish pilot I met at the works dance,' Lily said, blushing furiously.

Seeing the envelope hadn't even been opened, Edna did a double take. 'How do you know?' she exclaimed.

Lily waved the back of the letter at her friend. 'His name is on the back: Oro Chenko.'

'Well, read it, then,' Edna declared as she poured scalding-hot tea into two cups. 'I'll have a read of mine too.'

Still wearing her old woollen coat to keep warm in the chilly prefab, Lily sat on the battered brown utility armchair to read Oro's letter.

My dear Lily,

It was a pleasure to meet with you at the Saturday dance. I hoped we might meet again soon, if you are free. I have next Saturday off from my teacher flying school and so could meet with you, if you like this idea? We have a phone in the office of Polish squadron – here is the

number – 335. Please phone and ask for me, Lieutenant Chenko,
and we can fix good day to meet soon.

Yours with affection,
Oro

Lily looked up from her letter with a happy smile, but it faded when she caught sight of Edna's stricken expression.

'What is it?' she asked as she nodded at the open letter clutched in her friend's hand. 'Bad news?'

Edna nodded grimly. 'They're moving Kathleen – *again.*' Almost in tears, she scanned the letter once more and explained, 'It's from the woman who organizes the evacuees' placement in Kendal, she says the old couple who Kathleen's been allocated to can't manage any more due to the fact that the husband's been admitted to Kendal Infirmary with suspected tuberculosis.' Crumpling the letter in her hand, Edna fought back tears. 'This can't go on, Lily,' she cried. 'It's the third move for Kathleen in less than six months.'

'Is there nothing you can do, lovie?' Lily gently enquired.

Pacing the room, Edna cried, 'Go up there to see her, for a start!' Distraught, she exclaimed, 'God Almighty, I only wish the works nursery was open right now. If it were, I could bring Kathleen here to live with me, instead of her being shunted from pillar to post like a bag of potatoes, poor little kiddie – what a state she must be in.'

Feeling really sorry for both Edna and her daughter, Lily laid down her mug before saying gently, 'Lovie, it's not just a nursery place that you need for Kathleen, she'll need accommodation sorting out too. What's happening in that department?'

Gathering her thoughts, Edna recalled her recent meeting with the works accommodation officer.

'She told me that there is provision on-site for family units, but I told her I would like Kathleen to live here with us in Prefab Number Eight.'

'And what did she say to that?' Lily asked cautiously.

'She was very understanding, but she said she would have to check the suitability of the dwelling when I knew more about Kathleen's future plans,' Edna explained.

Impressed by Edna's motivation, Lily replied, 'That's a start at least. You don't want to bring Kathleen here, only to be told you've got to move her – that would be awful, after all she's been through.'

Suddenly flustered, Edna turned to Lily. 'Really, Lil, be honest with me. Are you sure you wouldn't mind sharing your home with my daughter?' she asked earnestly.

'Why would I mind sharing with a little girl who needs to be with her mother?' Lily answered compassionately.

Visibly brightening up, Edna said gratefully, 'Thanks, lovie. Offering to share your home with a child is very generous.'

With the bit between her teeth, Lily urged, 'Things are getting serious, Edna – now that you've got the accommodation officer on side, you really need to chase up the person in charge of the nursery list. You can't be the only mother on the site who's desperate for a nursery place.'

'I just wish there was somebody at work I could talk to. None of us new girls on the site have got kiddies apart from me – and I don't feel easy about asking the local lasses. I could ask Sid,' she said tentatively. 'He might know who could advise me.'

'Worth a go,' Lily agreed.

Putting down her teacup, Edna nodded towards the letter that Lily was holding. 'Tell me about your letter, lovie.'

Grinning from ear to ear, Lily announced, 'Oro has asked me out.'

'Course he has,' Edna beamed. 'Who could resist the belle of the ball?'

'Actually,' Lily replied, modest as ever, 'that title goes to you, Edna, in that red dress.'

Playfully dismissing the compliment, Edna asked, 'When are you meeting up with him?'

'He's suggested Saturday.'

'Can you manage that with your work schedule?' Edna asked.

Lily nodded hopefully. 'I'm going to try and swap with someone who has Saturday off,' she explained. 'Oro's given me his number to ring at the Polish air force base.'

'Can they speak English?' Edna naively asked.

'Well, Oro certainly can, so I presume his colleagues can too.'

'Well, then,' said Edna as she lit up a Woodbine. 'Looks like we're both going to be busy tomorrow; you sorting out leave, and me making some serious enquiries about a nursery place and accommodation for our Kathleen.'

The following day, Edna asked Sid if he knew anything about the procedure for applying for a place in the Bell Works nursery. Looking at her like she had just landed from an alien planet, Sid burst out laughing.

'Bloody hell fire, woman!' he exploded. 'We build fighter planes here – I've no clue about baby nurseries.'

Feeling a fool, Edna nevertheless pressed on. 'Who do

I need to talk to about seeing if I can get a place for my daughter when it opens?'

Sid just shrugged. 'Haven't a clue, mi duck. Mebbe enquire at the general office.'

Standing in the corridor that connected the shop floor to the canteen, dithering about what to do next, Edna jumped in surprise when she felt a tap on her arm. Turning round, she was even more taken aback when she saw Ruby standing before her.

'Did I just hear you asking about a place in the baby nursery?' Ruby asked.

Momentarily speechless, Edna nodded before blurting out, 'Yes, I've got a little girl up in Kendal, she's an evacuee. I want to bring her to Hucknall, preferably before Christmas, but I need to get permission for her to come here and live with me – and also see if I can get her a place in the nursery before I move her. I know the nursery's still being built, but do you know who I should talk to about getting her a place?'

Ruby's lovely dark-blue eyes sparkled. 'You've come to the right woman,' she smiled. 'I'm on tenterhooks myself, waiting to hear if my son has a place – he needs one as soon as possible.' Getting down to basics, Ruby added, 'It's due to open soon. I'd advise you to get your daughter's name on the waiting list right away.' Seeing Edna's panicked expression, she urged, 'Let's pop over to the admin department. I know the way well,' she added with a grin. 'We've just got time before the hooter goes.'

Very much aware of the hostility that existed between the two camps of female factory workers, Edna was overwhelmed by Ruby's generosity.

'I'd really appreciate it, if you've got time?' she whispered nervously.

Flashing her warm vibrant smile, Ruby replied, 'Of course I've got time, us mums need all the help we can get.'

While Ruby was busy introducing Edna to the woman who ran the works admin department, Lily was standing in the public telephone box in the entrance hall, nervously dialling the number that Oro had given her. When the call was picked up at the other end she quickly slipped in the coins.

'Er, may I please speak to Flight Lieutenant Chenko?'

'Righty-ho,' boomed a very authoritative upper-class English voice. 'I'll fetch him.'

A few minutes later, Lily visibly relaxed when she heard Oro's voice on the other end of the line.

'Chenko speaking.'

'Hello, it's Lily,' she said softly.

Obviously delighted, Oro exclaimed, 'Lillee! How nice to hear you.'

Thrilling to the sound of her name on his lips – pronounced as a soft 'Lillee' – she spoke shyly.

'I thought I'd let you know that I have this Saturday off work too.'

'So, you are free?' he asked excitedly.

'Yes, I'm free.'

'We can meet here, if you like?'

'The airbase?' she asked in surprise.

'Yes, if it's convenient for you?'

'Yes, all right.'

'Don't worry, I make you official visitor,' he chuckled.

'Nobody will throw you out as a spy,' he joked. 'Midday,' he suggested. 'I come and escort you, if you prefer?'

'No, I'll walk over, it's not far,' she quickly told him.

'If you like, Lillee,' he agreed.

Blushing with pleasure again at his pronunciation of her name, Lily brought the conversation to an end. 'See you on Saturday, then,' she said.

'Goodbye, I look forward to see you,' he concluded, with formal politeness.

Laying the receiver back down in its cradle, a smiling Lily slumped against the side of the telephone booth. Goodness, she thought to herself, just the sound of Oro's voice made her weak at the knees. Smiling at her foolishness, she opened the kiosk door and all but bumped into Edna who was hurrying across the hallway.

'Edna,' she called out. 'Wait for me.'

On their way back to work, Edna explained where she had been.

'You'll never believe this,' she cried, flushed with excitement. 'That lovely woman, Ruby, she took me to the admin department to help me sort out a nursery place for Kathleen. She's incredible! She knew just what to do. She was kindness itself. She's desperate for her little lad to get a place too.'

'Goes to show that not all Hucknall women are monsters,' Lily grinned. 'Did you get any idea about when the nursery might open?'

Edna nodded. 'Soon, definitely before Christmas. I'm imagining that people who've had their names down for some time will be the first to get places.'

'But at least Kathleen's on the list now,' Lily reasoned.

'On domestic sites like ours, there have got to be adequate arrangements for mothers and their children.'

'Though I'd be really sad if I had to move out of Prefab Number Eight,' Edna said.

'I wouldn't like it either,' Lily smiled. 'It would be lovely if the three of us – you, me and Kathleen – could live there together.'

Shaking her head in disbelief, Edna murmured, 'Ruby's taken a weight off my shoulders; I really owe her one.'

21. First Date

Lily was glad that she had decided to make her own way to the Polish airbase where Oro was stationed. While getting dressed for her first date with the handsome young pilot, she realized she was a bag of nerves. Usually the confident one who put others at their ease, she fumbled with zips and fasteners until Edna – aware of her friend's growing tension – laughed.

'Come here and let me do it,' she urged.

Turning her back, Lily let Edna pull up the long metallic zip on her best winter frock – a soft pink pleated woollen dress with a creamy lace Peter Pan collar.

'I bet the poor fella's just as nervous as you,' Edna chuckled.

'He didn't seem nervous when I phoned him, and he certainly wasn't nervous when we met at the dance,' Lily explained. 'I wasn't nervous then either, actually – but golly, I am now,' she laughed.

'You'll be all right once you're with him,' Edna reassured her friend.

When Lily met Oro, her heart skipped several beats. The sight of his golden hair glinting in the bright autumn sunlight and his green eyes sparkling with delight when he saw her approaching, made her feel ridiculously giddy and excited. With a huge welcoming smile on his face, he slipped her arm through his and set off.

'I have a surprise for you,' he announced.

Aware of how much taller he was than her, Lily craned her neck to gaze up at him. His hair was just as golden as she remembered, and his vivid green eyes were startlingly bright in broad daylight.

'Where are we going?' she asked as he signed her in at the sentry's office beside the heavily guarded front gate.

'For a walk – then comes the surprise,' he winked.

Walking Lily around the Nissen huts, storerooms, residential and admin blocks, Oro led her to a makeshift bench in front of a single-storey building that looked on to the runway.

'Here is nice and private, better than *kantyna* – that's Polish for NAAFI – where everybody stares at a pretty girl like you.'

Blushing at his compliment, Lily perched on the edge of the bench and curiously watched him take a Thermos flask from the canvas rucksack he had been carrying. Pouring hot liquid into two plastic cups, Oro smiled.

'Not boring English tea,' he told her. 'Strong black Polish coffee, we get sent from home. Here, taste,' he said as he handed Lily a steaming cup.

Cautious at first, Lily sipped the strong black liquid.

'It's sweet!' she exclaimed in delight.

'I stole the sugar,' he confessed. 'Not so good without.'

'It's delicious,' she enthused.

'I think so,' he agreed.

Sitting comfortably side by side, Oro pointed out a number of aircraft lined up on the runway.

'Hawker Hurricane, De Havilland Mosquito – best of all, the Spitfire,' he enthused. 'Beautiful, light and graceful, like you, a silver bird.'

Blushing again at his romantic compliments, Lily responded shyly.

'I love Spitfires,' she exclaimed. 'Not just because I build them. Like you, I love their lightness and speed. I've been reading up about the Mosquito twin engine – that's probably my second favourite,' Lily said, with genuine enthusiasm. 'But I agree, Spitfires are the best.'

Pouring out the last of the sweet black coffee, Oro asked more about her work at the Bell factory. Conscious of her lowly position compared to his rather illustrious role of both lieutenant and pilot in the Polish Air Force, Lily gave a little self-deprecating shrug.

'I'm just an engine girl,' she explained. 'I team up with another woman, we work in pairs on the factory floor, assembling aircraft. The place is so noisy you simply can't speak.' Suddenly aware that her high state of excitement was causing her to babble, Lily checked herself. 'Please tell me if I'm speaking too quickly.'

'I understand,' he smiled. 'Your voice is clear and sweet – like a bell. So go on,' he urged, 'tell me more about your job.'

Using her hands to illustrate the sort of cramped space that she worked in, Lily explained, 'The body of the aeroplane is in a tight wooden jig. We use a metal template that comes with rows of pre-drilled holes; we clip it on to the section of the aircraft we're working on and use it as a guide so we know exactly where to drill holes and rivet metal panels on to the cockpit's fuselage. It's pretty cramped, working side by side for hours on end. You soon get to know your working partner intimately,' she grinned.

Oro gave an appreciative nod. 'Engine girls are important for us pilots. We never have enough aircraft to compete with the Luftwaffe's output.'

Lily's head drooped. 'My heart flips with excitement, and at the same time sinks with fear, when I see our planes fly out. I always wonder as they disappear over the horizon, how long might it be until they're shot down?'

Looking severe, Oro said with great conviction, 'Getting shot down is bad indeed, but if you shoot enough enemy aircraft before that, it is worth the sacrifice – fewer Luftwaffe planes is always a triumph.'

Looking into his honest, open and smiling face, dominated by his dazzling green eyes and mop of golden hair, Lily felt a wave of admiration and affection sweep over her. I like this man, she thought. She liked his quirky imagination; producing strong black coffee to sip by the runway on a chilly autumn day was just delightful. She liked his enthusiasm for the war work he was committed to, and his passion for aircraft. His tall, commanding presence excited her, as did his broad shoulders and strong chest; recalling dancing in his arms, she felt yet another tell-tale blush creep over her cheeks. Frightened that he might be reading her thoughts, she averted her eyes until she had regained some composure.

'So, now we go flying,' Oro announced as he replaced the empty Thermos flask in his canvas rucksack, then got to his feet.

Thunderstruck, Lily exclaimed, 'Are you really serious?'

'It's what I suggested when we first met,' he grinned. 'I've not changed my mind – have you?'

'NO!' she cried, 'I'm just, well, taken aback,' she admitted.

Taking her firmly by the hand, as if they were going for a stroll in the park, he said, 'Come, follow me, this way.'

Leading her off the main runway, he guided her to a slip road that fed on to a connecting runway where, to her astonishment, she saw a Tiger Moth standing ready for action. Blinking at the glowing, bright yellow plane starkly outlined against a sodden grey sky, Lily found it difficult to be coherent.

'It's . . . gorgeous!' she blurted out.

Oro gave a proud nod. 'I built it with a fellow mechanic,' he said, with an undisguisable swagger.

'You *built* it?' she gasped.

'Yes – maybe I'm not so good a builder as you, little engine girl, but believe me, she goes like a bird.'

They were greeted by Oro's mechanic, who was waiting with two flying jackets.

'Steve and I work together and share the plane. This is my friend Lily,' Oro said, fastening the jacket around Lily's slender shoulders before slipping into his own.

'You'll be needing that jacket, miss, it's chilly up there. Hat and goggles too,' Steve grinned.

'I've never flown in a plane before!' Lily gasped as Oro secured the leather strap of the flying hat under her chin.

'Then it's time you did,' he teased.

'Up you pop, miss,' Steve said as he gave her a leg-up into the front seat of the open-cockpit biplane.

'It looks too delicate to fly!' Lily exclaimed as she gazed at the aircraft's wings and tail. 'It seems to be made of wood!'

'They're not solid metal, miss, but these planes are safe enough,' Steve assured Lily as she sank deep into her seat.

'Me and Oro here have flown her many a time, she goes like a dream. Enjoy!' he said as he stepped away.

'Put the wireless headset on,' Oro said from the seat behind her. 'I have a pair too,' he added as he adjusted his own set. 'We're connected, so we can chat during the flight.'

Staring at the wide expanse of the engine bonnet in front of her, Lily began to panic.

'Why am I in the front seat?' she cried.

Catching sight of her petrified face in the mirror, Oro burst out laughing. 'Don't worry, believe it or not, I'm in the driver's seat. Ready?'

Shaking with nerves and excitement, Lily adjusted her goggles. 'Ready as I'll ever be,' she gasped.

Oro gave Steve, who was standing on the runway, the thumbs up sign. 'Okay,' he called as Steve swung the propeller.

'Chocks away!' Oro called, even louder, as he released the throttle and the Tiger Moth started to taxi down the runway.

Lily gasped as the plane bounced along, then gathered speed as they approached the main runway – passing the bench where they had just sat to drink coffee. As the end of the runway loomed up, Lily closed her eyes and prayed, thinking they'd go crashing headlong into a ploughed field, but suddenly she felt the Tiger Moth lift and, with graceful ease, the plane took to the wide-open skies.

Opening her eyes wide, Lily laughed with sheer exhilaration.

'Hahhhh! It's so beautiful!' she exclaimed. And all her fears fell away as she gazed in wonder at the world below her.

Behind her, Oro smiled. 'There is nothing in the whole world like this.'

After flying out over the woods that fringed the airfield, the aircraft soared into the clouds, which cleared as the small plane lifted gently on the changing air currents. With the wind whipping around her, Lily peered over the side of the aircraft, excitedly pointing down to familiar landmarks below.

'Hucknall church! It looks tiny,' she cried.

They swooped over miles of rolling hills until they could see the dim outline of the city of Nottingham, and then Lily realized that Oro was already swinging inland.

'Are we heading home already?' she cried in disappointment.

'Certainly not before we've looped the loop,' he chuckled as he banked the aircraft higher.

Lily's stomach churned as, on a breathtaking nosedive, they dropped height before Oro took the Tiger Moth curling up and up again.

'*Wheeeee!*' She laughed as they dipped and soared.

'Feeling sick?' he asked.

'No,' she cried. 'I love it.'

On their journey back they flew over farms, villages and grazing cattle, criss-crossing the lines of railway tracks and roads where the few vehicles below looked like toys in a children's picture book. Finally, as the airbase loomed, they skimmed over the ploughed fields; closing down the throttle, Oro made his descent downwind, reducing speed, then with professional ease he skilfully landed the Tiger Moth gently back on the runway. After disconnecting their headphones, Oro hopped out of his seat before helping Lily out of hers.

Once safely back on terra firm, and wildly overexcited, Lily flung her arms around Oro and hugged him, still high on adrenalin.

'Thank you, that was wonderful,' she cried.

Holding her close, Oro gazed into her mesmerizing silver-grey eyes that sparkled with sheer exhilaration.

'I've never known anything like it,' she babbled on. 'The sky, the light, the wind, the moors – oh, but once we were up there, swooping and diving, I felt like an eagle soaring higher and higher into endless space.'

Lily's beauty, combined with her bubbling joie de vivre, took Oro's breath away, and before he could stop himself or even ask her permission, he pressed his lips to hers.

'Sweet Lillee,' he murmured as her lips parted under the pressure of his.

Limp in his arms, Lily could barely breathe. When she did pull away, it was to gaze into his eyes and dreamily ask, 'How am I ever going to get back to normal when I've just nearly touched heaven?'

'Is that what my kisses do to you?' he teased. 'One day, flying will become normal,' he assured her.

'No!' she exclaimed. 'I never want anything as wonderful and unique as that experience to become mundane and normal. It's sublime!' she passionately insisted.

'You should have seen your face,' he teased.

'I seriously couldn't believe it was happening – that you had planned such a thrilling thing for me.'

Standing on her tiptoes, it was Lily's turn to kiss Oro. 'Thank you, I'll never forget today as long as I live.'

'It is first of many flights for us,' Oro answered softly.

'Promise . . .' she whispered.

Kissing the tip of her small nose, he whispered back, 'Oh, yes, I can safely promise that, with all my heart.'

22. Day Nursery

Early the next week, Ruby's patient diligence in following the progress of the Bell Works nursery finally paid off. She was one of the first to receive a letter informing her that Archie had secured a place and could start right away. Ruby's immediate reaction of joy and relief gave way to anxiety. The last thing she wanted was to offend her mother. After all, she had put in so many hours minding her grandson – and even though it had taken a toll on her health, Mrs Fields had never complained. But when it came to making the announcement, Ruby's mum was fine, relieved even, Ruby secretly thought.

'There's no need for you to do anything,' Ruby explained after her mother had read the letter. 'The nursery hours are geared to our shifts, so I'll do all the drop-offs and pick-ups.'

'I wouldn't mind doing a bit of something to help out,' her mother kindly volunteered. 'It'll be a long day, without the little lad to look after,' she confessed. 'I'd be happy to pick him up when you're working extra-long hours.'

Grateful as she was for this offer, Ruby didn't immediately want to burden her mother with tasks she hoped she could handle herself. The whole idea was to ease her mother's load, rather than initiate a new regime of care and responsibility.

'That's good to know,' she said as she gave her mother a peck on the cheek.

With a starting day fixed later that week, Ruby turned her attention to Archie's needs. Trying not to think how much he might miss the familiarity of being at home with his family, Ruby concentrated on preparing him for the big change in his young life. Used already to being bottle-fed by his grandmother during the working day, Archie still enjoyed a breastfeed before bedtime. Cuddled close in his mother's arms, it was a time of deep contentment for both of them, and Ruby certainly didn't want that to change. All Archie really needed when the big day came was a spare change of clothes, an extra pram blanket, and his favourite cuddly toy – which in his case was a knitted pink pig.

When the big day dawned, Mrs Fields woke her daughter with a cup of hot tea even before the alarm had gone off, at 6 a.m. Offering to change Archie's nappy and bottle-feed him while Ruby got ready for work, Mrs Fields left her daughter preparing for the new day ahead. Ironically, while her mother seemed fine Ruby felt like a wreck. As soon as she had got into bed the previous night, she had created imaginary scenarios that kept her awake, and little Archie, picking up on his mother's restlessness, had grumbled and complained throughout the night. Ruby had finally hauled him into bed with her, where they both fell into a deep sleep.

After drinking her tea, Ruby hurried downstairs to the chilly lean-to bathroom tagged on to the back of the two-up two-down terraced house. Standing on the flagstone floor, with her feet frozen, Ruby washed herself at the sink before dashing back upstairs to get dressed. She brushed her long thick brunette hair, tucked it under a warm woollen scarf, then slipped on her winter coat, relieved her mother of her wriggling son, and settled him into his pram, snugly tucked under his blankets. There followed the usual struggle of heaving the pram out of the narrow front door into the cobbled street, then Ruby turned to say goodbye to her mother.

Mrs Fields suddenly had tears in her tired eyes.

'I'll miss the little lad,' she cried. 'I know I was not as good at minding him as I should have been, but I tried mi best, Ruby.'

Holding on to the pram handle with one hand, Ruby turned to hug her mother.

'You're not to talk like that, Mother, you've done a wonderful job of looking after Archie,' she insisted, with tears in her eyes. 'You know as well as I do that realistically we couldn't go on the way we were. With Archie getting bigger, he'll need more attention, plus I'm going to be working longer shifts. At least the nursery is designed to work around the factory's hours.'

Mrs Fields nodded. 'I know it's best all round,' she agreed. 'Now off you go, you don't want Archie to be late on his first day.'

Setting off, pushing the old Silver Cross pram, Ruby called over her shoulder, 'Bye, Mother – remember to get some rest.'

The new Bell Works nursery was a delight to walk into. Built with solid local red brick, it had a wide entrance hall from which a windowed corridor led into three large airy rooms, catering for all ages under five – babies, tweenies and toddlers. Outside there was a paved covered patio area, where prams and outdoor equipment were stored, while inside the baby nursery stood a row of little cots with a spacious changing area to one side, where piles of clean nappies were stacked tidily on shelves. Seeing the little cots and the neat kitchen area, with sterilized feeding bottles drying on the counter, Ruby felt a lump in her throat. Holding her son close, feeling his warm little mouth nuzzling her neck, Ruby had a fleeting moment of doubt. As if sensing her unease, Matron – who had welcomed Ruby on her arrival – held out her arms.

'Here, let me take him, dear,' she said firmly. 'Best to avoid too much emotion, or baby will pick up on it too.'

Though her words were brisk and businesslike, Ruby recognized the wisdom and experience in Matron's kind eyes.

'We know where to find you if we need you,' Matron assured Ruby, before she walked away with Archie in her arms.

All day long at work Ruby was anxious and preoccupied, to such an extent that Audrey – working alongside her in the jig supporting the fuselage they were fitting out – nudged her in the ribs.

'How did it go with the little 'un?' she asked.

Ruby gave a shrug before mouthing, 'Okay.' Then, nodding briefly, she turned her attention back to the job in hand.

At dinnertime, over mince and onion pie bulked out by mashed carrots and turnips, with apple fritters to follow, Audrey, seeing her friend's face was still strained, came straight to the point.

'I'm sure he's in good hands.'

'I know that,' Ruby blurted out. 'But I can't help wondering every five minutes how my little lad is getting on.'

'Course you can't,' Audrey responded. 'It's only natural. What kind of mother would you be if you didn't worry about your baby?'

Pulling herself together, Ruby continued, 'I know it's for the best all round – and after all, Archie's only a stone's throw away. Just so long as the shifts don't get too long, I'm sure he'll be fine.'

Leaning back in her chair, Ruby caught sight of Edna with her friends, sitting some distance away. It was an unspoken rule that the newcomers (all of whom lived in prefabs on the same site as Edna and Lily) sat at one side of the canteen's serving hatch while the established locals sat at the other end, and never so far had the twain chosen to meet or mix. But suddenly, before she could even think to stop herself, and aware that Mary and Audrey's eyes were on her, Ruby rose and moved purposefully towards the other side of the canteen counter.

'What's she up to?' gulped Mary. 'There's nobody over yonder she needs to talk to.'

'I think we're about to find out, mi duck,' Audrey muttered darkly.

Seeing Ruby approaching, Edna quickly stubbed out her cigarette and got to her feet. With half the occupants of the canteen watching them, the two women faced each other.

'I just thought you'd like to know,' Ruby started, 'that I dropped my son off at the Bell Works nursery this morning, and it seems very nice indeed.'

Smiling widely, Edna responded, 'I'm delighted to hear

it. Thank you for letting me know. How was your boy when you left him?'

'I think he might have been a bit taken aback to find himself in Matron's charge, but she was very competent, like she'd done it a hundred times before. I was a nervous wreck,' Ruby admitted. 'Matron more or less asked me to leave before I set Archie off.'

Edna giggled. 'I'll be exactly the same if I ever get my girl here. I'm quite sure Matron must have seen it all a thousand times before, though – it's the mothers who suffer.'

Suddenly aware that Lily and Jeannie were staring, if not actually gawping, with dropped jaws open wide, Edna remembered her manners.

'Lily, Jeannie, do you remember Ruby? She's the one who's been advising me on how to get Kathleen's name on the nursery waiting list,' she quickly explained. 'Her little boy started there today,' she added.

Jeannie gave a sweet smile. 'How could I forget? Ruby helped me out too, on my first day on the factory floor. I thought I would cry when Annie abandoned me,' she confessed. 'But you taught me the ropes, and I've not looked back since.'

Ruby gave a little shrug. 'That first day at the coal face is a nightmare.'

Desperate to hear more about the new nursery, Edna hurried the conversation on. 'What does the place look like now that it's finished? Does it look full up already?' she added breathlessly.

'Not really, though I think it will steadily fill up as time goes by,' Ruby explained. 'It's a lovely building,' she added enthusiastically. 'Big and light and airy; from what I could see there are three large nurseries for the different age groups. My Archie's in the baby nursery, I should imagine your daughter would be in the one up from that. Tweenies, I think they call it.'

Edna gave a little shiver of excitement.

'I've already asked the powers that be up in Kendal about the possibility of bringing my daughter here to Hucknall, and the accommodation officer here knows just how much I want Kathleen to live with me.'

'Keep checking with admin about a nursery place,' Ruby urged. 'Don't go waiting for the office to get in touch with you, you've got to keep nagging them. I must have badgered them at least two or three times a week,' she said, with a self-deprecating grimace. 'I suspect being a nag-bag paid off,' she joked.

'Then I'll make sure I'm a nag-bag too,' Edna joked back, grateful for the advice.

At the end of the conversation Ruby made her way back to her side of the canteen, where meek little Mary's eyes were as wide as saucers.

'What were you talking to her about?'

'*Her* is Edna, who needs some advice about nurseries,' Ruby announced rather loudly.

'Has she got children?' goggle-eyed Mary spluttered.

'For God's sake, lovie, they might be new here, but they are *human*,' Ruby exclaimed. 'They do have feelings,' she added with a teasing smile. 'They have boyfriends, family, children even. They're not shipped in from an alien planet, they're ordinary women, same as us,' she concluded.

Across the other side of the canteen Edna was having a similar conversation with her pals.

'Well, that's a turn-up for the books,' Jeannie remarked. 'A Hucknall lass mixing with us new folk.'

Suddenly weary of all the antagonism, Edna said, 'Oh, let it go, Jeannie, I need all the help I can get if I'm ever going to get our Kathleen down here. Ruby's a good kind woman, a mother just like me, who gave me some sound advice which I'm definitely going to follow.'

When the hooter finally blasted at the end of what seemed like a very long day, Ruby flew into the ladies' changing room to exchange her grease-stained dungarees for her day clothes, then dashed across the site to the nursery. Breathless with a mixture of excitement and apprehension, she rushed through the front door and all but ran down the connecting corridor to Archie's nursery. With her hand on the doorknob she paused to get her breath back, which was when she heard a sweet voice singing a lullaby. Opening the door as quietly as she could, she stepped into the nursery to find a young nursery nurse singing to Archie while she cradled him in her arms.

> Golden slumbers kiss your eyes,
> Smiles awake you when you rise.
> Sleep my darling, don't you cry,
> And I will sing a lullaby.

Startled by the sight of a flushed Ruby, the young girl smiled warmly. 'Hello, he's been just fine, good as gold.'

Gazing at her sleepy son, Ruby's heart melted with love.

'He's just had a feed,' the nursery nurse added. 'He seemed restless, so I thought I'd settle him with a song.

Not that I've got the best voice in the world,' she added self-deprecatingly. 'But Archie didn't seem to mind.'

'I thought you sang beautifully,' Ruby enthused.

'Here, he's all yours,' the nurse said as she passed Archie to his mother. 'I'm Gladys, by the way, I work here in the baby nursery,' she explained.

'Delighted to meet you,' Ruby smiled. 'I think I might have missed you this morning.'

'I'm on late shifts this week, so I would have missed any early morning arrivals.'

'And he really was fine?' Ruby enquired.

'He's been fine all the time I've been here, a really good little lad.'

Ruby smiled proudly.

'And there was I, worrying myself sick most of the day,' she said as she beamed down at her gurgling son.

'Every mother does,' Gladys said sympathetically. 'But they soon settle into the new routine.'

After collecting Archie's belongings, Ruby settled him in his pram and, after waving goodbye to Gladys, she set off for home. Though it was only six o'clock, it was already dark by the time she got back home – she would have been out of the house nearly twelve hours. But, she thought, it had been a good day, a momentous day. Archie had gone into day care at the Bell Works and, from the looks of him, as she gazed adoringly at her son lying contentedly in his pram, the day had gone well. Thank God, she sighed gratefully. All her careful planning had finally paid off.

I must remember to tell Edna tomorrow how well Archie's first day has gone, she thought. Recalling Edna's wide smile and kind dark eyes, she realized she was becoming unexpectedly fond of the newcomer; she seemed open and straightforward, and like a woman you could trust. They need all the help they can get, she mused. Poor souls, working just as hard as we are, but nowhere near home and family – and learning a new trade too. We're all in the same boat, or in our case, in the same aircraft fuselage, Ruby smiled to herself. Us engine girls are stronger united – divided we fall.

23. Nag-bag

One afternoon, while Lily and Jeannie were bolting sheet-metal plates into place under the aircraft's fuselage, Jeannie mouthed, 'Can I talk to you later?'

Pausing with the heavy drill in her hand, Lily cocked an eyebrow before answering back, 'Break time.'

'In *private*,' Jeannie responded emphatically.

When the hooter sounded out for a tea break, Edna dashed to the ladies' toilets. This gave Lily a chance to follow up, with Jeannie walking along beside her. Coming straight to the point, she asked, 'What's so urgent?'

'I've been thinking, maybe I should offer to swap my prefab with Edna's, if it strengthens her case for Kathleen to come and live here.'

'That's not a bad idea, and very generous of you to think of it, Jeannie,' Lily agreed. 'I would love to share with you,' she said warmly. 'But your prefab, like ours, is a two bed. So, there's no guarantee the second room would stay empty – especially if conscription becomes compulsory, as everyone seems to think is going to happen soon.'

'Mmm, I get your drift, Lil,' Jeannie murmured. 'What if a woman Edna doesn't get on with is given that berth?'

'Especially if that someone wasn't keen on sharing accommodation with a little girl,' Lily added. 'We really need to sit down together and talk this through.'

'Edna's got a lot on her plate,' Jeannie agreed. 'I know

she's hoping to go up to see Kathleen on her next week-end off. It's so difficult, trying to manage everything from so far away, when we're working long shifts all the time.'

'I think we should have that chat about Edna moving prefabs soon,' Lily insisted. 'It might help clarify her thoughts.'

Sitting cheerfully in front of the fire crackling in the pre-fab's small grate, later that night, the three friends sipped cocoa as they listened to the evening news on the little radio that Jeannie had bought second-hand from Hucknall's pawn shop. The news was all about the enemy's advance on Moscow.

'Odessa and Kharkov have already been taken, but now they're making tracks for Sebastopol,' Lily said anxiously.

'Who'd want to be heading into Russia just as winter's setting in?' Edna grimly remarked. 'It's a cold country – and a big one too.'

'They're coming at us from all sides; north, east and south, they're making inroads,' Jeannie murmured. 'God, at times I have to admit I wonder how we'll ever fight them off.'

Trying to be cheerful, Lily said chirpily, 'Well, at least we're in the right business, building planes to fight off the enemy.'

'What does that Polish boyfriend of yours say about the enemy's advance in the east? He must know all about the fighting going on there.'

Recalling their conversation on the previous Saturday, Lily replied, 'He says getting shot down and losing an air-craft is bad indeed, but the loss is worth it if you take out a Luftwaffe Messerschmitt. Oro says every fallen enemy aircraft counts.'

'But according to all the news reports, they're still producing more aircraft than we are,' Jeannie said glumly. 'No matter how hard we work, and how many hours we put in, we just can't match their output.'

Hearing the BBC announcer concluding the news, Lily switched off the wireless.

'Jeannie and I have been thinking about your domestic arrangements, Edna.'

'We were wondering if you'd like to swap prefabs with me, when Kathleen eventually comes down here to live with you?' Jeannie started.

'Can you move prefabs, just like that?' Edna asked as she snapped her fingers.

'I have made some basic enquiries,' Jeannie said shyly. 'Apparently, you can swap, as long as it's an official agreement between the tenants and the admin department,' she told Edna. 'Obviously, they need to have a proper register of where everybody is billeted.'

'You're such good friends to even come up with this idea,' Edna said gratefully.

'It's only a suggestion, to see if it helps – both of us want you and Kathleen to be happy,' Lily answered sweetly.

'I don't know what to do for the best,' Edna confessed. 'I really don't want us to be a burden to anybody.'

'You're not a burden, lovie,' Lily insisted. 'We're only trying to work out what's best for you and your little girl.'

After giving Lily a grateful smile, Edna continued. 'If they put me in a family unit, I could end up living in a bigger prefab with another woman who has a child or a baby, just like me.'

'Would that suit you more, lovie, being with other kiddies?' Jeannie gently enquired.

Edna shook her head. 'No!' she responded staunchly. 'I don't want to move into a prefab with a stranger, when I'm already settled with a housemate I'm very fond of. The accommodation officer knows that Lily doesn't mind sharing with me and Kathleen, we've already discussed it.' Throwing Lily a grateful smile, she quickly added, 'I hope you really don't mind, Lil?'

'Not at all,' Lily assured Edna. 'Best to sort out everything in advance of Kathleen arriving; we want her move here to be as smooth as possible for her.'

Edna nodded in agreement. 'Imagine if I did move into a new place, with somebody who I didn't get along with – or worse still, our children squabbled all the time. It would be a nightmare.'

'It's obvious you're happy and settled here with Lily, in Prefab Number Eight, which I have to admit is far prettier than mine,' Jeannie smiled. 'Anyway, the offer's on the table, so think about it before you go and talk to the accommodation officer again.'

A few days after the prefab conversation with her friends, Edna shyly asked Ruby if she might accompany her to the nursery to pick up Archie after she had finished her shift.

'I'd like to see the nursery, now that it's up and running,' she explained. 'Maybe one day soon, if things work out right, I'll be picking Kathleen up after work too.'

'Wouldn't that be lovely,' Ruby beamed. 'When are you hoping to see her again?'

'Just as soon as I can get weekend leave,' Edna told her. 'If the trains aren't delayed or rerouted, I think I might be able to make the journey to Kendal in a day, otherwise it's a weekend of travelling.'

When they walked into the nursery, Edna was warmed by the bright happy atmosphere of the place. Sounds of laughter and chatter drifted down the wide corridor, and from one of the nursery rooms she heard children chanting 'The Farmer Wants A Wife'.

'This is lovely,' Edna exclaimed as she gazed around in delight.

Ruby nodded in agreement. 'Matron is marvellous, a no-fuss-and-nonsense woman, with a real understanding of children, and her staff couldn't be nicer. Seeing them every day, twice a day, they've almost become friends. They're thoughtful about keeping me up to date with Archie's activities during the day, they don't miss a thing, everything he does they remember to tell me – I feel included, even though I'm not here.'

After Ruby had collected Archie from the friendly nursery nurse on duty, she tucked him up in his pram and set off for home, with Edna by her side.

'Have you been regularly checking the nursery waiting list?' she asked.

Edna gave a quick nod. 'Just about every other day. I've replaced you as the resident nag-bag!' she joked.

'It's the only way,' Ruby replied. 'It'll happen soon, I'm sure.'

'I've still got to get Kathleen down here, and I don't

know how long that will take. Obviously, I've been in touch with Kathleen's welfare worker in Kendal; she knows I'm not happy with the way my little girl has been passed around like a bag of potatoes, she says it's just bad luck the way things have panned out. I've told her that I want Kathleen with me just as soon as things can be arranged.'

'From what I've read in the papers, you're not the only mother who's trying to reclaim her child,' Ruby said. 'A lot of evacuees have already gone back home. I think the government shipped them off too early, and families have got fed up, they'd rather be together than torn apart.'

Edna gave a heavy sigh. 'My feelings exactly. But even so, I've got to do the right thing by Kathleen. The little 'un hardly knows her own mother, that's why my visits to Kendal are so important.'

When they arrived at the prefab site, the two women went their separate ways. As she walked back home through Hucknall, Ruby gazed at her sweet little son burbling happily away underneath his cosy pram blanket. Imagine not seeing him every day, she thought to herself, not kissing him goodnight or holding him in my arms when he's tired or upset. Life would be intolerable, but for poor Edna that was the norm.

The disbanding of families was one of the unfortunate features of war, a harsh reality that thousands of women and children were experiencing, throughout the land. It was a high price to pay for peace.

On one of her visits to the admin department Edna said rather apologetically, 'I know you must think I'm a blinking pest, but you see, I have to get things organized in Hucknall before I can even think of bringing my little girl down here to live with me.'

The admin secretary, who over the course of Edna's regular visits had got to know something of her situation, smiled sympathetically.

'I'd give you a place if I could, but I have to adhere to the rules, or I'll get my marching orders. But,' she added, dropping her voice to a whisper, 'if anybody above you on the list drops out, I'll move you up right away.'

Edna threw her a grateful smile. 'You're very kind.'

'I wish I could do more,' the thoughtful secretary said. 'I know families everywhere are rallying round to mind children. I even saw a poster the other day that said "Caring For A War Worker's Children Is A National Duty".'

'It's true,' Edna declared. 'It is our national duty, because if we don't, there'll be hardly any war work done.'

'But look at the stress it lays on the family,' the secretary sighed. 'I see it all the time.'

'I know,' Edna agreed. 'My friend Ruby's mother had to give up minding her grandson because it was making her ill. There's only so much you can take, whatever the government might recommend.' Edna's shoulders slumped. 'I really thought I was doing my duty, and the best thing for my little girl, when I sent her off as an evacuee. I believed that she'd be better off living with a family in the Lake District, rather than staying with me in Wigan, but now, knowing what she's been through, I sometimes think she might have been better off staying with me.'

24. Kendal

When Edna was granted the weekend leave she had applied for, she immediately informed Kathleen's welfare officer that she would be visiting her daughter. Thrilled that Edna would be seeing her little girl, thoughtful Lily asked about the situation at the Bell Works nursery.

'I took Ruby's advice about checking where Kathleen was on the waiting list – bless her, she knows from her own experience how to go about things.'

'You two are real pals these days,' Jeannie smiled.

'Now we've got the nursery and children in common, there's lots to chat about,' Edna explained. 'Plus she's a very kind and thoughtful woman,' she added.

'Haven't you noticed a slight thawing in the atmosphere at work?' Jeannie remarked. 'I don't just mean you and Ruby either.'

'Personally, I put it all down to Ruby,' Edna said staunchly. 'She's so kind to everyone – heavens, look how she's helped me.'

'She is remarkable,' Lily agreed. 'But really I think it's more general than that. It's difficult to maintain a grudge when we're all in the same boat – tired, hungry, and stretched to our limits. There's not much energy left at the end of the day – not even for a row,' she smiled.

'I wouldn't say Annie's there yet,' Jeannie added. 'She and a few others are still holding back.'

'They'll come around in the end,' Lily said with a confident smile. 'They'll just have to!'

Edna's journey north was not a comfortable one. Sitting in a corner of a packed carriage, she constantly checked the welfare officer's letter informing her of Kathleen's change of address. When she finally arrived in Kendal, it was well past lunchtime, and though her stomach rumbled, she didn't want to waste precious time queueing in a café for something to eat. Instead, she made her way to the address where Kathleen had been placed. With her heart thumping in her chest, Edna stood on the doorstep of a small cottage on the edge of town. Raising her hand to ring the bell, she stopped to listen to the happy sound of children's laughter.

When the door was opened by a smiling, rosy-faced lady bouncing a baby on her hip, Edna's smile widened.

'Hello, I'm Edna Yates, Kathleen's mother.'

'Nice to meet you, I'm Nellie Parks, and this is Charlie, six months old and a little monkey,' Nellie said as she bounced her plump baby boy on her hip. 'The welfare lady told me to expect you today. Come in, come in,' she said as she led the way into a cosy sitting room.

Edna's heart melted at the sight of Kathleen sitting on the sofa sucking her thumb and cuddling her teddy.

'There she is, good as gold,' Nellie said as she nodded towards Kathleen, absorbed in turning the pages of a dog-eared comic book. 'I'll pop the kettle on, I expect you're gagging for a brew.'

Though Edna was indeed 'gagging for a brew', her heart was so full of love she could barely speak. Seeing the tears in her visitor's eyes, Nellie tactfully bustled into the kitchen, still bouncing cheerful Charlie on her broad hip.

'Back in a tick.'

Laying down her handbag, Edna approached the sofa with caution. Sitting at the opposite end to her daughter, she drew a long, steadying breath. My daughter doesn't recognize me, she thought. Gazing adoringly at Kathleen, Edna's maternal heart lurched in her ribcage. You're so lovely, she thought. Kathleen didn't so far share Edna's physique; she was delicately built, on the thin side in fact, but she did have Edna's lovely pale skin and tumbling dark hair that fell around her narrow shoulders in big fat ringlets. She also had Edna's big dark eyes, but Kathleen's weren't sparkling and bright right now; if anything, they were serious, old for her age, as if she had lived through too much to actually articulate. My poor baby, a stricken Edna thought, giving an inward sigh.

Firmly putting her own emotions to one side, Edna searched around for something that might distract Kathleen from her book. Spotting a little knitted doll on the sofa, Edna picked it up and cuddled it in the same way that Kathleen was presently cuddling her teddy.

'Poor little dolly,' she said as she rocked the toy. 'Does she belong to you, Kathleen?' she tentatively asked.

Kathleen gave a solemn nod.

'But you're nursing Teddy?' Edna softly enquired.

'He's poorly,' Kathleen replied.

Looking at the toy bear's gnawed-off ear, Edna murmured, 'He'll get better soon, I'm sure.'

Turning her large serious eyes on Edna, Kathleen said with complete conviction, 'I'm his mummy and I'll make him better.'

Feeling tears rush into her eyes, Edna steadied her voice before she answered, 'Of course you will, sweetheart, that's what mummies are for.'

At which point Nellie came bustling back into the room. 'Do you mind taking Charlie while I fetch in the tea things?' she asked as, without any ceremony, she plonked the little lad in Edna's lap and returned to the kitchen.

Nellie came back a few moments later carrying a tea tray loaded with a pot of tea and toasted tea cakes.

'We've got a tiny bit of proper butter, lovely and fresh from the farm where mi husband's a shepherd.'

Tearing her eyes away from her daughter, Edna gazed in awe at the small pat of golden-yellow butter sitting in a pretty dish decorated with pink roses.

'My goodness, I don't know how long it is since I've seen butter,' she gasped.

Clearly enjoying the moment, Nellie carefully spread the butter on to the tea cakes, then both women, salivating at the sight, watched it disappear into the warm toasted tea cakes.

Handing a hot cup of tea and a tea cake to Edna, Nellie said, 'I expect you'll be needing to get that inside you after your long journey here?'

Sinking her teeth into the gorgeous buttery tea cake, Edna sighed with pleasure. 'It feels so good just to be here,' she answered as she rolled her eyes in Kathleen's direction. 'Would you like a bite of tea cake, darling?' she asked as she proffered the plate to Kathleen, who firmly shook her head.

Dropping her voice to a whisper, Nellie explained, 'She's not a great eater since she left the old woman. I had a heck of a job getting her to eat anything but hot milk and bread. She's picked up since, though. She loves the farm and all the animals, and she all but worships Charlie,' she said.

Hearing his name, the baby stretched out his chubby hands to Nellie, who eagerly relieved Edna of her charge.

'It's time for his feed,' she said as she unceremoniously undid the buttons on her blouse. 'He's got the appetite of a lion,' she added proudly.

Seeing her daughter in this easy and open environment, with a foster mother who seemed to have a natural gift with children and babies, Edna was grateful for this most recent home. She had imagined her daughter in all sorts of scenarios too grim to articulate – an orphanage, or an uncaring family who had only agreed to house Kathleen for the sake of the money they would get. Yet here she was, in the bosom of a warm loving family, with a foster mother who clearly had a heart of gold. While Kathleen was now preoccupied with colouring in a picture book, Nellie filled in some of the blanks for Edna as she fed a gurgling Charlie.

'When your daughter arrived here, she was in a right state. Hardly spoke a word. Me and mi husband – he's a good kind man,' she added fondly, 'we thought it best to leave Kathleen to settle in, rather than fuss over her. Like I say, she didn't speak much, but Charlie never stopped communicating with her in his own little way,' she chuckled. 'He'd laugh and giggle when she was near, and reach out to grab her hand, so it was him that broke the ice. Before long, the two of 'em were inseparable, and that's when Kathleen's language picked up. She started telling me what Charlie wanted, saying stuff like he's hungry or he's tired, and I'd agree, and together we'd sort out whatever it was Kathleen thought he needed.'

Overcome by the woman's sensitivity, Edna said gratefully, 'That's so clever of you, Nellie.'

'Not at all, just instinct,' Nellie answered dismissively. 'The more I accepted what she was saying about Charlie and agreed with it, the more confident she became – and to be honest, she's been a proper little helper, a real treasure.' Turning to her visitor, she added, 'You should be very proud of your little girl, Edna.'

'Oh, I am,' Edna assured Nellie. 'And I miss her all the time.'

'I'm sure you do; we'd certainly miss Kathleen if she left us.'

Taking a deep breath, Edna said, 'Actually, Nellie, that's a subject I'd very much like to discuss with you.'

25. A Mother's Love

Checking that Kathleen was happily preoccupied with her colouring, Edna continued in a low voice.

'You see, Nellie, I very much want Kathleen to come and live with me in Hucknall. I appreciate the stability you have given her here in your lovely home, she seems so content, but she's been through a lot of changes since she was put on that train in Wigan as a little evacuee. I've always felt guilty about letting her go, and I want to make up for that.'

Nellie gave a sympathetic nod. 'I certainly agree with you on that, she's been through a lot.'

Edna hesitated before she moved on. 'But seeing her here, so secure and cherished, I'm beginning to rethink my original plan. How can I possibly uproot her again, now that she's so happy? She clearly worships Charlie – I've only been here a couple of hours, and I already worship him myself,' she laughed.

Gazing lovingly at her baby boy, Nellie nodded in agreement with her visitor. 'He has a winning way, does our little Charlie.'

Slumping back into the sofa, Edna looked towards Kathleen. The little girl was now softly humming as she combed her dolly's long blonde hair.

Dropping her voice to a whisper, Edna said, 'To be honest, Nellie, I'd really appreciate your advice. Do you think, if I can sort everything out, now is the right time to move Kathleen?'

Settling Charlie on her other breast, Nellie didn't rush her reply, and when she did speak, it wasn't the answer Edna was hoping to hear.

'Though I understand your feelings,' Nellie said gently, 'if you want God's honest truth, my answer would be no.'

Even though she knew how true Nellie's words were, Edna's face fell.

'Before I say anything, I'm only speaking from your daughter's point of view. If I were a mother and some know-all busybody suggested to me that I should leave Charlie with a foster carer, when all I wanted was to take him home to live with me, I would snap their blinking head off!' As Nellie spoke, her cheeks flushed with genuine passion. 'But, seeing as you've asked, I'll speak mi mind. As I said, the little lass arrived here in a bad way. I've already told you how me and mi husband handled all of that, and Charlie helped.'

Seeing Nellie looking uncomfortable, Edna urged her to continue. 'I'm afraid to say it, but I feel you know my Kathleen better than I do, Nellie. Please tell me what you think, speak freely, for her sake.'

'The reason why I think you should leave the lass here is so she can gradually get used to you all over again. I think you need to reintroduce yourself as her mother, start calling yourself Mummy today. We'll do the same – to re-inforce it,' Nellie urged. 'You need to build up Kathleen's confidence, regain her love, have a bit of fun with *all of us*; for a short time we could be her one big extended family. God Almighty, there's a war on – let's pull together. Not just for the nation but for each other,' Nellie passionately concluded.

Edna, galvanized by Nellie's insight and wisdom, which was already chiming with her own instincts, was sitting bolt upright.

'My God, Nellie, you're better than any welfare worker I've ever spoken to!' she exclaimed.

Waving a dismissive hand in the air, Nellie retorted, 'Don't be so daft.'

Seeing Kathleen approaching Charlie, who was now wriggling restlessly in his mother's lap, Nellie asked, 'What is it, sweetheart?'

'Can I play with Charlie, Mama?'

Buttoning up her blouse, Nellie patted the space beside her. 'Course you can, lovie, but first I've got something important to tell you.' Holding Charlie in one arm and Kathleen in the other, Nellie said, 'Do you know who the lady visiting us today really is, sweetheart?'

Kathleen threw Edna a sweet but bland smile. 'Nice lady.'

Nellie nodded. 'A very nice lady, she's also your mummy.'

Clearly bewildered by this information, Kathleen cried, 'But *you* are my mummy. And Granny was my mummy before you!' she exclaimed.

Turning to Edna, Nellie shot her a look to take over.

Dropping to sit on the floor, so she was on the same level as her daughter, Edna said, 'Nellie's right, I am your proper mummy. She's been looking after you while I was away working, just like the granny lady looked after you before Nellie.'

'Granny went to help Grandad in hospital,' little Kathleen said sadly.

Putting one arm around her daughter's narrow shoulders, Edna said, 'That's right, I'm sure he'll get better soon.' Carefully picking her words, she continued, 'I'd like to come and visit you again soon. If you'd like that, Kathleen?'

Kathleen blinked in surprise. 'Will you visit Charlie too?'

Smiling widely, Edna replied, 'Of course! We can go for walks and play with your toys. Perhaps I can even bring some new toys for you and Charlie, next time I come to see you,' she added hopefully.

Suddenly struck by a thought, Kathleen enquired, 'Will you be Charlie's mummy too?'

Edna firmly shook her head. 'No, sweetheart, Nellie is Charlie's mummy, and I'm your mummy.' Sighing, she added, 'I wish I could stay here with you, lovie, but I have to get the train back to work today.'

Old beyond her young years, Kathleen enquired, 'Will you come back?'

'Oh, yes, darling,' Edna said, with a heartfelt catch in her throat. 'I promise I'll come back as soon as I can.'

Seeing Edna choking for words, Nellie quickly continued the conversation. 'Your mummy will definitely come and see us again very soon.'

Throwing Nellie a grateful look, Edna quickly swiped the tears from her eyes. Now certainly wasn't the time to overload her daughter with too much emotional detail; best to be calm and practical and stick to her promises about visiting again as soon as she was able.

Satisfied with this information, Kathleen turned to Charlie. Nellie was settling the baby boy on a rug before the fire, which was surrounded on all sides by a hefty metal fireguard. Sitting down beside the smiley baby, Kathleen patiently handed him toys to play with, and when he eventually made a grab for Kathleen's long dark curls, she giggled as she rolled around on the rug with him. Watching them play like two puppies, Edna knew in her gut that her decision to take things slowly and steadily – hard as it had been – was right. Kathleen was enjoying happy and carefree days here in Myrtle Cottage – days the war had stolen from so many – after the secure babyhood she had been denied. Edna thanked God that Kathleen was finally in a safe haven. As her mother, Edna would follow her instincts, as well as Nellie's wise advice; she would spend time and energy getting to know her beloved daughter all over again.

After spending a few happy hours with Nellie, Charlie and Kathleen, Edna found herself back on the train again. For all her reasoning she nevertheless felt devastated when it came to tearing herself away from her daughter, but she put on a brave face, kissed and hugged her, and promised she would be back soon. Turning her back, she walked away with tears streaming down her face. Don't look back, she firmly told herself, be brave, stay strong, you mustn't let Kathleen see you crying and upset.

Standing on Kendal station's cold and windy platform, Edna ached to have her daughter by her side. She imagined her there, holding her hand, looking up, excited to be going on a journey with her mother. One day soon, Edna comforted herself, be patient and wait, when the time is right, with God's help, it will happen.

As night fell and the steam train lumbered south, stopping and starting at random stations down the line, Edna was actually relieved that she hadn't dragged Kathleen along with her. Weary troops lay with their heads on their duffle bags, sleeping in crowded corridors; some were curled up in the overhead net carriage racks, while others stood miserably chain-smoking. It was not a sight that would lift any heart, especially a child's. Where were all these hundreds of young men going? Billeted to barracks in the middle of nowhere, awaiting orders that would ship them to the western front, or North Africa, even the Far East? Thinking of Kathleen, Edna reached into her bag to take out the little gift her daughter had handed to her just before she left Myrtle Cottage.

'For you, Mama,' she'd said shyly.

Gazing down at the little sheep made of woolly cast-offs, Edna had smiled in delight.

'A little lamb, just like the ones on the hills where you live,' she had exclaimed.

Looking now at the toy she was nursing in her hands, Edna's thoughts flew to Kathleen, safe in Kendal; was she having tea with Charlie or perhaps getting ready for bed? Knowing she was safe, warm, contented and well fed, was enough for now. The rest would come in good time.

When Edna walked into the prefab, Jeannie and Lily immediately sensed that she was utterly drained.

'I'll fetch some tea,' Lily said thoughtfully.

After tea had been drunk, and Edna had warmed herself by the fire, she told them about her visit and the decision she had made, based on Nellie's wise advice.

'It's what's best for my daughter,' she explained. 'I have to build up her trust.'

'You were right to put your daughter first,' Lily agreed. 'When it comes to sacrifice, nothing beats a mother's love.'

Jeannie nodded in complete agreement with Lily.

'It takes guts,' she declared. 'I'm not so sure that I could have done it.'

Edna gave a rueful chuckle. 'I talked it over with Nellie, she made complete sense.' Recalling her words and her kindness, she added, 'She's a wonderful person, I completely trust her with my Kathleen.' Yawning, she covered her mouth with a hand. 'I'm done,' she announced.

'Go and get ready for bed,' Lily urged. 'I'll bring you a hot-water bottle.'

'Night, lovies,' Edna said as she kissed her friends. 'Thanks for all your support – I seem to be surrounded by good women with wise counsel,' she said gratefully.

26. 'Them' and 'Us'

The following morning, Ruby was keen to see Edna and hear about her trip north, but there was no chance to talk until the hooter went for their first break of the day.

'Edna,' she cried, 'how did it go?'

Edna was sitting at a table with Lily and Jeannie. Touched by Ruby's concern, she pulled out a chair.

'Sit yourself down, lovie, it's a long story.'

By the time Edna had recounted the events of her visit, Ruby was wide-eyed with emotion.

'That was *so brave* of you, it must have been really hard,' Ruby finally spluttered.

'We felt the same too,' Lily admitted.

'You clearly did the right thing for the little mite,' Ruby declared.

Edna gave a philosophical shrug. 'I can only bring Kathleen down here when she's good and ready to make that move. I'd love her to be here for Christmas, imagine the fun we could have together, decorating a Christmas tree, maybe even building a snowman and throwing snow-balls.' Sighing, she dragged herself back to reality. 'I've been so preoccupied with all the practicalities of a move – getting her a nursery place seemed the most important thing of all, and it will be, once she's here – but seeing her up there, so little and vulnerable, so trusting and sweet, the last thing I want to do is drag her away to yet another new place. Yes, she would be with her mother, but in a strange place – and in a nursery too. It's going to take time, I just have to be patient and take my cue from Kathleen, and from Nellie too.'

Ruby laid her hand over Edna's. 'I respect you for that decision, mi duck, only a mother would put their child before their own desires.'

With tears in her eyes, Edna gulped and declared, 'You would have done the same for your son, Ruby – I'm sure of it. Mind you,' she added briskly, 'to make this plan work I've got to spend as much time as I possibly can visiting Kathleen. It's the only way.'

'It's a really good idea to slowly introduce yourself,' Ruby replied. 'The more you visit Kathleen the more familiar she'll become with you, and that will make the transition from Kendal to Hucknall all the easier when the time is right.'

Ruby jumped up as the hooter shrilled out.

'Whoops, back to work!' she exclaimed. 'Honestly,' she laughed, 'I seem to spend more time over here with you than over there with the Hucknall lasses.'

'You're welcome over here any time it takes your fancy, lovie,' Edna said, with genuine affection in her voice.

'Thanks, it's nice to know,' Ruby acknowledged the offer. 'And vice versa, of course.'

Glancing across the canteen to where Annie and the other Hucknall women were sitting, Jeannie pulled down the corners of her mouth.

'Mmm, I'm not quite sure we're there yet,' she muttered under her breath.

*

Since visiting Kendal and spending time with her sweet daughter, Edna was preoccupied with reappraising her life. In the light of her recent meeting with Kathleen, and Nellie's calming influence too, her thoughts of Ken had vanished overnight. Yes, she'd enjoyed the fun and the excitement of meeting him, drinking and dancing, but when she compared her attraction for Ken with the depth of her love for Kathleen, she knew that her relationship with the flirtatious Canadian had been nothing but a war-time fantasy.

After her brief trip north, Edna returned to work; this week she was working on the cockpit assembly line, paired with Lily. Unlike her friend, who was thrilled to be assigned to cockpits, Edna felt emotionally drained; the riveting gun in her hand seemed to weigh a ton as it pounded against the shining sheet metal, securing line after line of bolts. With her head throbbing, Edna blinked hard. Buck up, *concentrate*, she told herself. Luckily, Lily was completely focused on her work, deftly wielding a pneumatic drill up ahead of Edna. As she shifted position, Lily caught sight of Audrey and Ruby working on a jig further down the cockpit assembly line. Pausing briefly, eagle-eyed Lily noticed – even from a distance – that Ruby's riveting wasn't as clean and accurate as it should have been; it looked like the panels weren't fitting properly together. Wondering why Audrey, Ruby's partner, wasn't aware of what was going on, Lily felt a sense of unease.

She waved her hand to Edna, mouthing, 'Hold on!'

Climbing out of their cockpit, Lily crossed the space to Ruby's jig. She immediately realized what the problem was – the metal sheets Ruby and Audrey were working on were thinner and flimsier than usual, certainly nowhere near as strong as the sheet metal she and Edna were presently working on. Tapping Ruby on the arm, Lily pointed to the weak seam.

Following the line of her finger, Ruby gasped, 'Oh my God!'

Gesturing frantically, Lily shouted, 'There's something wrong! Report it to Sid, right away.'

Still holding the riveting gun, Ruby gave the thumbs up sign, and Lily returned to her position on the assembly line.

Edna was looking dumbfounded. 'What's going on?' she asked.

'Later,' Lily replied.

At break time both Ruby and Audrey joined Lily, Edna and Jeannie at their table where they were enjoying meat and carrot pasties with mushy peas.

'Heavens!' Ruby immediately exclaimed. 'Thank God you spotted that awful mistake. We had to strip the entire thing back and start from scratch.'

'Sid said the metal was from a new batch that had only recently been delivered,' Audrey went on to say. 'When we examined it closely, it was clearly inferior to the usual stuff we work with. Sid said it was a dodgy batch.'

Looking pale, Ruby added, 'Using shoddy material to build a fighter aircraft could cost a pilot his life. If you hadn't spotted it, Lily, God only knows what might have happened,' she murmured.

'You saved our bacon, mi duck, thank you for alerting us,' Audrey added.

Looking shocked, Lily said, 'I'm only glad I could help.

The minute I saw the panels all skewed and out of place, I knew something was wrong.'

'I know it's no excuse,' Ruby continued, 'but I was up all night with Archie. I had to drag myself out of bed this morning, by which time Archie was sound asleep. He brought the roof down when I got him out of his cot and put him into his pram. I hope he's all right now,' she added anxiously.

'I'm sure the nursery staff will be taking good care of him,' Edna reassured her. 'More to the point, how are *you* feeling?'

'Better after two cups of tea,' Ruby admitted. 'I don't think I'll ever get over the shock of seeing those badly fitted panels – God, it could have been a disaster,' she groaned.

Lily gave her a pat on the back.

'Luckily, it isn't,' she smiled. 'I hope Sid's sending that faulty batch back to the factory?'

Audrey grinned. 'Don't you doubt it, he's hopping mad. I wouldn't want to be the poor sod on the end of his wrath.'

When the hooter sounded out again, the five women rose to their feet.

'Back to work, ladies,' Edna chuckled.

Audrey gave a cheeky smile. 'You've got a nicer view on this side of the canteen.'

'Oh yeah, the windows give on to a grand view of the factory wall,' Jeannie said, with a mocking laugh. 'You should get yourselves over here more often,' she added warmly.

Looking at Edna and her friends, Audrey returned her smile.

'You know what, I might just do that.'

On her way down the corridor to the factory workshop, Ruby was stopped by Annie. The overseer took her by the arm and drew her to one side, to have a word in private.

'Sid's just told me what happened.'

'It was a real shock, Annie,' Ruby answered honestly. 'It was Lily Palmer who saved the day. She spotted what was going on from across the factory floor. We've a lot to thank her for.'

Annie gave a curt nod. 'Sid's fuming.'

'It just shows how good it is when people work well together,' Ruby added pointedly.

Annie gave a non-committal grunt. 'Nobody could argue with that; it was well spotted by that newcomer girl, you should let her know that.'

Clever Ruby gave Annie a tender smile. 'I think you could do that, Annie,' she said persuasively.

The overseer gave an awkward shrug. 'We'll see.'

Returning to her workstation, Ruby tried to hide her smile. Had she imagined it, or did she sense that Annie had finally acknowledged that the new girls might just be up to scratch?

27. Flying

Before her second date with Oro, excited Lily told her friends exactly what her boyfriend was planning. They were all gathered around the prefab fire, drinking cocoa, while listening to the BBC's late evening news.

'He's promised to give me flying lessons,' she blurted out.

Nearly spilling her boiling-hot cocoa into her lap, Edna gasped, 'God almighty! I'd rather walk the plank than take to the skies in an aircraft.'

Jeannie burst out laughing. 'Especially when you know who's built them!' she joked.

'Stop teasing,' Lily pleaded. 'I really loved my last day out with Oro.'

'As I recall,' Edna reminded her friend, 'last time you were a passenger. This time you might actually be at the controls.'

'I know!' Lily retorted passionately. 'I can't wait.'

'Do you know anything about how it's done?' Jeannie enquired. 'Like how you get the aircraft up there in the first place?'

Lily shook her head. 'Not really, Oro had the controls when we last flew – he was in the seat behind me, talking me through the procedures.'

'Well, all I can say is, the best of luck,' Edna remarked as she lit up a Woodbine. 'Hopefully, if I can juggle a day off, I'll be on a packed troop train heading north to see our Kathleen while you're having your flying lesson.'

Putting aside her own excitement, Lily smiled. 'I hope it works out, Edna. You must be so looking forward to seeing your daughter again.'

Edna gave a vigorous nod. 'I'll be even more excited if Kathleen remembers my name and gives me a big hug,' she confessed.

'It really is a long game of patience,' Jeannie sympathized.

'Worth it, though,' Edna declared. 'If, in the end, I get my daughter back.'

On compassionate grounds Edna did manage to swing leave – just a day off – though Sid reminded her that there wouldn't be many more granted.

'I can't be seen making allowances for you, Edna; there are other women in need of time off too, you know.'

'Of course,' Edna quickly agreed. 'I appreciate your understanding, Sid.'

'Like I say, we need the workforce on the shop floor – and that's a government order. I can't be seen as a soft touch; rules apply across the board, so don't push your luck.'

'Hopefully, my little girl will be living with me soon, so I shouldn't be troubling you much more in the future,' Edna smiled.

'Just make sure you're back in time for work,' he concluded.

While Edna was making her chilly train journey to Kendal, Lily was sitting in Oro's beautiful Tiger Moth aircraft.

Unlike her first trip, when she had been unprepared, Lily had carefully chosen clothes to keep her warm: tweed trousers, a woollen polo-neck sweater and a scarf. Nevertheless, she was still grateful for the flying jacket that Oro lent her. Fastening the buttons down the front of the jacket, he smiled tenderly at Lily's uplifted, pale delicate face.

'It's cold up there,' he said as he bent to kiss her pink lips, feeling them part under his touch. 'Nervous?' he asked.

Lily answered honestly. 'Yes, but looking forward to it. But *please*, Oro,' she quickly reminded him, 'don't scare me to death – remember I've only ever built planes previously. I've never flown one.'

'Are you afraid I'll loop the loop again?' he teased.

Laughing, Lily responded, 'I loved it while you were in control. But I certainly don't want to do it myself,' she admitted.

Stroking her shoulder-length silver-blonde hair, Oro answered softly, '*Ukochana*, dearest, I promise I won't do anything to frighten you.'

Standing on her tiptoes so she could put her arms around Oro's neck, Lily murmured, 'I know you won't, I trust you.'

Oro secured the leather flying hat under her chin. 'Let's get in the plane, is always best place to start,' he grinned.

Once in the cockpit, Lily's pulse started to race. Swaddled in so many warm clothes, she also began to sweat, but the cold autumn wind blowing straight down the runway soon cooled her down and she knew she would be a lot colder once they took off.

Oro leaned forward in his seat to talk to Lily.

'*Dobrze?* – that's Polish for "okay?"'

Lily grinned back.

'Okay, *dobrze*,' she echoed his words.

'Buckle up and I'll talk you through the starting procedure.'

Obeying his instructions, Lily listened carefully to what he had to say.

'When we're ready to go, Steve will start the engine by standing in front of the plane and manually turning the propeller.'

Nodding, Lily recalled seeing Steve, one of the ground staff, start the Tiger Moth by hand on her first flight out.

'Steve will also remove the chocks and guide us out.'

Gazing at the narrow cockpit's vast array of knobs, switches and levers, Lily squeaked, 'What are they all for?'

'Altitude, headwind, brakes – but don't worry about any of that right now. Your job, sweetheart, is to concentrate on take-off, steering, and following the waypoints on the map.'

Gulping nervously, Lily repeated what Oro had just said, 'Take-off, steering, mapping.'

Giving her a big confident smile, Oro said, 'Our headsets are connected; we have dual control. Remember, I'm right here behind you.'

Lily gave a nervous nod.

'Steve will start her up, then we wait for green light,' he told her.

A few minutes later, after the clearance light flashed and the chocks had been removed, Oro applied the throttle and waited for the air speed to increase in order to take off. As a rush of icy-cold wind hit her full in the face, Lily felt a huge burst of adrenalin rip through her.

'Ease the throttle forwards,' Oro instructed. 'I'm watching, I can see what you're doing.'

Gripping the wheel, Lily rolled the Tiger Moth out of its bay and on to the empty runway. She gasped as she felt the powerful Gypsy Moth engine surge.

'What now?' she asked.

'Push the joystick forwards, just like you saw me do when we last flew together.'

Gripping the joystick, Lily asked in a tense voice, 'Like this?'

'Yes, good,' he responded.

'How do I know when to go?' she asked.

'When you feel the lift, that's when you'll know when to go – just listen to the engine. And remember – I'm right behind you, darling.'

Thundering down the runway with the aircraft rapidly gathering momentum, Lily certainly did feel a lift – just as the tail lifted clear off the ground, the Tiger Moth took to the skies. Feeling exhilaratingly at one with the aircraft, Lily took her soaring higher and higher until they plunged through cloud and entered a clear blue world of stillness and tranquillity. With the wind swirling around them and the sky an arching dome of blue overhead, Lily felt unexpectedly cocooned in the cockpit.

Calling out to her, Oro said, 'Oh, this is just wonderful!'

'So beautiful,' she sighed, as her eyes drifted towards the distant horizon shimmering in a silver-blue haze.

As the clouds dispersed, she was able to gaze at the world they had just left – roads, railway lines, houses, fields, churches, farms and winding rivers. Down there, far below, she thought, people were working, children were going to school, her comrades in the Bell Works were building planes, soldiers were marching out of barracks and catching trains that would take them across the wide stretch of the North Sea to war-torn countries where they would be expected to lay down their lives for the cause of freedom. Tears filled Lily's lovely silver-grey eyes; so much beauty and perfection up here above the clouds, yet so much misery, struggle and fear down there.

Oro's voice quickly brought her out of her reverie. As if reading her thoughts, he said, 'It's easy to lose yourself up here.'

'It's so still and quiet,' she responded.

'Until an enemy plane zips into sight and all hell breaks loose,' Oro reminded her.

Looking nervously from left to right, Lily imagined how terrifying that would be. An enemy bomber tailing her, circling and firing. She knew from building Spitfires the exact dimensions of their small, cramped cockpits. Lily shivered as she imagined Oro flying out on enemy missions, solo, heading into strange territory with an enemy aircraft bearing down on him, zipping in and out, drawn into a deadly dog fight where only one would survive, while the loser tumbled into the darkness of the North Sea – 'the pilot's graveyard', as it was commonly referred to by airmen. She was grateful for the time off he had chosen to spend with her, but she realized, flying his Tiger Moth today, that most of his life was spent on sorties from which there was a very good chance he might not return. With such terrifying morbid thoughts filling her head, she realized she hadn't heard Oro's instructions.

'Sorry,' she hurriedly apologized. 'I couldn't quite hear what you were saying.'

Speaking to Lily through their connecting headsets, Oro said, 'Time to turn her around, sweetheart.'

Feeling like she had only been briefly airborne, Lily responded, 'Already?'

Repeating himself, Oro said, 'Yes, time to turn around. We need to take it easy on fuel,' he pointed out.

Gripping the wheel until her knuckles stood out stark white, Lily made the turn. As she did so, the horizon tilted and then levelled out as they emerged through cloud and dropped height.

'Watch me carefully as I guide her down slowly, gently . . .' Oro's voice sounded out.

As much as she could from her restricted position, Lily watched Oro make a very cautious descent for her benefit. As the ground came up to meet them, he eased on the brakes and brought the nifty little Tiger Moth to a stop.

Overcome with nervous excitement, Lily slumped in her seat.

Turning to her, Oro smiled. 'Hey, quite an experience,' he said.

Looking up, her dazzling eyes blazing with passion, Lily exclaimed, 'Oro, that was the best thing I've *ever* done in my entire life!'

28. Lord Byron

After the Tiger Moth had been safely landed, Oro surprised Lily by suggesting they go for a walk.

'Walking helps me settle nerves after a flight,' he explained. 'Of course, it's not always possible, but I take advantage when I can.'

Feeling highly overexcited herself, Lily instantly held out her hand so they could walk along together. Recalling her fears, she prompted Oro to talk about his working life.

'Tell me about your work here, Oro,' she urged. 'I know you live on the Polish base, but what do you do there?'

'*Ukochana*,' he smiled. 'You must understand that I can't tell you all that we do – and neither do I want to make you fearful of my work.'

'Often not knowing is more scary than knowing,' she pointed out.

'Well, okay,' he started slowly. 'When we're not in action, bomber pilots usually fly out daily. There's always a pre-flight briefing then the mission itself, which might be several hours, and a post-flight briefing. When we're not on a bombing raid, we cover reconnaissance, intelligence gathering and bomb damage assessment. And there's training too, I'm heavily involved in training up new recruits.'

'I'm surprised you have a minute to see me,' she teased.

'You are priority!' he said, with a laugh. 'But really, we work in shifts, leave is allocated – or not, as the case may be – sometimes on missions we might not sleep for thirty-six hours, other times we sit around for hours waiting for information to filter through, then it's action stations. Scramble! Scramble!' he mimicked. Then added on a more serious note, 'The feeling after an enemy attack is first of all complete relief that you've survived, but you're emotionally revved up, like an engine. It's hard to come down when adrenalin is still pumping through your body.'

'I can imagine how emotionally wrung out you must be after a bombing raid,' she said sympathetically.

'For sure, you dodge death up there.' He nodded upwards to the rain clouds gathering over Hucknall. 'Then there are people you kill, men sometimes whose faces you see through smashed windscreen, it's not such a good feeling to see someone go down in flames, even though you are glad to be the one who survives.' He gave a philosophical shrug. 'It could happen to us all, the risk pilot takes every time he flies.'

His words sent a shiver shooting down Lily's spine. Oh my God, she thought, here am I raving on about the thrill of flying, while Oro carries the burden of what might happen to him and his comrades every time they take a plane up. Cuddling up to him, she murmured, 'Promise me you'll always come back to me, dearest?'

Pulling her close, Oro pressed her slender body against his own.

'*Ukochana*,' he breathed. 'You are becoming so very precious to me.'

Lily caught her breath; a few minutes ago, she had thought that flying was exciting enough, but now her heart was pounding, not with nerves but with a sensation that made her light-headed and giddy.

Leaving the airbase behind them, the couple walked along Hucknall's narrow high street.

'Strange to think that we've only recently met,' Lily mused. 'I feel like I've known you much longer.'

'War brings men and women together in strange ways,' he observed. 'Look at me – a Polish airman flying aircraft in Nottingham.'

'And here am I – a fisherman's daughter building Spitfires. It's fate that brought us together,' Lily declared romantically.

'Fate, destiny, attraction,' Oro cried, grinning as he lifted Lily in his arms and spun her around before setting her back down on the pavement. 'A force of power pulled me to you, magic lady with shining silver eyes.'

Smiling at each other, they continued through the town until they reached a beautiful old grey stone church, set on a slight rise above the marketplace.

'This is what I want to show to you,' Oro explained.

Intrigued, Lily followed him up the church path that led to an ancient porch set under a huge stained-glass window. Glancing at the notice board inside the church porch, Lily said in surprise, 'St Mary Magdalene Church, burial place of Lord Byron. How extraordinary!'

'Nice church, always calm and quiet,' Oro told her. 'I like this Byron poet too. He is romantic like me,' he said, with a shy smile.

Inside the dark nave Oro led Lily to a side transept where, in a modest unobtrusive tomb, lay one of England's greatest Romantic poets.

'I thought such a famous poet would have been buried in Westminster Abbey – a grander place than St Mary

Magdalene in Hucknall, certainly,' she added as she took in the fine details of the ancient building. 'Though this is a very fine church indeed.'

'I understand this is Lord Byron's family land,' Oro said. 'It's good to rest in country you love after death.'

As they stood in thoughtful contemplation by Byron's tomb, Oro surprised Lily by quoting lines from one of his most famous poems.

> She walks in beauty, like the night
> Of cloudless climes and starry skies;
> And all that's best of dark and bright
> Meet in her aspect and her eyes . . .
> And on that cheek, and o'er that brow,
> So soft, so calm, yet eloquent,
> The smiles that win, the tints that glow,
> But tell of days in goodness spent,
> A mind at peace with all below,
> A heart whose love is innocent!

'You know it off by heart?' incredulous Lily asked.

Looking slightly self-conscious, Oro nodded. 'I learnt it because I like it. And now I have somebody lovely to speak it to, I like it even more,' he replied.

Outside, the rain that had been threatening all day was pouring out of a sodden grey sky. Sitting side by side on the narrow wooden bench that ran the length of the porch, Lily leant her head on Oro's shoulder and listened to the comforting sound of the pitter-pattering raindrops on the timbered roof.

'This is so peaceful,' she sighed.

'Lily, these times I spend with you, in the clouds and down here on the ground, are so special for me. My heart is filled with love that grows greater every time I see you,' he whispered earnestly. 'Will you be my girl, my sweetheart, my *ukochana*?' he asked, with the sweetest of smiles.

Leaning up to kiss him, Lily whispered back, 'Yes, Oro, I'll be your sweetheart, not just because you're handsome and take me flying but because – like you – I'm falling head over heels in love.'

29. Dark Thoughts

Thanks to Sid helping her to juggle her shifts, Edna did get the opportunity to visit her daughter again. Though relieved and grateful to have secured time off, Edna was not happy. Sitting on a sooty steam train, heading north, she felt troubled beyond words; she had begun to wonder if she might be pregnant with Ken's baby. Though she had told Jeannie and Lily about her night with Ken, she had never told them the whole truth – that she had made love with Ken in the park, and they had taken no precautions. Edna's heart plummeted as she considered her situation; what on earth was she going to do? Would she have to resort to a back-street abortion? Sick with fear, she wondered how much an illegal termination would cost. Even if she went down that terrifying route, what were her chances of survival? She had heard so many terrible stories about the fatal consequences of bad practice. What if she were to die in the process; leaving her daughter motherless, destined to be packed off to 'Granny Jack' for the rest of her life? And if she kept the baby, what on earth would she tell her husband who had been absent for the last six months?

Sitting on a packed train, inhaling the thick smoke-filled air, Edna recalled how foolish and self-indulgent she had been, talking about 'a new lease of life' – in effect, twisting the truth, when she was a married woman and the mother of an evacuated little girl. To add to her woes Edna had recently received letters from her dragon of a mother-in-law, demanding money for her upkeep. Edna knew only too well that the old bat missed Edna's ration coupons far more than she actually missed her daughter-in-law – or, for that matter, her granddaughter either. What made the situation even worse was that her husband, Jack, had taken his mother's side.

'She really needs the extra cash,' Jack had written in his letters home. 'If you could send her a couple of quid out of your wage packet, every now and again, I know it would make all the difference.'

Edna seethed at the thought of sending any of her wages to her mother-in-law, who she knew would only spend it on stout and cigarettes, when she herself needed every penny of her wage packet to cover train fares back and forth to Kendal, and all the little extras – bedding, clothing, shoes, food and nursery fees – which she would eventually need to provide for Kathleen. Though the Bell Works subbed the nursery, child care didn't come entirely free.

Edna's frantic thoughts were chased away by the sight of little Kathleen pounding up the platform to greet her.

Holding out her chubby arms, the little girl called out, 'Mummy! Mummy!'

The sound of her daughter's sweet lisping voice and the sight of those big trusting eyes brought tears to Edna's eyes, making her feel even more guilty about her shameful behaviour.

'Hello, my sweetheart,' she cried as she swooped Kathleen into her arms and kissed her rosy warm cheeks.

'We got your letter,' smiling Nellie said.

'Sorry it was such short notice,' Edna apologized.

'Don't worry, it's lovely to see you,' good-natured Nellie beamed. 'Kathleen's been counting down the days.'

Walking back to Nellie's cottage, pushing the big old Silver Cross pram with Kathleen perched at one end and chuckling baby Charlie tucked up warm and cosy at the other end, Nellie told Edna of her daughter's progress.

'Kathleen's doing really well,' she said. 'She chatters happily about you, and when I told her you were coming back, she was so thrilled. She's getting used to the idea of her new mummy.'

'Oh, Nellie, you give me such hope,' Edna cried, hanging on her every word.

'In my opinion, if she carries on like this, talking about you and missing you the way she has been recently, it won't be long before she's ready to join you.'

Edna's heart skipped a beat. How she yearned for that moment – except now she carried a dark secret that would take a dreadful toll on her little girl. Smothering the rising panic that threatened to engulf her, Edna dragged her thoughts back to the here and now.

'I'm hoping the move from here to Hucknall will be soon,' she told Nellie. 'I want to make sure everything's just right for Kathleen when she does join me. Oh, Nellie!' she cried, with a catch in her voice. 'I can't believe that it really is going to happen.'

The rest of the day was spent happily with Kathleen, Nellie and Charlie. Though the November day was short, and darkness fell early, they made the most of the daylight they'd got. When Nellie tactfully suggested that Edna and

Kathleen go out for a nice walk on their own, Edna eagerly jumped at the idea – a little privacy would give her the opportunity to talk to her daughter about living together in Hucknall. Kathleen, joined at the hip to Charlie, suggested they push the baby in the pram around the park, but Nellie said Charlie needed his nap. Winking at Edna, she urged the two of them outdoors.

Walking hand in hand, they made their way through the falling autumn leaves to the municipal park. After feeding the quacking ducks with some stale bread that Nellie had given to Kathleen, they strolled around the edges of the pond where seagulls vying for food greedily dive-bombed waterfowl.

Tentatively approaching the subject, Edna started, 'I've been thinking, sweetheart, that soon you might like to come and live with me in my little house in Nottingham?'

Little Kathleen stopped in her tracks and threw her mother a quizzical look. 'Can Charlie come too?'

Edna smiled and shook her head. 'No, lovie, Charlie lives with his mummy and daddy, but he might come and visit you when you live with me in my house.'

'Will I live with a mummy and a daddy?' Kathleen asked.

'You'll live with me; your daddy is a soldier, fighting far away in another country,' Edna said. 'When the war is over, and Daddy comes home, we'll all live together again.' Please God, Edna thought to herself, that's if Jack's not abandoned me once he knows I'm pregnant with another man's child. Pushing the thought from her mind, she hunkered down so that she could look directly into Kathleen's eyes. 'Would you like to come and live with me, sweetheart?'

Slipping her arms around her mother's neck, Kathleen

laid her head on Edna's shoulder. 'Yes, Mummy, I want to live in your house,' she sweetly agreed.

Overcome, Edna could only clutch her daughter and hug her tightly.

'I think we'll have fun together,' she promised. 'There's a nice nursery near my house, where lots of children go to play, I'm going to ask the lady in charge if you can go there too.'

'Will you come and play too, Mummy?'

Edna smiled as she shook her head.

'I'll be at work, sweetheart, building aeroplanes in the factory right across the way from your nursery.'

Kathleen's eyes widened in surprise.

'Aeroplanes that fly up in the sky?' she squeaked.

'That's right, darling.'

'Clever Mummy,' Kathleen said as she stretched up to kiss Edna.

After a welcome early tea in Nellie's warm kitchen – home-made fish pie with sprouts, followed by apple pie – Edna was reluctant to leave the warmth of the family home. With Kathleen curled up sleepily on her knee, and Charlie gurgling happily as Nellie breastfed him, Edna sighed heavily as she rose to her feet.

'I mustn't miss my train back,' she said.

Rubbing her tired eyes, Kathleen yawned. 'Stay, Mummy, please stay.'

Thinking of the long journey home on a cold smoky train, surrounded by exhausted servicemen, Edna's resolve crumbled. Sid would be furious if she didn't turn up for work, but right now Kathleen's happiness and a secure future for both of them were her priorities. In a reckless moment of intense emotion, Edna made a decision that would certainly have a huge impact on her future relationship with Sid. To hell with it, she suddenly thought, why shouldn't I have a night with my daughter? I'll be in a lot of trouble when I get back to work, but I'll have to live with it and pay the consequences. Right now, I just want to make my little girl happy.

Later, lying in Kathleen's narrow single bed with her daughter cradled in her arms, Edna had no regrets about staying over in Kendal – or the repercussions that would ensue. This was time well spent, precious time making up for all the weeks and months they had lost. When she considered the joy she felt lying peacefully beside her daughter, listening to her gentle breathing, Edna yet again chastised herself for allowing her relationship with Ken to develop. What she and her daughter shared right now was unquestionably real love; what she had shared with Ken was nothing but lust, which filled her with deep shame and regret.

The following morning, Nellie and Edna had a brief chat about Kathleen's move to Hucknall.

'I'll support your case with Kathleen's welfare officer,' Nellie said as she bundled Charlie into his big pram prior to all of them leaving for the railway station. 'You just make sure that you get everything sorted your end; we want everything to go as smoothly as possible for Kathleen's sake.'

'I've been working hard to make that happen,' Edna assured her new friend. 'Pestering the work's accommodation officer and the matron at the nursery too, they've all been more than helpful. But *you*, Nellie,' Edna added in a rush of emotion as she hugged her daughter's carer, 'you've been wonderful. I couldn't have got this far without your support.'

'I just want what's best for Kathleen, she's a sweet little girl,' Nellie said, with a catch in her voice.

'I hold Mummy's hand,' Kathleen announced as they all set off through the narrow winding streets.

Feeling the tight clasp of her daughter's little hand gave Edna the strength she needed to say goodbye. God willing, she thought, this would be the last time she made the journey alone; next time they would be travelling together.

When the soot-black train rolled in, Edna boarded it. After releasing the window with the stout leather strap, she waved goodbye to the little group on the busy platform.

'I'll be back as soon as I can,' she promised, with a tremulous smile.

Nellie was bouncing Charlie in her arms and called out, 'Safe journey.'

Waving goodbye, Kathleen solemnly said, 'I love you, Mummy, bye bye.'

When the train rumbled out of the station, spouting black smoke in its wake, Edna waved until the carriage turned a corner and her daughter disappeared from view. As they thundered over the rail tracks that edged the rim of Morecambe Bay, Edna pulled the window shut, with her daughter's words ringing in her ears.

'I love you too, my darling,' she murmured. 'Please God, let me be a good mother, even though I have made a terrible mess of things.'

30. Annie

As the frosty atmosphere in the workplace began to lift, Sid made no secret of his huge relief.

'All quiet on the Western Front,' he joked. 'I have to say, I never thought I'd see all you lasses mingling together, nice and friendly, like you are these days. Better than knives out, like it was before.'

'Apart from our Annie,' Audrey grinned.

'She'll come around in the end, just you wait and see,' Sid said confidently.

After Sid had gone on his way, little Mary blurted out, 'To be honest, I sometimes get a bit lost for words, if the truth be known. It's not like when I'm talking to mi pals, I'm never short of things to say. I know their families and where they live, where they went to school and how many kiddies they've got. When I'm around the new girls, I do get a bit tongue-tied.'

Smiling at Mary's touching naivety, Ruby said, 'Mary, lovie, I keep telling you, they're no different to us. They haven't just landed from outer space,' she teased. 'Just ask about their families and where they've come from, that'll soon get them nattering.'

'But in't it cheeky, probing into strangers' affairs?'

Audrey let out a loud hoot of laughter. 'Hell fire, you're not exactly asking how much money they've got in the bank!'

'And it's a lot better than ignoring them,' Ruby pointed out.

Blushing furiously, Mary added, 'Mi mam said I should mind mi manners, that I shouldn't let Hucknall folk down by asking outsiders overfamiliar questions.'

'Oh, for crying out loud . . .' Audrey murmured under her breath.

Putting an arm around skinny Mary's narrow shoulders, Ruby said gently, 'Lovie, just be yourself and stop worrying – you're not capable of upsetting anyone, no matter what your mother might think.'

Seeing Edna queueing up at the canteen counter, Ruby hurried over to join her.

'A little bird told me you didn't come into work yesterday,' she said, keeping her voice low.

'That little bird was right,' Edna winced. 'I'm sorry to let anyone down, but to be honest I just couldn't bear to leave Kathleen, it gets harder every time. When she begged me to stay, I hadn't the heart to say no. It was lovely spending the night with her,' she sighed. 'Mind you, did I get a roasting from Sid for not turning up for my shift yesterday morning! He was livid, said he'd cut my wages, which is fair enough. I couldn't tell him the truth, so I lied through my teeth and told him I'd missed the last train.'

When both women had collected their mugs of tea and a pile of chip butties, they settled down at the nearest table.

'The good news is, I don't think it will be too long before I can bring Kathleen to Hucknall,' Edna told Ruby. 'She's really getting comfortable with me. Nellie's sure it won't be long now. I try not to allow myself to think that she might be with me by Christmas.'

'Wouldn't that be wonderful!' Ruby cried. 'Christmas with your little girl.'

And a baby on the way, Edna thought miserably. She was going to have to tell Lily and Jeannie the truth soon, and the welfare officer too. She just hoped it wouldn't ruin her chances of being reunited with her daughter.

Breaking into her reverie, Ruby asked, 'Did you talk to Kathleen about the nursery?'

Edna nodded. 'Sweet little thing, she asked if I could go there and play too. Oh, I wish!' she laughed. 'I'd like nothing more than to spend all day playing with Kathleen.'

'I'm sure she'll like it,' Ruby assured Edna. 'The staff are so good, always warm and welcoming – and in Matron's world, baby always comes first,' she said knowingly. 'I never imagined Archie would settle down as quickly as he has. He chuckles every morning when Matron welcomes him, sometimes he even cries when he has to leave her, would you believe it? He just loves the Bell Works nursery.'

At the end of the working day, Ruby hurried over to the nursery as usual to collect Archie. He was already in his pram, snuggled up in his warm woolly twinset and matching knitted bonnet.

'He's had a good day,' Gladys, the beaming nursery nurse, told Ruby as she was stooping over the pram in order to kiss her baby's cheek. 'He's getting on nicely with the solids we're slowly introducing, nothing too lumpy,' she assured Ruby. 'Bit of mashed potato and a few teaspoons of stewed apple. My goodness, your lad's certainly got an appetite, walloped the lot back.' Smiling indulgently, the young girl waved goodbye to her charge.

Archie leant back against his pillows and babbled happily all the way home. Pushing the pram, Ruby turned a corner and almost bumped into the works overseer who was also on her way home.

'Annie,' she exclaimed. 'I'm sorry, I nearly knocked you over.'

Turning her attention to Archie, Annie cooed and fussed over him in a way that Ruby always found to be strangely at odds with her tough working persona at the factory.

'He's coming on a treat,' Annie enthused. 'How's your mam coping nowadays, without the little lad to mind?'

Walking companionably along together, they exchanged a few minutes of small talk before Annie came straight to the point.

'It's hard not to notice that you spend most of your time over on t'other side of the canteen these days, laughing and chatting with them newcomers. You seem to prefer their company to the Hucknall lasses.'

'I have to admit, I've made friends with "them on t'other side",' Ruby said with a smile. 'Lily, Edna and Jeannie, in particular. We work virtually opposite each other on the factory floor – and you must remember that it was Lily who spotted a fault on the aircraft I was working on and alerted me to it,' she reminded Annie.

Seeing Annie flinch, Ruby felt a twinge of guilt – the last thing she wanted to do was upset the overseer. But really, she had to accept that these days, with war raging across the world, the workforce had to join together and work harder than ever before. Petty squabbles in the workplace were a waste of valuable time and energy; new workers – all women – would soon be pouring into the factory to provide the fighter planes so desperately needed to beat the enemy. Was Annie angry simply because she was being obdurate? Ruby wondered. Or was there something else troubling her that was closer to home?

Knowing that Annie lived alone with her ninety-year-old ailing mother, Ruby switched the conversation from work to home.

Gently bouncing the pram, she asked, 'How's your mother getting along these days, Annie?' Seeing Annie visibly stiffen at the mention of her mother, Ruby proceeded with caution. 'It can't be easy for her, with you working all the hours that God sends and her alone in the house all day.'

With an agonized expression on her face, Annie suddenly turned to Ruby.

'It's awful!' she exclaimed. 'You're right, she is on her own all day, waiting for me to come home. She never touches the Thermos flask of tea and the few sandwiches I leave out for her before I set off. They're always there, exactly where I left them, when I get back. She's wasting away before my eyes,' she cried. 'I've begged her to see the doctor, but she refuses point blank, says he'll admit her to the workhouse – which she insists she'll never leave alive.' Shaking her head in despair, she continued, 'No matter how many times I tell her the workhouses were shut down long ago, she doesn't believe me. And because she associates the doctor with the workhouse, she won't let him through the front door.' Sighing heavily, Annie murmured, 'I'm terrified I'll come home and find her dead in her bed one day.'

Feeling overwhelmingly sorry for Annie, who usually kept her fears and anxieties to herself, Ruby asked, 'Is there anything I can do to help? I could pop in from time to time and pay her a visit,' she suggested.

Knowing that, on top of working full time, Ruby had a house to run and a young baby to look after, Annie firmly shook her head.

'Don't be silly, mi duck, you've got enough on your hands as it is. Mind you,' she added knowingly, 'your mother's burden must have lightened once you got little Archie into the works nursery?'

Ruby beamed her dazzling smile that always lit up her sparkling blue eyes and brought a dimple to her firm rosy cheeks.

'It's been a blessed transformation,' she replied. 'Changed all of our lives for the better – especially Archie's.' Suddenly catching her breath as an idea dawned, Ruby continued, 'You know what, Annie? Mother has time on her hands these days, I know she wouldn't mind visiting your mother. She gets a bit lonely too, now that she's no longer minding Archie.'

Looking embarrassed, Annie waved a dismissive hand in the air.

'I wouldn't dream of bothering her, Ruby, she's not well herself as it is.'

'She's much better nowadays,' Ruby assured her. 'I know she'd welcome a trip around the corner to pay your mother a visit. It would do them both good.'

Looking hesitant, Annie glanced nervously at Ruby.

'Why don't we ask them and see what they say?' Ruby urged.

'Well, if you say so,' Annie answered doubtfully.

'Nothing ventured, nothing gained,' Ruby responded

cheerfully, as they said their goodbyes and made their separate ways home.

It turned out that Mrs Fields wasn't at all averse to visiting an old neighbour. In fact, she and Mrs Barnes quickly got into the habit of having a cup of tea made by Mrs Fields, fresh and hot, and which Annie's mum enjoyed with the butties that her daughter had devotedly prepared for her.

'She's much happier,' Annie joyfully informed Ruby the following week. 'Eating better, and always got something to chat about when I get home from work. Your mother's visits have done her the power of good,' she added, with a grateful smile.

Smiling back, Ruby said proudly, 'My mother could charm the birds from the trees. She knows all the local gossip – who's flitting, who's expecting, who's walking out with who. I don't know how she keeps up with it all.'

'There's something else too,' Annie added. 'Mother's stopped talking about the workhouse. Did you say anything to your mother, by any chance?'

'Actually, I did,' Ruby admitted. 'I asked her if she could put your mother straight on the subject – reassure her that workhouses no longer exist, and she should stop worrying herself sick about it.'

'Well, it worked,' Annie beamed. 'Oh, lovie, really, I can never thank you and your mother enough.' Looking Ruby straight in the eye, she said, 'Is there anything I can do in return?'

Holding her gaze, Ruby gave a long slow smile. 'Yes, there is actually.'

As if sensing what might be coming next, Annie cocked an eyebrow at Ruby.

Without a moment's hesitation, Ruby stated, 'I'd like you to help the new girls a bit more. Really, Annie,' she added earnestly, 'they are nice women, good women who mostly chose to come here to Hucknall because they want to build fighter planes for the war effort. Doesn't that say something about them? They could have gone elsewhere – Southampton, Leeds, Scotland, Portsmouth – but they asked to come *here*.'

Seeing the light of understanding beginning to dawn in Annie's eyes, Ruby rammed her final point home.

'Just drop your guard, Annie – you might be pleasantly surprised.'

First thing the following morning, Lily, Jeannie and Edna – who were sleepily enjoying a cup of tea before the hooter shrilled out – all but fell over in shock when Annie, with Ruby at her side, approached their table. Clearly primed by Ruby, Annie was looking tense but determined.

'Ruby tells me that your little girl might be starting at the Bell Works nursery,' she said, speaking directly to Edna.

Though completely flabbergasted, Edna replied, 'I'm hoping she might be able to join me soon – before Christmas, with a bit of luck.'

Looking awkward, Annie nevertheless continued. 'When the time comes, if you need to clock on a bit later of a morning, at least to start with, I'll quite understand. I'm sure we can sort that out between us, while your little girl settles in like.'

'Thank you very much, Annie,' Edna gratefully responded. 'I really appreciate your kind offer.'

'Just let me know and I'll see what can be done,' Annie concluded before she turned and walked away, clearly relieved that she had done the right thing.

Giving the cheekiest of winks, Ruby joked, 'You all look like Her Majesty the Queen has just invited you to the palace for tea!'

Flopping back in her chair, Edna spluttered, 'Did I just dream that?'

'No, it was real,' Ruby whispered before dashing off after Annie.

Left alone, Edna, Jeannie and Lily shook their heads in disbelief.

'I think our Ruby should join Churchill's war cabinet,' Jeannie chuckled. 'Talk about crossing into enemy territory. That was a cunning diplomatic move – and kind too,' she acknowledged.

Humbled by what Annie had done, and so publicly, Edna blinked back tears. 'That must have cost her a lot,' she gulped.

31. The *Ark Royal*

On the day that the nation reeled after hearing about the sinking of the *Ark Royal* by a German U-boat, the talk in the factory was only of the terrible tragedy. Gone were the days of 'them' and 'us'; right now everybody was anxiously listening to the works wireless. Hanging on to the BBC newsreader's every word, the stunned workforce listened to the announcements that continued throughout the day. Targeted off the coast of Gibraltar by a German submarine, the *Ark Royal* – a vast aircraft carrier, known as the 'Lucky Ship' because of all its famous exploits on the high seas – was presently listing.

'Oh my God!' Audrey gasped as more details came through. 'Only one man dead out of one thousand and five hundred crew, that's nothing short of a miracle.'

'Rommel must have had his eyes on *Ark Royal* for a while,' clever Ruby announced. 'She's been active all summer, delivering aircraft to Malta and escorting convoys around the Med.'

'It must have been a heck of a blast to take her out so quickly,' Lily added.

'And she split in two before she went down,' Audrey said. 'The crew and officers must have been transported off even as she was listing.'

Throughout the animated conversation Edna remained strangely quiet. Normally, she would have been glued to the news; like all of her colleagues she was addicted to the BBC announcements, but today she was quiet and uncharacteristically withdrawn.

'Everything all right, lovie?' Lily whispered as they went back into the factory after a short tea break.

Turning to her friend, Edna shook her head. 'No, something apart from the sinking of *Ark Royal* is troubling me,' she blurted out.

Raising an arched eyebrow, Lily threw her a questioning look. 'What is it, what's wrong?'

'I'll tell you tonight,' Edna said as the din of the factory drowned out any further conversation.

In the prefab that evening, after a simple supper of beans and baked potatoes – which Jeannie shared with Edna and Lily – the girls gathered by the fireplace where crackling logs threw out a cosy golden warmth.

Edna, sick of being tense and pent up, didn't wait for Lily to start the ball rolling.

'Girls, the thing is, I'm expecting Ken's baby,' she blurted out.

Visibly stunned, Lily and Jeannie could momentarily only stare at Edna.

Jeannie, the first to find her voice, gasped, 'Oh my God!'

Throwing up her hands, Edna cried, 'I know, I know – stupid, *stupid* me! I've taken myself to task a hundred times. You warned me from the beginning –' she gave a hopeless shrug – 'but I thought I knew better, just a bit of fun . . . What a fool I've been.' Putting her head in her hands, Edna let out an anguished groan. 'Just as I've got Kathleen sorted, I get myself in the family way. Oh Jesus, what a bloody mess.'

Exchanging a despairing look, Lily and Jeannie wondered how they could best comfort their distraught friend.

Desperately searching for the right words, Lily nervously asked, 'Might you consider going home to have the baby?'

'NO!' Edna cried. 'My mother-in-law would be down on me like a ton of bricks. I can never go back there. And then there's Jack; how can I explain to him that I'm pregnant, when I've not seen him for months?' She sobbed as she abandoned herself to grief.

As Lily took weeping Edna into her arms, Jeannie whispered, 'I'll go and put the kettle on,' before tiptoeing softly out of the room.

Lily smoothed Edna's dark hair and soothed her with gentle words. 'It's undoubtedly tricky, lovie. At the moment there's a lot of questions, and not many answers. You can't deal with everything in an instant. Let's start with you, sweetheart – what do you want to do?'

'I want to bring Kathleen here to Hucknall, like I always planned to do. No matter what, I don't want that arrangement to change. She mustn't suffer because of my selfish actions.'

Given her friend's radical change of circumstances, Lily wondered how this arrangement would now work; keeping her doubts to herself, she stayed calm and focused as she listened to Edna.

'Maybe I'll be able to work until I'm nearly due. Then after the baby's born, I could leave it in the nursery along with Kathleen.'

Thinking how much hard work this plan would involve, Lily nevertheless nodded. 'That way, you won't have to do any explaining to your mother-in-law,' she said.

'But then there's Jack,' Edna wailed as Jeannie returned with a loaded tea tray. 'What on earth am I going to tell him?'

Handing Edna a mug of strong tea, Jeannie responded to her question. 'The truth,' she said flatly. 'You're not the only lass that's got herself pregnant while her husband's been stationed abroad.'

'He'll go berserk,' Edna whispered. 'He might even leave me.'

'He might stick by you,' Jeannie said. 'I've heard of fellas claiming the baby as their own, even when they know it's not the case.'

'Then resent them as they grow up – the cuckoo in the nest,' Edna cried.

Thinking of practicalities, Lily tentatively asked, 'I wonder just how long you'll be able to work in the cramped conditions that we endure every day? Bent over double, stretching up to grab drills and riveting guns, not to mention working on our hands and knees in an oily fuselage for hours on end.'

Edna nodded in agreement with her. 'It's all right for now, but it will be really uncomfortable when I'm bigger. Course, by that time everybody will know I'm expecting, and they'll be wondering how that came about,' she sighed.

'There are other pregnant women working in the factory,' Jeannie pointed out.

'Generally, those women have husbands who have recently been home on leave,' Edna cried as she started to sob all over again. 'What possessed me to have anything to do with that wretched Canadian?'

Lily and Jeannie exchanged another meaningful look;

though they had barely met the man, their first and lasting impression of him was a flirt and a womanizer.

'Will you tell him about the baby?' Lily asked.

'Why would I do that?' Edna asked.

'Because he has a responsibility – it's his child, after all,' Lily pointed out.

'I've not seen him since I let him have his way with me,' Edna replied. 'If he's not interested in me, he'll be even less interested in a baby.' Shaking her head, Edna concluded, 'No, Lily, I'm on my own, and it's my own stupid fault, there's nobody else to blame but me.'

Darting a quick look at Jeannie, Lily firmly took hold of Edna's trembling hands.

'No, sweetheart, you are not on your own, you've got friends . . . you've got us.'

32. Sid's Girl

When Sid heard that Lily was having flying lessons, he was deeply impressed.

'Oh, aye,' he bragged, 'we don't just make aircraft at the Bell Works, some of our lasses are bright enough to fly 'em too.'

Embarrassed by Sid's praise, Lily protested. 'My boy-friend's only taken me up a few times, Sid,' she firmly told him. 'Four at the most.'

Sid, who had had no success flirting with any of the visiting ferry girls, gave a loud scoffing laugh. 'Them bloody ferry girls think they're the bee's knees, coming in here all toffee-nosed, when one of our own lasses can do just as well as them.'

Seeing poor Lily blushing, Ruby added, 'Lily's doing well, we're all really proud of her.'

Throwing Ruby a grateful glance, Lily said, 'I'm not qualified yet – but I do love flying.'

Looking incredulous, Sid guffawed, 'You can get the bloody thing up there! That's quite an achievement, as far as I'm concerned.'

Later, with Ruby, Audrey and Mary seated at a canteen table beside her, Lily was once again made to feel uncomfort-able – this time by Mary, who picked up where Sid had left off.

'I've never known anybody who can fly a plane,' she said, with a meek little smile. 'Least of all a woman.'

Cheeky Audrey tittered. 'Hell fire,' she teased. 'You'll be asking for Lily's autograph soon.'

Seeing poor Mary squirming with embarrassment, Lily quickly changed the subject. Knowing just how much Mary loved her grub, she brightly asked, 'What's on today's menu, lovie?'

Without a moment's hesitation, Mary responded, 'Rissoles with mushy peas and baked potatoes – followed by jam roly-poly.'

And mercifully, that was the end of Lily's embarrassing conversations for the rest of the day.

Lily was thoughtful when she returned to the cockpit assembly line where she and Edna were riveting long slim sheets of shaped alloy inside the cockpit's cramped interior. Crawling after her workmate, Lily watched Edna drill a series of neat holes in the metal seam, after which she stretched forward to grasp the riveting gun to secure the section she had just drilled into place. Catching sight of Edna straining to lift the weighty tool, Lily wondered just how long her pregnant friend would be able to work as an engine girl. How much reaching, stretching, squatting and bending could she realistically do as the months went by? And there was the climbing too, up and down the precarious ladders, to work on the jig.

Though Edna was tough and determined, there was only so much the body could take – and even though Edna fobbed off all offers of help, Lily could see at first hand the increasing strain her dear friend was under. She tried to imagine what she would do if she were in Edna's situation. How would she begin to tell Jack, her loyal and loving husband, that she was pregnant with another man's child? Even if he agreed to accept the baby as his own, Lily wondered if he would always resent it.

She vividly recalled the night of the Bell Works dance, where Edna – looking sensational in her red satin evening gown – had emanated a vibrancy that had drawn men to her, like bees to honey. The evening, a giddy night of fun and flirtation, had gone to Edna's head, the consequences of which, Lily thought sadly, would haunt Edna for the rest of her life.

Later that week, Lily spotted a young woman dressed in a pilot's coat sitting alone in the canteen. Assuming that she was a ferry girl, Lily screwed up all of her courage to approach the visitor.

'Excuse me,' she started nervously, 'am I right in thinking that you are a ferry girl?'

Unlike the previous snooty ferry girls, this young woman flashed Lily a wide and welcoming smile.

'Yes, I am.'

'Er, would you mind if I asked you a few questions?' Lily nervously continued. 'You see, I'm learning to fly and –'

Not waiting until she had got to the end of her sentence, the stranger pulled out a chair.

'Please sit down, it's nice to have company,' she grinned.

Eagerly accepting the offer, Lily quickly sat down.

'I'm Geraldine,' the visitor told her. 'How can I help you?'

Before she lost confidence and bolted, blushing Lily blurted out, 'As I said, I'm having flying lessons.'

Looking at Lily's working clothes – her engine girl's grubby oil-stained dungarees and her bright spotty turban – Geraldine cocked a curious eyebrow.

'Oh, so you build planes and fly them too?'

Lily self-consciously explained, 'I've only been flying for a very short time, with my boyfriend – he's a Polish pilot at the airbase up the road –'

'Polish?' Geraldine interrupted as she took out a silver filigree cigarette case. 'They're good chaps, brave and massively underestimated.'

Though Lily completely agreed with Geraldine's sentiments, she didn't dwell on them.

'What I'd like to know, if you don't mind,' she blurted out to Geraldine, who was now lighting up a cigarette, 'is how can I become a ferry girl like you?'

Geraldine gave a dismissive shrug. 'If you're already flying, I'd say that qualifies you for the job.'

'But I've only ever flown with my boyfriend!' Lily pointed out.

'The Polish pilot?' Geraldine said, with a teasing smile. 'I imagine he's an excellent teacher?'

'He's very good,' Lily answered proudly.

Suddenly serious, Geraldine said, 'So, let's be clear, you can take off, fly, follow landmarks on a map, make a descent, and land on an airstrip?'

Lily gave a hesitant nod.

'Yes, but so far only in a Tiger Moth with Oro in the cockpit, with our headsets connected. I've never flown solo,' she stressed.

'There's always a first time for everybody,' Geraldine said as she stubbed out her cigarette in an ashtray. Holding

Lily's direct gaze, she asked, 'Are you seriously interested in transporting planes to wherever they are most needed?'

Lily didn't hesitate for a second.

'Yes, absolutely . . . but I don't know whether I qualify.'

'I can tell you honestly that girls with less experience than you have delivered aircraft to airfields all over England. We're really up against it,' Geraldine said, nodding towards the nearest window with a view of the stack yard. 'Look at the Spitfires you girls have built out there, every one of them is urgently needed in Lincoln, Norfolk, Suffolk, Essex – *everywhere*, in fact. These aircraft are the only way we will ever win the war. There are no pilots available to deliver them; with chaps gone, women have got to step up to the plate.'

Breathless with nervous excitement, Lily earnestly asked, 'Do you really think I could deliver one of our Spitfires?'

'Really, darling, I know female ambulance drivers who in an emergency have taken a plane up after a few test runs. Under pressure, you can do anything, believe me.' Rising to her feet, Geraldine said, 'Two of us were supposed to pick up today but my pal had an accident, sprained an ankle while landing a Lysander this morning. I know this is out of the blue, but if you really are serious about flying, I'd be grateful to take you up on your offer.'

Beginning to shake with excitement, Lily nervously spluttered, 'Help! I'm supposed to be back at work in a few minutes – I'll have to get permission off my supervisor before I agree to anything.'

'Righty-ho, off you go,' Geraldine urged. 'And don't be long, conditions are good for take-off right now,' she called after Lily.

Spurred on by Geraldine, and with adrenalin pumping

around her body, Lily frantically searched around for Annie. She finally spotted her in the far corner of the canteen.

'Excuse me, Annie, sorry to bother you,' Lily said breathlessly. 'I need your permission to leave the factory.'

'Oh, and why's that, then?'

'Well, you see, there's a ferry girl over there.' Lily pointed in the direction of Geraldine. 'She needs help to transport an aircraft out of here.'

Surprised, Annie asked, 'Really, can you do that?'

Lily blushed. 'I think so. I've been having flying lessons.'

A slow smile crept across Annie's face. 'You little dark horse!' she chuckled. 'You never let on.'

Lily gave a self-conscious shrug. 'It was in my time off, with my boyfriend.'

Seeing the excitement gleaming brightly in Lily's silver-grey eyes, Annie gave her a quick pat on the arm.

'Off you go, duck,' she said. 'Take care, and come back safe.'

Lily found Geraldine out in the yard with Sid at her side. Both of them were standing by the Spitfire that Geraldine had been allocated. When Lily joined them, panting after running across the yard, she heard Sid loudly grumbling.

'I was under the impression that two lasses were coming to pick up today?'

''Fraid my pal had an accident, sprained an ankle this morning.'

Sid gave an anxious tut. 'God knows how we'll get this lot dispatched,' he muttered as his eyes swept over the rows of aircraft awaiting collection.

'Well, I could make a suggestion,' Geraldine said, with a glint in her eye.

'And what might that be?'

Nodding towards Lily, who was walking quickly towards them, Geraldine said, 'I suggest this young lady flies an aircraft to Woodbridge, in Suffolk.'

Absolutely thunderstruck, Sid – for all his bragging about Lily's prowess – could only gawk in disbelief.

'Is she fit for purpose? I don't want ow't nasty happening to her,' he blustered.

Geraldine gave a slow deliberate nod. 'I'd say so. From what I've gathered, I think she can deliver.' Addressing Lily directly, she repeated what they had only recently discussed. 'Correct me if I'm repeating myself – you can fly, you're able to follow waypoints and landmarks on a map, and you can land an aircraft?'

Throwing back her shoulders, Lily replied, 'Yes, I can do all of those things.'

Glancing up at the shifting clouds in a heavy grey sky, Geraldine urged, 'Then let's get on with it – and the sooner the better, I don't fancy flying through a storm if I can avoid it.'

For all his bravado about Lily's know-how, Sid suddenly looked startled. 'Is she dressed for the occasion? We don't want the lass freezing to death up there.'

'Is there a flying jacket hanging around?' Geraldine asked. 'Goggles, and gloves too,' she called after Sid.

The foreman raced off to find Lily appropriate clothing. Left alone, Geraldine looked Lily straight in the eye.

'Seriously, love, you're about as qualified as I was on my first flight – and by the way, my commission came out of the blue, just like this one. Remember, this isn't a lark, this war is being fought in the sky, aircraft are being blown up and gunned down every minute of the day. The more planes we can generate, the greater our chances are of beating Hitler. I promise I'll be ahead of you, guiding you all the way, out there and back in. Now, tell me, honestly – are you ready for this?'

Holding her gaze, Lily responded with a passion that actually surprised her.

'Yes, I'm ready.'

33. Destination Woodbridge

Sitting alone in the cockpit of a brand-new Spitfire – one she wondered if she might have helped assemble – Lily took deep breaths. She had built enough of these aircraft to be familiar with their layout. Obviously, it didn't look the same as a Tiger Moth, but the principles were the same. The only problem was that Oro wasn't close by, supervising her every step along the way, but Geraldine had promised that she would be there, guiding and directing along the route.

As if reading her thoughts, Geraldine said briskly over their connecting headsets, 'Righty-ho, I'll take off first, just follow me down the runway. When you've gathered enough speed, advance the throttle and let the plane do the rest. We'll keep below cloud level, so hopefully you won't lose sight of me. Have you familiarized yourself with the map and the waypoints along the route – rivers, railway lines, junctions, towns – to help you map your route? I'll be following exactly the same waypoints – all you have to do is tail me. Woodbridge isn't far, so it's a nice easy introduction. Chocks away!'

While Geraldine waited for clearance, Lily took a few minutes longer to closely study the map, checking the waypoints as Geraldine had suggested. When she saw Sid giving her the thumbs up and removing the chocks, Lily's heart began to thud. Holding her breath, she watched

Geraldine taxi out on to the runway. Once Geraldine was clear, Lily released her Spitfire's brake and rolled forwards too. Hearing Geraldine's calm, matter-of-fact voice through her headset, Lily started to breathe easier.

'I'm starting her up . . .' Calling out instructions, Geraldine's voice crackled over the airwaves. 'Applying the throttle full on, waiting for the air speed to increase in order to take off. When I feel the power surge, I'll take her up,' Geraldine explained as she gathered momentum and thundered down the runway.

Hardly daring to take her eyes off Geraldine's aircraft, Lily watched the Spitfire rise from the tarmac, skim briefly over barren winter fields and then, gaining height, take to the air.

'Your turn now.' Geraldine's calm clear voice sounded in Lily's headset.

Speaking into her mouthpiece, Lily responded immediately. 'When my speed's high enough, and the power surges, I pull back on the joystick and take her up?'

'Exactly,' Geraldine answered. 'Good luck.'

Doing exactly as she was instructed, Lily rolled the aircraft faster and faster down the runway. When she felt the powerful surge of the Merlin engine, she pulled back hard on the joystick . . . and the Spitfire was airborne. Filled with a mixture of sheer elation and utter terror, she cried out loud, 'OOOH!'

Geraldine's chuckles sounded in Lily's headset.

'That feeling never goes away,' she said. 'Now concentrate and stay alert, we're going to make a right-hand turn, then maintain a straight course heading east.'

On this trip Lily had no time to gaze around and wonder

at the beauty of the world, way down below; all she could think of were the controls and the all-important waypoints that charted their route to Suffolk. Grateful that they were below cloud and that she had Geraldine always in her sights, Lily kept a steady course. Feeling she was in safe hands, she began to relax just a little. Astonished that she had actually got the Spitfire airborne, she checked her speed and position on the map. Suddenly, to her amazement, the ancient Suffolk forests of Thetford and Rendlesham loomed into view, and she looked down at the vast sweep of winding rivers and estuaries criss-crossing their way over vast stretches of marshland and isolated beaches. Time had literally flown since she had taken off, and now another challenge faced Lily – safely landing the Spitfire.

'There's the airbase,' Geraldine instructed. 'We'll make a slow steady descent, but first turn her around, nice and easy on the steering.'

Gripping the joystick, Lily made the turn. As she did so, the horizon tilted then levelled out as she positioned the Spitfire in line with the looming airbase.

'When we get the green clearance light from the airbase's tower, I'll make my descent. Wait for me to land, then start to make your own descent,' Geraldine instructed as they waited for clearance.

With her heart in her mouth, Lily followed Geraldine in. Using the air speed and the descent rate that Geraldine instructed, she kept her aircraft in line with the runway; reducing her air speed, she made a cautious descent. Trying to keep her steering steady, Lily's heart jumped as the wild easterly wind hit the aircraft side on and sent it lurching from right to left.

'Concentrate, woman,' she told herself through gritted teeth.

As the tarmac came up to meet her, Lily wanted to close her eyes and scream. Instead, she kept her nerve, and guided the plane down – and just like when she had been flying with Oro, she virtually collapsed over the wheel as the aircraft came to a very bumpy stop.

Too weak to stand, Lily took several deep breaths then jumped as a red-faced mechanic tapped loudly on her windscreen.

'Follow me in, miss,' he called.

Nodding feebly, Lily took hold of the controls and slowly guided the Spitfire down the runway where several mechanics were waiting to take over. After shutting down the engine, Lily rose to her feet and realized she could barely stand up. All the strength seemed to have gone out of her trembling legs.

'I feel like my legs have turned to jelly,' she gasped as she steadied herself.

Clambering out of the cockpit, Lily was met by a grinning Geraldine on the tarmac.

'Oh my God!' Lily spluttered.

Giving her a hearty clap on the back, Geraldine boomed, 'Well done! You excelled yourself.'

Dazed and euphoric, Lily was overwhelmed by the conflicting sensations she had just experienced – fear, terror, exaltation, panic, gratitude – and could only shake her head.

'How does anybody *ever* get used to that?'

Having successfully landed the Spitfires – which had been instantly claimed by the mechanics, who assured the ferry girls that they would be in operation within days – Lily and Geraldine went into the NAAFI for a cup of tea and a bite to eat. Grateful for the hot strong tea and the toasted tea cakes, Lily felt her body start to relax and come down from the high she had been on since leaving Hucknall. Indefatigable Geraldine, after a chat with the officer in charge who had briefly joined them in the canteen, had yet another surprise in store.

'Looks like we're flying a couple of Spits back to Hucknall.'

Completely flabbergasted, Lily put down her mug of tea before she spilt it all over the metal table they were sitting at.

'I thought we were making our way back by train,' she protested.

'I thought so too,' Geraldine honestly answered. 'But there are a couple of aircraft that need some minor repair work, so we've been asked to fly them back to the Bell Works right away. Better than hanging about waiting for a troop train from Ipswich. We should be home in time for tea,' she ended cheerfully.

Wondering how anybody could always be so jolly and optimistic, Lily felt her stomach plummet. You can't carry on reacting like this every time you get an order to fly, she firmly told herself. Think about the bigger picture and stop panicking.

'Righty-ho,' Geraldine said as she swiftly polished off her mug of tea. 'Let's get back into the saddle.'

Once outside, Lily's heart sank when she saw how grey and drizzly the skies were. Catching sight of her tense expression, Geraldine waved a hand in the air.

'Don't worry about the weather,' she reassured Lily. 'We'll stay below the clouds, just like we did on the way over here.'

Looking at the Spitfires they were due to fly out, Lily's eyes widened; battle-scarred and dented, these weren't shining and new like the aircraft they had just delivered.

'Are they safe to fly?' she asked the mechanic.

'Absolutely! A bit of body repair should see them as good as new,' he answered cheerfully.

Once inside the cockpit, Lily immediately noticed the difference between the two fighter planes; the interior and the controls in the older Spit were battered and damaged from constant action.

'Same routine as before,' Geraldine announced, before moving out first on to the runway. 'We'll follow the same course; you'll recognize the waypoints home. Just sit back and relax.'

After adjusting her headset, Lily settled back in her seat. At least this time she had some idea of what she was expected to do – and the knowledge of that gave her a sudden boost of confidence.

'I can do this,' she said out loud as she rattled down the runway after Geraldine and took to the air, with considerably more expertise than on her first solo flight.

Darkness started to fall towards the end of their return journey, but with Geraldine up ahead Lily kept a steady course. When she saw the green clearance light flash from the Hucknall tower, she kept her aircraft in line with the runway, guiding the Spitfire down from the stormy sky with a new confidence, though the clanking in the rear of the aircraft did suggest it urgently needed some mechanical attention.

When she finally switched off the aircraft's engine in the docking bay, Lily didn't slump forward over the wheel but instead fell back in her low bucket seat.

I can fly, she thought as the smile on her delicate heart-shaped face widened. 'I really can fly!' she said out loud.

At which point she saw Oro through the cockpit's wind-screen – and from the expression on his face he didn't look one bit happy.

34. Crossed Wires

Once Lily had signed off her Spitfire to the mechanics waiting on the runway to receive it, she hurried to say goodbye to Geraldine.

'Never doubted you for a minute, darling,' she enthused, full of warm praise for Lily. 'Natural-born flyer.'

Blushing with pleasure, Lily spoke the truth. 'I was terrified – but I *loved* it!'

'Of course you did,' Geraldine laughed. 'And now you can ferry planes out of here whenever the call comes.'

Seeing Oro approaching, Lily tensed as she noticed his uncharacteristically brooding expression. Quickly introducing him to her new friend, she said proudly, 'This is Oro, my boyfriend. It was him who taught me to fly.'

Grabbing his hand, Geraldine shook it in her hearty manner. 'Delighted to make your acquaintance. Polish, I believe?'

Oro clicked his heels and nodded. 'Lieutenant Chenko, Polish Flying Squad.'

'Well, you've done an outstanding job with this young lady, she's an absolute trooper.'

Though Oro smiled politely, Lily instinctively knew that something was irritating him.

'Lily is an excellent student,' he agreed. 'However, I am surprised that she thinks she is at the stage where she can fly solo.'

So that's it! Lily thought. He's displeased with me for going up without his permission. Feeling herself going hot with embarrassment, Lily focused on what Geraldine was saying.

'I'm afraid to say, Lieutenant Chenko, that it is entirely my fault,' she said generously. 'Originally, two of us were scheduled to transport the aircraft, but unfortunately my partner was held up. Two Spitfires were urgently needed at the Woodbridge airbase, and this young lady stepped in at the last minute. She was tremendous.'

Wishing Geraldine would stop praising her, Lily shuffled uncomfortably.

'Anyway, now I must love you and leave you, dear,' Geraldine boomed. 'I've got a lift into Nottingham, from where I'll catch a train back to London.' Throwing her arms around diminutive Lily, she gave her a huge bear hug. 'I hope our paths cross again soon, darling,' she said, before striding away across the empty factory yard.

As soon as they were alone, Oro turned on Lily. 'What in God's name were you thinking of, Lillee?'

Quick to defend herself, Lily responded, 'I wasn't thinking of anything – to tell you the truth, I was in shock. Geraldine was stuck, she said she needed help.'

'Did you tell her how inexperienced you are?' he cried.

'Absolutely.'

'And she still went ahead?'

'Yes, she assured me she would lead me in and out . . .' Lily's voice faltered as the adrenalin rush that had kept her going all afternoon began to ebb and fade. 'I suppose I just trusted her.'

'You could have died up there!' Oro exclaimed.

'That did cross my mind,' she answered grimly.

'I didn't teach you to fly so that you could become a ferry girl and risk your life delivering aircraft all over place.'

Stung by his words, Lily quickly retaliated, 'So *why* did you teach me to fly, Oro? Just to impress me?'

Looking hurt and offended, Oro responded with passion. 'To enjoy sharing the pleasure *together* – not to risk danger.'

Now angry, Lily exclaimed, 'Women are doing men's work everywhere these days. Oro – look at me,' she commanded. 'I used to be a pretty little waitress in Whitby, calming customers and serving tea, and now I'm an engine girl, building planes to kill the enemy. Why shouldn't my flying skills, modest as they are, be used for the greater good?'

Seeing the sudden blaze of anger in her cheeks, and the dangerous flash in her bright silver eyes, Oro started to backtrack.

'Lillee, please, you misunderstand me. I respect that you and other women do a good job – the country would be lost without your courage – but seeing you flying alone, making your descent on runway, it gave me shock of my life.'

Now thoroughly riled, Lily took his words the wrong way.

'Do you think I shouldn't be flying – that I shouldn't be left alone in charge of an aircraft?'

'I never said that!'

'Anyway,' she suddenly asked, 'how did you even know I was flying? It was a spur-of-the-moment decision. Who told you?'

'I came to Bell Works to deliver letter to you. When I arrive here, Sid told me you were flying,' Oro explained.

Sid! thought Lily. It would have to be him, telling the world and his dog that Lily was now a pilot, as good as any of them snooty ferry girls. Dear old, silly old Sid. He really had gone and put his foot in it this time.

Realizing she was still wearing the borrowed flying jacket over her oily dungarees, Lily said, 'I have to get back to work.'

'Me also,' he muttered. 'Maybe you consider going for walk with me tomorrow, Lillee?'

'Maybe,' she muttered furiously as she turned on her heel and walked away.

In the evening of that eventful day, emotions were riding high in Prefab No. 8.

In recent days, having had a roasting from Sid – who had been furious with her for staying overnight in Kendal – Edna had nevertheless gone begging, cap in hand, to Mr Lovelace. Like Sid, he didn't condone her recent late return to work and the trouble it had caused his foreman, but seeing the desperate look in Edna's eyes and knowing full well her struggle to reclaim her daughter, Lovelace had eventually granted her another brief compassionate leave, though his parting words to her carried a warning.

'Don't let me down,' he had said firmly. 'This is a special dispensation, Edna, then you buckle down to work like the rest of the engine girls in my factory.'

'He was decent enough about it,' a grateful Edna later told her friends. 'While I was with him he actually checked with the admin secretary – who I've been nagging to death on an almost daily basis – on where Kathleen is on the nursery's waiting list.'

'Lucky he's sympathetic, after the ticking-off you got from Sid,' Jeannie remarked.

'To be fair, Sid was only doing his job,' Edna reasoned. 'If everybody bunked off like I did, there'd be fewer Spits leaving this factory, that's for sure.'

Lily, who had seen a softer and kinder side of Sid recently, defended their foreman. 'He's got a good heart has Sid.'

Continuing, Edna added, 'Mr Lovelace even told me he would prioritize my case with the accommodation officer. He's been more than kind to me.'

'He has indeed,' Jeannie agreed. 'Nevertheless, make sure you double-check your arrangements with the accommodation lady before you leave for Kendal; it's important for Kathleen's sake that there are no last-minute slip-ups.'

Edna gave a quick nod. 'Don't you worry,' she answered firmly. 'I'll call into the nursery first thing tomorrow to have a word with Matron. Please God, she can squeeze Kathleen in, she's right at the top of the list, I saw it with my own eyes when Mr Lovelace was checking it today.'

'So how did you leave it? When are you going to Kendal?' Jeannie asked.

'Tomorrow, as soon as I get everything sorted,' Edna replied. 'I'll only need a day and a night at most, then I'll be back at work – and hopefully Kathleen will be installed in the Bell Works nursery.'

After catching up with the accommodation officer – who came to visit Prefab No. 8 to check its suitability for a young child, and also to discuss with Lily her feelings about sharing her home with a child – the arrangement had been signed off, on condition that the officer would make another inspection after Christmas. He had also said he would discuss Kathleen's progress with the matron and staff at the nursery.

By evening, after meetings with matron and the accommodation officer – and having worked throughout most of the long day – Edna was completely exhausted.

When Jeannie arrived later, to help Edna pack her few belongings in readiness for her journey north the next day, she found Edna feeling terribly sick in one bedroom and Lily in floods of tears in the other bedroom. Going between her two closest friends, Jeannie was trying her hardest to soothe both. Telling Edna to sit down and rest by the fire, she finished packing her things, after which she slipped into the back bedroom to see how Lily was getting on. Finding her lying still and prostrate on her narrow single bed, Jeannie was just about to slip away when she heard a strangled sob.

'Oh, lovie,' she murmured as she hurried to Lily's bedside where she perched to pat her friend tenderly on the back. 'Why don't you come next door and I'll make us all a nice cup of tea?'

Looking up with bloodshot eyes and a flushed red face, Lily obediently nodded. She followed Jeannie into the sitting room and joined Edna, slumped on the sofa in front of the fire.

'Well, we're a right pair,' Edna groaned.

'I can't believe I've fallen out with Oro,' Lily wailed.

'And I can't believe I'll ever make it to Kendal and back without passing out somewhere along the way,' Edna wailed.

Clutching each other's hands, the two women gazed miserably into the crackling fire.

'God almighty, what a mess,' Edna sighed.

Arriving with mugs of tea, which she quickly handed out, Jeannie was determined to lift the mood. She said in her cheeriest voice, 'Here we are, nice and hot and strong.'

Just the smell of the stewed tea turned Edna's queasy stomach. 'Sorry, sweetheart, I might just have water instead.'

Lily, on the other hand, clutched her mug of tea and used it to help steady her trembling hands.

'I still can't get over how cross Oro was with me,' she murmured.

Playing the part of the peacemaker, Jeannie hesitantly suggested, 'Maybe he was just worried, love?'

'I was worried too, Jeannie,' Lily protested. 'And scared witless.'

'When I heard you were flying a Spitfire out of the Bell Works, I thought I was hearing things,' Edna exclaimed. 'I tell you, Lil, half the factory workers were gawping out of the windows. I couldn't watch,' Edna confessed. 'I had to close my eyes.'

Blushing to the roots of her hair, Lily blurted out, 'Are you telling me you were all watching me take off?'

'Oh, aye, led by Sid. Hell fire, you had quite an audience,' Edna laughed. 'Everybody cheered when you were airborne!'

Setting aside her mug of tea, Lily gasped. 'Was I wobbling all over the place?'

'Like I say, I had my eyes shut most of the time,' Edna giggled, 'but Annie said –'

'Was Annie watching too?'

'She was riveted, she and Sid were vying for the best view at the window,' Jeannie chipped in. 'I thought you were marvellous, sweetheart. I was so proud of you.'

'I'm beginning to feel like I dreamt the whole thing,' Lily spluttered. 'All I did was go up and chat to Geraldine – the next thing I know, I'm in the cockpit of a Spitfire heading for Suffolk.'

Smiling mysteriously, Jeannie asked, 'And do you happen to know who fitted out that particular Spitfire?'

Lily shook her head. 'Absolutely no idea.'

'Here's a hint,' Jeannie continued. 'Somebody you know well.'

'You?' Lily joked.

'No, a Hucknall lass.'

'RUBY!' Lily cried.

'Ruby and Audrey to be exact,' Jeannie continued. 'They knew it was their aircraft because of some riveting detail they did on the tail – they recognized it as their own.'

'So, I flew Ruby's plane to Woodbridge.' Lily shook her head in disbelief. 'I should tell her that she did a good job. The guys at the airbase couldn't get their hands on her Spit quick enough. I hope she survives her first run,' she added thoughtfully. 'The aircraft we flew back were badly battle-scarred and in need of attention.' Recalling her thrilling experience, Lily was suddenly overwhelmed. 'Oh dear,' she said, with an emotional catch in her voice. 'All I did was fly to Suffolk. What must it be like for those young chaps who fly into the face of the enemy?'

*

Lily, exhausted both physically and mentally by the dramatic events of the day, decided to have an early night. Hoping she wouldn't lie in bed tossing and turning, worrying about Oro, she did in fact fall into a deep sleep.

She woke early the next morning, ready to accompany Edna to the local railway station. Seeing Edna looking pale and faint, Lily immediately took possession of her travelling bag.

'Let me have that, lovie,' she urged.

Grateful for the offer, Edna handed over the bag. 'I just wish I could stop feeling sick all the time,' she sighed as they walked up the road, arm in arm together. 'I don't remember it being this bad with our Kathleen.'

'Are you sure this is the right time to bring Kathleen down here to live with you, Edna?' Lily tentatively asked. 'I mean, you being so sick all the time – couldn't you hang on for a few more weeks until you feel a bit stronger?'

Edna vigorously shook her head. 'No, I promised Kathleen last time I saw her that we would be together soon. I can't go breaking that promise just because I'm the one that's made such a blasted mess of things.'

'I understand,' Lily quickly responded. 'It's just bad timing for you, lovie.'

'I can't make Kathleen suffer for my wilfulness; bad timing or not, I won't go back on my word,' Edna miserably protested. Throwing back her shoulders, she added, 'Once she's with me, things will be a lot better.'

Looking at her already exhausted friend, Lily wondered if she shouldn't offer to accompany her on her journey north.

'I've got the day off, I could come with you,' she insisted.

'Give over,' Edna retorted. 'I'll be all right once I see my little girl, she won't want to see her mother weak and feeble. I'll get by,' she assured Lily.

The two friends stood on the platform of the little railway station, lost in thought as they waited for the train to pull in.

'What're you planning to do on your day off?' Edna asked.

Lily shrugged. 'Oro suggested we go for a walk, but I was so cross with him after he'd ticked me off, I just walked away in a grump.'

Giving Lily a hard penetrating stare, Edna replied, 'I said this yesterday, and I'm saying it again now, I think you've misread the man's intentions. I mean, for crying out loud!' she exclaimed. 'When I heard you were taking a Spit up, I all but had a heart attack! I know you've been having flying lessons, but to tell the truth I thought it was all a bit of fun, a laugh with your fella. I never thought in the world of God that you could *fly*, really fly.'

Lily slowly nodded as she took in her friend's words. 'I felt the same too,' she smiled. 'I thought Geraldine was having me on, at first. But when it became clear that she was deadly serious, I was terrified – thunder-struck, in fact.'

Holding up a hand, Edna said, 'Hold it right there, you just said you were scared stiff, right?'

Lily quickly nodded. 'Like I said, terrified.'

'So, if you were scared, why wouldn't Oro be scared too?'

The deafening roar of the train thundering up the line drowned out all further speech.

When the train shunted to a rumbling halt, Edna said

with a cheeky smile, 'I leave that thought with you. Perhaps you owe the poor fella an apology?'

Lily gave a guilty shrug. 'I was rather overwrought,' she confessed.

'Then sort it out, lass, Oro's a good lad.' Edna grinned as she kissed Lily goodbye.

Handing over the travelling bag, Lily returned Edna's kiss. 'Good luck, lovie,' she murmured. 'See you when you get back.'

35. Riber Castle

Deep in thought, Lily walked back home with Edna's words ringing in her ears; why shouldn't Oro have been scared stiff on her behalf too? After her first solo flight, high on adrenalin, Lily had seen his words as a criticism, a reprimand for going behind his back, without his explicit permission. So, what did you expect? she asked herself. A pat on the back, a fanfare of trumpets, a big hug? Was Oro in a state of shock just like she was? Starting to squirm, Lily realized that she might have overreacted. Gazing up into the clear but cold blue sky, she rather regretted her decision not to go walking in the country with Oro; it was the perfect day for it, and after all the stresses and strains of the week it would be a joy to stretch her legs and breathe in fresh country air.

Too late now, she thought to herself.

When she turned the corner of her street on the Bell Works site, Lily caught her breath; Oro sitting on the doorstep of Prefab No. 8 was the last thing she expected to see.

Before she could stop herself, she called out in delight, 'ORO!'

Jumping to his feet, he responded with equal pleasure, 'LILLEE!'

Approaching him shyly, Lily's heart contracted when she saw the look of doubt and uncertainty in his green eyes, wondering if her own eyes reflected the same emotions.

She searched for the right words to say. Finding none, she just stuttered, 'I, er . . . I . . . ?'

Grabbing her hands in his, Oro squeezed them hard. '*Ukochana*, darling, I am so sorry.'

Throwing him a shy smile, Lily exclaimed, 'Oh, me too, Oro, I'm really sorry.'

Hugging each other in relief, they both smiled as happiness replaced anxiety.

'I said everything wrong way round,' he blurted out. 'I should start with the thrill of seeing you fly solo, but truth is I was full with fear, *ukochana*, dearest, I thought you would die, and I would lose the wonderful girl that I love.'

Lily's heart lurched. Had Oro, while apologizing, admitted that he was in love with her?

'And I got the wrong end of the stick,' she willingly admitted. 'I thought you disapproved of my actions because I wasn't experienced enough,' she honestly admitted.

Equally honest, Oro added, 'I would say in truth that you were not ready to fly solo, but maybe I was wrong.' He shrugged. 'From what I see you do, your descent and landing they were good. I was in shock, thinking how you got up there in first place.'

At which point Lily burst out laughing. 'Sweetheart, how I got up there shocked me too.' Cuddling close to him, Lily stood on her tiptoes to reach up and kiss his cheek.

Running his hands through her lustrous blonde hair, Oro sighed. 'Oh, my sweet Lillee,' he murmured into her hair. 'Let's forget this fighting and go for walk,' he suggested. 'I have car –' he nodded in the direction of an old jeep parked close by – 'let's go walking in hills and spend day together.'

Kissing his warm lips, Lily smiled. 'I can't think of anything nicer.'

On the drive over to Matlock, Lily asked Oro how he had managed to get hold of a jeep and the petrol that was in the tank.

'We can use Jeep if we request and give good notice, the petrol comes with a bit of exchanges.'

'Wheeler-dealing!' Lily laughed.

Nodding, he grinned. 'Schnapps in exchange for few cigarettes, that kind of thing.'

'Well, I'm very grateful.' She smiled as she reached out to take his free hand. 'It's a real pleasure to be out in the country.'

'I feel same thing,' he agreed. 'I always see rolling green hills and English countryside from high up in the sky; today we will walk the lovely green hills and breathe good fresh air.'

They fell silent as they drove through narrow winding lanes flanked with hedges, spiky and bare, devoid of their summer colours. Grateful that the day was dry and clear, they enjoyed the wild landscape unfolding before them. When they reached Matlock, Oro didn't stop in the fine grey-slate town but carried on driving.

'I have surprise for you,' he told Lily with a wink.

'You're full of surprises,' she answered, giving him a teasing smile.

When Oro brought the car to a halt at the base of a majestic castle adorned with flamboyant towers, turrets and battlements, Lily gasped in delight.

'Riber Castle,' Oro announced as he leapt out of the car and opened the door for Lily.

Grabbing a rucksack from the back of the jeep, Oro slung it over his shoulder. Then, with one arm wrapped around Lily's slender waist, he led her along the track that led up the grassy mound to the castle.

In a sheltered spot under one of the towers Oro set down his rucksack from which he took out a picnic blanket, a Thermos flask and several parcels.

'I bring picnic to eat here.'

Delighted by his thoughtfulness, Lily quickly helped him spread the blanket on the ground. She watched, completely fascinated, as he unfolded several little parcels all carefully wrapped in brown paper.

'Some special Polish salami . . .' he said as he laid his offerings out on the picnic blanket, 'Polish black bread, pickles and good strong Polish coffee.'

'Where did all this come from?' delighted Lily asked.

'Poland, of course – food parcels from home,' Oro proudly announced.

Sitting side by side, out of the cold wind, they shared the wholesome food, which Lily loved.

'The salami is so delicious; I've never tried anything quite so tasty before.'

'It goes well with bread and pickles,' Oro said appreciatively as he laid several slices of salami on his thick wedge of black bread. 'These pickles are from home, from my mother's kitchen,' he said, with a catch in his voice.

'You must miss her,' Lily said softly.

'I miss all of my family very much,' he admitted. 'One day, when this war is over, I hope you will meet them.'

Replete with good food, they leant against the tower wall to sip the sweet black coffee that Oro had brought in the Thermos.

'Try bit of this,' he said, with a mischievous glint in his eye as he produced a miniature bottle from his uniform pocket and poured a splash of liquid into Lily's black coffee. 'Schnapps, from apples and pears.'

Taking a sip, Lily gasped as an explosion of fire went off in her mouth.

'Hah! It's strong.'

'Very strong,' he agreed as he took a gulp from the bottle. 'Warms the body.' He laughed as he drew her close and held her in the fold of his arms.

Happy and relieved that they were close again, Lily murmured, 'Oh, Oro, I'm so sorry for upsetting you.'

'Lillee, there is something I have to tell you, to explain my feelings – why I was so upset yesterday.'

Holding her breath, Lily nervously wondered what he was going to say next. When he did start to speak, he took her breath away.

'My sweet Lillee, I am so proud of you. I see how good you are . . . natural, you say.'

Feeling self-conscious, Lily took a cautious little sip of the mixture of coffee and schnapps in her Thermos cup.

'I never thought to see you fly so soon. I was scared, and also very, very guilty – because of me and what I had done, teaching you, I believe I could have killed you.'

Seeing his stricken face, Lily protested. 'It was nothing to do with you, darling, it was my choice that I agreed to Geraldine's request. Without your tuition I could never have done such a thing.'

'And this was my problem – that *I* taught you to fly,' he added. 'Maybe next time, I will be ready, but first time was troubling.' He shook his head in disbelief.

'I think we both overreacted, for different reasons,' she agreed. 'But look, we're here now, happy together, let's enjoy this precious time.'

Nodding vigorously, Oro replied, 'Yes! But promise you will let me give you more flying lessons before you go up again with Geraldine woman?' he begged.

'Of course,' she cried. 'I would really appreciate all the extra help I can get.'

'Good,' he said, with a teasing smile. 'Because your landing was bit on wobbly side!'

36. Bedtime Stories

After weeks of worrying about not hearing from Frank, Jeannie was thrilled when a backlog of letters arrived.

'Just like buses,' Lily grinned. 'You wait for hours, then three turn up all at the same time.'

'I don't care,' said Jeannie as she hugged the letters even before she opened them. 'Not hearing anything since his leave ended, I thought he might have gone off me.'

'Gone off a sweet lady like you!' Lily scoffed. 'Don't be daft!'

'I'm not good-looking like you, Lily,' Jeannie modestly pointed out. 'I don't have fellas chasing after me, and to be honest I've never been that bothered – well, not until now. But I do like Frank – even though I've only met him twice,' she smiled.

Gazing at the clutch of letters gripped in her hand, Lily smiled back.

'Going off how many letters you've got there, I'd say that he likes you too.'

Later that day, it was Lily who suggested that Ruby and Archie join the welcoming party at the station when Edna returned to Hucknall with Kathleen.

'Edna's always telling us how much Kathleen loves babies,' she pointed out. 'Seeing Archie in his pram on the platform when she gets off the train might make Kathleen feel more at home.'

'That's not a bad idea,' Jeannie agreed. 'That's if Ruby can spare the time to join us.'

So, when Edna stepped off the train on a dank November Sunday morning, holding her daughter's hand firmly in her own, she was thrilled to see her friends gathered on the platform, all waving and smiling as she approached.

'How lovely to see you all!' she cried. Peering down at Kathleen, wrapped up warm in her brown tweed coat and with a ruby-red beret pulled down over her tumbling dark-brown curls, Edna smiled. 'Say hello to my daughter, Kathleen.'

Before either Ruby or Jeannie could say a word, Kathleen boldly took a step towards Archie's big Silver Cross pram.

'BABY!' she exclaimed.

'Baby Archie,' Ruby said.

Lifting the gurgling baby boy from his cosy covers, Ruby bounced him on her hip.

'Archie . . .' Kathleen said as she took hold of his chubby hands.

In response Archie tried to nibble her fingernails, which made Kathleen giggle.

'Shall we put baby back in the pram, and then we can all walk home together?' Ruby suggested.

'I used to sit in Charlie's pram,' Kathleen remembered.

'She likes riding in prams,' Edna smiled.

'You can sit in Archie's pram,' Ruby volunteered. 'I'll put him at the top and you can sit at the bottom with your legs over the end of the pram. Would you like that?'

'Yes, please,' Kathleen nodded.

Once the children were safely installed in the old capacious pram, Ruby set off walking with Jeannie and Edna.

'How was it, leaving Kendal?' Jeannie enquired.

Dropping her voice, Edna answered, 'Better than I thought, actually. Kathleen was so excited about the train journey, she didn't make too much of a fuss about saying goodbye to Charlie. Seeing you waiting for us with little Archie was a stroke of genius,' she added gratefully.

'It was Lily's idea in the first place,' Jeannie told her. 'She's back at the prefab, getting everything ship-shape for you and Kathleen – she can't wait to see you.'

It was lovely and warm in the prefab's big main room. Thoughtful Lily had lit a fire and spread the table with a bright cloth on top of which was a vase of evergreen branches and a little china plate piled with a few boiled sweets and some date biscuits.

'This is where you're going to live, darling,' Edna said as she led her daughter into the prefab. 'Here's your bedroom,' she added as she showed Kathleen a little truckle bed covered with a bright quilted bedspread. 'Here's your bed – and this is Mummy's,' she said, patting her own narrow single bed. 'We'll be cosy and close every night at bedtime.'

Sitting solemnly on her own bed, Kathleen asked, 'Where's Archie's cot?'

'Archie lives with his mummy in another house very close by,' Edna explained. 'He goes to your nursery, so you'll see him every day. Come on,' she urged as she held out her hand. 'Let's go and see what he's up to now.'

They found little Archie on his tummy struggling to sit up on a blanket in the sitting room. Kathleen immediately hunkered down with the little boy and proceeded to play with him and his toys, while Lily passed around welcome cups of tea to Edna, Jeannie and Ruby.

'Thanks for making everything so welcoming, Lily,' Edna said as she sipped only water. 'Kathleen's so excited about her new home – and to have Archie to play with on her first day here is a real treat.'

Noticing the strain on Edna's face, Ruby asked, 'How are you feeling, sweetheart?'

'Not great,' Edna sighed. 'But at least we made it; now I can get Kathleen settled into a new routine. With Archie around she might not pine so much for her little pal, Charlie.'

'Picking up from nursery and getting back home after a long shift is hard work to start with,' Ruby warned. 'But at least you're on-site, and you don't have to walk back home through Hucknall every night.'

'And we can do some pick-ups once Kathleen's got used to us,' Jeannie generously offered.

'It's all going to work out,' Lily assured Edna, who didn't look convinced.

In a low whispered aside Edna groaned, 'If only I wasn't in the family way. I should be dancing around, jumping for joy that everything's worked out and I've finally got my Kathleen here with me. Instead, I'm worried sick. Wondering how we're going to manage – and how in God's name I'm ever going to explain my condition to my husband.'

Wishing that Edna had thought of this before she met her Canadian airman, Lily kept her mouth firmly shut. It was too late now to turn back the clock; Edna's predicament would only get worse as the months passed. The best they could do was keep their promise and support their friend through the hard times that lay ahead. Nevertheless, Lily couldn't help but reproach herself. She had stuck her neck out, right at the beginning, when Edna – wild with excitement about 'a new lease of life' – had cheated on her husband. But Lily's judgemental remarks had backfired and Edna had taken offence. Now, with the knowledge of hindsight, Lily chastised herself for not sticking to her principles. But would it have helped to chastise Edna further? Lily wondered. Would she have pursued Ken and a fantasy relationship anyway? If she had carried on criticizing Edna's immoral behaviour, they would certainly have fallen out, which would have made life uncomfortable in their shared prefab. But wasn't discomfort a small price to pay in comparison with what Edna was going through now?

Edna had been so reckless, so determined, Lily recalled. I probably couldn't have stopped it, she thought, but maybe I should have tried a lot harder.

Dragging herself back to the here and now, Lily heard Ruby (who hadn't seen her husband, George, in months) ask, 'Is Jack due home on leave soon?'

'No, thank God!' Edna exclaimed. 'It's awful of me to be even thinking that way, but it's the truth. I know I'm going to have to face reality soon enough, but I'm holding off the awful day for as long as possible.' Feeling a little hand reaching out for her, Edna turned to smile at Kathleen.

'Mummy, can we go and feed the ducks with Archie?'

Feeling like she had barely got the strength to stand up, never mind go walking around Hucknall town centre, Edna smiled feebly.

Ruby saw her weary expression and quickly volunteered. 'Why don't we leave Mummy here to unpack while you, me and Archie go for a walk instead?'

'Yes, please,' Kathleen said, with an eager smile.

*

The days that followed in Prefab No. 8 took on a whole new pattern after Kathleen's arrival. Up an hour earlier than usual, Edna helped her daughter to get dressed, then they would set off for nursery, often with Edna piggy-backing Kathleen if the little girl was sleepy. Luckily, Edna didn't have to bother about preparing breakfast as the nursery provided a wholesome meal for the children on their arrival. Remarkably, Kathleen didn't make too much fuss when it came to mother and daughter saying their farewells; as long as she had a friend to take her mind off the leave-taking, she seemed perfectly content. This was a huge relief for Edna, who continued to suffer from dreadful morning sickness. Very often, Ruby and Edna would walk in the early dawn light across the site to the Bell Works, after dropping off their charges. Ruby's expert advice comforted Edna when she felt nervous and guilty about leaving her daughter.

'I feel terrible when I have to shake her awake and make her get up in the dark,' she fretted. 'She's so good, rarely complains, but when I think what a happy little life she must have had up in Kendal, rolling out of bed whenever she woke up, then sitting down for a nice hot breakfast – instead of being lugged across a chilly factory yard as dawn is breaking.'

'The most important thing, Edna, is that she has *you*,' Ruby insisted. 'Nobody can replace a mother.'

'And I'm so happy to have Kathleen here, but her life in Kendal was a lot more relaxed and secure. Then there's the baby, that's bound to turn her world upside down before very long.'

Ruby nodded. 'Obviously, you've not told her yet?'

Edna quickly shook her head. 'No, I'll wait till I start to show, then I'll try to explain what's happening.'

'And when the baby's born?' Ruby gently enquired.

'God knows . . .' Edna sighed. 'Lily insists we can all live together in the prefab, but really, two kiddies in such a small space, not to mention all the washing and clutter that goes with having a new-born. You know what Lily is like, generous to a fault, she says we can manage, but she hasn't a clue what's up ahead. A baby in the house will have a massive impact on her life too. It's just not fair.'

'You know Lily,' Ruby said fondly. 'She has a heart of gold.'

Dropping her voice, Edna added in a confidential whisper, 'Actually, I've been thinking about having this baby adopted.'

Knowing adoption would have been the very last thing she would have wanted when she was pregnant, Ruby waited for Edna to continue.

'It's an awful thing to say, but I feel nothing for this baby,' Edna blurted out. 'When I was expecting Kathleen I was so excited, but this pregnancy is different. I'm just worried sick all the time.'

Seeing her friend's agonized expression, Ruby soothed, 'One step at a time, dear. You've got a bit of time to consider future plans.'

Edna nodded in agreement. 'It's good to actually voice what I've been thinking about,' she confessed.

'You can talk to me any time, you know that,' Ruby smiled. 'Now, come on – let's grab a cuppa and some toast before the hooter goes off.'

*

Fortunately, as time passed, Edna was able to tolerate tea, but she very quickly became uncomfortable and awkward in the confined quarters of a Spitfire's fuselage. By the end of the day, her back felt like it would break, and the weight of the drill or the riveting gun, held at awkward angles for hours on end, brought on cramps that had her doubled over in pain.

Picking up Kathleen, usually at the same time that Ruby was picking up Archie, was the very best time of the day. She loved to see her bright-eyed daughter racing up the corridor to greet her; the warm smell of her daughter when she bent down to hug her, and the feel of soft kisses on her cheeks – they were all new and joyful experiences. Often Kathleen would have a little gift for her mother – a crayoned drawing of Edna, or a painting of a dog or a cow, or sometimes (if the group had been baking) a little jam tart or a gingerbread man. These were precious little gifts, given with great love and pride.

Walking home on the dark winter nights, hand in hand, with Kathleen chattering non-stop as she skipped along beside her mother, they would catch up with each other's day. Who Kathleen had played with, what she'd had for a snack, who she'd sat next to at dinner time, and which nursery rhymes she liked best. After tea, while Edna washed up, Kathleen would snuggle up with either Lily or Jeannie and ask for a story before bedtime. There were no picture books in the prefab – and though Edna planned to buy some, she hadn't had a free moment to go into Nottingham to choose some books with Kathleen. Luckily, it turned out that Jeannie was a natural-born storyteller, and as it was approaching Christmas, she started making up charming little stories about Father Christmas's elves working in Toyland preparing presents for children all over the world.

Wide-eyed with wonder, Kathleen gasped, 'Will Father Christmas bring me a new dolly, Jeannie?'

Realizing the amount of hardship they were all facing, and how every child this Christmas would be suffering as a consequence of rationing and lack of cash, Jeannie back-pedalled.

'He'd like to, sweetie, but it's a difficult time for everybody, even in Toyland they're cutting back this year,' she explained.

It broke Jeannie's heart to see Kathleen's hopeful expression fade.

'So, I can't have a dolly with long curly hair?'

'I'm sure he'll bring you a nice big surprise,' Jeannie promised.

Afterwards, Jeannie apologized to Edna, 'I shouldn't have gone and mentioned Christmas so soon, getting Kathleen's hopes up like that, she was really excited.'

'Christmas is on the horizon, after all; we can't dodge that bullet, even though we've got nothing much to offer,' Edna said glumly. 'Hell fire, the way the war's going at the moment, we'll be lucky if we're not invaded before Christmas.'

'Don't be like that, Edna,' Lily pleaded. 'You know what they say: don't panic – and carry on.'

'Aye, I know it all right, it's putting it into practice that's the hard bit. But,' she said as she threw back her shoulders, 'I'll do my best to make my little girl's Christmas a happy one. She deserves it, poor mite, and it's not like it's her fault that there's a world war raging.'

*

Lily and Edna were astonished when, night after night, Kathleen curled up in a sleepy bundle on Jeannie's lap, listening to made-up story after story.

'How do you do it? I could sit and listen to you all day,' Edna exclaimed.

Jeannie gave a modest little shrug.

'My Irish grandma was a natural storyteller. She was never taught to read – was barely educated, in fact – but, my God, she could reel off tale after tale. Some were folklore and fairy tales, others she just made up.'

'So, she taught you?' Edna asked.

'Well, it wasn't exactly teaching, more an inherited gift. I always loved her stories and remembered them, then I started to make up my own stories, for my nephew and nieces. I like reading children's fairy tales too, though some would scare the pants off little Kathleen,' she smiled. 'I modify them, to make them entertaining rather than terrifying.'

'Well, I'm impressed,' Edna conceded. 'As you say, it really is a gift.'

Looking a little embarrassed, Jeannie said, 'Frank's been an influence too.'

Surprised by her comment, Lily asked, 'Really? Considering you barely know him, how has that come about?'

'He's such a good storyteller,' Jeannie said proudly. 'He tells me funny stories about his friends, which make me laugh. Recently, I've plucked up the courage to write my own funny stories about us engine girls.'

'God help us!' Edna exclaimed.

'It's all good fun, nothing serious, or personal, a bit like a diary,' Jeannie hurriedly told her. 'I really love writing to Frank, I only hope he enjoys writing to me too.'

Kathleen was certainly enjoying Jeannie's bedtime stories. Every night, spellbound by Jeannie's magic storytelling skills, she asked for one or more stories before she went to bed. While Jeannie entertained the sleepy little girl with the adventures of Snow White or Sleeping Beauty, or other more original stories, Lily and Edna would slip into the freezing-cold kitchen to tidy up. When the clock struck seven, Edna would scoop her daughter off to bed.

'Say goodnight to Jeannie and Lily,' she'd whisper.

Removing her thumb from her mouth, Kathleen would whisper, 'Night night, God bless.'

When they were left alone, one typically cold November evening, Jeannie and Lily caught up with each other's news.

'So, how is your nice young man?' Lily asked.

Jeannie gave a fond smile. 'He writes every week, without fail, and I write every other day if I've time,' she replied.

'Heavens!' Lily laughed. 'Is there enough to write about every other day? It's not like we do much more than go to work and come back again.'

Jeannie gave a self-conscious smile. 'There is, now I'm making up stories to entertain him.'

Curious, Lily asked, 'What do you write about?'

'Like I told you, I write about us girls, and Sid and Annie too. Sometimes I don't even have to make things up, I just recount events that happen at work. I try to weave them all together in a cheerful and humorous way, nothing too gloomy – them lads over there have got enough on their plate. Frank insists it cheers his mates up. I didn't even know he was reading my stories to his pals,' she blushed.

'If they're as entertained by your storytelling as we are, I don't think for a minute that Frank is just being polite,' Lily insisted.

Giggling, Jeannie continued, 'Frank says he'd rather read my engine girl stories than have somebody playing a harmonica badly, right in his ear.'

Struck by an unexpected thought, Lily's bright silver eyes suddenly flew wide open.

'Jeannie, I've got an idea – you should write a book!'

'Don't be daft,' Jeannie scoffed. 'I'm not a writer. That's only for clever folk.'

'Absolute nonsense! You make up wonderful stories – entertaining troops and children alike. It's an amazing gift, lovie. Don't knock it.'

Jeannie gave a dismissive shrug.

'It's now't really, just a bit of fun.'

Determined not to be fobbed off, Lily exclaimed, 'Jeannie, if ever there was a time for finding happiness in unexpected places, this is it! Life's grim but we can still dream. Look at me – a waitress from Whitby who has learnt to fly. The world is not the same place that it was when war broke out, everything's been turned upside down. Why shouldn't you write stories, especially if it's in your genes?'

Now thoroughly embarrassed, Jeannie tried to change the subject. 'Let's see how it goes.'

Thoroughly galvanized, Lily persisted. 'Lovie, if I can fly, you can write!'

37. Tobruk

Ruby was also busy writing, not stories but letters, to her beloved husband, George, who she believed was waiting to be sent overseas. Like thousands of other wartime wives she was familiar with often erratic wartime postings; nevertheless, she became worried when weeks had passed and there was still no word from her husband. When she finally received a strange-looking blue triangular-shaped letter, Ruby's heart plummeted. Having never seen one like it before, her hands began to tremble. Was this a missive bearing bad news?

Hardly daring to breathe, Ruby ripped the blue envelope open and started to read George's dramatic news.

Darling, please don't be alarmed by this 'bluey' sent to you from overseas. It might be unfamiliar to you, but 'blueys' (a nickname used by the lads over here) are the Army Field Post Office's standard stationery.

Clutching the letter, Ruby fell on to the nearest kitchen chair.

'OVERSEAS! Oh my God, no,' she gasped.

All through the year there had been ongoing news of fighting from North Africa. Tobruk, a deep-water port in Eastern Libya – essential for the Axis advance on Alexandria and Suez – had recently been wrested from the Italians. As if anticipating his wife's alarmed response, George wrote of his recent overseas posting.

I'm so sorry for the long delay between our letters, you must be worried sick. I would have told you of our new posting, but we had no idea until it was sprung upon us by the powers that be. Suddenly, our regiment was shipped out overnight to Liverpool, from where we sailed to Tobruk via Durban in South Africa. What a wonderful place Durban is, perfect climate, sunny, with beautiful scenery – you could almost forget there was a war on. We had a terrible sea passage to Durban! Not only were we seasick in that leaky old tub we sailed in, we also had U-boats on our tail and the threat of aerial bombing. We were so grateful to drop anchor and walk on solid land once more. Unfortunately, there was no time for hanging about sunning ourselves, or even a minute to pen a letter, it was a quick turn-around, with hundreds of troops once again boarding ships – some, like me, directed to the Western Desert while others went the other way, to Singapore.

I tell you, we hit the ground running on arrival here. We're under constant artillery and air bombardment. And as if that weren't enough, the heat is stifling, there's sand where you thought it never could go, snakes, fleas, flies and scorpions. But at least we're alive. I'll never complain about rain again. Supplies of food and water aren't plentiful, but morale is high. The Ozzie fellas fighting alongside us are a laugh a minute, they seem to be better at coping with the heat than us Brits and always look on the bright side of life. We all take heart and are proud that we're holding a vital stronghold that the Germans desperately want to secure.

My other news, sweetheart, is that now we're posted over here we won't be leaving in a rush. The leave we were counting on has been withdrawn, so we're all a bit down in the mouth about not getting

*home and seeing our families as we were expecting at Christmas time.
I was bitterly disappointed when we were informed, I'd give anything
to be with my little son when he opens his eyes on Christmas morning.*

*Enough of me, my sweet, how are you and my little boy? I miss
you both like an ache, some days. I look at Archie's photo, crumpled
from being in my uniform pocket – khaki desert combat drill, these
days. His image is faded with the kisses I give him every night before
I turn in, usually praying that I won't be bitten by a scorpion or a
rattlesnake. I kiss your picture too, my gorgeous girl, with the beautiful radiant smile and wonderful big blue eyes. I have only to think
of your long silky brunette hair and I go weak at the knees – you
are the most beautiful girl in the world, I can't believe you agreed to
marry me. With your looks you could have married a prince.*

*Though there's not much time for daydreaming over here, I do
occasionally think of home – of Hucknall, the local pub, the high
street, the picture house, and the lovely hills outside the town where we
did most of our courting. I tell you, sweetheart, it seems like another
world, literally half the world away from this wild desert landscape
littered with bombed-out rusted vehicles and shattered weaponry.
Now that I'm here, and not in transit, I'll be able to write to you
more. Try not to worry, my dearest love. 'We'll Meet Again', as
Vera Lynn says, the day can't come soon enough.*

*Your adoring husband,
George*

Folding up George's love letter, Ruby wiped tears from
her eyes. She'd dreamt of waking up beside her husband
in their big double bed on Christmas morning, with Archie
tucked in between them, opening little stockings contain-
ing simple gifts. Even cooking a meal together would be

a joy; nothing as fancy as turkey or a joint, just a meat pie and roast potatoes accompanied with a few bottles of beer would be a feast these days. Anything shared with George was a joy, but now even that fantasy was gone. And how could she even think of complaining? Not with her husband and his regiment now posted to the Western Desert, surviving on poor rations and living in intense heat. Oh, but how she yearned for George; to be held in his arms once more, to feel safe and secure, protected and loved, to have a shoulder to cry on, and a man she could cuddle up to at night and enjoy the pleasures of the marriage bed with. Like every woman in the land she put on a brave face, maintained a stiff upper lip, and just had to keep carrying on. Or, as cheeky Edna put it, 'Keep buggering on!'

'I am so sick of this blasted war,' Ruby said.

She carefully folded up her first bluey from the African desert. Standing up tall, she straightened her shoulders.

'If George can do it, so can I,' she said, through gritted teeth, before she walked into the kitchen where her mother was feeding Archie boiled eggs and soldiers.

Later that day, seeing Ruby unusually quiet in the ladies' changing rooms, Audrey in her usual direct manner asked, 'What's up, mi duck?'

Too miserable to choose her words carefully, Ruby blurted out, 'George is in Tobruk – and he's not going to be home for Christmas, which is what we've all been hoping and praying for.'

Halting midway in knotting her green spotted turban, Audrey gaped at her friend. 'Hell fire, there was I thinking he was still stationed somewhere in England.'

'Me too,' Ruby answered glumly as she stepped into her huge heavy boots. 'Africa's the new front; a lot of troops are being deployed over there these days.'

'Actually,' Audrey added thoughtfully, 'Jeannie was talking about her young man going to Tobruk, you should have a word with her.'

Hours later, during their afternoon break, Ruby caught up with Jeannie and Edna over a cup of tea.

'Audrey tells me that your young man might be in Tobruk, where my husband has just been posted,' Ruby started.

'To be honest, I've not known Frank long,' Jeannie admitted. 'He was fighting in France, evacuated from Dunkirk; then in recent weeks he thought his regiment would be posted to North Africa.'

'One picnic after another,' Edna grimly joked. 'Poor sods, what they must have endured.'

Producing George's odd-shaped triangular blue letter from the pocket of her dungarees, Ruby asked, 'Have you had one of these from your Frank? This one took me quite by surprise.'

Looking carefully at the flimsy blue envelope, Jeannie shook her head. 'I've never seen an envelope like that in my life.'

'George tells me they're called "blueys",' Ruby explained.

Curious, Jeannie asked, 'When did you get it?'

'Only this morning,' Ruby replied. 'After weeks of hearing nothing, it finally arrived.'

'I've not heard a word from Frank since he wrote about his possible posting overseas,' Jeannie told her. 'How is your husband?' she thoughtfully asked.

'Hot, hungry and homesick,' Ruby smiled. 'But you know, bearing up, making the most of it.'

Edna shook her head. 'You wonder how our lads do it, with that terrible heat and not enough water – not to mention the enemy bombing raids.'

'They're brave lads,' Ruby said proudly.

Blushing, Jeannie suddenly asked, 'I wonder, when you next write to your husband, could you ask him if the Lancashire Regiment have landed? It would be a huge relief to know that Frank's regiment have arrived safe and sound.' Looking concerned, she added, 'What's odd is that Frank's normally a good letter writer; since we first met, we've kept up a constant stream of letters. I even write him stories about our daily life here in the Bell Works, just little anecdotes he reads out loud to amuse his mates when there's nothing else to do. It's a bit of a jolly ongoing thing between us. I still write stories for Frank,' she sighed wistfully, 'in the hope that whenever he gets them, wherever he might be, he'll have something to entertain him. I hope to God he does . . .' her voice drifted.

'It is a worry, not knowing where they are,' Edna agreed. 'I'm beginning to wonder if my husband might be on the move too. He's a terrible letter-writer – last time I heard from him, he was waiting to be posted overseas. If your two fellas are anything to go by, and North Africa is the new front line, my husband could be on a troop ship heading out there too.'

'Well, at least we know that Ruby's husband has landed safely,' Jeannie said warmly. 'Maybe we'll have news soon too, Edna.'

Falling quiet, Ruby recalled George's words.

It was a quick turn-around, with hundreds of troops once again boarding ships – some, like me, directed to the Western Desert while others went the other way, to Singapore.

With a sinking heart, Ruby wondered if Jeannie's boyfriend's regiment had in fact been directed the other way, to Singapore? If that was the case, Jeannie might not hear from Frank for quite some time. But, Ruby cautioned herself, she definitely wasn't going to mention that to Jeannie now. If Frank was in a Far Eastern location, even further away than North Africa, news would probably travel very slowly; she'd keep her fingers crossed that Jeannie would hear something from her boyfriend very soon, hopefully before Christmas.

38. The Ramsholt

True to his word, Oro arranged another flight in his Tiger Moth for Lily.

'You're the pilot – you're going to do everything,' he told her. 'I'll be the passenger; I don't expect to use the controls. If you plan to be a ferry girl, then you must take total responsibility.'

Giving a brisk nod, Lily didn't argue. Though still nervous, she drew confidence from the fact that she had been taught to fly by an experienced pilot and she had (miraculously!) managed her first solo flight thanks to Geraldine's calm tutoring. Though it hadn't been text-book perfect, she had nevertheless accomplished the mission and got back safely to tell the story. Not only was she eager for more flying experience, she also wanted to demonstrate to Oro that she had made progress and was a competent pilot. Gazing up at Oro's fragile, brightly coloured Tiger Moth, Lily secretly wished it was a Spitfire. In truth, right now she would have preferred to be settling down in the bucket seat of a Spitfire, rather than sitting behind Oro in the Tiger Moth's pilot seat – but this she kept tactfully to herself.

Zipping up the bulky flying jacket that Oro had provided, Lily chatted to Steve.

'Several little birds have told me that you got your flying colours recently,' he chuckled.

Throwing a brief glance towards Oro, who was chatting with one of the other mechanics, Lily put a cautionary finger to her lips.

'Shhh,' she smiled, 'I was in Oro's bad books for a while.'

Steve handed Lily her goggles and a leather helmet.

'Not for long, miss,' he grinned. 'The boss was in a state of shock when he got back here after seeing you land a Spitfire, but he got over it.'

Lily gave a sheepish grin.

'It was a very wobbly landing, even though I tried my best to keep the runway in line with the aircraft, the wretched wind blew me all over the place.'

Steve gave a non-committal shrug.

'These things happen when you're dealing with the elements, miss. Heck, it could have been worse – an easterly wind combined with ice on the runway wouldn't have been much fun. Anyway, I can tell you that the boss, after he'd talked to the chaps in the clearance tower – who told him you'd handled the flights pretty well, given the circumstances – he was proud as Punch of his girlfriend.'

'Let's hope I handle myself even better today,' Lily beamed.

Gazing up at the cold blue winter sky, Steve gave an experienced nod.

'Good day for flying, miss.' Seeing Oro approaching, he called out, 'All set, sir?'

'You should be asking the lady that question,' Oro grinned. 'She's flying today, I'm just the passenger.'

Realizing that Oro was making a point, Lily grinned back.

'I'm all set, Steve, just give me a minute to sort myself out.'

'No problem, miss, I'll swing the propeller and shift the chocks when you're good to go.'

Turning to Oro, Lily asked, 'One very important question – where are we going?'

'I thought we would repeat your flight with Geraldine. It might be less terrifying second time,' he smiled mischievously.

A wave of relief washed over Lily; knowing the terrain and waypoints, not to mention the location of the Woodbridge base, immediately made her feel more relaxed.

'Good idea,' she agreed.

Climbing into the cockpit, Lily settled into her seat and quickly belted up before studying the map for all the familiar waypoints. When she was ready, she gave Steve the thumbs up and he manually started the aircraft before removing the chocks. Rolling out of the bay and heading for the runway, Lily was concentrating hard on all the manoeuvres, barely aware of Oro in the seat in front of her, and though their headsets were connected, Oro remained silent and didn't offer advice. After getting the green light clearance signal from the control tower, Lily started to taxi. Then, as the air speed rapidly increased, she applied the throttle; feeling the wind biting her face and her hands growing numb with cold, Lily thundered down the runway gathering momentum. As the engine power surged, she pulled back hard on the joystick and took the aircraft up.

She gained height, skimming briefly over muddy fields, and though high on adrenalin she focused on keeping a straight course east. Checking her air speed and position on the map, Lily made out the waypoints she had flown over with Geraldine as her guide. Glad that she was below cloud level and therefore able to recognize familiar landmarks – church spires, winding riverbeds and railway junctions – Lily maintained her course eastwards. When the sprawling Suffolk forests and the vast sweep of criss-crossing estuaries and stretches of marshland loomed into view, Lily made a smooth turn; as she did so, the horizon tilted and then levelled out as she positioned the Spitfire in line with the runway. When she got clearance from the Woodbridge control tower, Lily gripped the joystick and started to make her descent. Gradually dropping height, she kept the aircraft level with the fast-approaching runway. As the aircraft landed, she braked hard and actually smiled to herself as it came to a halt.

When the roar of the engine fell silent, Oro's words through her headset were music to her ears.

'Very well done, pilot.'

After a safe landing, Oro yet again surprised Lily by suggesting they go for a walk before making the return flight home to Hucknall.

Glancing at her little silver wristwatch, Lily asked, 'Have we time? You know how quickly it gets dark at this time of the year.'

'We've got time,' he replied. 'There is something I would like you to see.'

Leaving the airfield, they threaded their way along winding sandy paths through a deep forest thick with ancient yews and young pine trees. They walked in deep silence, broken only by the stirring of the wind soughing through the treetops and the noisy cackle of pheasants running as they broke for cover.

Intrigued, Lily asked, 'How did you find this place?'

'I told you, when is possible, I like to walk after flying.'

Lily nodded. 'You said it relaxes you. But seriously, I don't know how you find the time.'

Grinning, he turned to her. 'I'm an adventurer,' he teased. 'No, really, I like to explore the places I go to, when I have the chance to do so. Sometimes on a late-night flight to Woodbridge I stay over. This is time when I go walking, to find new places; Suffolk is very beautiful, peaceful place.'

When they emerged from the deep belt of evergreens that fringed the forest, Lily gasped in wonder.

'Goodness,' she exclaimed as her eyes took in the view laid out before them.

The deep, wide River Deben that swept by Sutton Hoo and then through Woodbridge, now at high tide, was swiftly making its way out into the North Sea. Holding Oro's hand, Lily allowed him to expertly guide her along the stony coastal path, lapped by the cold estuary waters as the tide rushed out. Clambering up a grassy bank, they followed the path that wound its way to an ancient red-brick pub perched on a small mound, well above sea level. In the little quay that nestled below, red-sailed Norfolk wherries bounced on the waves alongside little fishing boats anchored in the bay.

'This is lovely,' Lily exclaimed as she settled on a wooden bench in the pub garden.

'The Ramsholt,' Oro announced. 'Nice Suffolk pub, with very good beer.'

While Oro hurried indoors to fetch some drinks, Lily sat out of the wind and leant back in her seat, giving a deep sigh of happiness. Thank God she and Oro had sorted out their misunderstanding; it had been horrible when they had briefly fallen out, but the squabble had made her realize just how much she cared for her sweet Polish boyfriend, who was always full of surprises. His imaginative excursions, whether to castles or rivers, came out of the blue, delighting her with his boyish sense of adventure.

When Oro reappeared, bearing a tray with two glasses of shandy and a plate of sandwiches, Lily realized that she was starving.

'Crab sandwiches, straight from Felixstowe,' he said as he laid the tray down on the bench. 'Eat, *ukochana*,' he urged.

'Mmm,' Lily murmured as she bit into the homemade bread, thickly spread with fresh tangy crab flakes. 'Delicious!'

Replete with unexpectedly good food, they sat side by side, Lily's head resting on Oro's shoulder, enjoying the wintry sunlight.

'This is good,' he whispered as he pressed her hand in his.

Staring dreamily at the river as it plunged inexorably towards the North Sea, Lily gripped Oro's hand and turned to kiss him softly on the cheek.

'Darling, this is wonderful. So peaceful,' she murmured. 'Who would believe that a war is raging just across the water from us? It seems wrong to be so happy when others aren't as fortunate as we are.'

Nodding, Oro agreed with her sentiments. 'It's true, *ukochana*, my darling, this is special time, like dream.'

Smiling, she cuddled closer to his warm body. 'Thank you for all the special times,' she said softly. 'I hope you never stop surprising me.'

Tilting her small chin so he could look into her upturned face, Oro continued more seriously, 'Lillee, I have news to tell you.'

Feeling her stomach plummet, Lily immediately thought the worst. Was Oro also leaving, like so many other servicemen, to fight in North Africa?

'I've been dispatched to train new recruits,' he told her. 'Secret destination,' he hastily added.

'For how long?' she asked.

Oro shrugged. 'Until job is done. Not long time, I hope,' he said as he threw her a smile that melted her heart. 'Will you wait for me, my Lillee?'

Throwing her arms around his neck, Lily hugged him tightly.

'Of course, my darling boy,' she cried, and she kissed him passionately on the lips. 'Just promise me you'll come back safely – and that you'll come home soon.'

39. S.W.A.L.K.

As Frank's long silence continued, Jeannie, though worried sick, never failed to write to him as often as she could. All of her letters included engine girl stories – which she hoped would entertain Frank and his soldier pals.

'I don't know what you find to entertain him,' Audrey declared one day over their morning break. 'Writing about us lasses must be as interesting as watching paint dry.'

'You wouldn't believe what there is to write about,' Jeannie replied. 'There's always something with a bit of a twist, unexpected news, or a sudden event that might raise a smile.'

Sounding distinctly grumpy, Edna growled, 'I hope you don't go telling him private stuff about us? The last thing I need is for my condition to go public.'

Looking shocked, Jeannie protested, 'Don't be daft, Edna! That's your business and not for me to proclaim,' she remonstrated. 'I just write amusing anecdotes, like the time that new young apprentice was told to go to the warehouse for a left-handed spanner. She was searching all morning until somebody put her out of her misery and let on that we were mucking about, having a laugh at her expense.'

'Hmm, it sounds innocent enough,' Edna conceded. 'But I don't know where you get the time or the energy to write the stuff.'

'In bed at night, or during my time off,' Jeannie explained. 'It entertains me too,' she admitted. 'Takes my mind off the war and the suffering all around us.'

Though Jeannie put on a brave front as the days passed and still there was no word from Frank, her resolve began to weaken. Finding their friend in tears in the ladies' toilets, Ruby and Lily immediately comforted her.

'Is it Frank?' Lily asked as she rocked her sobbing pal in her arms.

Gulping back tears, Jeannie nodded.

'I can't help but think the worst, Lily,' she cried. 'If he'd been sent to North Africa, surely I would have heard something by now? It's not like Frank's bad at keeping in touch, he's a good writer, and regular too.' Shivering in fear, she added in a whisper, 'I *know* in my bones that something is wrong.'

'Can you contact his family?' Lily asked.

Jeannie shook her head. 'No, I have no way of contacting them; we never got close in that way, there wasn't time really. We only met once after the works dance, and then his leave ended. Our relationship grew as we corresponded – we both liked writing and telling each other funny stories. I just wish there'd been time to get to know him a bit better,' Jeannie said as she wiped tears off her cheeks. 'He's such a lovely lad, I just hope and pray he's safe.'

Having held back information previously, Ruby took a deep breath.

'Jeannie,' she started nervously, 'I'm sorry to have to say this, but from what my husband told me in one of his letters, Frank might well have been sent to Singapore.'

'Why do you say that?' Jeannie cried, thoroughly alarmed.

Racking her brains, trying to remember exactly what George had written, Ruby tried to explain. 'George said that when his troop ship docked at Durban, men were dispatched in two directions; one lot went to North Africa while the other lot went to Singapore, which might explain why I've heard from George and you haven't heard from Frank.'

Not certain of the exact geographical location of Singapore, Jeannie muttered, 'Is Singapore much further away?'

'Yes, it's in the Far East,' Ruby replied. Then, in an attempt to comfort Jeannie, she added, even though she wasn't at all sure about the relative efficiency of the Singapore postal service, 'And I'm sure forces' post from over there must be very slow.'

Sighing, Jeannie murmured, 'Singapore . . . poor Frank, I hope he's okay.'

Seeing Jeannie's anguished expression, Lily gave her a warm hug.

'Wherever Frank is, he'll want to hear from you, sweetheart, so you must keep writing to him,' she urged. 'Once you do know where he's stationed, you can send him all your engine girls stories to cheer him up.'

Jeannie gave a weak smile. 'You're right, I'll keep on writing and pray that Frank gets in touch soon.'

The next day, despite no letters having arrived from Frank, to Jeannie's surprise she had an unexpected visitor, a soldier from the Lancashire Regiment, a pal of Frank's who turned up at the Bell Works in the afternoon.

'He's in the entry lobby,' Annie told her. 'He's got a parcel for you. Best take him into the canteen, don't be long.'

Hurrying into the lobby, Jeannie was astonished to see a tall, dark young man wearing black-rimmed glasses waiting for her.

'Sorry to bother you at work, miss,' he said as he shook her hand. 'I'm Eddie Perkins, a friend of Frank's. As I was in the area, I thought it might be a good time to drop off this package.'

Stupefied, Jeannie stared at the brown paper parcel in his hands. 'Who's it from?' she gasped.

'Frank,' he replied.

Fearing the worst, Jeannie went weak at the knees. 'Is he, is he . . . ?'

Holding up a hand, Eddie tried to calm Jeannie.

'As far as I know, he's all right, miss.'

Suddenly frantic, Jeannie cried out, 'Have you heard from him?'

'Yes, in a manner of speaking,' he answered. Seeing the anguished expression on Jeannie's face, he quickly added, 'You see, miss, some of the lads were recently posted to Singapore, and Frank was one of them. I didn't go because of my eyesight,' he said, with a self-deprecating smile. 'I'm presently having a bit of treatment and hoping to join my regiment overseas soon.'

'So, you were sent home when they went?'

'That's correct,' he answered. 'Anyway, Frank left a box of letters when we were clearing the barracks, they're the stories you wrote for him. I know how much he appreciated them, we all did, but there's a weight limit on luggage when you're on the move like he is now. So, not wanting them burnt or destroyed, he asked me to deliver them if I was ever over this way. I live in Yorkshire but I was visiting relatives nearby, so here we are . . .' Smiling shyly, he held out the box. 'You are the writer, they belong to you.'

Feeling tears suddenly pricking the backs of her eyes, Jeannie took the box from his hands. 'Thank you,' she murmured, 'that's very thoughtful of you.'

Seeing his tired face, looking so strained, Jeannie suggested they get a cup of tea in the factory canteen.

'Won't you get into trouble, miss?'

'I'll be all right for ten minutes,' she smiled.

After she had collected two mugs of strong tea and a round of toasted tea cakes with barely a lick of marg, Jeannie hurried to join Eddie at a nearby table.

Without any preamble the young man said, with great enthusiasm, 'Me and the lads used to look forward to hearing your engine girls stories. We called you the "Spitfire Kids",' he chuckled.

Amused, Jeannie chuckled too. 'Nice title,' she grinned.

'You've got a way with words, miss,' he continued shyly. 'You really caught the camaraderie in the factory and the growing sense of fear on the home front; you made us smile with your jolly anecdotes, took our minds off the war.' Smiling, he recalled, 'Sitting in the barracks, lying on our beds with a cup of tea, listening to Frank reading them out loud. He was dead proud of you, miss.'

Blushing with pleasure, Jeannie asked about her young man.

'How was he when you last saw him?'

'Gung-ho, I'd say,' Eddie replied. 'Glad to be seeing a bit

of action. Mind you, the order came out of the blue – it all happened quickly, virtually overnight. I was gutted not to go,' he murmured miserably. 'Damned eyesight's always been a problem, even before the war, when I was working as a postman.'

Behind the thick lenses that he wore Jeannie could see that the kind boy's eyes were a piercing bright blue.

'When does your treatment start?' she enquired.

'It's already started, miss; eye drops and tests to rectify the weakness in my right eye. I just hate being out of action,' he added gloomily.

'With a bit of luck, you might join your mates soon,' she said encouragingly.

'What wouldn't I give to be out there now, alongside my pals in Singapore.'

Feeling a shudder run down her spine, Jeannie resisted saying how lucky Eddie was not to be out there, alongside his pals in Singapore – which, from all the accounts she had read of the Far East, was a really tough posting. Seeing the time on the canteen wall clock, Jeannie hurriedly finished her tea.

'I'd better get a move on,' she murmured.

Rising to his feet, Eddie quickly said, 'Before you go, miss, can I ask if you're still writing your stories?'

Feeling foolish and self-conscious, Jeannie nodded. 'I write them for Frank, for when he comes home,' she said, with an emotional catch in her throat.

'I'm pleased to hear it, miss,' Eddie beamed. 'Like I say, he was dead proud of you, and your stories really cheered us all up, made us laugh out loud at times. That one about the young apprentice and the left-handed spanner was a scream – as if there's any difference! A spanner's a spanner, whether you're left- or right-handed, the tool doesn't change,' he chuckled. 'Keep it up; you might one day find somebody who'd like to publish your Spitfire Kids.'

Liking the sound of Eddie's catchy title, Jeannie nevertheless answered shyly, 'Maybe – though I don't think for a minute I'm up to that standard.'

'Frank never doubted it,' Eddie answered staunchly. 'So why should you?'

After she had said goodbye to Eddie, Jeannie peeped into the box he had left. Catching sight of a letter with Frank's favourite acronym, S.W.A.L.K., on the back, she smiled.

'Sealed with a loving kiss,' she murmured as she ripped open the envelope and read Frank's last letter to her.

My dearest sweetest Jeannie,

I'm snatching a moment to write to you as, all of a sudden, we're being deployed overseas. We've only just been told, so we're all in a flat spin, packing and writing letters home. I'm told it will be a long journey by sea via South Africa, to North Africa or Singapore. Not sure of our destination at this point, but it should be quite an experience. I just hope I don't get too seasick. I even get dizzy on the fairground dodgems! I can't take your precious letters and your lovely stories with me, so I've asked my pal Eddie to keep them safe and deliver them to you when he's over your way.

You have such a gift, a real talent for putting words together, you bring scenes to life so vividly, I almost feel I know your friends at the Bell Works. The lads love hearing about your foreman, Sid, chatting up the ferry girls who knock him off his perch. Cocky devil! They like hearing about Annie too – how she's come around after being such a dragon to start with. I think you're wonderful; please don't stop writing just because I'm going away. Keep up the good work, then I can read all about the Spitfire Kids when I'm back home again.

The sergeant's just walked into the barracks – barking orders as per usual – got to go, my sweet. I'll think of you all the time and carry your stories in my heart.

Your ever-loving, devoted
Frank xxxx

Stifling a sob, Jeannie slipped Frank's letter back into the S.W.A.L.K. envelope. Then, after safely stowing the box in her locker, she dashed back to work before she got a ticking-off from Annie.

After her shift had finished, while Edna was picking up Kathleen from nursery, Jeannie walked back to Prefab No. 8 with Lily. Once home, Lily immediately lit the fire while Jeannie made a pot of tea in the kitchen. The two friends settled down on the sofa before the crackling fire as it gradually warmed up the icy-cold prefab.

'Who was that chap who turned up today?' Lily enquired.

'Eddie Perkins, a friend of Frank's, they're in the same regiment,' Jeannie explained. 'He told me that the Lancashires have been posted to Singapore, nearly all of them. Apart from him, he was kept back for medical reasons,' Jeannie added. 'He brought me all the engine girls stories I've written for Frank; he thought they would get destroyed if they were left in the barracks.'

Seeing Jeannie's sad expression, Lily quickly said, 'That was kind of him. Did he have far to come?'

'He said he was visiting relatives in the area, but I think he might live in Yorkshire. I didn't enquire further,' Jeannie admitted. 'I was in such a state of shock after he told me that Frank had been shipped off to the Far East.'

'It's good to know at last where he's been posted,' Lily insisted.

'So far away from here . . .' Jeannie's voice cracked as she let out all the emotions she had been holding in all afternoon. 'When I saw Eddie, I panicked – I thought he had come with bad news about Frank. I felt myself starting to shake all over, then when he said Frank was all right, and that he had just come to deliver my stories, I thought I was going to faint with relief.' Wiping tears from her cheeks, she added feebly, 'I suppose it explains why I've received no letters from Frank in what feels like ages, at least I know he's not gone off me.'

Lily smiled gently. 'He's too nice a boy to do that, he was smitten the moment he saw you on the dance night.' Sighing, she added, 'We're all waiting to hear from our loved ones – you, Ruby, and now me with Oro.'

'Have you any idea when he'll be back?' Jeannie asked.

Lily shrugged. 'Not a clue. He said he was training recruits, but who knows? He might be in action on a top-secret bombing raid and he's keeping it quiet, for all I know.'

'We're all in the same boat,' Jeannie said miserably. 'Worrying about the men who mean the world to us.'

Lily threw her friend a sympathetic glance. 'Except some of our men are much further away than we thought.'

'The only one of us who's not missing their man is Edna,' Jeannie pointed out. 'And who can blame her, given the circumstances? I still can't believe that horrible Canadian airman has made no contact with her,' she finished crossly. 'Like Edna said, he got what he wanted, he's probably chasing other women by now. Poor Edna,' Jeannie murmured. 'She looks so worn out. What with work and looking after Kathleen – and being pregnant.'

'All we can do is support her and Kathleen as much as we can,' Lily said staunchly.

'Are you enjoying sharing the prefab with her little girl?' Jeannie enquired.

Lily's bright smile lit up her pretty voice. 'Oh, yes, Kathleen's a little poppet. So sweet and chirpy, she's settled in a treat.'

Their conversation was interrupted by Edna and Kathleen arriving home. Rushing to sit between Jeannie and Lily, Kathleen gave them both a hug.

'How was nursery today?' Lily asked the excited little girl.

'We played a game,' Kathleen announced. 'I was the farmer's wife!'

Remembering the children's ring game that she played as a child, Lily started to sing, 'Eee-i adio, the farmer wants a wife.'

'Was that fun?' Jeannie asked.

Kathleen solemnly shook her head. 'The farmer's wife wants a baby – but I *don't* want a baby.'

Catching sight of Edna, who was standing directly behind the sofa on which her daughter was sitting, Lily could see her friend choking up.

'Don't worry,' she whispered to her friend. 'It's only a child's game, Kathleen doesn't mean it.'

Swallowing tears, Edna whispered back, 'But she's right – I don't want a baby either, Lily, especially not this one.'

40. Solo

Lily was delighted when she saw Geraldine in the canteen again, only a few weeks after their first meeting.

'Come and join us,' Geraldine called across the crowded room.

Hurrying over, Lily was introduced to Geraldine's companion, a tall gangly middle-aged woman wearing a flying jacket.

'This is Emily, she's the one that had the fall on the day you stepped into the breach,' Geraldine explained.

'Pleased to meet you,' Lily answered with a warm smile.

Seeing the smartly dressed pilots in their tweed trousers and knitted polo-neck jerseys, Lily suddenly felt self-conscious about her appearance – she was dressed in her habitual dirty, oily dungarees, with big boots and a red spotted turban that was sure to be covered in grease. She hid her grimy hands under the rim of the canteen table.

'Jolly good of you to do the honours when I was out of action,' Emily said in a posh, clipped voice. 'Bally inconvenient, I'm sure. Has to be done, though.'

'I told Emily what a brick you were, going up like that on your first solo flight,' Geraldine explained.

'We've all got to go it alone eventually,' Emily cheerfully continued. 'No point in making a fuss.'

Rather overwhelmed by the visitors' completely gung-ho manner, Lily finally manged to get a word in edgeways.

'What've you been up to recently?' she eagerly asked Geraldine, who was lighting up a cigarette.

'Not supposed to gossip about our sorties,' her new friend said with a wink. 'Let's just say we've been busy delivering all along the east coast.'

'Bloody freezing it's been too,' Emily added. 'Those north-easterly winds are an absolute beast when it comes to landing and take-off. Not to mention the wretched sea mist – ghastly conditions for landing.'

Staring at the visitors, Lily felt a rush of envy. How she wished she could fly on a mission again. She had loved her last flight with Oro; being in control had made it a memorable occasion, and she would never forget their romantic walk afterwards, to the Ramsholt Inn by the beautiful River Deben in Suffolk. But flying fighter planes to airfields was altogether another experience; it was a mission with a purpose that filled her with both high excitement and tension.

As if reading her thoughts, Geraldine said without any polite preamble, 'Fancy another run, an urgent delivery?'

Startled, Lily blinked. 'What, now?' she gasped.

'First thing tomorrow morning,' Geraldine explained. 'Two Spits out to Norfolk, new terrain for you.'

Spluttering, Lily replied, 'Yes, I'd like that very much. I'll have to get permission, of course.'

'Sure,' Geraldine shrugged. 'Any problems, let me know and I'll sort it out.'

'Sid was okay last time,' Lily hurriedly said.

'Sid . . . ? The tubby chap who has an overblown high opinion of his charm with the ladies?' Geraldine joked.

'He's nice really,' Lily assured them. 'He's given up on you snooty ferry girls,' she laughed. 'He gets nothing but dirty looks and the cold shoulder.'

Emily let out a loud, dismissive hoot. 'No time for slap and tickle when there's vital war work to be done.'

Quickly turning the subject away from poor Sid, who Lily was increasingly fond of, she enquired, 'What are the arrangements?'

'I'll be back later tonight after our drop-off,' Geraldine told her. 'Em's got a morning pick-up in Derby, which is why I need you to step in. Last minute, as usual,' she said with an apologetic grin.

Rising to her feet, Emily urged, 'Come on, old girl, better get a move on if we're going to be back here later.'

Rising too, Geraldine added as she zipped up her flying jacket, 'I'll leave you to sort it out with the boss, Lil. Wanna come and watch us take off?'

'I'd like nothing more,' Lily cried.

Curious eyes turned to Lily as she left the canteen with the ferry girls.

'Oi, what are you up to, leaving us already?' cheeky Audrey called out.

'I'll explain later,' Lily called back.

Finding Sid in the repair shop, Lily breathlessly asked if he could spare her for half an hour while she accompanied the ferry girls into the yard.

'Aye, all right, mi duck,' he wheezed. 'Them bloody ferry girls have come down from their high horse now that they know one of our own lasses is a pilot.'

Blushing, Lily said, 'It's not quite like that, Sid.'

'If you're not a pilot what are you?' he pragmatically demanded. 'At the end of the day, it's you that's flying the bloody plane!'

Grabbing her coat, Lily ran out into the yard where she found Emily and Geraldine already strapped into their cockpits, wearing headsets and goggles.

Sliding open her window, Geraldine explained, 'Just waiting for the green light.'

'Safe journey,' Lily cried.

'See you later,' Geraldine said as Emily started to roll her Spit out of the bay.

Hearing the ground staff calling out, 'Chocks away,' Lily stood well back as Geraldine followed her colleague down the runway.

Shielding her eyes against the low-lying winter sun, Lily watched the two brand-new Spitfires take to the skies. Admiring both pilots' skilful manoeuvring of their aircrafts, Lily wished she had their easy confidence. Squinting, she tracked the disappearing Spits whose metal fuselages glinted silver-bright against the ice-cold blue sky, watching them until they disappeared from sight.

Lily returned to work with her heart racing.

This time tomorrow, she thought, I'll be piloting a war plane to Norfolk.

After work, when Lily told her friends about her plans for the next day, there was a general cry of dismay.

'I know you love it, but it puts the fear of God into me,' Jeannie exclaimed.

'Me too,' Edna agreed. 'I can build Spitfires, but my God I never *ever* want to fly one.'

Kathleen was sitting on her mother's lap, intrigued by the conversation. 'Has Auntie Lily got wings?' she announced.

Smiling gently, Lily replied, 'I fly aeroplanes, sweetheart.'

'Ooooh!' the little girl gasped. 'Can I come flying in the sky with you?'

'God forbid,' Edna muttered under her breath.

'Perhaps one day, when you're a big girl,' Lily said hesitantly.

Utterly fascinated, Kathleen laughed. 'Will I need wings to fly?'

'The aircraft has wings, lovie,' Lily explained.

Kathleen jumped off her mother's lap and raced around the room flapping her arms. 'Look at me – I can fly!'

Shaking her head, Edna chuckled. 'Hell fire, you've got her going now.'

The following morning, Lily was up even earlier than usual, terrified that she would miss her rendezvous with Geraldine. Arriving before the hooter went for the early shift, she found Geraldine in the canteen drinking tea and smoking a cigarette.

'All set?' she enquired.

'All set,' Lily told her. 'I've got official permission.'

'Jolly good,' Geraldine said briskly. 'So, same procedure as before; deliver two and pick up two. Only difference is this time I'll be heading to Lincoln for my final drop-off and you'll be flying home solo.'

Lily let out a little gasp of surprise. So far, she had never flown without somebody either up ahead guiding her or sat close by her in the aircraft.

Seeing her shocked expression, Geraldine robustly

observed, 'Nothing to worry about. If you can find your way to Woodbridge and back, you can certainly make your way home from Norfolk. The thing to concentrate on as we fly out are the map pointers. Hopefully, we'll be below cloud cover, so focus on all the major waypoints – railway intersections, church spires, bends in the river, road junctions.'

Recalling her recent flights, Lily nodded; Geraldine's practical advice was reassuringly logical, she would certainly follow it.

'Righty-ho,' Geraldine continued as she stubbed out her cigarette. 'Let's head off to Egmere.'

Bewildered, Lily asked, 'I thought we were going to Norfolk?'

'We are – Egmere, in Norfolk.'

Lily's early morning take-off started without a hitch. When they saw her approaching, the Bell Works ground staff waiting by the Spits smiled a welcome.

'You're quite a familiar sight these days, miss,' one of them beamingly teased.

Feeling self-conscious and stuck for words, Lily didn't know what to say.

'You're doing a grand job, miss,' the airman continued enthusiastically. 'The country needs women with your pluck.'

Blushing, but thanking him for his kind words, Lily was relieved to climb into the cockpit where she immediately put on her headset before studying the map for waypoints on their route. Hearing Geraldine's voice crackling in her headset, Lily immediately responded.

'Have we got the all-clear sign from the tower?' she asked.

'Just waiting, which gives you time to check out the landmarks en route; remember you'll be flying back alone, so note them well.'

'As if I could ever forget,' Lily grimaced.

'We've got an early start, so hopefully you'll be flying back mid-afternoon before it goes dark,' Geraldine continued.

God forbid that I should ever fly back in the dark, Lily thought.

'All set?' Geraldine asked, with her usual cheerful bravado.

'Wish me luck,' Lily responded.

Touching down at the Egmere airbase was almost a disappointment; Lily had enjoyed the flight over the Norfolk landscape so much, she wanted to keep flying over the salt marshes and vast golden beaches fringed with pine trees. On a clear, bright cold day like today, the North Sea was not a menacing steel-grey 'graveyard' – as the pilots who regularly flew over named it – instead, its tumbling waves reflected the pure blue of the chilly winter sky.

Once the Spits were safely grounded and immediately claimed by the groundsmen, Geraldine wasted no time in organizing the next leg of their journey.

'We'd both like to be out of here sharpish,' she told the staff.

'Righty-ho, miss, grab a cuppa and we'll have 'em ready to go.'

In the NAAFI, over mugs of tea and some stale fish-paste sandwiches, Geraldine suddenly turned serious.

'Listen here, lovie, if you're not up for this, we can sort something else out.'

Lily seriously considered her words before she answered. 'I'm up for it, as long as I can take off and hopefully get back while there's daylight.'

'Good gel, knew you would!' Geraldine responded by giving startled Lily a firm clap on the back.

While waiting for the usual take-off procedures and the green-light clearance, Lily checked her aircraft's gauges. Just before Geraldine started moving out of her bay, she said to Lily through their connected headsets, 'Good luck, love, see you when I'm next in Hucknall.'

Waving from the cockpit, Lily grinned as she spoke. 'Thanks for all your advice.'

Taxiing after Geraldine, Lily concentrated on her colleague's every move. This time around you are on your own, she told herself. After Geraldine had soared away, Lily felt a twinge of emotion; she had grown in confidence with this woman who had accepted her and welcomed her as an equal. She was lucky – no, Lily thought, it was more than that – she was blessed to have Geraldine as a friend and mentor; she had been an inspiration to her.

I'll do her proud, Lily thought, as she too took to the skies and started to make her way home.

The journey home, flying over Norfolk, mercifully still in daylight, was a real pleasure. Even while concentrating hard, picking out all the important waypoints en route, Lily nevertheless drank in the beauty of the landscape; vast beaches that gave on to pine forests and rolling countryside dotted with farms. Making sure her attention didn't wander too far, Lily marvelled at the sand spits and inlets, and the winding channels that flowed out into the North Sea. Though she had imagined she would be lonely, just her and the Spit she was flying, she realized with some surprise that she actually enjoyed the intense solitude and the thrilling experience of being at one with her aircraft.

Hours later, after she had landed the Spit in need of repair, Lily signed off all the paperwork with the airmen. Weary to the bone, but jubilant that she had made a successful flight back, she enquired after Geraldine.

'Has she landed safely in Lincoln?'

'Not sure, miss,' one of the ground staff answered. 'I can check with the control tower, they're bound to know.'

Though tired, cold and starving hungry, anxious Lily couldn't rest until she knew her pal had safely landed. Hanging about in the yard, waiting for the airman to come back to her, Lily anxiously checked her wristwatch. Seeing the airman approaching, she called out, 'All well?'

'Your pal landed in Lincoln,' he started.

'That's a relief,' she said, before noticing the pained expression on the airman's face, at which point her pulse started to race. 'What is it?' she cried out. 'Is Geraldine all right?'

The airman answered, with a catch in his voice. 'I'm afraid not, miss. It looks like the aircraft she was delivering for repair work had a bit of a problem.'

Feeling like her knees were going to give way, Lily gasped, 'What kind of problem?'

'I'm sorry, miss, it's bad news,' the airman grimly replied. 'Your colleague's aircraft . . .' He paused to steady his voice. 'It crashed on landing.'

Reeling with shock, Lily exclaimed, 'Oh my God, is she . . . ?' Hardly daring to breathe, she couldn't finish the sentence.

The man shook his head. 'Sorry, miss, by all reports the young woman died instantly.'

41. Sharing the Load

The following morning, Edna was busy getting Kathleen up and ready for nursery. She urged red-eyed Lily, who had been awake nearly all night, to rest and stay in bed.

'No,' Lily strongly protested. 'That's the worst thing I could do.'

'Look at the state of you, lovie,' Edna cried. 'Worn out with crying.'

'I'm better off at work,' Lily insisted. 'If I stay here on my own all day, I'll only dwell on it.'

Struggling to get Kathleen buttoned up in her warm winter coat, Edna sympathized. 'Such a terrible loss, a brave young woman like that.'

'I keep thinking, what if I'd been given that run, that aircraft? I might be dead and Geraldine alive,' Lily murmured as she sipped the mug of tea Edna had made for her. 'I need to know what happened,' she fretted. 'Was it the aircraft that failed, or did Geraldine mistime her landing? She was so experienced, so confident, I can't believe it would be that. In which case, if it was the aircraft,' she exclaimed, as she started to cry all over again, '*why* did anybody even allow it to leave the airfield?'

Kathleen, impatient to be on her way, tussled with her mother, who was now trying to tie the laces on her winter boots.

'Mama, be quick, go to nursery,' the little girl urged.

'All right, lovie, just let me give Auntie Lily a kiss,' Edna replied.

'I kiss her too,' Kathleen said as she rushed at Lily and hugged her tightly around the neck. 'Love you,' she lisped.

'I love you too, my sweetheart,' Lily murmured, with an emotional catch in her throat. 'See you at teatime.'

'Byeeee,' the little girl cried as she ran to the front door. 'Ready, Mama?'

Hurrying after her eager daughter, Edna called over her shoulder, 'See you later.'

Lily dragged herself into the bathroom – another freezing-cold room – and washed her face, cleaned her teeth, brushed her long silver-blonde hair, performing every action on autopilot. Then, in the bedroom, she slipped out of her nightdress and got dressed for work.

'This time yesterday, Geraldine was alive. I was having a cuppa with her before we took off for Norfolk. Dear, brave Geraldine – what a damn waste of a fine young woman.'

Throughout the day, Lily continued to brood about Geraldine, but as the morning wore on, she suddenly caught sight of Edna reaching up to grasp a hefty length of sheet metal that was dangling from metal chains attached to an overhead gantry.

Tapping Edna on the shoulder, she shouted, 'STOP! It's too heavy for you, in your condition – let me do that.'

Lily was strong and muscular – as a consequence of all the hard, physical graft that aircraft building entailed – and effortlessly lowered the sheet metal into the cockpit.

Edna, grateful for her friend's thoughtfulness, mouthed, 'Thanks, lovie.'

Picking up the heavy drill, which was suspended from an overhead electrical cable that ran the length of the factory ceiling, Lily hunkered down beside Edna. Working in tandem, as they always did, with one drilling holes to secure the length of sheet metal into place while the other riveted, Lily's thoughts inevitably drifted to Geraldine again, vividly recalling her waving brightly through the cockpit's sliding window, giving the thumbs up sign as she called, 'CHOCKS AWAY!' and taking off into the bright blue sky.

Life was so precious, so fragile, and in some cases so tragically fleeting. Where was Oro now? Lily wondered. She hadn't heard a word from him since his departure for the mystery training camp; she hadn't expected to either, but at times like this, how she longed to be held in his strong arms, pressed against his warm body, strengthened by his love and support. Thinking of the aircraft he might be using for training his new recruits – Hawker Hurricanes, De Havilland Mosquitos, as well as Supermarine Spitfires – Lily prayed they would be safe. Remembering her own training, she marvelled at her ignorance, and at Oro's patient responses to her string of naive questions. Though scared stiff, she had been so thrilled and excited; the adrenalin that shot through her entire body told her that flying was something she instinctively responded to. Now, with some experience under her belt, she was steadier, more cautious. Flying was undeniably wonderful, but right now – after Geraldine's untimely death – she was more sober about the risks that came with it. After drilling the last bolts into the Spitfire's fuselage, Lily said a silent prayer for all the men who might pilot her in the war. God bless you all, God speed and bring you home safe to your loved ones.

*

These days, unlike the bad old days, the engine girls – Ruby, Mary, Audrey and Jeannie – regularly gathered together for a gossip and a catch-up. Sometimes even Annie plonked herself down for a quick cuppa. In the middle of all the chatter and laughter, Edna had a quiet word with Lily. Typically, she came straight to the point.

'So, what's going on, missus? You don't need to do my work for me.'

Dropping her voice to a whisper so that all around wouldn't hear, Lily replied, 'You know what's going on, Edna, you can't go lifting and carrying the way you are. It's bad for you.'

Looking mutinous, Edna glowered. 'Hold on a minute,' she declared. 'It's me that got miself into this blasted mess, I can't allow folks to do my share of the work just because of my own stupidity.'

Thinking that Edna's protests might be overheard, Lily pressed a cautionary finger to her lips. 'Shhh, keep your voice down, Ed.'

Turning to the intimate group of engine friends, Edna said forcefully, 'It's not a secret, everybody here knows I'm expecting.' Addressing them all, she said, 'I was just saying to Lil here that she can't take on my work just because of my condition.'

Trying to explain herself, Lily quickly said, 'I was concerned. As you all know, our work involves a fair bit of stretching and lifting.'

'I'd have done exactly the same thing,' Ruby answered robustly.

'Thank you for your consideration, Ruby, but my point

is – why should anybody cover for me when I'm the one who created the problem in the first place?'

'It takes two to tango,' Jeannie said cryptically.

'I am not looking for sympathy,' Edna said hotly. 'It's up to me to pay for my own mistakes.'

Knowing just how proud and stubborn her friend could be, Lily spoke with equal determination. 'I am *not* standing by and watching you harm yourself. So, Edna dear, you'll have to lump it!'

Audrey burst into a loud peal of laughter. 'Well said, Lily. Edna's been well and truly put in her place.'

Edna gave a wry smile. 'I love you for your thoughtfulness, Lil,' she said as she reached over to kiss her friend on the cheek. 'I'm sorry for being grumpy, it's just my way of hiding my feelings. Thank you, sweetheart.'

Mary, who had been following the conversation with her usual wide-eyed innocent expression, spluttered, 'I still don't know how you can be expecting if your husband's not here?'

Having talked to Mary several times on the subject of her untimely pregnancy, Edna rolled her eyes.

'I've already told you, Mary, I've been a naughty girl. To be blunt – my husband's not here, so it can't be his baby, can it?'

Mary blushed bright red with embarrassment.

'Listen, lovie, has your mother ever talked to you about the birds and the bees?' Ruby asked gently.

Squirming, Mary replied, 'She's told me how cats and dogs get born.'

'Well, it's the same thing with humans, lovie. Just a bit more romantic and exciting,' Ruby assured her.

'You should be so lucky,' Edna muttered darkly, under her breath.

Their conversation was cut short by the sound of the hooter.

Walking back to work, with Jeannie and Lily on either side of her, Edna said with genuine gratitude, 'Really, I'm touched by your thoughtfulness, I couldn't have better friends.'

'We always said we'd take care of you, lovie,' Jeannie assured her.

'That's good,' Edna said, with tears in her eyes. 'Cos you two are all the family I've got right now.'

42. A Long Game

As Germany made more advances in Eastern Europe, the nation, though galvanized by Prime Minister Winston Churchill's moving patriotic rhetoric, began to fear. Could the Germans really win? Had they sufficient armaments to keep on fighting?

There certainly weren't enough planes to compete with Hitler's endless wave of aircraft that nightly decimated the country. Engine girls at the coal face knew this better than most. Working around the clock, assembling Spitfires and reassembling battle-torn aircraft, their output never stopped.

Though stalwart and determined, there was nevertheless a creeping fear – could the Allies do it? The Commonwealth countries were supporting them, with brave lads shipped in from halfway across the world, but America was still slow on the uptake.

'They're playing a long cautious game,' Ruby said over a brief tea break.

'What's stopping them from fighting alongside us? Are the Yanks frightened of burning their fingers?' Audrey scoffed.

'Political manoeuvres,' Lily said. 'Who knows what goes on in the corridors of power?'

Edna gave a dismissive shrug. 'So, while Hitler storms

across Europe, we sit and wait for the Yanks to come to our aid.'

Audrey said wretchedly, 'When war broke out, I was so gung-ho – we would not be beaten, not *ever*. We were right to defy tyranny, but now – after two years and all the talking – we're not much further forward.'

Ruby was outraged. 'You can't talk like that, Audrey, so many have died already, we can't just give up now.'

'I'm *not* giving up,' Audrey protested. 'I'm just scared,' she admitted.

'We're all scared, if we're honest,' Jeannie said. 'But we're a brave nation too – look what happened at Dunkirk. I'll never forget hearing about all those little boats that sailed across the Channel to bring our troops back home.'

'If I'd got a rowing boat, I'd have gone miself,' Edna passionately announced.

Though busy working full time and looking after Archie, Ruby never failed to write to her husband at least once a week. Later that day, while her sister played with Archie, lying on a rug with his toys in front of the fire, she did just that.

My darling George,

I hope life in North Africa is not too gruelling. I think of you all the time, pestered by the heat and flies, and worry that you don't have enough water and food. I hope and pray you're safe, my own precious love. Though we hear little about the goings-on over there, the news on the radio and in the papers is all about the war here in Europe gathering momentum, with Hitler's advance on Russia and the siege of Sebastopol, and now it looks like Moscow's coming under attack. It really is a world war, with enemy fighting spreading like a flame across the globe, where will it ever end?

We all continue to work hard; the Bell Works is pushing out aircraft at such a speed you would think that we are winning the war. So many aircraft come back to the factory, bashed and battered by enemy fire, in need of immediate repair before they are whisked off again. It's round-the-clock work, long shifts (admittedly with good overtime pay), but sometimes we are hungry and dirty, working in small cramped spaces. I feel I've been bolting war planes together for a hundred years! Don't get me wrong, sweetheart, it's war work that I'm happy to do, proud to do, but when I think of me as a young girl, running over the moors, hand in hand with my handsome boyfriend, I can hardly believe that we were ever so young and carefree.

I struggle to imagine what it will be like to live in peace, when all of this fighting stops. Towns and cities all over the country will barely exist after the bombing raids the Germans have put us through – Coventry so far being the worst. Poor souls, what they must have gone through beggars belief. The country will have to rebuild, even if we triumph over the enemy, but how many years will it take to rebuild Britain? I'll change the subject – I'm sure you don't want to hear my morbid thoughts.

Some good news, Mum is thriving. It began with Archie starting nursery, and that load being lifted from her shoulders. Since then, she's been out and about a lot more, mostly visiting Mrs Barnes; you may remember her, the old lady who lives around the corner whose daughter, Annie, is my overseer. She wasn't at all well, so I persuaded Mother to pop in and see her, and it's done them both the world of good. They chat and drink tea, put the world to rights, and generally support and advise each other. Friendship is a great thing, it's cheered both of them up, and now they're inviting other old friends

to join them for a cup of tea and a scone – sometimes they even play
whist. It makes me smile.

Archie continues to love his nursery; he loves the staff and they
certainly love him. He's the sunniest baby, always smiling unless he's
teething. He's got a new little playmate, my friend Edna's daughter,
Kathleen. She's a bit older than Archie, and such a little mother;
she stands on her tiptoes and stretches up to push his pram when we
walk home from nursery. Edna lives in one of the prefabs on the Bell
Works site. The prefabs are freezing cold; our terraced house seems
so warm and cosy compared to those ugly metal temporary homes.
With talk of female conscription becoming obligatory, I think we'll
be seeing a lot more prefabs on the Bell Works site to house the female
workers who'll be called up.

Archie's crying for his supper – there's no denying your little lad
food, he has the appetite of a horse! Take care of your dear precious
self, and please write, I've not heard from you in weeks. It might be
the post, or just that you're too busy, but I get worried sick when I
don't hear from you, my darling.

Yours ever,
Ruby xxxxx

After bathing a wriggling Archie in the tin bath in front of
the fire, Ruby laid her son on her lap and rubbed him dry
with a big warm towel. Laughing as she tickled his small
dimpled body, she revelled in the joy of motherhood. She
might not be with her son all day long, but moments like
these were so precious for mother and son.

Ruby settled her sleepy son in his cot and sang to him
until he dozed off, then she crept downstairs to make a
cup of tea for her younger sister and her mother. It was

their nightly habit to sip a cuppa while listening to the BBC news. After her mother and sister had gone upstairs to bed, Ruby washed up their cups, all the time preoccupied with thinking about Edna. How was her friend ever going to manage? Working long shifts, with early morning drop-offs at the nursery, was gruelling enough, but as her pregnancy advanced, she would inevitably become more tired and uncomfortable. And then there was the problem of offering too much help – which clearly offended Edna.

She seems to want to punish herself, but she can't go on like that, Ruby thought. And she's yet to face the music, address the grim reality with her husband, Jack.

After locking up and going to bed, exhausted by her long day, Ruby slept peacefully until dawn, when Archie woke up for his first feed of the day. As she bottle-fed him, sitting up in her bed, Ruby little realized that Edna's problems were soon going to get a whole lot worse.

When Edna walked into the canteen with a face like thunder, her friends instantly knew something was badly wrong. Ruby threw a questioning look at Lily and Jeannie, who had accompanied Edna, but couldn't gauge from their expressions what the problem might be.

The tight-knit group of friends didn't have to wait long for the answer.

'My husband's just written to say he's coming to see me at the weekend,' Edna blurted out.

Alarmed, Ruby gasped before she could stop herself. 'That's tricky!'

'Very tricky,' Edna groaned. 'He's got a short leave; he's

staying at his mother's and getting the train over here to see me and Kathleen.'

Realizing that she would need privacy with her husband, Lily immediately said, 'I'll get out of your way, Edna. So you and your husband can have some nice family time together,' she added awkwardly.

'Nice!' Edna scoffed at the word. 'It'll be a nightmare, believe me.'

Nobody doubted for a moment that the imminent meeting would indeed be a nightmare.

'Apart from my own bombshell news, I'm worried sick about Kathleen. Of course I'll tell her that her dad is visiting us, but she won't have a clue who he is – she's barely seen him since she was born.'

'It'll be a big shock,' Ruby said, with a sympathetic smile.

'She knows Nellie's husband up in Kendal better than she knows her own dad,' Edna said glumly.

'What will you do?' Audrey cautiously asked. 'Go for a walk, make him some dinner, sit and chat?'

'We'll have to do summat, we can't sit in the prefab all afternoon, but I'm worried he might see the change in me when I'm walking about,' Edna confessed.

Ruby threw her friend an appraising glance. 'Mmm, you're not that big, lovie.'

'And what if he touches me?' Edna cried. 'And he will – after all, he *is* my husband. Most couples can't keep their hands off each other after a long separation, it'll look odd if I keep avoiding him.'

'It might be better to tell him from the start,' sensible Lily suggested. 'Give him time to get over the shock, then you can spend the rest of the day trying to work something out.'

Mary, who had barely opened her mouth, innocently said, 'He might be so pleased to see you both, he might not mind.'

'Oh, sweetheart, he will mind,' Edna said with great conviction. 'He'll go crackers. Nice lad that he was when I last saw him, what man in their right mind would want their wife playing around with other fellas? Still, it might take his mind off talking about his mother,' she grimly joked. 'Imagine what that old bag will be like when she hears I've been unfaithful to her son, she'll never let me in the house again.'

Patting Edna gently on the arm, Ruby advised, 'One thing at a time, Edna. Deal with Jack first, worry about his mother later.'

43. Sortie

At the beginning of December, Lily was relieved to see Emily in the works canteen. Not hesitating for a second, she hurried across the noisy room to join the ferry girl.

Without any preamble Emily bluntly said, 'Rotten luck about Geraldine.'

Seeing Emily acting so brave and matter-of-fact, Lily forced herself to hold back the tears that threatened to spill over.

'They should never have allowed the girl to fly that Spit, I was told the back end was ropey,' Emily protested. 'Knowing Geraldine, she would have just nodded and got on with it. To be fair, it was going dark, so maybe she couldn't see the extent of the damage. Or maybe there was further damage that occurred during the flight,' she shrugged. 'I suppose we'll never know, the aircraft's a wreck, and Geraldine is dead.'

With Emily's sharp words ringing in her ears Lily murmured sadly, 'She was a wonderful friend; I'll never forget her. I want to honour her name,' she quickly added. 'She encouraged me to be a ferry girl and I want to carry on her work.'

'That's good news,' Emily grinned. 'As I have a mission in mind for you.'

Feeling the familiar flutter of excitement in her tummy, Lily held her breath.

'A couple of deliveries, to Lincoln and Suffolk,' Emily confirmed.

Lily gave a quick eager nod.

'If you can sort out permission, we'll leave first thing in the morning, then hopefully we'll return here before nightfall.'

'Righty-ho. Where are you off to now, Emily?' Lily asked as the ferry girl rose to her feet.

'Suffolk, then back here for an early morning start.'

Now used to having their own ferry girl on-site, Sid put up no argument – quite the opposite, in fact.

'I only hope them posh ferry girls appreciate the sacrifices we make here in Hucknall, allowing our engine girls to help them out with their blinking deliveries.'

'Delivering aircraft is vital war work, Sid,' she reminded him. 'You know better than most how our planes need shifting to nearby airbases that are always urgently in need of new aircraft. I can help do that – more than that, I *want* to help.'

'Aye, you're a good lass,' he said, with an affectionate smile. 'Just take care of yourself, we don't want any more nasty accidents, do we?'

'I'll take great care, Sid, I promise.'

Up at first light the following morning, Lily found Emily calmly smoking a cigarette in the factory's stack yard.

'All set?' she enquired.

Lily nodded as she zipped up her flying jacket and secured the leather straps of the flying hat under her chin.

'Lincoln first, immediate turnaround to Woodbridge,

then back to Hucknall, probably flying an aircraft in need of repair.'

Lily felt a lick of fear creep up her spine. Geraldine had died returning a damaged Spitfire; this was a commission that right now she hoped she might avoid.

You have to be as brave as Geraldine if you're to honour her memory, Lily firmly told herself.

As if sensing her fears, Emily urged, 'Let's get on with it.'

Lincoln being a new destination, Lily had been thorough in her preparation for her first flight there, studying the map and the waypoints en route. Taking off after Emily, she felt a rush of sheer pleasure as she took to the air and banked higher and higher until Hucknall was just a little toy town, hundreds of feet below.

Though it was wet and cloudy when they landed in Lincoln, the early morning flight had been straightforward, with useful waypoints to guide them, particularly rivers and vast stretches of black fens across the Lincolnshire Wolds. The new Spit handled well and came down on the wet runway with barely a wobble.

'Well done,' Emily said as they queued up for mugs of tea in the NAAFI. 'Grab a sandwich, then we'll leave for Suffolk before it gets too misty.'

Desperate not to be flying through mist, which would obscure the waypoints that Lily depended on, she quickly ate a rather stale meat-paste sandwich and gulped down her tea. Ten minutes later, they were back on the runway, zipping up their warm jackets while they waited for the airport ground staff to prepare the aircraft they were flying out.

'Know your way from here?' Emily enquired.

'I'm not familiar with the first leg of the flight out of

here, but I'm familiar with the Suffolk run, I've done it a few times now.'

'Good, see you at the Woodbridge base later on,' Emily said as she strode over to her aircraft.

After Emily had taxied her Spit on to the runway and taken off, Lily quickly followed. Concentrating hard on the rivers and channels winding their way through the fens that were so characteristic of the eastern part of the region, Lily was surprised to suddenly see more familiar landmarks emerge as she flew over Suffolk. As the wide flowing estuaries and tidal creeks loomed into view, her mind flew back to that wonderful day she and Oro had spent in a charming old-fashioned pub on the banks of the River Deben, a world away from war. It had been a golden day to cherish, Lily recalled.

Tearing her thoughts away from Oro, Lily focused on her descent. But as she did so, the mist that they had been trying to avoid all day descended like a grey blanket. Squinting, she tried to make out landmarks that would have been obvious and familiar in the bright light of day, but there were none visible. Trying to fight down a rising sense of panic, Lily reminded herself that the green clearance light would flash when she was approaching her landing point.

'All I have to do is get there and land her safely,' she doggedly reminded herself.

To her enormous relief the mist suddenly cleared, and Rendlesham Forest swung into view.

Nearly there, she told herself. Look out for the green signal and pray the mist holds off.

Checking her descent speed, Lily approached the airstrip

where she had successfully landed Spits previously. Lining the aircraft up with the runway, she waited for the green light, which suddenly pulsed out. Slowly dropping speed, she started to make her descent, at which point the mist suddenly descended, completely obscuring her vision.

Sweating with fear, Lily firmly admonished herself, 'Keep on a straight course.'

Even though blinded by mist, and tense with fear, Lily managed to keep on track and brought the aircraft down, landing with a resounding bump on the runway.

She jumped as the tyres hit the ground. 'Thank God!' she said out loud.

At this point she unexpectedly felt the aircraft tilt, and suddenly she was rolling sideways. Not knowing where she was going, or what was to the right or left of her, Lily's thoughts flashed to Geraldine. Was this what she had experienced before she died? Slamming down hard on the brakes, she slowed the careering Spit, which spun sideways, still out of control. She gripped the steering wheel and, not knowing which way to turn, cried out as the aircraft's nose smashed into a brick storage unit at the end of the runway.

Braking wildly, Lily (still belted into her seat) put out a hand to protect herself as the windscreen caved in and she felt an agonizing pain shoot up her left arm. Trembling and terrified that the aircraft might burst into flames, Lily scrambled to unstrap her belt, but it wouldn't instantly release. As smoke began to pour from the engine, Lily caught sight of an orange lick of flame. Gasping, she screamed into the headset.

'HELP! I'm choking, my aircraft's on fire.'

Finally managing to snap open her seat belt, and knowing

that she had to escape from the smoke and flames that were spreading through the cramped cockpit, Lily gritted her teeth. Fighting against the pain in her arm, she crawled towards the door and managed to swing her legs out, but not before the fire really took hold and the fuselage started to burn and fall apart around her. Tumbling out of the cockpit and landing on the runway, Lily lay bleeding on the ground. She saw arc lights flashing and heard the sound of sirens shrilling out.

The last thing Lily saw, before pain completely engulfed her, were ground staff running towards her bearing a stretcher.

When Lily didn't return home to Hucknall that evening, there was a great sense of concern. After work, worried sick, Jeannie hurried back to Prefab No. 8 in the hope of finding Lily at home and making tea. When she found the prefab dark and empty, her heart sank.

'Oh, Lily, love,' she murmured into the darkness. 'Where are you?'

A long night passed, with no sign of Lily. Her absence troubled Kathleen, who was used to having her aunties around when she returned from nursery. Jeannie did her best to entertain the little girl with her stories and fairy tales, but eventually, weary at the end of a long day, Jeannie said goodnight to Kathleen before returning home to her own prefab.

Giving Edna a hug as she left, Jeannie murmured, 'Hopefully we'll learn more first thing tomorrow morning.'

'I hope so,' Edna replied. 'This waiting around, not knowing, is terrible. She's always come home safely before.'

Both women remembered hearing from Lily about how Geraldine had died flying an aircraft. They clung on to each other for support.

Searching for comforting words, Jeannie said, 'She's probably been held up or had to stay overnight somewhere. Please God, she'll show up tomorrow with an explanation.'

44. Ipswich Hospital

Gathered around a canteen table the next morning, an anxious Jeannie told Audrey and Mary that they had heard no further news of missing Lily. When Edna and Ruby appeared, after dropping their children off at the Bell Works nursery, Mary was white-faced with worry and in tears.

'Somebody must know where she is.'

'Surely Sid's phoned the airbase that she was flying to by now?' Audrey insisted.

'I've been awake all night worrying about Lily,' Ruby confessed. 'If only we knew something,' she added desperately.

An hour later, Annie came hurrying across the factory floor to the fuselage that Jeannie and Edna were working on. She waved to the two women where they were standing on the high jig, securing long lengths of sheet-metal strips to the underside of the aircraft.

'Sid wants to see you. NOW!' she called out.

Exchanging a look of fear, the two women laid aside the pneumatic drill and riveting gun they were using and made their way down the ladder. Going weak at the knees, they followed Annie as she led them off the factory floor to Sid's office.

When he saw the tension in the women's expressions, Sid immediately pulled out two chairs and came straight to the point. 'I got word through this morning from the officials at Woodbridge airport where Lily landed her plane,' he started.

Unable to bear the suspense a minute longer, Edna cried, 'Is she alive?'

Smiling and nodding, Sid answered, 'Aye, thank God, she's alive.'

Slumping back in their spindly wooden chairs, Edna and Jeannie struggled not to burst into tears.

'What happened to her?' Jeannie asked, once she had got her breath back.

Sid held up his hand and started to explain. 'Lily had an accident yesterday afternoon. She landed the plane in thick mist; it skidded off the runway and caught fire.'

Edna gasped in shock, lost for words.

'Where is she now?' Jeannie enquired.

'She was taken by ambulance to Ipswich Hospital.'

'Hospital!' Jeannie exclaimed. 'Can we see her?'

'I'll make enquiries,' he promised. 'If she's in intensive care they might not allow you in, but I'll do my best. Though I can't spare both of you – one of you will have to stay here and carry on working.' Sighing, he added with an emotional catch in his voice, 'Brave little lass, doing a dangerous job like that.'

During the morning break, when Jeannie and Edna told Lily's friends that she was alive but hospitalized, a wave of both relief and concern rippled around the canteen table they were sitting at.

'Oh my goodness,' Ruby sighed. 'Thank heavens she's safe, I only hope she's not badly hurt.'

'What she must have gone through,' Mary whispered. 'I'd be petrified – she's a proper hero is our Lily.'

'How terrifying – imagine not being able to see a thing,' Audrey murmured.

A sudden thought struck Ruby. 'I wonder if we should tell her boyfriend?'

'Lily told me he's away, she said she didn't know his whereabouts. It's top secret,' Edna added. 'I've no idea how we would contact him.'

'He should be told,' Ruby insisted. 'I'll drop off a message at his airbase anyway, on my way home. Lily would want him to know.'

'We've asked to see her,' Jeannie continued. 'Sid's going to make enquiries on our behalf.'

Later that day, Sid approached Edna.

'I've arranged a visit to see Lily, but only one visitor is allowed,' he told her.

Realizing that she would have to look after Kathleen, Edna immediately said, 'It'll have to be Jeannie. I've got to look after my little girl.'

'Righty-ho, tell Jeannie she can take tomorrow off – troop trains allowing, she should be able to get to Ipswich and back in a day.'

Early the next morning, Jeannie took a packed troop train to Ipswich, where she caught a bus on to the hospital. Sitting in a draughty corridor until the bell went for visiting time, Jeannie's thoughts were in turmoil. What were the extent of Lily's injuries? Would she be conscious? Would she be able to walk, or talk even? Immersed in worrying thoughts, she jumped when the visitors' bell clanged out.

Jeannie's heart contracted at the sight of her friend lying

in bed with her arm in plaster and her sweet, pretty face covered in cuts and bruises.

'Sweetheart,' she murmured as she dropped into the chair beside Lily's bed. 'How are you?'

Trying to smile, Lily grimaced as she exclaimed, 'Ouch! I cut my lip and had to have stitches, so it's painful to smile.'

'Then please don't,' Jeannie begged. 'Is it all right to speak?' she asked nervously.

Lily nodded. 'Yes, yes,' she insisted. 'I might be a bit slow and slurred, but I'll do my best. Oh, Jeannie, it's so lovely to see you.'

'Everybody sends their love,' Jeannie told her friend. 'Mary, Annie, Sid, Audrey, Ruby, Edna, Kathleen, even baby Archie – they all send their warmest wishes for your speedy recovery.'

With tears in her lovely silver-grey eyes, Lily murmured, 'I'm so lucky to have friends like you.' Gazing solemnly at Jeannie, she added in a more serious voice, 'I'm lucky to even be alive.'

Jeannie gripped her hand, close to tears herself, and whispered, 'Oh, lovie, we were so worried when you didn't come home.'

'I'm sorry I frightened you all,' Lily apologized. 'Everything was going well,' she recalled. 'Emily and I dropped off two Spits at the Lincoln airbase, then quickly took off with two more. She said heavy mist was forecast, so we didn't hang about. In fact, I barely encountered any mist until landing, when it descended like a thick blanket.'

Seeing Lily's delicate heart-shaped face looking strained and white, Jeannie urged, 'Sweetheart, don't upset yourself.'

Lily shook her head. 'It's good to talk,' she insisted. 'I keep thinking about it, over and over again. I landed the plane in the mist, but then it tipped on the runway and went skidding out of control.'

'You must have been so scared!' Jeannie gasped.

'I was – but I was confused too, I couldn't see a thing, and I didn't know which way to steer. When the aircraft hit a building and the front end burst into flames, I couldn't release my belt and I thought I would be burned alive. Jeannie, I was so frightened.'

'Sweetheart,' Jeannie said as she gently stroked her friend's hand. 'It's a miracle you got out at all.'

'I know,' Lily said, with a long shuddering sigh. 'I was very lucky.'

'Ruby said she would drop a note off to Oro at the Polish airbase, to let him know.'

'That's kind of her, but he won't be there,' Lily pointed out. 'In fact, I've no idea where Oro might be.'

'It might get passed on to him, wherever he is,' Jeannie said hopefully.

'I hope so,' Lily sighed. 'I'd love to see him.'

Smiling reassuringly, Jeannie spoke soothing words. 'We'll keep on trying to get through to Oro.' Seeing her friend looking tired and in discomfort, she added, 'I'm sorry, lovie, all this talking is wearing you out.'

'I am tired and the painkillers are wearing off,' Lily admitted. 'But it's so nice having somebody here with me.' Reaching out, she took hold of her friend's hand. 'I need to talk to you about something that's worrying me,' she whispered. 'You see . . .' She paused as a tear rolled down her cheek. 'After what's happened, I think I should give up flying. I was out of control after I landed that aircraft – I could have killed somebody else as well as myself.'

Carefully choosing her words, Jeannie responded, 'From what you've just told me, you landed in mist.'

'Yes, and then everything spun out of control, which is my point,' Lily breathlessly insisted. 'Was that a mechanical failure or my inexperience?'

Out of her depth, Jeannie thought carefully before answering. 'I wouldn't know that, Lil. All I know is that you did your job – you landed the plane – it was the mist that was the problem. You were disorientated, not out of control, lovie. You survived, just thank God for that.'

'I do, but I'm beginning to doubt myself.'

'Hardly surprising, after what you've been through,' Jeannie robustly responded. 'Realistically, it's going to take you a while to get over this, maybe it would be wise not to fly again right away. You'll need to recoup your strength in both mind and body,' she added tenderly.

When the visitors' bell went, an hour later, Lily was clearly exhausted. Having asked about Edna and Kathleen, Ruby and Archie, and all of her friends at the Bell Works, she let Jeannie do the talking, which seemed to soothe her.

The ward sister approached, pristine in her starched white uniform and frilled cap, and Jeannie quickly rose to leave.

'One of us will be back soon to visit you; everybody's queuing up to see you,' she said as she stooped to kiss her friend's hot forehead.

'I'm hoping they'll move me to a hospital nearer Hucknall soon. Apart from my broken arm I've only got minor burns and a few cuts,' Lily said.

'Let the hospital make the call on that one, dear. Now get some rest,' Jeannie murmured. 'Bye, sweetheart, take care of yourself.'

Though Jeannie got home very late, she called into Prefab No. 8 to give Edna an update.

'You look worn out,' Edna said.

After hanging up her coat, Jeannie sat by the crackling fire where she warmed up her cold hands.

Edna offered Jeannie some tea from the pot keeping warm on the hearth, and asked, 'How was she?'

'Brave, but my goodness she looks a sight,' Jeannie answered. 'Her broken arm is in plaster, and she has some cuts and burns. She's on drugs to control the pain, so she gets a bit woozy.'

'It must have been a huge relief to see her,' Edna smiled.

'It was, she sent love to all of us,' Jeannie told her friend. 'She's hoping to be allowed home soon.'

'It would be marvellous if she could get back to us,' Edna replied. 'You look done in, lovie, get to bed,' she urged. 'Early shift tomorrow morning – come hail or come shine – and everybody will be asking after Lily, so brace yourself.'

Standing up and stretching, Jeannie smiled. 'I'm sure I'll sleep well tonight, it's been a long day,' she yawned. 'See you first thing tomorrow morning.'

Little did the two women know what shocking news would shake the entire world the next day, when the Japanese Imperialist forces launched an attack on the United States naval station at Pearl Harbor. The Bell workers heard news of the destruction of eight US Navy battleships and the deaths of over two thousand Americans as the news trickled in throughout the day and the night. President Franklin Roosevelt declared December 7th 'a date which will live in infamy'.

'They're well and truly in it now,' Edna announced as they all sat down together for their first morning tea break. 'The Yanks will never back down after this.'

'We've been waiting long enough for them to join us,' Ruby pointed out. 'I'm surprised it's taken a tragedy such as this to make them jump in.'

'You can't sit on the fence when your own men are being targeted,' Jeannie pointed out.

When Sid turned up to enquire after Jeannie's visit to Ipswich, he was relieved to hear how 'His Favourite Girl' (his own nickname for Lily these days) was progressing.

'Hopefully, she'll be back with us soon,' he commented, before adding, 'God knows, we'll be needing all the engine girls we can get our hands on after what's happened at Pearl Harbor. Mark my words,' he warned, 'war productivity will escalate now like you've never seen it rise before.'

45. The Visit

Jack's visit loomed over Edna, who hardly slept the night before he arrived. Kathleen picked up on her mother's mood; she was missing Lily – who she was devoted to – and became awkward and argumentative. Luckily, Jeannie broke the tension with her bright and breezy presence when she popped in just before breakfast.

'What's all this?' she asked, when she saw Kathleen's bowl of cold congealed porridge on the kitchen table.

'Don't want it,' Kathleen grumbled. 'Want Auntie Lily.'

Playfully tickling the little girl, Jeannie laughed, 'Won't Auntie Jeannie do for now?'

Wriggling away from Jeannie, Kathleen smiled. 'Please can I have a story?'

Turning to Edna, still in her nightdress and completely unmade-up, Jeannie cocked an eyebrow. 'Is that a good idea?'

Edna quickly nodded her head. 'Yes, it'll give me time to tidy my bedroom and get dressed.'

Jeannie read *The Three Bears*, *Cinderella* and *The Three Little Pigs* from a picture book she had bought in a second-hand bookshop in Hucknall village. Meanwhile, Edna whizzed around her untidy bedroom where Kathleen's clothes were strewn everywhere.

If I have my way we won't be coming in here, she thought, as she made the narrow bed.

Knowing they might go for a walk during Jack's visit, Edna had borrowed a big baggy coat that Ruby had worn during her own pregnancy. With the coat wrapped around her body and loosely tied at the waist, Edna was confident that it camouflaged the changes in her body and felt easier about going for a stroll around Hucknall with Jack. After brushing her dark hair, which had lost its rich lustre since she fell pregnant, Edna applied some make-up; if anything, it made her face look more drawn and thin.

'It's the best I can do,' she sighed as she studied her image in the mirror on her bedroom wall.

Could this be the same woman who – radiant in a red satin dress – had taken the Bell Works dance floor by storm just a couple of months ago? Slumping down on to her bed, Edna wondered what Jack might be like these days. After all, it was so long ago that she last saw him – way before she arrived in Hucknall, in fact. She certainly felt like her world had been turned upside down in the last few months; how must he be feeling, with war raging across the world? Edna groaned as another miserable thought assailed her: Jack's dreadful mother.

'Please God, don't let him start pestering me to give her money,' she said out loud. 'It's bound to cause an argument if he pushes me too far.'

She had decided that if she could get away with not telling Jack that she was expecting, she would. If he rumbled it then she would have to explain herself. But as far as she was concerned, the longer she could keep it from him the better. Who knows what the outcome might be? she thought bitterly to herself. The way she felt about Ken had certainly not endeared her to the baby she was carrying;

she felt no bond with this child at all, and was still seriously considering having it adopted. That would certainly be one way of solving the problem – and it could be one way of keeping her pregnancy and infidelity from Jack too, if she could avoid seeing him for that length of time.

Anxious that Edna might find it stressful looking after Kathleen as well as entertaining Jack, Jeannie had suggested she take the little girl off her hands for at least some part of the day.

'Just in case you might want to spend some time alone with Jack?'

'No, thanks,' Edna exclaimed. 'I'm as nervous as hell. The more Kathleen can distract and entertain him during his visit, the better for me.'

'And have you got enough food to feed him?' Jeannie asked as she did up her coat in readiness for leaving.

'I've got what my ration coupons allow – a tin of corned beef to make some butties, plus tea, milk, bread and meat paste – not a feast, but it should be enough. He'll only be here for the afternoon,' she pointed out, 'then he'll be heading back to his mother's.'

When Jeannie had left, Edna sat on the battered leatherette sofa, feeling tense and nervous; though she had lit the fire against the bitterly cold December weather, the room was still chilly.

Reminding her daughter that they were expecting an important visitor, Edna said, 'Remember to be nice to your daddy.'

'I don't have a daddy,' Kathleen answered defiantly.

'Yes, you do, sweetheart, he's coming to see you today.'

When Jack knocked loudly on the front door, Edna

jumped to her feet, smoothing down her pleated skirt and Fair Isle cardigan. She checked her hair in the mirror before she went to open the door.

'Hello!' Jack cried as he strode into the narrow hallway. He took Edna in his arms and all but squeezed the life out of her. 'Where's my little girl?'

Edna was taken aback, barely recognizing the big burly man who entered the small sitting room, completely claiming the space. He was louder and far more confident than the skinny lad she had waved off to war – and he seemed taller, if that were even possible. His head was almost shaved of hair, his face was heavier, and a heavy growth of stubble darkened his chin.

'Hello, Jack, how was the journey?' she asked politely.

'Terrible, packed troop train from Liverpool – mind you, I did get in a few rounds of cards with some of the lads on the train. Won too,' he winked.

Seeing his little daughter playing with her toys, he rushed forward to pick her up and swing her high in the air.

'Here she is!' he boomed.

Shocked and terrified by the total stranger who had her tightly in his grip, Kathleen struggled out of his arms, crying, 'MUMMY! MUMMY!'

Once he'd put her back down, Kathleen hid behind her mother's skirts and peered out at her father, who looked less than pleased.

In shock herself, Edna nevertheless tried to calm her anxious daughter. 'Shhh, lovie,' she soothed. 'It's just your dad come to see you.'

'Humph,' he grunted as he threw off his soldier's greatcoat and lit up a cigarette. 'She's a right mardy lass!'

Bridling at his words, Edna immediately went on the defensive. 'Jack, you have to understand that Kathleen's been through a lot since you left, evacuated at two years old and moved from place to place; she's only just settling here with me, in fact.'

'Aye, mi mam said you should never have let her go. She said you were keen to get shot of her.'

Stung to the quick by his harsh words, Edna exclaimed, 'Kathleen was evacuated for her own safety! You know better than anybody how unsafe Wigan was, with enemy planes bombing Liverpool almost every night.'

'Aye, that's as may be, but mi mam says you couldn't get away from Wigan quick enough, once the kiddie had gone.'

Though guilty of recent infidelities with Ken, Edna nevertheless staunchly defended herself. 'I came here to work as an engine girl,' she protested. 'It's well-paid work — and as soon as I could, I brought Kathleen here to live with me.'

At which point, hearing raised voices, Kathleen started to cry.

Hearing his daughter grizzling, Jack scooped up the protesting little girl and plonked her on his knee. Trying one more time to woo her, he said, not unkindly, 'Come and sit on your dad's lap and tell me what you've been up to.'

Kathleen was now thoroughly frightened of the burly stranger. She jumped off his lap to run into the kitchen.

'I'll make us some tea,' Edna said as she hurried after her child.

'And a few butties,' he called after her. 'I've had now't to eat since I left Wigan, mi stomach thinks mi throat's been cut — I'm bloody starving.'

Hugging Kathleen in the kitchen, Edna whispered, 'Try not to cry, lovie, we'll go to the park after we've had something to eat, and you can feed the ducks.'

Coaxed into helping her mother make corned-beef sandwiches, Kathleen calmed down a bit. When the sandwiches were made and the tea was brewed, Edna set them down on the little table in front of the fire.

'Now then,' she said, on a bright cheerful note, 'tell me your news.'

Gulping down the hot tea and voraciously chewing the sandwiches, Jack responded with his mouth full.

'More training than fighting,' he told her. 'It could be worse, we're a good regiment, good lads all of 'em, we get up to some fun when we can.'

Edna wondered exactly what sort of fun they actually did get up to.

'I've not heard much from you, though I have tried to keep in touch,' she said, knowing full well that since she had fallen pregnant, she hadn't had any inclination to write to her husband.

'We've been moving around all over't place, hardly got a minute to write love letters,' he scoffed. 'The good news is,' he continued as he polished off the final corned-beef butty, 'we're on track for North Africa; we'll be heading off there soon. That's where the action is these days. The desert should be a nice change from endless training exercises in muddy fields.'

My God, Edna thought, how he's changed.

She could hardly equate this loud-mouthed man with the awkward boy she had married. What had happened to him? What had made him so coarse and insensitive?

Incredulous, she realized that her husband appeared to be enjoying the war. He seemed to relish the idea of fighting in the desert – which, from what she had heard from Ruby (where her own husband was serving), was a nightmare environment.

After the food had been demolished by her seemingly ravenous husband, Edna knew that she couldn't keep nervous, restless Kathleen indoors. *She'll be better off at the park, where she can at least run around and get away from her dad,* she thought, as she buttoned up Kathleen's warm tweed coat and they all set off for town.

As they walked through the narrow streets, Jack carried on showing off about his regiment and his pals; insensitive to his wife and daughter, he recounted stories unsuitable for a child's ears.

'Us lads get up to all kind of pranks,' he chuckled, 'especially with them cheeky little local lasses.'

Thinking guiltily about her own condition, Edna felt she was in no position to judge. Jack, however, quickly censored himself and backtracked.

'Not me, of course – us married folk toe the line, don't we?' he said, with a conspiratorial wink, which made Edna cringe in shame.

To her relief Jack spotted a pub near the park, which he immediately headed into.

Calling over his shoulder, he said, 'I'll catch you up later.'

For nearly an hour, Edna happily entertained Kathleen on the swings and roundabout, until Jack reappeared slightly the worse for wear. Speaking blearily, he put an arm around his wife's waist, which made Edna stiffen in horror.

'Let's get back home and have a little man-and-wife time together, shall we, sweetheart?'

Feeling her heart start to race, Edna whispered, 'Remember Kathleen, we don't want to do anything to upset her.'

'She won't see what's going on if she's playing with her toys,' he murmured rather drunkenly in her ear. 'Come on, sweetheart, you can't deny your husband his rights.'

Once back in the prefab, Edna began to panic. Without ado, Jack urged Kathleen to play with her toys in the sitting room. He quickly shut the door on her, then grabbed Edna's hand and led her unwillingly into the bedroom. Quickly removing her coat, he started to fumble with the buttons on her cardigan.

'Jack,' she whispered urgently. 'What if Kathleen walks in?'

'She won't,' he muttered thickly. 'She's busy with her toys.'

'But she might hear us,' Edna protested wildly.

Shutting her up with a kiss that nauseated Edna, he leant her back on the bed and hurriedly started to remove her underclothes. Thoroughly repulsed by the smell of his beery breath, Edna started to struggle.

'For God's sake, woman, do your duty,' he grumbled as he threw his trousers on to the floor.

Feeling his hands on her breasts, and knowing he would soon be touching the rest of her body, Edna tried to sit up.

'Don't move,' Jack grunted as he struggled with the hooks on her bra.

At this point Kathleen came running into the room.

Seeing her mother sprawled across the bed, and her father half naked, she started to scream.

Edna leapt to her feet and quickly rearranged her underwear.

'It's all right, lovie. Me and Daddy are just having a little cuddle.'

Thoroughly frustrated, Jack struggled to find the clothes he had abandoned, swearing and cursing loudly.

'Damn and blast it – where are my bloody trousers?' he snarled.

Stumbling to his feet, he slipped on the trousers he had drunkenly discarded and fell backwards on top of Edna, who had turned to pick Kathleen up. The weight of Jack's hefty body sent her spinning to the ground; she landed hard on her hips and ribs, sprawled on the cold lino. Winded, she cried out in pain.

'Mama, Mama, get up,' Kathleen begged as she ran to her mother's side.

'I'm all right, lovie,' Edna croaked as she lay stunned on the floor.

After Jack had pulled on his trousers, he moodily held out a hand to help Edna to her feet. 'Are you all right?' he asked curtly.

Rubbing her bruised ribs, Edna didn't make a fuss; though winded, her only thought was to get Jack out of the bedroom.

'Yes, I'm fine,' she quickly answered. 'Shall I make us a cup of tea?' she offered.

'Don't bother,' Jack answered grumpily. 'I've a train to catch.'

Once they were all back in the sitting room, Jack

shrugged on his heavy khaki overcoat. 'I'd best be off,' he grunted as he lit up yet another cigarette.

Overjoyed that his visit was coming to an end, Edna tried not to show her true emotions. 'Oh, so soon,' she murmured.

'Aye, Mam's cooking mi tea,' he told her. 'Then I'm meeting the lads in't pub, that's if the bloody trains are running to plan.' Turning to his daughter, who had remained behind her mother's back, he grunted, 'Let's hope you'll be happier to see me next time, missy.' Then he turned to Edna and added moodily, 'And the same goes for you too, lady, I was expecting a warmer reception than this.'

Desperate for him to just leave, flustered Edna mumbled, 'Hopefully it'll be better next time, when we're not so rushed.'

Throwing open the front door, Jack scoffed, 'It'd better be, that fiasco was hardly worth the bloody train journey.'

Watching Jack walk away, Edna waited tensely until he had turned the corner and then disappeared from sight. In shock, and weak with nervous exhaustion, Edna returned to the sitting room. She slumped down on the sofa with Kathleen clutched in her arms. The entire visit had been a nightmare for both mother and daughter; Jack had clearly not enjoyed it either. Originally she'd been worrying about him discovering that she was pregnant, but now she could only wonder what in the name of heaven had happened to her husband. Is this what war did to an innocent young man who, even when they were married, barely had the confidence to make love to her?

'Will that horrible man come back?' Kathleen whispered.

'No, not for a while,' Edna promised.

'He shouted a lot, and he was mean to you, Mummy.'

Emotionally worn out, Edna fell asleep with Kathleen curled up beside her.

When Jeannie tapped on the door some hours later, Edna was relieved to find her friend standing on the front step, rather than Jack. She feared he might have come back.

'All clear?' Jeannie tentatively enquired.

Edna nodded grimly. 'Yes, he's gone.'

Over a welcome cup of tea Edna recounted the events of the day to Jeannie.

'It was awful,' she whispered. 'Though the good news is, I kept my condition hidden, which is a huge relief.'

Seeing her friend utterly drained, Jeannie suggested Edna have a lie-down while she gave Kathleen a bath in front of the fire. Rubbing her sore hip, which was starting to ache, Edna filled a hot-water bottle to take to bed with her.

'I must have fallen harder than I thought when I tripped over in the bedroom,' she said.

Alarmed, Jeannie whispered, '*What* exactly happened in the bedroom?'

Checking that Kathleen was occupied with her toys, Edna dropped her voice to a whisper.

'He tried to, you know, get into bed with me.'

'With Kathleen around?' Jeannie gasped.

Edna gave a quick nod.

'She was in here playing, to start with, but she came running into the bedroom when Jack was trying to have his way with me, which is when I put up a bit of a struggle and fell over.' Turning to her little girl, who was presently

346

peacefully playing with her toys on the rug by the fire, Edna murmured, 'Oh, Jeannie, he's not the lad I knew. God knows, I've done some bad things, and I'm paying for them now, but he's changed so much, physically and mentally. If I'm honest, I must admit that I didn't like seeing him at all. When he started talking about his mother and the things she said about me, I thought to myself, I can never go back to living with them.'

Seeing Edna looking very pale, and clearly in pain from her fall, Jeannie urged her to go and lie down.

'You've a lot to deal with right now, just take one step at a time,' she said soothingly.

An hour later, glad that her friend was having a nice long rest, Jeannie was lifting Kathleen out of the tin bath to dry her on a big warm towel in front of the fire as Edna walked in.

'Hello, lovie, shall I put the kettle on for a brew?' Jeannie said, glancing up.

Edna looked even paler than before she had gone for her rest. She was holding on to the door frame for support.

Seeing her mother weakly swaying, Kathleen called out, 'MAMA!'

Before Jeannie could get up to help her friend, Edna's legs seemed to just give way beneath her and she slumped to the floor.

46. A Long Night

Hurrying over to her friend after popping Kathleen on the sofa, Jeannie bent down to Edna who, thank goodness, hadn't lost consciousness.

'Come on, dear, if I help you stand, let's try and get you back into bed,' she urged gently.

She slowly managed to haul Edna to her feet and support her friend's tentative steps, but as they got to the bedroom, her eyes were immediately drawn to the bedsheets, stained red with blood. Jeannie tried her best to stay calm and practical, asking her friend nervously if she was still bleeding.

'I didn't know I was, but I'm in awful pain,' Edna replied as she gripped her tummy.

Wondering how she was going to look after both Kathleen and her mother, Jeannie said tensely, 'I need to get help. Will you be all right if I just nip next door and ask your neighbour to keep an eye on Kathleen, while I go and fetch Ruby?'

Edna nodded weakly. 'Yes, but be quick, I'm scared,' she admitted, seeing the bleeding for herself now.

After talking to the neighbour, who said she could nip in for half an hour, Jeannie ran through the streets of Hucknall until she got to Ruby's house. Banging on the door, she was disappointed when Ruby's mother opened it.

'I'm sorry to trouble you, but is Ruby in?'

'Sorry, love, she's gone to the pictures with Audrey, I'm minding Archie.' Seeing the look of pure panic flash across Jeannie's face, Ruby's mother added, 'Is there anything I can do?'

'I urgently need help,' Jeannie answered. Then she suddenly had a thought. 'Do you happen to know Annie Barnes' address?'

'Aye, she lives just around the corner, number three, Downham Avenue,' Ruby's mother told her.

'Thanks very much. Please tell Ruby I called, when she gets back.'

Hurrying down the road, Jeannie wondered how Annie might react when she turned up on her doorstep. Never mind that, Jeannie firmly told herself. I need all the help I can get right now. When Annie opened the door to Jeannie, she did register surprise. Without any preamble Jeannie blurted out her news.

'Annie, Edna's really poorly . . .' Feeling uncomfortable about filling in the details, she mumbled, 'I can't look after both little Kathleen and her mother . . . I need help.'

Annie's answer was instantly supportive. 'I'll just sort out Mother for the evening. You run along back to Edna, and I'll catch you up – I promise I won't be long.'

When Jeannie got back to the prefab, she found Edna in the bathroom and Kathleen with the next-door neighbour in the sitting room.

Breathless from running all the way into town and back again, Jeannie gasped, 'Thanks for helping out.'

'Not a problem,' smiled the kindly neighbour as she left. 'Any time.'

When Annie turned up just behind Jeannie, Kathleen announced, 'Mummy's poorly.'

'That's a shame,' Annie said kindly. 'Shall I go and see how she is?'

Jeannie gave a quick nod in Annie's direction.

'And we need to get you ready for bed, sweetheart. I've got a surprise for you,' she added mysteriously. 'You're going to sleep with me in Auntie Lily's bed, won't that be fun?'

Smiling too, Kathleen asked, 'Where's Auntie Lily going to sleep?'

'She's got her own nice bed in hospital where the nurses and doctors are making her better,' Jeannie thoughtfully explained.

Relentlessly asking questions, Kathleen said, 'Will you always sleep in our prefab?'

'No, I'll go back home to mine when Auntie Lily comes home,' Jeannie responded, with a cheerfulness she certainly didn't feel.

While Kathleen played with her toys on the rug, Jeannie joined Annie in Edna's bedroom to search for the little girl's nightie and slippers.

'Edna's still in the bathroom – she's lost so much blood, I think she must be miscarrying,' Annie whispered urgently.

'That's what I feared,' said Jeannie sadly, frightened for her friend.

'Kathleen mustn't see what's going on,' Annie quickly added. 'She'll get alarmed.'

Jeannie gave a quick nod. 'You sort Edna, I'll see to the little girl.'

When white-faced Edna emerged from the bathroom, Annie took her by the arm and steered her back into bed.

'Come on, mi duck, let's find you some fresh clothes,' she urged.

Once Edna was sitting on the bed, Annie replaced Edna's stained dress and under-slip with a warm nightie. Then, laying a towel across the bed, she gently helped Edna to lie down. Completely worn out, Edna slumped back against the pillows and closed her eyes.

'Thanks for coming to the rescue,' she said feebly. 'I fell over this afternoon, while mi husband was visiting us, the bleeding started shortly after he left.'

'Should I get a message to him?' Annie enquired.

'No, best not,' Edna answered quickly. Sighing heavily, she confessed, 'It doesn't take much to work out that it's not his child, Annie.'

'I see,' Annie answered diplomatically. 'Now what are we going to do, young lady?' she continued. 'Shall we try and get you to the hospital?'

Edna shook her head. 'The bleeding's heavy, but I think I can handle it here at home. I'm not that far gone,' she added, with a deep blush.

Tucking the blankets in around her, Annie said, 'Are you in a lot of pain?'

'Yes, they're like strong period pains.'

'Have you got any painkillers?' Annie enquired.

'We might have some in the bathroom cabinet,' Edna told her.

Out in the hallway Annie had a quick word with Jeannie. 'I suggested Edna might like to go to the hospital, but she insists on staying here.'

'Can you manage?' Jeannie asked. 'I'm having trouble settling Kathleen, because she obviously can't sleep with her mother like she normally does. I'm putting her in Lily's room. Oh goodness, what a mess, both of my best friends in trouble,' she murmured, with tears in her eyes.

Giving her a firm pat on the shoulder, Annie said determinedly, 'We'll get through it. Though it might be a long night,' she added, with a bleak smile.

When Jeannie returned to Kathleen, now finally sleepy and nursing her dolly, she thought how extraordinary life was. Here was Annie Barnes in their prefab, nursing a woman she wouldn't even have spoken to a few months ago; the 'outsiders' and 'foreigners' had become part of the Hucknall community, and if anybody wanted any evidence of that, they had only to see how tender and caring Annie Barnes was with a woman from Wigan who quite clearly had become a friend.

The night of Edna's miscarriage was long indeed; both women took it in turns to help poor Edna back and forth to the lavatory. By dawn, when Edna was in a deep sleep of exhaustion, Annie – who had been up most of the night – felt able at last to return home to see to her mother before she clocked on at the Bell Works.

'I can't thank you enough, Annie,' Jeannie said as she hugged the older woman and said goodbye. 'I could never have got through it, what with Kathleen needing company and reassurance.'

'You did the right thing, mi duck,' Annie assured her.

'Do you think Edna will be all right if I go into work today?' Jeannie anxiously asked. 'I can drop Kathleen off at nursery and pop back here during my dinner break?'

Annie nodded. 'She'll sleep after what she's been through. We can take it in turns to keep an eye on her through the day, I'll sort it out with Sid.'

When Ruby saw Jeannie clocking on in the marbled entry hall of the factory, she immediately apologized for not being available the night before.

After Jeannie told her about the dramatic events, and how Annie had stepped in to help, Ruby said, 'Thank God for friends.'

'Exactly. Who would have thought she'd be the hero of the moment?' Jeannie remarked.

'When Annie's your friend, she's a friend for life,' Ruby added knowingly. 'Do you think it was the shock of seeing Jack that brought on Edna's miscarriage?'

Jeannie shook her head. 'We hardly had time to discuss it. I don't even know if she actually told him she was expecting – she wasn't planning to. She told me she just had a fall.'

'Poor lamb,' Ruby said anxiously. 'Don't worry about Kathleen,' she added, 'I'll pick her up from nursery later on. I'll try and see Edna when I drop Kathleen off at home.'

'I've just been back to the prefab to make Edna a cup of tea and a sandwich; she's a bit better, just weak and tired, but the bleeding's stopped at last. She's in no state to come into work this week.'

Lying in bed in the empty prefab, huddled under the satin eiderdown that kept slipping and sliding every time she turned over, Edna – though utterly worn out and drowsy with painkillers – nevertheless could not stop replaying Jack's visit in her head. It wasn't just how he had talked and behaved towards her, he had been so brash with Kathleen; the little girl had clearly been scared to death.

'He's my husband,' she said under her breath, 'but I don't know him, and I certainly don't like him. He seems closer to his mother and his pals in the regiment than he does to me and his daughter.'

At least he hadn't found out that she was pregnant – and now that she had lost Ken's child, he never would. One thing's for sure, Edna thought bitterly, I don't want any more mad foolish flings with anybody. In truth, I don't even want my husband any more. At this point she had no idea how she would leave Jack, but one thing was crystal clear in her head: she was never going back to him and his mother in Wigan.

From now on, Edna thought grimly, it's just me and Kathleen.

47. Home Truths

Lying on her hospital bed, examining the cuts and grazes on her hands that were slowly starting to heal, Lily looked up in surprise when the ward sister appeared at her bedside.

'Good news, dear,' Sister said cheerily. 'You're fit enough to be moved by army ambulance to a hospital nearer home.'

'Wonderful,' Lily exclaimed. 'When can I leave?'

'Hopefully tomorrow, if we can arrange transport to Nottingham Hospital,' Sister explained.

'Thank you,' Lily smiled gratefully. 'It will be good to be nearer my friends.'

'By the way, this has just arrived for you,' Sister added as she handed Lily a letter. 'Get some rest, I'll be back later to check your dressing.'

Left alone, Lily quickly tore open the letter.

Dearest Lily,

I'm writing in haste, as I think you should know what's going on here. Sad news. Edna's lost her baby. It happened shortly after her husband's visit this week. I was at my wits' end, wondering how I could manage both Kathleen and Edna, but Annie stepped in, she was magnificent, and we got through the awful ordeal together. Edna's presently taking it easy, she'll need to build her strength back up, so I suspect she'll be off work for a week. It was an awful shock for her but I think the relief of not having to hide her pregnancy is enormous, plus she no longer has to worry about Jack finding out about her relationship with that dreadful man, Ken. From the sound of things, I don't think Jack's visit went well. Kathleen regularly tells me that a horrible man came to see them, she says he shouted a lot and was mean to her mummy. She's frightened of him coming back. I don't know the ins and outs of the meeting, but I keep telling her not to worry, he won't be coming back for a while, which seems to calm her down. Poor little kiddie, she's had so much to put up with recently.

We're just about managing here, but missing you terribly; Kathleen especially misses her pretty Auntie Lily, she can't wait to see you. I hope you're getting better, sweetheart? Do you know when you might be moved to another hospital, or come home? It would be quite something to have two patients in Prefab Number 8. I hope you don't mind, but I'm presently staying in your room. It's simpler this way; I can keep an eye on Edna and drop Kathleen off at nursery in the mornings on my way to work. Ruby brings her home at night, which is nice. She and Edna have a chat, which cheers Edna up.

Have you heard from Oro? We haven't seen him, but then we wouldn't expect to – I only hope he's picked up the messages that Ruby left for him at his airbase, or that one of his pals has passed on the news of your accident.

Must rush, Kathleen's begging for her tea! Let me know your news just as soon as you can. Take care of your dear self.

With much love,
Jeannie

PS: I hope you don't think I'm being big-headed, but I've enclosed a couple of my Spitfire Kids stories. Frank and his pals enjoyed them – made them smile, he said – maybe they'll pass the time of day as you lie on your hospital bed. The characters may remind you

of a few familiar faces in Hucknall! Just seeing my stories again,
and recalling the funny, catchy title that Frank gave them, makes
me realize how very dear that boy is to me. He's wise beyond his
years, and he thinks well of everybody. I miss him so much. He's
been such an inspiration in my life. Anyway, I hope you enjoy the
Spitfire Kids as much as Frank does x

Though looking forward to leaving Ipswich Hospital and moving closer to home, Lily nevertheless felt uneasy. She was healing well, she was lucky to be alive, but her heart was heavy. In all the time since her plane crash and hospitalization she hadn't heard a single word from Oro. Like Jeannie, she hoped the message Ruby had left at Oro's airbase would have found its way to him – and even if it hadn't (she reasoned), surely one of his airmen pals would have notified him of her crash in Suffolk? The Woodbridge airbase would be in touch with other local airbases; Oro might not be in Hucknall, but his mates surely must have heard about an aircraft accident involving a ferry girl. And if they had, they just might have passed that information on to him. Tears slipped down Lily's pale face as she considered what might have prevented her boyfriend from getting in touch with her.

Who knows? He may have met a glamorous female pilot, Lily fretted. Or come to that, several glamorous female pilots might have caught his eye.

Though she knew full well that Oro had never come across as a flirt, she also knew without a doubt that men, good men, were scarce on the ground these days. With his charm and good looks he could have his pick of young women training to be pilots. Had he found somebody better than her? After all, she was only an engine girl, previously a Whitby waitress, with aspirations to become a pilot.

But he's not like that, Lily told herself. His absence might be down to something far more sinister; he might have been posted elsewhere or be on a dangerous bombing raid.

With her head beginning to throb, Lily reached for Jeannie's stories. Maybe these will cheer me up, she thought, groaning at the pain in her damaged arm, or at least they'll take my mind off Oro.

The following day, after a gruelling ambulance journey north through towns and villages on the east coast that were being ravaged with constant bombing, Lily was grateful to be admitted to Nottingham Hospital. Once she'd been issued with a bed on a female ward, she instantly fell into a deeply troubled sleep filled with nightmare images of orange flames, black smoke and her hands gripping the steering wheel as the Spitfire rolled inexorably into a brick wall.

Sweating and thrashing under the starched white bed-sheets, Lily groaned as she opened her eyes. Confused and only half awake, she blinked hard several times when she saw a dark shadow by the side of her bed.

'*Ukochana*,' a dear, familiar voice whispered. 'Darling, shhh . . .'

Slowly coming round, Lily realized she wasn't dreaming – she was wide awake, in fact, and gazing up into the face of her beloved.

'ORO!' she cried as she struggled to sit up, then yelped in pain as she caught her damaged arm.

'Darling, *ukochana*, please, lie still,' Oro urged as he gently lowered her back down on to the pillows. Smiling, he stroked her silver-blonde hair off her cheek. 'Sweet girl,' he murmured.

Delighted to see him, Lily gasped, 'How did you manage to find me?'

'A good friend informed me only this week that you had crashed your plane; he had heard about a ferry girl accident at the Woodbridge base, and being my pal, he did a bit of investigating and discovered that the ferry girl was in fact you. When I found out, I was out of my mind with worry, but nobody can leave camp without special dispensation. I applied for compassionate leave,' he explained. 'I got a lift from the south coast with a pilot who was delivering an aircraft to Hucknall.' Holding her good hand tightly in his own, he murmured, 'Oh, my love, what happened to you?'

Lily gave a long shuddering breath before starting her story. 'I landed in a heavy mist, then spun out of control on the runway. The nose of the Spit caught fire but I managed to scramble out before the entire aircraft went up,' she briefly told him.

'And now, dearest, how are you feeling?'

Smiling sweetly, she answered, '*So*, *so* happy to see you, Oro!' Reaching up with her free arm, which she curled around his neck, Lily pulled him down to her level so she could kiss him deeply on the lips. 'I've missed you so much, sweetheart.'

'My love . . .' he whispered as he kissed her back.

Locked in each other's arms, they became suddenly aware of footsteps approaching.

'Sorry, sir,' a smiling young nurse said. 'Visiting time is nearly over.'

Drawing apart, the two young lovers gazed adoringly at each other.

'When will I see you again, darling?' Lily anxiously asked.

'I'm hoping my senior recruiting officer can find another tutor to replace me. If he can get someone then I'll be able to return to my base – though I will be back in action – but at least I'll be nearer to you, my sweetheart,' he said fondly.

Though Lily dearly wanted her boyfriend close to her, she realized that he was in fact safer teaching recruits than flying on enemy bombing missions with his Polish squadron. Nevertheless, she was grateful for his thoughtfulness.

'I desperately want you close by,' she answered as she gripped his hands. 'I already feel better and stronger just for seeing you.'

'I have to return to the recruiting centre to tidy things up, then I'll come back as soon as I'm allowed, I promise. All you have to do is get well, my sweet Lily.'

'I'll do my best.' She smiled at him as he bent to kiss her goodbye.

Watching him walk away down the long ward, lined with metal beds arranged in rows on either side, Lily's heart contracted with love: she was so proud of her handsome pilot and so relieved that he would soon be coming back to his Hucknall base. Thinking excitedly of all the lovely things they could do together, Lily's heart raced. Then she caught sight of her broken arm, lying heavily on the bed, and gave a resigned sigh.

'No flying for me for the moment,' she cautioned sternly. 'That's one thing that will have to wait.'

During her time in Nottingham Hospital, Lily was thoroughly entertained by Jeannie's charming, funny, light-hearted stories that would resonate with readers. The warm tone, light style and happy camaraderie delighted and distracted Lily as she lay on her hospital bed. One afternoon, while she was deep into one of Jeannie's stories, who should turn up but Edna.

'Edna! What you are doing here?'

Carefully giving her dear friend a hug, Edna grinned as she sat down on the metal bedside chair.

'When I heard you'd moved hospitals, I just had to see you, lovie.'

'But, should *you* be out of bed?' Lily panicked.

Edna shrugged. 'Really all I did was walk up the street and catch the bus here. Anyway, I've got to build up my strength – I'm planning on going back to work next week. To be honest, I've had more than enough of lying in bed, day in and day out, thinking about what a mess I've made of things,' she said, with a bitter smile. 'I thought a little outing would do me good.' Lowering her voice, she added, 'I tell you straight, Lil, you put the fear of God into the lot of us.'

'It was a terrifying experience, I was lucky to survive,' Lily confessed. 'But I am on the mend now, which is why they let me leave Ipswich Hospital and come here. It's so nice to be nearer home.'

'It's nice for us too. We can see you more often now.'

Lily gave a secret smile. 'I've had a visit from Oro.'

361

'I thought I saw a little sparkle in your eye,' Edna grinned.

'It was so good to see him after so long. I thought he might have gone off me,' she admitted, with a self-deprecating smile.

'Never! Not with your stunning looks – he'd be mad,' Edna laughed.

Lily gave a romantic sigh. 'He looked so strong and handsome.'

'Love's young dream,' Edna teased.

Breaking out of her reverie, Lily said, 'Enough of me, tell me how *you* are.'

'As I said, improving, looking forward to getting back to work.'

'You must take care, Edna, you know how tough it can be on the factory floor, all that heavy lifting and straining, take it slow to start with.'

'You seem to have been saying that to me for weeks now,' Edna said. 'I'm not pregnant any more: it's been a shock, but I think in the end it will be for the best.'

'How did it happen?' Lily asked.

After Edna had related the incidents leading up to the accident, she added in a sombre voice, 'Something snapped in me that day, Lil – I feel like I never want to see Jack again.'

Stunned by the harshness of her words, Lily waited to hear what she might say next.

'He's not the boy I loved, or the man I married, he's coarse and loud-mouthed, rude – and I suspect a bit of a drinker, from the way he dived into the nearest public house as soon as he could.'

'What are you going to do?' Lily asked nervously. 'After all, you're still married.'

'Aye, and there's a war on, and mi 'usband is more than likely heading off to North Africa. I won't be getting in touch with him in a rush – and hopefully, he won't try and get in touch with me either.'

'What if he does? There is Kathleen to consider, she *is* Jack's child,' Lily reminded her friend.

'I'll just ignore his letters and hopefully, over time, we'll drift apart; we've certainly not got much in common these days,' Edna told her glumly. 'Luckily, he seems fonder of his mother than he is of me – maybe he'll settle for a woman she approves of, rather than one she detests.'

Thinking of her own recent rapturous reconnection with Oro, Lily was sympathetic. 'What a horrible situation to be in.'

'It's terrible what war can do to a person. And who am I to judge?' Edna said bitterly. 'Take me, for example, living the dream, so I thought, a second lease of life, flirting for England. Hah!' she scoffed. 'Look where I ended up.'

'We live and learn,' Lily consoled her.

'Aye, we live and learn the hard way.' Clearly keen to change the subject, Edna added, 'Jeannie's been living with me since I had the accident, she's been a godsend, but she'll be moving back into her own prefab when you come home.'

'I wish we could all live together, rather than in two separate prefabs,' Lily said.

'Maybe after Christmas we could ask for a transfer to a bigger prefab,' Edna suggested.

Lying back on her banked-up pillows, Lily said incredulously, 'Christmas . . . it doesn't feel like it usually does to me.'

'Me neither,' Edna agreed. 'When I think of the Christmases before the war, poor as we were, there was always a good spread on the table on Christmas Day, and presents under the tree – aye, they were happy days.'

'I used to love working in the hotel on Christmas Day,' Lily recalled. 'It was so exciting, with all the guests in the best of festive spirits. We ran around all day serving food and drink, but the staff had plenty of fun too, and we always sat down to a feast once the guests were fed. Roast goose and duck, always a side of ham in those good old pre-rationing days, Christmas pudding, custard, Wensleydale and Stilton cheeses, port and brandy if you fancied it. It seems like a dream now.'

'Stop it!' Edna begged. 'God knows what we'll scratch together for our Christmas dinner: sprouts and potatoes, if we're lucky, with a sausage and a bit of stuffing thrown in. Though I must sort out a little stocking for our Kathleen, and I'm saving my clothing coupons for a new coat for her. Hopefully, we can put up a Christmas tree for her to decorate.'

'I'd love that!' Lily exclaimed. 'Let's really make this Christmas as good as it can be.'

'After all the help and support I've had recently, I would love to include the local lasses in the festivities; Ruby, Audrey, Mary, Annie, we feel like a family these days, I'd hate them to be excluded from any of our celebrations.'

'I think that's a wonderful idea,' Lily enthused.

Suddenly excited, Edna said, 'We could go carol singing round Hucknall and get to know the locals. When I think what it was like a few months ago, that horrible "them" and "us" atmosphere. How did we manage to get our wires crossed so badly?'

'Thank God, all of that is behind us,' Lily mumbled in a sleepy voice.

'I ought to leave you to get some rest, lovie,' Edna said.

'I am a bit sleepy,' she admitted. 'I've been reading Jeannie's stories, "The Spitfire Kids" she's taken to calling them. They are so entertaining. She told me that her young man, Frank, says she's got real talent. I agree with him. I think she should try and get them published.'

'I've been thinking the same thing,' Edna said conspiratorially. 'Being laid up, you probably aren't aware that the local paper is running a short story competition.'

Lily's eyes visibly brightened. 'Are you thinking what I'm thinking?'

Edna nodded. 'The thing is, I'm quite sure Jeannie won't submit them – she says the stuff she writes is just a bit of fun – but I think she might stand a chance.'

'You mean if we leave it to her, it might not happen?'

Edna grinned as she nodded again. 'Do you think it would be wicked to submit them without asking her?'

'She might be furious if we go behind her back,' Lily replied.

'She wouldn't be if she got through successfully,' Edna said, with a knowing smile.

Too tired to argue, Lily agreed. 'All right then, send a few of her stories in, and let's see how far they get.'

48. News

As soon as Edna was fit enough to return to work, she threw herself into organizing Christmas activities.

Worried about Edna's health, Annie insisted, 'You should be taking it easy and getting your strength back, not organizing carol singing events.'

'Actually, I'm not feeling so bad,' Edna told her. 'Anyway, it takes mi mind off more troubling matters.'

'Nevertheless, Edna,' Annie persisted. 'Don't go lifting and carrying huge weights, at least not for the time being.'

'I won't – in fact I can't!' Edna laughed. 'Jeannie's constantly on my back, she's taken over Lily's guardian angel role.' Smiling fondly at her thoughtful friends, Edna said, 'I can't be ill forever, you know.'

Adamant Annie spoke on behalf of the entire group. 'We're all keeping an eye on you, whether you like it or not.'

Throwing up her hands, Edna declared, 'All right, you win, let's change the record and talk about my carol singing idea. Kathleen hardly stops singing "Jingle Bells" and "Rudolph The Red-Nosed Reindeer" these days, so I thought we should pick up on the festive cheer and organize a carol singing event.'

'And who's going to be doing the singing?' Mary asked.

Sweeping out an arm to include everyone, Edna answered, 'We are! The Bell Works Carol Singers,' she announced.

'And exactly where are we thinking of holding this grand event?' Audrey joked.

'Hucknall church,' Edna answered. 'Me and Kathleen walk over there most Sundays, it's a gorgeous little place.'

'You'll have to get the vicar's permission,' Ruby pointed out.

'I'll make enquiries next time I see him,' Edna replied. 'Lily told me that Lord Byron is buried in St Mary Magdalene Church.'

'Hell fire! We've a lot to live up to, then,' Audrey chuckled.

'If the vicar agrees, we'll hold the service on Christmas Eve, just as it's going dark. We'll light candles to create a nice atmosphere. It'll be lovely,' Edna enthused.

Thinking of others as usual, Ruby murmured, 'It really is a lovely idea, Edna, though we should bear in mind that for people without their loved ones Christmas time might be very hard indeed.'

'Aye, they might think there's now't much to sing about,' Audrey added.

'That's exactly why we've got to put our hearts into the carol service and sing for the ones who are not with us,' Edna insisted. 'It might make some people sad, but it might make some people happy, especially the kiddies. Why should they be denied happiness? They weren't the ones who created the war,' she added staunchly.

Ruby threw Edna a ravishing smile. 'You're right, lovie, let's do it for the kiddies, make Christmas 1941 one they'll remember.'

Grinning, Edna clapped her hands together. 'Right, so are we agreed? We'll organize a Christmas Eve carol service at St Mary Magdalene – courtesy of the vicar, of course.'

After a general chorus of agreement, Mary was feeling increasingly nervous. 'Will anybody bother coming to listen to us lot?' she asked. 'After all, we're only engine girls, not proper trained singers.'

'It's the thought that counts,' Ruby reminded her. 'Especially if we can involve all the kiddies in the event.'

Getting carried away, Edna continued, 'We could pin up posters around the town inviting everyone to the Bell Works Carol Service. And we could pass a plate around during the service for donations – which we could give to the Bell Works nursery. They're keen to buy new outdoor equipment, maybe a slide and some swings, for when the weather gets warmer. They'd be grateful for anything they could get.'

Now utterly panic-stricken, Mary finally blurted out the truth. 'I can't sing for toffee!'

'Look, lovie, if you're that anxious, just pretend to sing,' Edna laughed.

Over the next few days, the Bell Works Choir steadily grew. Though the women were working, they tried their best to attend the choir rehearsals in Hucknall church. Those with a family, like Ruby, often turned up late but it was always worth the effort. It wasn't just the singing that drew them, it was the camaraderie they shared on those chilly evenings, standing in the nave, wrapped up in their warmest coats against the cold, holding their song sheets and singing all their favourite festive songs together. Like Edna smilingly said, 'It's not King's College carols at Christmas, it's just Hucknall lasses having a bit of fun!'

To make the best use of their free time, the choir often practised in the canteen or in the ladies' changing rooms during their dinner breaks. Their repertoire extended to all the popular carols, and when it was discovered that Ruby had the voice of an angel she was given solo parts in 'Once In Royal David's City' and 'See Amid The Winter's Snow'. Keen to be part of the choir but not disgrace herself, Mary obediently opened and shut her mouth, never letting a squeak out, but she seemed to enjoy the fun and laughter that accompanied the rehearsals.

'Such a pity that Lil's not here – she would love it,' Edna said, at the end of one of their practices. 'She's got a lovely voice – and the face of an angel to go with it.'

An armaments factory in wartime never closes, so the management worked with Sid on rotating shifts, which meant that those who wanted time off could take limited leave while those who wanted to carry on working did so with an overtime bonus. Apart from the rehearsals there was decorating the church to arrange and the posters to create; these were drawn by hand, during several tea breaks, ready to distribute around the town. Even as the cold weather worsened and food rationing tightened, the atmosphere of excitement and anticipation grew as they all counted down the days to Christmas. It was Annie who came up with the idea of them all sharing Christmas dinner together in the church where the carol service was going to be held.

'After the vicar agreed to let us sing there on Christmas Eve, I asked if he would mind if we congregated in the church on Christmas Day for a bring-and-share Christmas dinner. He actually asked if he could come too,' she smiled. 'Don't think he fancied eating on his own in his draughty cold vicarage.'

'We can't eat our dinner sitting in pews!' Audrey cried. 'It wouldn't feel right, wearing a paper hat and pulling crackers in the central nave.'

'There's an area to the side where they hold social events, mother and toddler sessions, and little prayer groups – it's all laid out with tables and chairs,' Annie explained. 'The vicar said we were welcome to gather there, just so long as we cleared up after the event.'

'I think that's a wonderful idea,' Edna agreed. 'Anything's better than sitting in a freezing-cold prefab.'

'Let's draw up a list and see how many friends and their families might like to come,' Ruby suggested.

Edna nodded enthusiastically. 'And if we share our food, hopefully there'll be more to go around.'

In the midst of all the preparations, Edna received a letter that made her even more excited. Hugging the letter to herself, she visited Lily in hospital after work, leaving Ruby minding Kathleen for an hour before bedtime.

'You're never going to believe it,' Edna declared as she plonked the opened letter on Lily's bed. 'This arrived today.'

Lily glanced at the envelope. 'It's addressed to Jeannie, at Prefab Number Eight,' she noticed.

Edna nodded. 'I couldn't have them sending a reply directly back to Jeannie, when she knew now't about what we've been up to,' she explained. 'Have a read,' she urged.

Holding the letter in her good hand, Lily read out loud.

Dear Miss Bradshaw,

After sifting through the many submissions that we received for our story competition, it is with great pleasure that we can announce you as the winner. We read your 'Spitfire Kids' with great enthusiasm, and admired your ability to create a workplace with a sound war ethic, while vividly bringing to life the women who work there. We look forward to publishing your stories in our newspaper and to sending you the £10 winner's prize very soon.

Meanwhile, please accept our sincere congratulations.

Yours faithfully,
The Editorial Team

'Oh, Edna,' Lily exclaimed. 'This is wonderful news. Have you told Jeannie yet?'

Edna shook her head.

'No, ideally I'd like to tell her when you're there too. Maybe we could both come to see you, if I can get Ruby to babysit for an hour.'

'I must admit, I'd love to see her face when she reads that letter,' Lily mused.

'I always knew her stories were good,' Edna said, with a satisfied smile.

'She'll be shocked sideways,' Lily predicted. Sighing wistfully, she added, 'I wish I was at home so I could celebrate with you.'

'Me too,' Edna agreed. 'When do you think they might discharge you?'

'I'm sure I'm fit enough to leave now,' Lily said robustly. 'I'll have my arm in plaster for a bit longer, but the cuts and burns have almost healed.'

'Just as long as you're home for all the Christmas activities.'

'The factory will be on full production, Christmas or not,' Lily pointed out.

371

'The war doesn't stop for Christmas,' Edna agreed, 'but Sid's organized rotas so that those who want to spend the day with their family can, while those who aren't fussed can work all the overtime they can get.'

'Good old Sid, what would we do without him?' Lily wondered.

Continuing excitedly, Edna added, 'It's not just the carol singing. We're going to decorate the church with holly and mistletoe, and put little home-made presents under a Christmas tree next to the crib. Sid's promised to locate one for us,' she said, with a wink.

'We're not short of trees, being so near to Sherwood Forest,' Lily joked. 'How many are coming to the dinner on Christmas Day?'

'About twenty of us,' said Edna. 'It's going to be great – I can't wait.'

When Edna returned home from her hospital visit, she found Jeannie in the prefab, in Lily's bedroom, sobbing her heart out. After quickly settling Kathleen with her toys in front of the fire, protected by a large wrap-around fire guard, Edna hurried to comfort her friend.

'Sweetheart – what is it?' she asked, 'Whatever's the matter.'

Holding up a crumpled, tear-stained letter, Jeannie cried, 'It's Frank. Oh, Edna, Frank's dead!'

Edna folded her arms around her distraught friend and held her close as she tried to soothe her.

'His friend Eddie – the lad who returned my stories to me a short while back – he wrote to me. Here . . . read it,' she said as she thrust the letter into Edna's hand.

Quickly scanning the lines, Edna read the news.

Dear Jeannie,

I'm writing to you with some very sad news. As you know, I didn't move on to the Far East with my regiment, due to my current medical treatment. I've heard little news from my regiment since they left, but I have heard from Frank's family. He and I live in the same village, just outside Hebden Bridge on the Yorkshire moors, our families have known each other since we were both lads at school, and we've kept close ties ever since.

It was through my mother visiting Frank's mother that we heard how Frank, along with hundreds of other soldiers, struggled with the heat and living conditions in Singapore. Mother saw the official letter that Frank's family had received from the War Office; it said that the poor lad died of a tropical fever shortly after arriving in the colony.

We are all in shock; he was such a good lad and would do any-thing for anybody. I don't think his mother will ever recover. I'm told she is inconsolable. I'm sorry to be the bearer of bad tidings but I thought you would want to know the news, no matter how bad it is. Keep writing your 'Spitfire Kids' stories – do it in memory of a brave lad who lost his young life in the service of his country.

Maybe we will meet again in happier times.

Yours respectfully,
Eddie

Slowly folding the letter, Edna sighed, 'Oh my God, Jeannie, what a terrible shock.'

Jeannie shuddered. 'I just can't take it in. He was so young and full of life. I can't believe he's dead,' she wept.

'That's the bloody war for you,' Edna answered bitterly.

'It's happening all over the world right now, and there's now't folks like us can do about it.'

Dabbing away her tears, Jeannie murmured, 'It's so good of Eddie to get in touch. It can't have been easy for him, writing a letter like that.'

Edna nodded. 'If he hadn't taken the trouble to let you know, you might never have found out – not being next of kin or knowing his family.'

Tugging nervously at her lip, Edna wondered what to do; should she tell Jeannie the good news about her stories, even though Lily wasn't present? Or would it dreadfully backfire, given the tragic circumstances.

'Er . . .' she started hesitantly.

'What's troubling you, Edna?' Jeannie asked, seeing her friend's strained expression.

'Actually, I've got some news too . . .' Edna started cautiously.

'Not more bad news!' Jeannie cried.

'No, no, in fact, it's good news . . . but it might not be quite the right moment to tell you.'

Thoroughly alarmed, Jeannie insisted, 'Please, Edna, just spit it out.'

Taking a nervous breath, Edna said, 'I've gone and done something without your permission. You see . . .'

When Edna came to the end of her confession, Jeannie could only gape at her.

'You sent my stories to the local press?' she spluttered.

'It was me, and Lily too – we both agreed your stories were good enough but we knew, if we asked, you being backwards at coming forwards, you would say they were no good and tell us not to send them.'

Looking incredulous, Jeannie shook her head.

'The timing is extraordinary,' she murmured. 'Frank always said my stories were good; he encouraged me all the way, he even gave me the title for the series. Hearing of his death at the same time as hearing that I've won a competition he would have encouraged me to enter, makes me feel so close to him, as if something of him lives on in the stories.'

Jeannie somehow managed to smile through her tears. She spoke in a voice that resonated with gritty determination.

'I'm going to carry on writing. "Spitfire Kids" will keep Frank's memory alive – I'll make sure of that.'

49. Conscription

Shortly after hearing of Frank's death, Jeannie went to visit Lily. The two friends were longing to see each other.

'Sweetheart, how are you feeling?' Lily asked.

Jeannie settled in the bedside chair. 'Since I heard about Frank's death, I've been all over the place, if I'm honest,' she confessed.

'Not surprising,' Lily reassured her. 'I only met him once, at the dance, but he was a lovely lad. Have you managed to get into work since you got the bad news?'

'Yes, I'm better off at work than moping around at home,' Jeannie sighed. 'It's so sad. Frank and I were only just getting to know each other; we only met twice but we really got on, I felt easy in his company, and I missed him a lot when he went away,' she said, with tears in her eyes. 'He was a good correspondent, wrote whenever he could, telling me about life in the army, which is what got me started on "Spitfire Kids". We entertained each other,' she smiled shyly. 'We even talked about spending time together at Christmas – if he was home on leave, that is. He wanted to introduce me to his family – they live up north – God, just imagine what those poor souls are going through. As if losing a beloved son weren't bad enough, losing him so close to Christmas, with all the memories that brings. It's odd, you know,' she murmured. 'It's not like I've lost a husband or a blood relative, but I feel like I've lost a real soulmate.'

Stroking her hand, Lily murmured, 'Grief is something you can't quantify; we all handle it differently. Whether it's the death of a husband, brother or friend, it's an awful shock.'

Jeannie nodded in agreement. 'The fact that I'll never see him smile again, or read a letter from him, just seems impossible. He was so young, with all his life ahead of him, and now he's gone – and from the sound of things, he suffered from a horrible fever before he died.'

Desperate to cheer her friend up, Lily said tentatively, 'He certainly had a great influence on you, Jeannie. Look what you've achieved because of him.'

'I know,' Jeannie exclaimed. 'It's wonderful that I won the competition! And before you ask, I don't mind that you and Edna went behind my back; like Edna said, I am a bit backwards about coming forwards. I'd never have had the confidence to enter a writing competition, so thanks for doing it for me.'

'What are you going to spend your winnings on?'

Jeannie blushed. 'A second-hand typewriter,' she announced. 'The editor has asked me to write a weekly "Spitfire Kids" article, so I'll need one. I'm going to compile all my stories into a book I'll dedicate to Frank's memory. When I think it's good enough, I'm going to circulate it to some publishers,' she shyly explained.

'That's such a lovely idea!' Lily exclaimed.

'It's as if Frank's pushing me, from beyond the grave, to do things I would never have dreamt of,' Jeannie murmured. 'Sometimes I feel embarrassed, and I worry people might think that I'm a big-head – you know, have grand ideas above my station – but quite honestly, with Frank somehow guiding and directing me, I don't care what folks think any more.'

'Good for you, lovie. Do the right thing by the lad and make him proud of you, up there in heaven.'

Smiling gratefully, Jeannie added, 'Thanks for supporting me and encouraging me too, Lil, you're a great friend. We all miss you so much at home.'

'I've got good news,' Lily beamed. 'I've been discharged, I'm coming home.'

'In time for Christmas!' delighted Jeannie cried. 'Edna will rope you in to her choir, there's no stopping her these days, it's "Jingle Bells" from dawn to dusk in Prefab Number Eight.' Pulling herself up short, she quickly added, 'I'll leave your room nice and tidy for you.'

'I was hoping that you might stay on in Prefab Number Eight,' Lily said eagerly. 'We could share my room, if we get hold of another single bed. It would be lovely for us all to be close together, and Kathleen would love it. Ruined by adoring aunties!'

'I'd love to live with you all,' Jeannie admitted.

'We've all been through so much these last few months: my plane crash, Edna losing her baby, and now you hearing your sad news about Frank. We need each other more than ever before. Now's not the time for you to go back to a prefab you might soon be sharing with a stranger,' Lily insisted.

Jeannie gave a slow nod.

'Our friendship has kept us going, kept us strong and determined. And I include the Hucknall lasses in that too – nervy little Mary, cheeky Audrey, lovely Ruby, and baby Archie – we're a real family these days.'

'Don't you go forgetting Annie,' Lily reminded her.

'She's a trooper if ever there was one,' Jeannie smiled. 'You should have seen the way she handled Edna when she was miscarrying; nothing panicked her, she took it all in her stride, firm but kind, she just got on and did what she had to do.'

'So, we agree,' Lily said decisively. 'We'll both share my room?'

Smiling happily, Jeannie nodded. 'Of course I'll have to register my move with the accommodation officer, but yes! I'll look into getting another bed. If all else fails, I'll unscrew my bed and carry it round to your prefab in pieces!'

'I wish I could be more helpful, I feel so useless, lying here,' Lily groaned. 'I want to get back to work, be with people, enjoy Christmas, even go flying again one day. Obviously, that will have to wait, but really the sooner I get back in the saddle the better. I've lost a lot of confidence,' she admitted.

'You crashed a plane that caught fire, so it's hardly surprising you lost your confidence,' Jeannie pointed out. 'You'll need to take your time, lovie.'

'I don't want to stop flying, Jeannie,' Lily continued. 'I've had a fright, but I'm alive, thank God.' Sighing, she added, 'You've no idea how wonderful it is being up there, above the clouds. It literally is another world.'

'Just be patient, I'm sure Oro will support you when the time is right.' Struck by a sudden thought, Jeannie asked, 'How are you going to get home once you're discharged?'

Lily flashed her most radiant of smiles. 'Oro's going to borrow a jeep from his base, and he'll drive me home. We might turn up when you're all at work, but I've got a key so we'll be able to let ourselves in.'

When the bell went for the end of visiting time, Jeannie paused in the doorway to wave goodbye to her friend, little knowing that the next day would bring even more significant news than the prospect of Lily returning home.

Early the next morning, Audrey was running up Hucknall High Street, late for work, having missed her alarm going off. She called out a friendly hello as she dashed past a friend from her school days, who was opening up the local paper shop where she worked.

Waving a morning paper, her friend yelled after her, 'Oi, Audrey! Come here – tek a look at this.'

Briefly backtracking, Audrey looked at the newspaper her friend thrust in her face.

OFFICIAL CONSCRIPTION FOR WOMEN

Breathless, not just from running but from shock too, Audrey gasped, 'Hell fire!'

'We knew it were coming,' her friend said lugubriously.

'Aye, and not before time!' Audrey cried. She quickly set off running again, wondering how much this news would change life for them all on the factory floor.

In the ladies' changing room, Audrey scrambled out of her home clothes and into her grubby dungarees before announcing to those who hadn't heard the momentous news, 'Female conscription is blinking official – I saw it in't paper on my way here just now.'

'Good news, if you ask me,' Ruby said as she secured her spotted green turban over her tumbling brunette hair. 'The more people building planes to fight the war the better.'

'You're right there, Ruby,' Edna instantly agreed. 'Hopefully, the new conscripts will be pouring into the Bell Works very soon.'

Without thinking, naive Mary exclaimed, 'The place will be overrun with newcomers.'

All heads turned to the young girl.

'Now then,' Ruby cautioned. 'Let's not go there, mi duck.'

Feeling embarrassed, Mary quickly apologized. 'Sorry, that was uncalled for,' she muttered, blushing.

Tying up her bootlaces, Annie said generously, 'Like Ruby just said, we don't need to revisit past times. If all the conscripted lasses are as good as the ones we've got here already, we'll be lucky.'

Edna's eyes locked with Annie's. Feeling emotional, she recalled the bad old days, which now seemed trivial and of no consequence. Annie had shown devotion at a point in her life when she needed somebody she could completely trust; as far as Edna was concerned, Annie Barnes was a friend for life.

Always the practical one, Audrey said, 'So, where are these new engine girls going to live, I wonder?'

'There are loads of empty prefabs,' Jeannie pointed out. 'I'm quite sure they can throw up loads more. They're now't but pre-fabricated sections; a Spitfire is better built than any prefab.'

'And there's the nursery too,' Edna added. 'There's bound to be women arriving in need of nursery care. Me and Ruby can help them there, knowing the ropes as well as we do now,' she smiled.

Reflecting back on her own arrival in Hucknall, Edna

wondered how she would have got through those early autumn days at the Bell Works without Lily and Jeannie's friendship. In reality it wasn't like she was ever homesick. Once Kathleen and Jack had left, and she was stuck on her own with her ghastly mother-in-law, Edna couldn't get out of Wigan quick enough. She actually wanted to leave home, start afresh, and enjoy a new lease of life. The latter experience had been a disaster, and best left to history, but despite this, coming to the Midlands and living in Hucknall had been the best thing that ever happened to her. Her desire to do her bit for her country to win the war had been the impetus, but along the way she had found the best of friends, the kindest community, a beautiful historic part of England, and she had got her precious daughter back. It had been a frosty start, for sure – and she hoped that the newly conscripted engine girls, who would soon come pouring into the factory, would be treated better.

As if reading her thoughts, ever-generous Ruby addressed the circle of women.

'We'll make sure the new recruits get a warm welcome, won't we, ladies?'

'Aye, the more engine girls we can train, the more aircraft we send into the sky to fight Hitler and win this blasted war,' Audrey added.

'Everything is bound to speed up now,' Ruby agreed. 'Women are going to be busier than ever in armaments factories all over Britain,' she predicted.

Mary gave a meek little smile. 'What would all them big noises running the country do without us women?'

'They'd be up the creek without a paddle,' Edna chuckled. 'Even the Prime Minister, Winston Churchill, calls us women his "Secret Army". You mark my words, there'll be millions of us fighting the war in workshops and factories, behind closed doors, in places that aren't even marked on the map; women will be assembling components for guns, tanks, aircraft and artillery.'

'It makes me shiver with pride to think what we might achieve,' humble Mary murmured.

'Let's bear in mind that when the new girls arrive, a lot of them might be young and homesick,' Jeannie added.

'I'd be devastated if I had to leave my mam,' Mary blurted out.

'We know that, lovie,' Jeannie smiled. 'So, it's just as well she lives in Hucknall, and you will never have to leave home.'

'Unless you get wed,' Audrey teased.

'I'm not getting wed,' Mary declared. 'Men frighten me to death.'

'Eeh, you're a soppy sod,' Audrey teased.

Annie brought the conversation to a close before the hooter sounded out, and the women had to return to work.

'The most important thing to bear in mind is that we do a good job of training up the new engine girls. We want every Spitfire that leaves this factory with our name on it to be in tip-top condition when we dispatch it to fight the Luftwaffe. That's our mission, ladies, never forget it.'

50. Auntie Lily

When Oro drove Lily home to Prefab No. 8 on the day that conscription became legal, she was pleased to find another single bed in her room, already made up with Jeannie's bedding. Her friends had damped down the fire with embers before they left for work that morning, to keep the prefab warm and welcoming for Lily's return. There was a card propped up on the kitchen table, next to a vase of holly leaves brightly speckled with big red berries. Kathleen had drawn a sweet little picture of Lily along with a message.

Welcome Home, Auntie Lily!

'This is lovely,' Lily sighed as she gazed around the prefab.

There was bread and marg on the kitchen table and a tin of corned beef, plus a little apple turnover that Kathleen had baked.

'I have something for us to eat too.' Oro grinned as he opened his rucksack.

'Oh, I do hope it's more of that delicious salami, and your special Polish black coffee,' she smiled.

'You are getting to know me well, *ukochana*.'

After stoking up the fire, the happy couple sat down, side by side, to eat the food he had brought – the strong coffee and salami that Lily especially liked, plus black bread and cheese.

'Beats corned-beef butties,' she giggled as they sipped the hot coffee.

'You must promise me that now you are home, you will rest.'

'I'll try,' she nodded. 'Even though I really do feel full of energy.'

'This is exactly what worries me, little silver busy bee,' he said fondly. 'Please don't forget you have arm in plaster.'

Waving her left arm in the air, Lily grumbled, 'How could I ever forget? But really, Oro, how am I going to pass my time if I'm not flying or building aircraft? I'll go out of my mind with boredom.'

'It might be cosy to sit and read in front of the fire,' he suggested.

Shaking her head, Lily said, 'I'm sure I could do something . . . ?'

'You write with your right hand, yes?'

Lily nodded.

'Maybe you could do something useful with your right arm? Painting, for example.'

'It's possible I could paint,' Lily agreed, 'as long as whatever I was painting was bolted down.'

'Ask your friend Sid if you can return to work after Christmas,' Oro suggested. 'It's only a week away.'

'I will,' she agreed. 'A week from now, we'll all be gathering in St Mary Magdalene Church for a Christmas feast, I hope. Will you be able to join us, my love?'

'That depends on what the Luftwaffe decide to do,' he replied solemnly. 'We could be in action on bombing raids all day and night.' Seeing Lily's excited smile fade, he quickly added, 'If things go quiet, I could take five minutes to cycle down here to see you,' he promised.

'Yes, come and join us at the church, and bring your

friends too. Audrey, in particular, would be thrilled if she could find a nice young man.' Reaching up to kiss his cheek and stroke his shining blond hair, Lily whispered, 'I don't need to find a nice young man – I already have one of my own.'

Tired after her journey, but happy to be home, Lily felt warmed by the fire and good food, and drifted off to sleep in Oro's arms. When she awoke, she was being tucked up in her narrow bed by Oro.

'I have to go, sweetheart, I thought I would put you to bed before I get the jeep back to base,' he whispered.

Snuggling down, sleepy Lily asked, 'When will I see you again?'

Oro shrugged. 'If we're on manoeuvres, you won't see me. But if I can, I will try to check out my beautiful patient.'

'Thanks for taking the time to bring me home.'

'Pleasure is all mine, my sweet Lillee.'

When Kathleen arrived home from school, she couldn't believe her eyes when she saw Lily sitting on the sofa cutting out paper-chain decorations.

'Auntie Lily – you're home,' she cried as she hurled herself into Lily's arms.

'Careful, sweetheart,' Edna warned. 'Auntie Lily's got a poorly arm.'

'Are you very poorly?' Kathleen solemnly asked.

'I'm fine everywhere, apart from this arm – which will be better very soon,' Lily said brightly.

'Mama said you crashed your plane?'

Lily nodded.

'But you didn't die?' Kathleen asked in all seriousness.

'No, I was very lucky,' Lily said, then swiftly changed the subject. 'Will you help me make some decorations?' she asked. 'If you hold the paper, I can cut it more easily, and then we can colour them.'

Delighted, Kathleen quickly sat down beside Lily, who did as much as she could manage with her right hand.

After making a pot of tea and putting some potatoes into the oven to bake, Edna and Jeannie joined Lily in the sitting room, where they quickly caught up on each other's news.

'Talk of conscription has been non-stop all day in the factory,' Edna told her.

'It was nice to hear everybody so positive about welcoming new workers,' Jeannie added. 'I expect the first wave will arrive after Christmas, girls as young as eighteen; they'll be in for a shock. Long shifts, hard work – not to mention terrible dungarees,' she laughed.

'Good pay, though, and lots of overtime,' Lily added. 'Far better money working in an armaments factory than on the land.'

'Urgh!' Edna shuddered. 'I would seriously hate to be a land girl; better off here building planes than milking cows before the sun comes up.'

Cutting and colouring the festive paper chains, Kathleen contentedly hummed 'Jingle Bells'.

'Sing with me, Auntie Lily,' she begged.

After several rounds of the popular song, Lily asked if she could join her friends' rehearsal group the next day at the Bell Works.

'I have to catch up with Kathleen,' she joked.

'It's all the old favourites, with lots of kiddies' songs thrown in,' Edna explained. 'You'd be welcome – the more the merrier.'

After their short choir practice – this time in the changing rooms, as lots of the diners in the canteen wanted to hear the latest BBC midday news – Lily wandered on to the factory floor. She stood gazing up at the aircraft in different stages of assembly. Technicians at one end were labouring over plans and designs, while at the other end of the factory Spits secured to jigs were being constructed. Seeing the gleaming metal fuselages taking shape – the nose, the cockpit and tail – made Lily shiver; her passion for aircraft had crystallized in this factory, entirely reshaping her life in the process. Miles away, and lost in her own thoughts, Lily jumped when Sid came and stood next to her.

'Hello, my favourite girl,' he said, with genuine affection. 'Thinking of taking one up?'

Giving Sid a friendly hug, Lily smiled. 'I wish that were the case, Sid, I already miss flying. But I'm going to have to build up my confidence after that nasty crash.'

Chuckling, he said, 'Hell fire, mi duck, you were a bit too keen, if you ask me. You jumped at the chance when them ferry girls asked you to transport aircraft for them – it was impressive but very hasty,' he said judgementally.

'I suppose it was,' she shyly admitted. 'But it was all so exciting, Sid. Learning to fly was something I never imagined would ever come my way.'

Slightly backtracking, he added, 'And it were a job that needed doing. These buggers,' he said, nodding at the range of aircraft all around them, 'are not going to fly themselves out of Hucknall. There's a desperate shortage of pilots, as we all know. I should be grateful to you, rather than rebuking you – but Christ, you put the fear of God in us that day you crashed.'

As his eyes suddenly filled up, so did Lily's. Dear old Sid, for all his bluster and banter, was a big softie at heart, worrying about his workers, like a fussy mother hen.

'I can't do any flying until I'm fully recovered,' she pointed out.

'That's a relief, you took ten years off my life,' he winked.

'I'm hoping I can come back to work after Christmas, Sid,' she grinned. 'There's nothing wrong with my right arm, so I could do a bit of painting; and once my broken arm is fixed, I really have a duty to deliver aircraft to where they are most needed.'

'Aye, but do me a favour, mi duck – next time, make sure you know a bit more about landing a Spitfire in the mist. None of us at the Bell Works want to go through all that worry again.'

51. A Partridge in a Pear Tree

The countdown to Christmas was filled with mounting excitement as each day passed. Any one of the inhabitants of Prefab No. 8 would burst into 'The Twelve Days Of Christmas' at the drop of a hat. Though she was still quietly grieving for Frank, and sadness overwhelmed her at the most unexpected moments, Jeannie was determined not to spoil Kathleen's Christmas. Listening to Lily chanting 'A partridge in a pear tree' as she washed herself in the bathroom sink, Jeannie reflected on the Christmas happiness (sometimes against all the odds) that she and her friends were enjoying together.

'It's like living in Father Christmas's Grotto,' Edna laughed as she ducked under the decorated paper chains that Lily and Kathleen had hung in festoons all over the sitting room. 'Can you please start making some other decorations before I strangle myself in paper chains?' she joked.

'We need to start decorating the church,' Jeannie reminded everybody as they drank cocoa by the fire, after Kathleen had gone to bed.

'Especially now that Sid has got us a Christmas tree,' Edna told her friends.

'I'm going to pick some holly and ivy to decorate the tables in the church. I might even find some mistletoe,' Lily giggled.

'And who will *you* be kissing under the mistletoe?' Edna teased.

Lily flushed as she said, 'There's only one man I want to kiss under the mistletoe.'

'Don't tell me,' Edna laughed. 'It's Sid!'

'He's been very kind to us,' Jeannie pointed out. 'We should invite him too.'

'I already have,' Lily confessed. 'I suggested he pop into the church for a bite to eat, and maybe a glass of something.'

'A glass of water, if he's lucky. Where are we going to get booze from?'

'You've got a point, Edna,' Lily agreed. 'Would it be a good idea to draw up a list of all the contributions we might expect?'

'Aye, we don't want to finish up with twenty-two baked potatoes and half a dozen nut rissoles!' Edna joked.

'I've got more time than anybody else,' Lily volunteered. 'I could come into work tomorrow and find out what all the guests are planning to bring; even if it's only a rough plan, it will give us an idea of quantities.'

'There'll be about twenty people, including family and children,' Edna reminded her. 'Annie's bringing her mum, Ruby's bringing her mother and sister, and little Archie of course. I don't need to tell you that Mary is bringing her mother.'

All three women exchanged a knowing smile. 'It'll be good to meet the woman who totally controls Mary, at last,' Jeannie smiled.

'I've heard so much about "Mi mam", I feel I already know her,' Edna chuckled.

Lily's Christmas list was diverse and unusual. Ruby's mock goose, made of breadcrumbs, herbs, egg, leeks, lentils and spices, and moulded into the shape of a goose with sausages placed as drumsticks on either side of it, was the most elaborate, others not quite so complicated. Rabbit casserole, wild herb and nut stuffing, roast potatoes, Yorkshire pudding, black pudding, wartime mince pies, and Christmas pudding made predominantly from carrot, potatoes, some fruit, spices and rum all steamed in big earthenware basins for hours beforehand and served with white sauce laced with brandy. Jelly and custard were on the list too, as well as tinned peaches, carrot cake with condensed-milk icing, sloe gin, elderflower wine, sherry and some bottles of home-made beer.

After scanning the long list, Edna was flabbergasted. 'Who'd a thought we could get that much food together?'

'Once word got around, I think our expected twenty guests rose to thirty,' Lily said.

'As long as everybody makes a contribution, they're all welcome,' Jeannie said.

Holding up her hand, Lily added with a mysterious smile, 'Wait for the best bit.'

All eyes turned expectantly towards her.

'Sid is in a pig club.'

An incredulous silence followed. Pig clubs were private arrangements between friends and families who bought, reared and fed their own pig for months, often in their own backyard or garden plot, sometimes keeping it a secret from the local government pigman, who kept a register of all pigs in the district.

'Hell fire!' Edna broke the silence. 'A pig club.'

Lily grinned as she nodded her head. 'He told me in private, whispered it like it was a state secret.'

'Folks do tend to keep their pigs a bit of a family affair, they don't want somebody thieving the beast they've been feeding up. It happens,' Edna said knowingly. 'I've seen grown men fighting in the street over the whereabouts of a pig.'

'Sid said he's got a side of boiled ham he'll bring to the Christmas feast,' Lily told her delighted friends.

'Mmm, I can almost taste it, served with parsley sauce and roast potatoes,' Jeannie murmured. Smiling, she added, 'If folks hear of Sid's pig, we could have quite a crowd.'

'Then we'd better keep it quiet,' Edna advised.

'I've told everybody who is coming to arrive at St Mary Magdalene Church after the morning service, about twelve thirty,' Lily explained. 'They can bring their dishes and we'll keep them warm or cold, as the case may be, in the church kitchen. We'll need to make sure we've got all the tables set and decorated beforehand.'

'I'd like to go to the Christmas morning service,' Jeannie said.

'Kathleen wants to go too, though she'll be tired after the carol singing on Christmas Eve.'

'Never mind,' Lily smiled. 'Christmas only comes around once a year.'

During the final rehearsal, on the afternoon of Christmas Eve, all those who weren't on shift work gathered in the prettily decorated church, which now housed a little crib in front of the altar and a tall Christmas tree adorned with twinkling tinsel and some gold and silver baubles. With Annie at the piano, they kept the rehearsal short as everybody present needed to get home for tea, then come back again, washed and dressed up for the first event of Christmas.

Just as Ruby was finishing her solo number, 'Silent Night', the door of the church creaked open. To everybody's astonishment, a young man in soldier's khaki drill walked down the central nave. Jeannie, sitting in the front row of the choir, saw who it was. She was pleased, but astonished, and had to wait for Ruby to finish singing before stepping forward.

Waiting politely for the carol to finish, the young man apologized. 'Please forgive me for interrupting, but I've come to see Jeannie.'

'Eddie!' Jeannie spluttered as she made her way towards him.

Staring awkwardly at her, the young man suggested they go outdoors.

'I've got something for you,' he said shyly.

Blushing, and turning to Annie at the piano, Jeannie asked, 'Can I slip outside for a minute?'

'Go on, then,' Annie smiled. 'We've just about finished anyway.'

As the youngsters walked down the nave, some of the choir singers hid their smiles.

'Shhh!' hissed Edna. 'That's the fella that brought all them stories to our Jeannie – the ones she wrote a while back, when she was walking out with that nice young lad, Frank.'

'Why's he come to see Jeannie on Christmas Eve?' curious Mary asked.

Striking the keys, Annie drew everybody's attention. 'Final carol,' she announced. 'It's "Hark! The Herald Angels Sing".'

Outside in the frosty graveyard, bright with holly berries growing in clumps on spiky green leaves, Jeannie and Eddie sat on an old wooden bench under a vast yew tree.

'What a lovely surprise,' Jeannie murmured, genuinely so pleased to see him.

Looking self-conscious, Eddie explained why he had made the journey to see her.

'I found a few more of your stories,' he said. 'I thought I'd better deliver them to the author,' he smiled shyly, 'before I'm posted elsewhere.'

Reaching into one of the pockets of his greatcoat, he pulled out a bundle of papers and handed them over to Jeannie.

Equally shy, Jeannie scanned them and said, 'You've gone to such a lot of trouble. It's very kind of you,' she exclaimed.

Eddie shrugged. 'It's nothing. I know how much Frank treasured them.'

Happy to see Frank's best friend, Jeannie urged, 'So, tell me your news, Eddie.'

'I've had an operation on my right eye, which went well, and I'll be reporting back for duty early in the New Year. I can't wait to rejoin my regiment,' he announced. 'Also,' he blushingly stumbled on, 'I wondered, please don't be offended by my question, I just wondered if you might consider writing to me while I'm away?'

Flabbergasted, Jeannie was briefly lost for words.

'I know it's a bit of a cheek,' he blurted out. 'But some-how I liked you before we even met, admired you in fact, you really lightened our lives with your funny stories. Then when I came to see you, I liked you even more. I just want you to know that, before I'm posted overseas.'

Seeing him looking so shy and embarrassed, Jeannie laid a hand over his.

'I like you too, Eddie. Of course I'll write – and thank you for your sweet words.'

Gripping her hand, Eddie grinned in relief. 'I was wor-ried you'd give me a telling-off for being . . . well, a bit insensitive, if you get my drift,' he confessed.

'I know Frank liked you, Eddie. I'll never forget him,' she told him honestly.

'Neither will I – he was a good lad, and a grand friend too.'

Sitting peacefully holding hands, Jeannie mused, 'Fancy you turning up on Christmas Eve. How did you get here?' she asked.

'On my motorbike,' he told her. 'Once I decided I was going to pay you a visit, I started saving up petrol.'

'So, you've been planning it for a while?' she teased.

'Let's just say, it was difficult to forget you, Jeannie,' he told her, and leant forward to give her a modest kiss on the cheek.

Jeannie insisted on making Eddie a hot drink and a sand-wich in the little church kitchen before he left. She waved him off, before returning to Prefab No. 8.

Kathleen was dressed in her new blue velvet winter dress – which doting Edna had saved all her clothing coupons to buy – in readiness for the carol service. She was standing in the centre of the sitting room, having her long hair plaited.

Smiling knowingly at Jeannie's radiantly happy face, Edna teased, 'I think we'll be seeing a lot more of that nice young man.'

'I hope so, Edna,' Jeannie said as she giddily grabbed hold of Kathleen and started to waltz around the room with her. 'He's asked if he can write to me!'

Lily was putting her make-up on in front of the mirror over the fireplace. 'And what did you say?' she asked, grinning.

'I said YES!' Jeannie laughed. 'I like him, he's a lovely boy.' Her face fell as she added, 'He's been posted abroad, just like Frank.' Suddenly panicking, she murmured, 'Oh my God, what if Eddie dies too?'

Taking her firmly by the hand, Lily sat Jeannie down on the sofa.

'Listen to me, lovie, even though there's a war on and we hear of death and danger all the time, we can't give up on hope. In times like these, caring for somebody means taking a risk. But isn't being loved and treasured worth taking a risk for?'

With tears in her eyes, Jeannie hugged her dear friend. 'You must worry about Oro all the time.'

'I do, and he worries about me too.' Lily smiled dreamily. 'But that doesn't stop us loving each other.'

Wearing their nicest and warmest dresses, Lily, Jeannie and Edna, with Kathleen running excitedly between them, made their way to St Mary Magdalene Church as a full moon rose in a frosty dark sky. Hearing the bells ringing from the ancient tower, the three friends smiled at each other.

'Who would have thought a year ago, when we didn't even know each other, that we'd become the best of friends and would be walking, arm in arm, to church on Christmas Eve?' Lily mused. 'Now I can't imagine life without any of you.'

'Kathleen's got so many nice aunties these days,' Edna chuckled.

Catching her mother's words, happy Kathleen chanted as she skipped along.

'Auntie Lily, Auntie Jeannie, Auntie Annie, Auntie Ruby, Auntie Audrey and Auntie Mary.'

While the choir took up their places, Kathleen sat with the children in front of the crib. The little group was supervised by Ruby's mother, holding Archie on her knee.

'Don't they look angelic,' Ruby whispered.

The children gazed in wonder at the carved wooden statues of the shepherds and their lambs gathered around the manger where Baby Jesus lay.

'Kathleen's drawn a picture of a donkey for Baby Jesus,' Edna whispered to Ruby. 'She left it in the manger this afternoon.'

Seeing Ruby's eyes sparkling even more than usual, Edna said, 'I know it's the festive season, but you look especially happy tonight. It can't just be the carol singing that's put a skip in your step.'

Dropping her voice to a whisper, Ruby said, 'I got a letter from my George this morning – the best Christmas present I could ever wish for.'

'You must be so relieved, lovie,' Edna smiled.

'To tell you the truth, I've been worried sick. The forces' post from North Africa is erratic, but today I got three letters posted weeks apart, yet they all arrived on the same day.'

'Just like buses, when they all come at once,' Edna chuckled.

'George is well,' Ruby told her. 'I wouldn't say he's happy, but he's surviving and he's with a great bunch of friends. Seriously, I couldn't ask for more.'

'Any news of him coming home?' Edna whispered back. Ruby shook her head.

'I think that would be too much to ask for. Getting three letters at Christmas has put my mind at rest. When I think of what other women must go through at this time of the year – like Jeannie, waiting to hear from Frank and then discovering he's died of a fever. I'm lucky, Edna,' she murmured humbly.

Thinking, guiltily, that if she never heard from her husband again she would be more than happy, Edna was relieved when Annie played the opening chords to 'Once In Royal David's City' and the packed congregation rose to their feet.

The evening's service ended with the sweetest rendition of 'Away In A Manger', which the local children sang. Though Kathleen had begged Ruby to put Archie in the manger – because he was 'a real baby' – Ruby had patiently pointed out that he was, in fact, too big for Jesus's little manger and was better off sitting on his nana's knee.

After the vicar's final blessing, the congregation drifted outside where, to the delight of the children, soft snow was falling, covering the gravestones in a pure white blanket. Sleepy Kathleen, almost too tired to walk, begged for a piggyback home.

When Edna swung her daughter on to her shoulders, a yawning Kathleen asked, 'When is Father Christmas coming, Mummy?'

'Sweetheart,' Edna promised, 'he's on his way.'

52. Christmas Day

Christmas morning was a happy time in Prefab No. 8; though their presents to each other were modest, they were thoughtful. Lily got her favourite Victory Red wartime lipstick, Edna was delighted with a thick woolly scarf Jeannie had knitted, and Jeannie was thrilled with an old-fashioned fountain pen her friends had bought for her in a second-hand shop in Hucknall. Kathleen went wild with excitement when she found a bulky stocking at the bottom of her bed on Christmas morning.

'Look, Mama, he's been!' she cried as she reached into the stocking and pulled out the little gifts that Edna had dropped in the previous night, before she went to bed: nuts and boiled sweets, an apple, colouring pencils and a small hand-knitted teddy bear that Edna had bought at a church bazaar.

As they prepared for the Christmas morning service they sang along to the popular songs and carols playing out on the radio. Kathleen was thrilled when the strains of 'Jingle Bells' filled the sitting room. In the hearth a fire, lit by Jeannie as soon as she'd got up that morning, crackled brightly. Their usual meagre breakfast of tea, toast and marg was enhanced by two chunks of Fry's dark chocolate, which Jeannie doled out.

'I've been hoarding this for a few weeks,' she grinned.

With her mouth full of sweet chocolate, Kathleen cried, 'Can we have chocolate every day for breakfast?'

'No, lovie, this is Christmas Day chocolate.' Edna smiled as she gave her daughter her own portion. 'A treat from your kind Auntie Jeannie.'

Laughing and still singing, they walked to church through the snow that had fallen quite heavily overnight. With flushed cheeks they arrived at St Mary Magdalene's, where friends and neighbours were filing in through the old church porch. Wishing each other a Merry Christmas, the congregation settled on the ancient pews to listen to the service, then rose to sing the rousing festive carols, ending with the all-time favourite, 'Hark! The Herald Angels Sing', which almost raised the church roof.

Once the service was concluded, everything went into overdrive as plates, bowls and tins of food were dropped off at the church kitchen, including Lily, Edna and Jeannie's contributions. The cold dishes were laid out on a long trestle table, decorated with pretty paper chains and sprigs of holly and ivy; the hot dishes were kept warm in the gas ovens, already heating up. All three women were astonished at the amount of food that continued to appear.

'People are so generous,' Edna exclaimed as she laid out a plate of spicy mince pies and carrot flapjacks.

'Everybody deserves one day in the year that's happy and carefree.' Lily was beaming as she positioned Ruby's mock goose in pride of place on the buffet table. 'A day when you can eat as much as you want, for a change.'

'And have a drink too,' Edna grinned. She nodded at the drinks table, filling up with bottles of stout, a bottle of port, sloe gin, ginger wine and elderflower cordial.

Outside, Kathleen was building a snowman when Annie arrived with her mother, along with Ruby and her family.

Archie in his big old Silver Cross pram giggled with pleasure when he saw Kathleen. The little girl made him laugh even more when she put her striped black and white bobble hat on top of her snowman. Suddenly, to the children's delight, the sound of jingling bells filled the sharp frosty air. Turning in the direction of the noise, they saw a little grey pony trotting through the snow pulling a small pony trap, and driving the trap was the colourful figure of Father Christmas! Clapping and cheering, a crowd of children rushed towards the pony and trap, which pulled up outside the lych gate. Father Christmas stepped out, with a sack flung over his shoulder.

'HO, HO, HO!' he boomed in a voice that was not dissimilar to Sid's. 'Merry Christmas.'

'MERRY CHRISTMAS!' they all bellowed back.

Skipping after the portly figure, the children followed him into the church where, standing under the Christmas tree and surrounded by expectant children, Father Christmas untied his sack and handed out presents.

'Let's start with all the boys and girls who have been good this year,' he teased.

'Me, me, me, me!' chorused the children as they surged forward to receive their gifts.

One curious boy said, 'I thought Father Christmas spent Christmas Day sleeping, after delivering presents all over the world?'

Father Christmas gave a cheeky wink. 'I thought I'd make Hucknall my last drop-off of the day,' he explained.

Once the children had settled down to play with their toys, Father Christmas revealed his true self in the church kitchen.

'Bloody hell, it was hot in that outfit,' Sid chuckled as he laid the red velvet coat, trimmed with white fur, to one side.

'Such a lovely thought, Sid,' Lily exclaimed as she gave him a big hug. 'Surprising the children like that – you've made their day.'

'Give us a stiff drink, lovie,' Sid grinned. Gratefully downing the liberal glass of port Lily poured out for him, he added, 'I've got to get yon pony back home, then pick up that side of gammon I promised you.'

Thinking of the lovely ham she was so looking forward to eating, Lily urged him to be on his way. She escorted him out of the church (where none of the children recognized him as the Father Christmas who had walked in) then stopped in her tracks as she heard the steady hum of aircraft flying overhead. Looking up, she squinted into the bright low-lying sun that was casting a dazzlingly bright light on the freshly fallen snow.

Gazing up too, Sid said, 'Spits . . . from the look of it, on their way east.'

Thinking of the airfields she had flown to in that direction, Lily's heart raced with a combination of fear and excitement.

'No rest for the wicked,' Sid grimly observed as he heaved himself into the pony trap. 'Don't start dinner until I get back.'

'I won't,' Lily promised. 'Everybody is gagging for slices of your boiled ham!'

After Sid's little pony had trotted off with its reins jiggling, Lily gazed upwards to watch the line of Spitfires disappear over the horizon. Seeing Oro today would complete her joy, but the reality was that he was likely to be on duty, which meant she probably wouldn't see him until all the Christmas activities were concluded.

Pity, she thought, as she retraced her footsteps indoors. Oro's Polish salami and schnapps would go down a treat with Sid's boiled ham and Ruby's mock goose!

As it turned out, more than thirty people joined in the Christmas feast – even the vicar invited a few friends along – but the contributions, accompanied with homemade pickles, chutneys, red cabbage and local Red Leicester, were eked out and there was enough for everybody. Though all the guests admired Ruby's creative mock goose, there was no doubt that Sid's glorious boiled ham stole the show. Wielding a carving knife and fork, he deftly carved slim pieces of the pork, fragrant with the smell of sage and rosemary that garnished the succulent crackling. Served with gravy, potatoes, sprouts, cabbage and carrots, it was utterly delicious. Pleased with his culinary success, Sid – tipsy after several bottles of stout – beamed at everyone around the table.

'If I say so myself, that were a right fine pig!' he announced.

'Hear, hear!' everybody chorused as they raised their glasses in grateful appreciation.

'A lot of time and thought went into that pig,' Sid continued. 'Not to mention slops served up, morning and night. We were all fond of him, but the terrible day came when . . .' He slowly drew a finger across his throat.

'Shhh, Sid,' Edna hissed. 'You'll frighten the kiddies.'

'I suppose all good things must come to an end,' Sid finished, rather sentimentally.

While the children eagerly accepted bowls of jelly and

custard, and the adults enjoyed the frugal Christmas pudding laced with fiery-hot brandy sauce, Lily started stacking the dirty dishes in the church kitchen; the clutter of empty pans, tins, bowls, cutlery and plates looked like a bomb had gone off. As she was tying on her pinafore to start the first batch of washing-up, she heard a little tap at the door. Thinking it was a child who had locked themselves out, Lily flung the door wide open, then cried out in delight when she saw Oro standing there holding a bunch of mistletoe over his head.

Pulling her to him, he whispered, 'Happy Christmas, *ukochana*, my darling.'

Lily threw herself into his arms and stood on her tiptoes to kiss his warm lips.

'Sweetheart,' she exclaimed, once he released her from his grip. 'You've missed dinner.'

'We had something at the base. I just slipped out to see you, but I have to get back. I did not want to miss you on our first Christmas together.'

Laughing, Lily removed the mistletoe from his hand and held it over her own head.

'Kiss me again,' she teased.

Showering her face and neck with kisses, Oro lifted her off her feet and spun her around until she was dizzy and breathless. When Sid walked in, Oro immediately put Lily back on her feet.

'You remember Oro, my pilot friend from the Polish base in Hucknall?'

'Oh, aye, you're the one that's been teaching my favourite girl how to fly?'

Oro clicked his heels. 'I have had that pleasure, sir.'

Wagging his finger, Sid added, 'You make sure you take good care of the lass, she's a little treasure.'

Grinning, Oro immediately said, 'I promise I will treasure her, sir.'

Sid returned to the party games now taking place in the church hall, and Oro said his goodbyes too.

'Sweetheart, I have a present for you,' he smiled. 'But I cannot give it to you until tomorrow, Boxing Day, when I get time off. Is all right, you are free?'

Lily gave a quick nod.

'I told Sid I'd be back at work after Christmas. So it's fine, darling.'

'Very good!' he beamed. 'Tell your friends you're going on a short trip.'

'Oro, what are you planning?'

'*Ukochana*, we're going flying!'

53. Two Turtle Doves

On Boxing Day morning, Lily couldn't believe her eyes when she found Kathleen curled up on the sofa in front of the fire with a little ginger kitten in her arms.

'Look, Auntie Lily, Cinderella's come to live with us.'

Laughing, Lily turned to Edna. Her friend rolled her eyes in amusement.

'You'll never believe it, Cinderella is Annie's Christmas present to Kathleen. By the way,' she said, lowering her voice, 'Annie didn't call her Cinderella; it's Kathleen's favourite name since Jeannie read her the story.'

Lily was puzzled. 'I don't recall seeing Kathleen with a kitten yesterday.'

'Annie didn't want to bring the kitten to St Mary Magdalene – she thought the Christmas dinner would be too loud and noisy for a little kitty, so she dropped her off here this morning.'

'She's gorgeous,' Lily said as she leant over to stroke the little bundle of warm ginger fur. 'Make sure you take good care of her, Kathleen,' she advised.

'I will,' the little girl answered solemnly.

Turning back to Edna, Lily shook her head. 'Dear old Annie, who would ever have thought that under that hard granite exterior was a big softie?'

'I know,' Edna smiled fondly. 'I'll never forget as long as I live how well she looked after me when I was ill after

Jack's visit. Annie's like the best granny to Kathleen these days, unlike the battle-axe in Wigan who is her real granny. Life's full of surprises.' Suddenly registering the warm clothes Lily was wearing, she exclaimed, 'Good God. You look like you're going mountain climbing.'

Lily grinned. 'I'm going flying, with Oro,' she announced.

Looking fearful, Edna said, 'You won't try landing an aircraft in thick mist like you did last time?'

'I'm not a ferry girl on this trip,' Lily assured her. 'This is Oro's Christmas present to me – a mystery overnight trip.'

'Ooooh, *overnight?*' cheeky Edna teased.

Walking into the room, still in her nightie, Jeannie caught the end of the conversation. She snuggled down on the sofa next to Kathleen's kitten, having seen her earlier that morning.

'Who's staying overnight?' she enquired.

Blushing deeply, Lily said, 'I'm going away with Oro.'

Also teasing, Jeannie said, 'Don't do anything I wouldn't do.'

Throwing up her hands, embarrassed Lily insisted, 'It's a surprise – I don't know anything about it.'

Smiling, Kathleen said, 'Cinderella was my Christmas surprise.'

Over a cup of tea and some leftover fruit pie, the girls discussed the events of the previous day.

'It was a great success,' Jeannie said. 'Everybody loved it, especially the children.'

'You could have knocked me down with a feather when Sid turned up in that pony and cart,' Lily chuckled.

Rolling her eyes towards Kathleen, Edna gave her friend a dig in the ribs. 'Father Christmas,' she said rather loudly.

Getting the message, Lily quickly added, with a smile, 'It was very kind of Father Christmas to spare the time.'

'I was so excited about our day at St Mary Magdalene's, I wrote another chapter of "Spitfire Kids" after you two had gone to bed last night,' Jeannie told her friends. Smiling shyly, she added, 'I think I've nearly got enough stories to send them off to a few publishers. My new year's resolution is to try and get "Spitfire Kids" published in 1942.'

Raising her mug of tea, Edna said, 'Amen to that!'

'Best of luck,' Lily added as she leant over to kiss her friend. 'Now, if you'll excuse me,' she grinned, 'I've got a date!'

When she arrived at the Polish airbase, Lily was signed in by Oro.

He took her by the hand. 'Come with me, *ukochana*, I have to pick up bag from my room, then we can be on our way.'

Now familiar with the layout of the base, Lily nevertheless inspected with curiosity the interconnecting runways, the large hangars and the many red-brick buildings that housed the communal, domestic, administrative and technical sites, plus the sick bay; at a distance from the domestic area were found the bomb disposal block and the bomb store.

'Don't let my cheeky Polish friends embarrass you,' Oro whispered as they hurried past airmen who threw admiring glances at pretty Lily. 'They all tell me I'm a lucky man having beauty like you for girlfriend.'

Throwing him a teasing smile, Lily joked, 'Have you told them I'm a lucky woman having a handsome pilot like you for my boyfriend?'

Oro laughed and said, 'You wait in *kantyna* while I fetch my bag, don't talk to any Polish pilots.'

Overwhelmed by the sight of so many curious men staring at her, Lily was way too shy to queue up for a cup of tea at the canteen counter. Instead, she sat shyly waiting for Oro to return. When he did appear, with a rucksack slung over his shoulder, his friends cheered and whistled as he escorted poor blushing Lily out of the building.

'Your friends seem starved of female company,' Lily observed. 'We should organize another dance so they can meet some nice local girls,' she suggested. 'If it weren't for that dance at the Bell Works in the autumn, you and I would never have met.'

'I never forget that wonderful night, my sweet Lillee, the loveliest girl in the room, with silver-blonde hair, wearing a blue dress. I thought I was dreaming when I saw you for the first time. Then when we danced, just the feel of you in my arms. I was lost to you,' he declared.

Though a little embarrassed by Oro's romantic memories, Lily vividly recalled the night of the dance herself. Spinning around the dance floor with Oro, gazing into his green eyes, and admiring his stunning golden hair. That memorable dance night, and meeting Oro, had changed her life forever.

As they walked across the tarmac to the parking bays, Lily smiled with pleasure when she spotted Oro's blazing, bright yellow Tiger Moth.

'She's so stunning,' Lily enthused.

'She's my favourite girl – after you,' Oro teased. 'Hop in.'

Briefly holding back, Lily said, 'Oro, you've still not told me where we're going.'

'*Ukochana*,' he grinned. 'I promise you soon find out.'

*

Though it was freezing cold, the views that winter morning were breathtaking. Snow had transformed the landscape, leaving the world spread out below the aircraft glowing white and glistening bright. The familiar waypoints looked different too; church spires glinted against the snowy landscape, and rivers, turned to ice, glistened as they snaked their way through the countryside. Sitting in front of Oro, Lily spoke to him through their connected headsets.

'It's more beautiful than ever,' she cried as Oro banked the aircraft.

Then, looping the loop, he brought them plunging down through arching blue space on a breathtaking nosedive.

'Feeling sick?' he asked.

'No, I love it,' she laughed.

When the ancient trees of Rendlesham Forest loomed into view, Lily immediately knew where their destination would be.

'We're en route for Woodbridge,' she cried in surprise.

'I hope you don't mind, *ukochana*,' he said cautiously. 'It is the only way for me to get you to the place I want us to be,' he said, with an enigmatic smile.

Not answering immediately, Lily considered his question; she wasn't in a rush to see the airbase where she had nearly lost her life, but she realized it would be good for her to revisit it sooner rather than later. Anyway, it would have to be done if she was to continue to fly as a ferry girl. At least she was making the journey with somebody she loved and trusted.

Telling the truth, she simply said, 'It's fine.'

Peering out of the window, Lily gazed out on to the wonderful Suffolk waterways, winding and twisting through the flat terrain, draining into estuaries that emptied out into the North Sea. With the wind whipping around her, Lily felt the aircraft lifting gently on the changing air currents. Feeling as excited as a child, she pointed out the vast stretch of shingle beaches, washed by the incoming tide.

'I love this county,' she sighed.

'Me too,' Oro responded through his headset. 'Maybe one day I live here.'

Surprised, Lily spoke through their connected headsets. 'I always imagined you would want to go home to Poland?'

'I love Poland, but England is a good place to live. Even in wartime I like this country – and you live here, my *ukochana*, so now is very dear place for me.'

When Woodbridge airbase came into view, Oro waited for the clearance signal, before making his descent downwind. Closing down the throttle, he reduced speed and then, with professional expertise, skilfully landed the aircraft on the runway. He disconnected his headset and hopped out of his seat to help Lily; with one arm still in plaster, she was unsteady when it came to clambering out of an aircraft.

When she was once more on terra firma, Lily gave Oro a kiss.

'Thank you for bringing me here,' she said, with a grateful smile. 'It's good to face my demons.'

'Demons?' he puzzled. 'Where are these demons?'

'I mean I need to confront what I'm most frightened of,' she explained. 'I had an awful experience here, but life goes on.'

*

The day was full of surprises for Lily, each one more wonderful than the one before. Leaving the charming little port of Woodbridge, they took a ferry boat down the River Deben, passing the Ramsholt Inn on their way. When she saw the charming old pub, perched above the tidal inlet, Lily assumed they would be stopping there, but, smiling mysteriously, Oro shook his head.

'Mystery tour,' he teased.

The cold, sharp frosty weather brought a rosy flush to Lily's cheeks; her silver eyes sparkled with delight as she gazed at the riverbank, from left to right, where flocks of scuttling wading birds, avocets, curlews, sandpipers and snipe dibbled on the ebb tide for crustaceans with their long pointed beaks. As the estuary widened out and the vast swell of the North Sea came into view, Lily seriously wondered if Oro was going to take her sailing right out to sea. Instead, the ferryman pulled the boat into a jetty where, once the boat had been secured, they stepped out. After paying the ferryman, who prepared to make his journey back upriver, they stood on the sandy bank in the fast-fading light of day.

Casting about the desolate spot, Lily said, 'It's nearly dark. Where on earth are we?'

'Bawdsey Manor,' Oro told her as he linked her arm through his.

They walked through an open metal gate that led on to a long winding drive. Close by, owls hooted as they began their nightly search for food. Lily jumped as a large barn owl with outstretched silver wings drifted low just up ahead of them, silent as a ghost. Foxes barked as they too began their nightly hunting excursions. Up above them the winter sky was a dark navy blue, speckled with a myriad of twinkling stars, and low on the horizon a new moon rose over the dark brooding sea. Shivering in the cold north wind that seemed to slice through her coat, Lily snuggled closer to Oro.

'Nearly there,' he told her. 'You'll be warm soon, I promise.'

Following the bend in the drive, Lily gasped as a huge manor house rose into view on a high rocky promontory. In the dark it was difficult to make out the details of the structure, but what was clearly visible in the slanting moonlight were four magnificent turreted towers at each corner of the building.

'This is where we are staying, my darling,' Oro informed her.

Delighted, Lily cried, 'It looks like a picture out of one of Kathleen's fairy-tale books.'

'Believe me, this is real,' he grinned. 'Welcome to Bawdsey Manor.'

Inside the manor house, they were met by the housekeeper, who kindly offered them tea and scones in the library.

A huge log fire was crackling in the vast marble fireplace.

'This is lovely,' Lily exclaimed as she sat in a large wing chair by the fireside.

'I'll be back shortly with your tea,' the housekeeper said as she left the room.

Once they were alone, Lily sprang up from the chair and started to explore the library.

'How on earth did you find this extraordinary place?' she asked Oro.

'Bawdsey Quay is the site of an operational radar station; its remote location is perfect for the work they do here. There are a string of similar radar stations dotted all along the east coast. They do a great job intercepting enemy aircraft flying over from Germany.'

'It feels like it's built on the very edge of the land mass,' Lily observed. 'How on earth did you discover it?'

'One of the Hucknall technicians told me about Bawdsey Manor, which offers limited accommodation to fighter pilots on leave,' he explained. 'I've been lucky to book us in for two nights.'

Lily smiled adoringly at him. 'Fighter pilots as brave as you, my darling, deserve a rest.'

Running his hands through her lovely silver-blonde hair, Oro murmured, 'What I really need is time alone with you, Lillee.'

Moving to embrace each other, they both jumped as the door opened and the housekeeper walked in bearing a tray of tea and scones.

'Have something to eat, and get warm,' she said in a homely Suffolk accent, 'then I'll show you to your rooms.' Smiling, she explained, 'Here, the tradition is always that men sleep in the white tower and ladies in the pink tower.'

Thinking of the tall looming towers, gilded by moonlight, Lily nervously asked, 'Will there be any other ladies sleeping in the pink tower apart from me?'

'For sure,' the housekeeper answered. 'All the girls attached to the radar station live in the pink tower. Though if the truth be told, working round-the-clock shifts as they do, the ladies only come back here to have a quick lie-down before they're called out to do another shift. Don't fret yourself, miss, you won't be on your own.'

'Will we be able to have supper here?' Oro asked.

'You're welcome, sir, it's all good local fare. When you've finished your tea, I'll show you to your towers.'

Oro waited in the vast, freezing echoing hall while the housekeeper escorted Lily to her room in the pink wing. Though it was damp and cold, Lily was charmed by the old-fashioned decor and the view from the window, which faced out on to the North Sea.

'I've put a hot-water bottle in your bed,' the housekeeper said. 'Though you might want to have another, as it's a cold night. Dinner's at seven.'

54. Bawdsey Manor

The housekeeper was right; dinner was delicious, exactly what the young couple, both starving after their flight and chilly ferry journey, needed. Oro, as usual, produced a surprise from his rucksack.

'Polish red wine we serve on base, try some, it's very rich and fruity, like Polish plums.'

As Lily sipped the strong red wine – which enhanced the tasty cottage pie and boiled cabbage, followed by spotted dick and custard, served up by the housekeeper – she felt a rush of pure happiness. They were on the extreme easterly edge of England with the enemy barely a hundred and fifty miles away, just across the sea, but here in this isolated place she felt safe, cherished and warm. Though there were a few other diners in the room, the housekeeper had thoughtfully put Oro and Lily in a nice private corner.

'The manor reminds me a bit of the hotel where I worked as a waitress before I joined up,' Lily said.

'The prettiest little waitress in Yorkshire,' Oro beamed. 'Everybody must have loved you!'

'I was popular,' she admitted. 'I was happy in my work and enjoyed meeting the guests; I never imagined while I was working in the Dolphin Hotel in Whitby that one day I'd be flying war planes.' Glancing up, she asked, 'Did you always want to fly?'

'Yes, since I was small boy, I always love planes, but really I am surprised to find myself flying aircraft here in England and not in Poland.'

'Everybody says the Polish pilots are the most fearless.'

Oro gave a proud smile. 'They are fearless and brave, for sure, but not everybody likes us, you know.'

'People will change their minds when they know what you do and what you risk,' Lily assured him.

After they had finished their meal and Oro's plum wine, they made their way back to the library, lit now only by a standard lamp and the firelight.

Sitting with her head on Oro's shoulder, Lily asked, 'What surprises have you got in store for us tomorrow?'

'Long walk,' he promised. 'Wrap up warm, it's cold on the east coast.'

Walking on the beach below Bawdsey Manor was blustery indeed. In between all the sea defences, spiked with metal bars and reinforced with solid blocks of concrete, there were shingle beaches where, tucked under overhanging pine trees, they could at least get out of the bitterly cold wind. Warmed by each other's hugs and kisses, they walked the few miles to Shingle Street where artists' cottages stood in a long row, some with smoke puffing from their chimney pots. An old fisherman and his collie dog ambled by with lobster pots, and an artist painting the coastline in thick oils offered them tea from his flask.

'No, thanks,' Oro politely refused. 'I have my own flask; we needn't deprive you of yours.'

Huddled up against a flint-built outhouse, Oro took out his flask.

'I hope it's your Polish coffee,' Lily giggled. 'It's just what I need right now.'

'You guessed,' he said as he handed her a cup of coffee and a thick wedge of salami.

Warmed by the thick strong coffee, Lily's silver-bright eyes grew dreamy as she gazed out across the North Sea. Crashing waves broke on the wide empty shingle beach.

'I could stay here with you in this peaceful place forever,' she whispered.

Draping an arm across her slender shoulders, Oro drew Lily close. 'My Lillee, it is forever I wish to talk to you about,' he whispered.

Feeling her heart skip a beat, Lily pressed herself closer into his side.

'From first moment I saw you, I knew you were the girl for me; clever, beautiful, brave . . .' Kissing her as he said each word, he chuckled as he concluded, 'And a pilot – I never thought I would make proposal to a pilot.'

Lily caught her breath. 'Oro,' she started to say, but he stopped her with another kiss.

'Listen, *ukochana*, I have something here for you.' Reaching into his blue airman's greatcoat, he brought out a small faded red velvet box. 'Please open . . .'

Nervously taking the box from him, Lily did as he asked. Flipping the little gold clasp open, she gasped in delight when she saw an old-fashioned diamond and sapphire ring.

'It's exquisite,' she cried.

'It belonged to my grandmother who died before the war broke out. She left it to my mother who said I could have it when I find the right girl.' Slipping the ring on to her wedding finger, he murmured, 'Here now is my right girl. My sweet Lillee, please will you marry me?'

Overwhelmed by his tender words, and the emotions churning inside her, Lily burst into tears.

'Yes, yes,' she sobbed. 'I love you so very much, Oro.'

As the high stormy waves smashed on to the empty beach, dragging pebbles and seaweed back and forth on the outgoing tide, the young lovers fell into each other's arms. Holding her delicate heart-shaped face in his hands, Oro kissed her soft pouting lips and felt them open to his touch. Hardly daring to let go of each other, they kissed over and over again, until Lily thought she might faint for lack of breath.

'I'm going to be your wife,' she said incredulously. 'And to think we only met a few months ago.'

'In these times of war, a man and a woman get to know each other quickly. Feelings are high and intense. I see you from very start as strong, brave, patriotic woman who loves her country – like me. We both fight for the countries we love.'

'You're right, darling,' she agreed. 'I know that life without you would be unbearable. It would be an honour to be your wife,' she said as she wiped away her tears.

Stroking her long blonde hair, Oro gave a deep sigh of happiness.

'Thank God, I was so scared you would say no. I thought you might want to marry a Yorkshire fisherman,' he joked.

Gazing curiously at her engagement ring, now glitteringly brightly on her wedding finger, Lily asked, 'How on earth did you get your grandmother's ring to England?'

'I asked a Polish pilot recently posted here to bring it for me. I kept it until the right moment, to propose to you in a beautiful place like this, today.'

Glowing and full of love, Lily sighed contentedly. 'I'll never forget this place or this moment,' she promised. 'I'll remember them both for the rest of my life.'

Early the next morning, they left Bawdsey Manor, where they had again spent the night in separate bedrooms.

'One day soon, *ukochana*, we will spend our wedding night together,' Oro had whispered to Lily as they said goodnight before going their separate ways to the chilly white tower and the pink tower.

'Maybe we could have a tower all to ourselves, just for newlyweds?' Lily joked.

'We could lock ourselves in and throw away the key.'

Sitting in the ferry that had come to collect them, Lily watched Bawdsey Manor disappear in a thick sea mist that engulfed the river all the way up to Woodbridge.

Seeing her looking nervously up at the sky, Oro said reassuringly, 'Don't worry, sweetheart, it's only morning mist, it will lift soon.'

Which it did, to Lily's relief; by the time they arrived at the airbase, the sky was bright and clear. Climbing into the cockpit of his Tiger Moth, Oro gave the thumbs up sign to the mechanic standing on the runway.

'Chocks away,' the man called as he swung the propeller and Oro opened the throttle.

Rolling down the runway, with its light wood and wire frame bouncing and rattling, the Tiger Moth gathered speed and then lifted like a great golden bird and with graceful beauty took to the wide open skies. As church bells rang from little villages lining the long sweep of the east coast – Felixstowe, Aldeburgh, Clayhive, Dunwich and Southwold – Lily gazed dreamily at her beautiful engagement ring. What would her friends say when she arrived home? she wondered. She imagined all of them would be happy for her. Though Annie (who had never married) might suggest she was too young, Lily thought, with a smile. Edna, after her recent impetuous action, might advise caution, while Ruby would be thrilled. Mary would worry that she was marrying a Polish pilot and might go away, and Audrey would volunteer to be her bridesmaid. Thinking of which, Lily imagined herself walking down the aisle flanked by all of her closest friends dressed in pastel-coloured dresses, with Kathleen, her pretty little flower girl, leading the way down the aisle of St Mary Magdalene Church. Oro, smart and handsome in his Polish airman's pale blue uniform, would be waiting for her at the altar and she, in flowing white satin with a long white lace veil trailing behind, would take his hand in hers and together they would make their marriage vows.

Sighing romantically, Lily wondered where she and Oro, once they were husband and wife, would live. Certainly not Prefab No. 8 on the Bells Works site. Maybe married quarters in Hucknall, she thought, but there was no doubt that life in the future would be different.

Staring down at the landscape, way down below, Lily reflected on the old year that was fast coming to its end. What would 1942 bring for her, for Oro, for her friends and her country? Would Britain and Europe, strengthened by the United States, bring the war to a rapid conclusion, or would they battle on for years to come? She had found love in her short time in the Midlands and forged deep friendships that would never be broken. She and the engine girls she had grown to love would go on building war planes; drilling, hammering, riveting and welding. They would continue to climb into their grubby dungarees every morning and unstintingly work their fingers to the bone for the country they loved.

'Bless them all: Edna, Jeannie, Ruby, Audrey, Mary, Annie,' Lily prayed as the wind snatched the words from her mouth and hurled them into the arching blue sky from where Oro was slowly starting to make his descent.

As the Hucknall airbase loomed into view, Oro lined up the aircraft with the runway. Then, braking gently, he expertly landed her on the tarmac.

Thinking ahead to the future, to 1942, Lily felt a shiver run down her spine. She was proud to be building and flying planes. Geraldine had gone, but she had picked up her mantle, her legacy. Lily would do all that she could, in the hope that her work and commitment would honour the passing of Geraldine and the other heroic women who had sacrificed their lives for others, for freedom and for the country they loved.

Acknowledgements

Writing *Engine Girls* was an entirely new brief for me. Moving location from the north of England (where most of my previous sagas were set) to the Midlands was a big change, but it did mean I was able to explore stunning countryside and create a whole new set of characters, which has been a joy. Accompanied by my friends and local guides Clare Birdsall and Jane Todd, who both have a great sense of pride in local history, we started to explore the Nottingham area. On a rainy day in Hucknall church (where Lord Byron, one of England's greatest poets is laid to rest) we met a group of lively and knowledgeable locals, most of whom grew up during the war. Vividly recalling stories of their childhoods dominated by heavily bombed airbases and secretly located armaments factories, they completely fired my imagination. There was no doubt after meeting them that Hucknall was exactly the right place to locate the Bell Works factory and its domestic site where my 'Engine Girls' would spend their war years.

I'd like to thank the kind and talented people who helped me along the way, starting with Hilary Dupere in Cambridge, who coordinated meetings and phone calls between myself and her son, Iain Dupere, Associate Professor of Aeronautical Engineering at De Montfort University, Leicester. Iain's clear explanations and diagrams on the structure of the Spitfire's Rolls-Royce Merlin engine were invaluable, while his knowledge of the assembling of a Spitfire, from tip, tail to fuselage and cockpit were literally riveting – it was rivets, thousands of them, that secured the aircrafts, bolted in by hundreds of engine girls working around the clock in an attempt to compete with the output of the Luftwaffe. Former pilots Pam and Nigel Fuller helped me when it came to the intricacies of learning how to fly, carefully taking me through details for take-off, landing and navigating waypoints along flight paths. Roger Morton of Cambridge explained the workings of the graceful Tiger Moth, which puts in a brief appearance in this book. My thanks, as always, go to my editor Rebecca Hillsdon at Penguin Random House, who came up with the Engine Girls theme, and to Clare Bowron and Shan Morley Jones for their fine editorial skills. Finally, my greatest debt is to Neil Storey, writer, TV presenter and established advisor on the First and Second World Wars. His humour, advice, knowledge and editorial contribution to the plot lines have been priceless, helping me explore a historical genre rich in characters, events, breathtaking bravery and rapidly developing aviation skills that helped Britain build aircraft to win the war in the skies over Europe.